FORWARD AND BACK

Michael Pickard

This is a work of fiction. Names, characters, businesses, places, events, and incidents are either the products of the author's imagination or used in a fictitious manner. Any resemblance to actual persons, living or dead, or actual events is purely coincidental.

DEDICATION

In memoriam to Randy J. Wortman, former Roosevelt High School Advanced Placement Physics teacher, who role-modeled how teaching can be successful when mixed with a healthy dose of humor.

ACKNOWLEDGMENTS

Sincere gratitude to Temple Beth Israel Writers for ideation and planning, and to Cheryl Pickard, editing consultant. Thanks to the Schaumburg Writers Meetup Group, the Wilmette Critinomicon Group, Shut Up & Write! ® Fort Collins, and The Writers of Glencoe for feedback.

Irwin Friedman, Elyse Malamud, Donald Meyer, Richard Rotberg, Judith M. K. Kaufman, K.L. Ardrey, and Heather Hein delivered unique insights, keen eyesight, and prose hindsight as beta readers.

Background graphic by Pawel Czerwinski
Cover design by Daynya Quigley

Day 0

[1] Monday, January 24, 2011

Faith moaned, "Randy, something weird is going on."

Instead of being woken by my public radio station, my wife kicked me in the ass. So much for a good night's sleep before my experiment to cure cancer.

I blinked in the dark. The clock radio read 4:06. My plan had been to leave for work early. Just not *this* early. I wanted to be at ChiLabs before nine for my make-or-break attempt to create super-heavy ions that would obliterate cancerous tumors. "Is the baby kicking again?" I reached out to share the experience, which never got old.

Faith pushed my hand away. "It's not a kick. It could be contractions, but I'm not sure."

"Craig isn't due for four weeks." We'd been overjoyed to find out the gender at Faith's ultrasound.

Her voice was a sandpaper groan. "Randy, what's going on?"

I had no clue. This was our first child. We'd scheduled the Lamaze classes to end just before the due date. So far, we'd taken three of six and hadn't gotten to the contractions and delivery topics. "Do you want some chocolate?" I'd made sure there was plenty in the house when I learned that was her pregnancy craving. "I can get you a Hershey Bar." I groped for and found Faith's hand under the covers.

"I'm not hungry. Do you think Craig's coming?"

Faith was experiencing something, but I had no facts upon which to make an assessment. At least she hadn't described it as painful. She deserved an answer. "I don't think so. You told me late births run in your family." What did we cover in the last class? "Take some cleansing breaths. Whatever it is, it'll pass." She'd been out and about all day, coordinating a food drive to restock the community pantry. Maybe she violated doctor's orders and lifted a heavy box and strained something. It was often difficult for her to rein in her dedication to her causes.

"I'll try." I felt her roll to the side, her hand slipping from my grasp.

"The best thing for you and Craig is getting a good night's sleep." *Me too.* I pulled up the comforter, which had slipped halfway to my stomach. I was just about to doze off when her foot struck me again. "Would you *please* stop doing that?"

"What would you prefer? Have me suffer in silence? I felt it again."

"The Lamaze instructor warned us about false labor." Maybe it was indigestion from our Chinese carryout dinner. "Okay, I'll be right back."

I slid out from beneath the covers. The cold made me need to piss. I stumbled down the hall to the guest bathroom. Maybe her stomach would settle and she'd fall asleep.

One step in, my foot collided with something. "Shit!" I reached out. The kitchen step stool? I flicked the wall switch. No ceiling light. "Damn." The stool must have been Faith's not so subtle reminder to replace the burnt-out bulb. At least she didn't try to do it herself. I never would have forgiven myself if she or Craig were injured in some stupid accident. I'd replace the bulb at a more reasonable hour.

I felt my way along the sink. She'd also left what felt like a newspaper on the closed toilet seat cover. No time for reading, especially yesterday's stories. I dropped it into the nearby wastebasket.

While I emptied my bladder in the dark, I settled on a technique to gather some relevant data about what was happening with Faith. I washed up, grabbed a legal pad, a pencil, and a watch with a second hand from my home office and peeked into the bedroom.

Faith sat up against the bolstered headboard, her nightstand lamp on. "What happened? I heard you yell."

"Nothing." I sat on my side of the bed, assuming the same sitting position. "Okay, when you get one of those aches, let me know and I'll write down the time. We'll see if there's a pattern."

"If you say so." She rested her arms on her prominent stomach. "That's the downside to being married to a scientist who lives and breathes data."

How else would Faith expect me to help us make assessments? I couldn't help but doze off while we waited. Sometime later, she grunted.

"Is that one?"

She nodded.

I marked down the time.

"Randy, I'm worried. Am I losing the baby? Is this what a miscarriage feels like?"

I'd never seen such fear on her face. "You're not miscarrying, not thirty-six weeks into the pregnancy. We'll figure it out."

I'd almost fallen asleep again when she yelped.

"Another?" I checked my watch and wrote down the current time under the first one. About ten minutes in between.

I watched the second hand make its rounds, hypnotizing me.

"Oooh. There's one," she said.

I opened my eyes, wrote down the time and subtracted. Ten more minutes had passed. Could she be right? We didn't have to worry, did we? Hospitals have lots of experience in handling premature births. Craig's timing stunk. Why couldn't he wait until later in the day, after my experiment?

Faith grunted. Another twinge, another ten minutes. Even if Craig was ready, we weren't.

She half-rolled towards me. "Do you see a pattern?"

"Yes." I put down the paper and pencil and strapped on the watch. Assuming these were contractions, I had no clue what to do. "Let's call your doctor."

"Good. He'll know."

I grabbed my phone from the charger in the kitchen and dialed the obstetrician's office number. An answering service picked up the call and promised a doctor would respond.

I stuck my head into our bedroom. "Somebody's going to call us back. You should get dressed, just in case."

4

I pulled on a shirt and pants from the closet in my office. No time for a shower if the doctor told us to come in right away.

Seven minutes later, the phone rang.

It was Faith's doctor. "I've been at the hospital all night," he said. "One baby after the other. I pulled up my notes from Faith's last office visit. A perfect check-up. No indication that the baby is going to arrive early. Faith is likely experiencing a false alarm. First-timers are always so anxious. Did she eat something spicy?"

The egg rolls had been bland. "Hot and sour soup?"

"As I expected. Heartburn or indigestion can be painful in pregnant women. Give her an antacid."

"But I timed her pains. People don't get heartburn every ten minutes like clockwork."

The doctor hummed. "All right. One of my colleagues will start his shift in about an hour. If it will ease her worry, come in then."

I hung up and strolled into the bedroom. "He suggested an antacid." I shared his offer about seeing one of his colleagues.

"It's not my stomach." Faith sat on the bed wearing a sweatshirt, her expandable jeans and ski socks. Her short blonde hair sprouted in all directions. "I want to go now!"

"Okay, okay." No arguing with a very pregnant wife.

Faith had written "pack for hospital" on our family calendar one week before Craig's due date. I grabbed a shoulder duffel bag from a shelf in the hall closet and made an executive decision for one change of clothes for her: a bulky sweater and corduroy slacks.

I filled my pockets from the contents of the wooden valet on the kitchen counter next to my wall charger: wallet, keys, and company badge. I pulled my phone from my pocket and sent a simple text to Soson Grudovich, my associate: *Taking Faith to hospital.* Then I fetched my red fall jacket from the entry closet. Faith was already in the family room buttoning her oversized winter coat. "Looks like you're ready for Alaska."

She stood at the door to the garage. "I checked the outside temperature. It's below thirty."

The previous day had been sunny and warm for a Chicago winter, so her weather report was a bit of a shock, but nothing compared to what I saw when I raised the garage door. The driveway was covered by half a foot of snow.

Faith stood next to me in the doorway and pointed at my empty parking stall. "Where's your hotshot all-wheel drive Audi when we need it?"

"At the dealer, getting snow tires installed." *One day too late.*

I swapped my jacket for my parka and added a wooly hat. In the garage, I helped Faith into her front-wheel drive Honda SUV. "The ride won't take long."

She rubbed her belly, something she'd done almost non-stop for the last month. I figured she was trying to calm our soon-to-be son.

I pulled out of the garage, snow crunching under the tires. Footprints in the otherwise pristine snow crossed the driveway near the garage door, not on the

6

sidewalk. Was someone stalking the house in the middle of the night? Maybe I should research alarm systems for protection.

I closed the garage with the press of a button on the remote control. "Don't worry." I patted her hand. "I remember how to drive in snow."

As opposed to the rest of humanity, who slid into curbs and oncoming lanes in front of us.

Faith held her stomach with gloved hands. Her lips moved but no sound came out. Was she whispering to Craig, telling him not to be impatient to start his life?

I'd memorized the optimal route to North Suburban Community Hospital in Arlington Heights. Flashing lights one block down from our subdivision confirmed that some idiot had forgotten how slippery the roads were during a snowstorm.

"They're still happening!" Faith squirmed in her seat. "Why aren't we moving?"

I fell back on the only thing I remembered from our last class. "Deep breaths. Take deep regular breaths."

"Screw your breathing! Get us to the hospital!"

Faith needed a distraction, something to take her mind off Craig. I turned the radio on. Faith turned it off. "What's on your calendar for next week, assuming this is a false alarm?" I asked.

"I don't know. Let me think." She repositioned herself in the passenger seat. "I'm supposed to lead the inventory and forecasting efforts for the Food Pantry next week. And I'm the primary author of the annual report on voter registration. This is terrible timing."

Craig's early arrival messed with both of our plans. I wanted to distract Faith, not get her more upset. "Aren't there other people who can do this work?"

"Well, I guess so, but I volunteered because I know what's involved. After all, I've done those things for years."

"What do you think will happen if you're not available?"

Faith took her time to answer the question, hopefully no longer concentrating on what her body was doing. "I guess someone else will have to step up."

"Exactly. Think of it as an opportunity for others in your organizations to grow. That will make them better. "

"I guess you're right." She heaved a heavy sigh. "I don't feel so bad, when you describe it that way."

As we inched forward, I saw a tow truck had gotten stuck attempting to pull two crashed and conjoined vehicles out of the way at an intersection.

Faith craned her neck to see out the driver's side. "What happened? Do you think everyone is all right?"

"Let's just worry about you, okay? I'll get us to the hospital as quick as I can."

"You better not get into an accident, Mister Hot Coupe."

Faith had reluctantly agreed to the Audi TT when I'd received a large work bonus, but only if that was my one and only impractical car purchase and I didn't drive like Mario Andretti.

8

A policeman manually handled traffic control. After twelve minutes, it was our turn to squeeze past the wreckage. Paramedics and firefighters surrounded the vehicles, which seemed to contain victims.

"Your experiment is this morning, isn't it?" she asked. "I'm sorry about the timing, not that I had any control."

Her inquiry about *my* schedule was tit-for-tat. "Yes, but I prepared everything in advance. Besides, Soson will be there to look after things." *Damn it all.* One critical test would determine either continued funding or my termination and a demolished reputation.

Faith grunted at the mention of Soson's name. "You trust him, right? You've told me so many times how critical this test is."

"I'm where I need to be. At your side." No way would I leave my wife, false alarm or not. If Hamza Bashir, one of the Labs' directors, made any claims on a successful result, Soson would set things straight.

Faith's smile twisted to a grimace as another contraction struck. *Her doctor has his head up his ass.*

A drive that should have taken twenty minutes, based on previous solo dry runs, was taking twice as long. The highways were mostly clear except for slush, although traffic was dense for such an early hour. Had everyone left early to get to work on time?

After twenty more minutes, I slid Faith's SUV into the curved, covered emergency driveway. I ran in and got an orderly who brought out a wheelchair and took Faith inside while I parked.

9

As I walked from the lot to the hospital, I pulled up our neighbor Patrice's phone number and called.

"Hello?"

By the slurred tone of her voice, I'd woken her. "Patrice? It's Randy. Faith is having the baby."

"She's not due for four weeks!" Her voice was loud enough to wake her husband and neighbors on both sides.

"Well, Craig's not waiting. We just arrived at North Suburban Community." My watch said 7:06. "I know you planned on being here."

"Damn right. I promised Faith I'd be there for support. After my three brats, I know the drill. Be right there."

"It's going to take you longer with the snow. Drive safe." The last thing I wanted was Patrice injured while doing Faith a favor. "Oh," I added, "there was a big accident—" Too late. She'd hung up.

The emergency room receptionist directed me to Faith's stall, a partitioned area with a closed drape.

A nurse intercepted me. "We're waiting for a doctor to confirm your wife's condition before allocating a labor room. Things are a little crazy here. Seems like every pregnant woman in a twenty-mile radius decided to give birth starting last night."

"You don't mean that literally, do you?" The mathematical odds would be worse than winning the lottery.

"Oh, no." She giggled. "We're just really busy, that's all. Thank you for your patience."

"I don't think Faith or I can convince Craig to stay put if he wants to come out." I stepped through the curtained entrance.

Nurses had dressed Faith in a hospital gown, her clothes stuffed into plastic bags on a chair in the corner.

Periodically she writhed on the bed, the gown slipping off her body. On our vacations, she'd wear a one-piece suit. Now, she was exposing herself as if she were on a nude beach. Did she even realize what she was doing?

The nurse added a light sheet for modesty.

"The Lamaze instructor said it might hurt, but I had no fucking clue!" Faith gritted her teeth, her body contorted on the mattress.

I remembered the teacher's advice about worse case scenarios. Maybe she had no good way to describe levels of pain. I'd seen increased anxiety in the faces of the other expectant mothers in class but not Faith's.

I blushed as I straightened the sheet, embarrassed on my wife's behalf. She laid quiet for about ten minutes. With the next contraction, her gyrations displaced the sheet again. I gave up running from one side of the bed to the other.

Periodically, a nurse would come in, push Faith's sheet and gown aside and check her progress. Then she'd make a note on Faith's chart. "The dilation has started all right, but it's progressing very slowly. That's good. Less chance for tearing. And your water hasn't broken." She put a cup and a damp cloth on the rolling tray table alongside the bed. "Ice chips only."

11

"I guess the doctor was wrong." I sat next to Faith, holding her hand. "How are you doing?"

"How do you *think* I'm doing?" Faith's face gleamed with perspiration. "I feel like I'm trying to shit a cinderblock. It hurts like hell. Look what you're making me go through."

What I'm *making* her *go through?* Other new fathers at work had advised me that their wives cussed them out and blamed them for their condition during the birthing process. I was getting off easy. "Like we had the option of *me* carrying?"

"God help us." Faith attempted a smile.

"I bet I can find some chocolate candy in a vending machine." I cursed myself for not bringing some from home. "Should I get you one?"

"Didn't you hear the nurse?" Faith tsked. "She told me nothing but ice chips."

If I'd heard, it hadn't registered.

Patrice rushed into the room. "God, I can't believe I made it in one piece. Why didn't you tell me to avoid Roselle Road?" She stomped over to the bed, leaving a slushy trail.

"Patty!" Faith reached out for our neighbor. They shared an awkward hug.

"Dear lord, how about a little modesty?" Patrice stood on the opposite side of the bed from me and straightened Faith's sheet. I didn't advise her that trying to keep Faith covered was pointless.

Seven forty-five. They'd be powering up the linear accelerator about now. Soson might know enough to troubleshoot any last-minute issues. I prayed that he was having an undistracted day.

12

Faith's doctor arrived in soiled scrubs. "I couldn't leave without seeing my favorite patient." He scanned Faith's chart. "Let me check for myself." He took his turn examining Faith. "Well, bless my soul. You *have* gone into labor. Given the speed of your dilation and the fact that your water hasn't broken, this is going to be a while." He checked his watch. "We're talking five hours, maybe six, certainly after lunch, my best guess. Meanwhile, I'll have you wired up so we can keep track of the heart rate." He nodded at the presiding nurse. "I'll advise an on-duty doctor from my practice that you're here." His head hung between slumped shoulders. "And now, I'm going home."

Faith grabbed the sheet and pulled it to her neck. "Thank you, Doctor."

The nurse lubricated Faith's belly and moved what looked like a hockey puck around until we heard Craig's heartbeat. The nurse strapped the device in place. "Our son."

My cellphone beeped and broke my attention. It was a text from Soson. "*The weather is horrid. Stay home.*"

Faith panted between contractions. Craig's heart raced. "Who was that?"

"Soson." I stared at the screen. "He told me not to come to work." After Craig was born, I expected to get an extra firm pat on the back and probably a cigar from him.

"Does he know we're at the hospital?"

Patrice brought the cup of ice chips to Faith's lips.

"Yes, I texted him." I reread his message. "He knows how important today is." I stiffened my spine. "If not for the storm, I'd think he had some reason for keeping me away."

"Doesn't he live close to the Labs?" She pushed the cup of ice chips away.

Patrice put it back on the tray.

"About ten minutes. His commute is trivial." Soson had described his location criteria to me when he'd moved a couple of years previous.

"Maybe he's just concerned for your safety. You have to admit, the roads are dreadful."

"You're right." I tapped the phone's screen to start a reply but couldn't decide what to say. Tell him I was okay with delegating oversight of the experiment to him? "You know, he and Hamza have been really close the last couple of years." Hamza, who'd hovered around my project, attempting to learn as much as he could about it. No matter his intentions, I felt threatened. "Why do I feel like there's something going on behind my back?"

"I thought you trust Soson."

"I do. It's just . . ." The pending doom in my gut based on a speculated Soson/Hamza collaboration wasn't easily describable. "I'll tell Soson I'm putting him in charge." I started typing a reply. "And to keep Hamza away from it."

"Wait." Faith's head tilted up, her eyes on the schoolroom-style wall clock. "Don't you complain that management is upset because they haven't seen any results from you? This is your last shot, right?" Faith was calm between contractions. "It makes sense for you to be there. You've put your heart and soul into this project."

I stopped typing. My failures to-date and this critical test had been a dinnertime topic for months, always giving me indigestion. "Yes, but—"

"You're on thin ice, and Craig and I need a reliable bread-winner." She batted her eyelids and smiled, until another contraction took her attention.

I gave Faith my hand. She squeezed all the blood from it.

Patrice looked at me with wide-open eyes. "You can't go. Faith's in labor. How can you possibly consider leaving?"

I dealt with the pain of crushed fingers, surely less than what Faith was experiencing. "No worries. I'm staying right here." I had confidence this experiment would produce heavy ions, given the settings I'd slaved over. Soson was perfectly capable of administering the experiment without me. It was mostly standing there while it ran. I just hoped he wouldn't get a burst of creativity and mess things up. "The laborious part is analyzing the results, and that will take weeks if not months."

"Can you hand me the ice?" Faith reached in Patrice's direction. "You heard the doctor. It's going to be hours."

Patrice held out the plastic cup. "Here you go."

"Are you going to sit here and watch me go through hell?" A few ice chips slid into Faith's mouth.

"That's my job at the moment." *Why does she keep suggesting I leave?*

Her speech was a bit garbled. "If I were in your shoes, I'd go. Patty can keep me company."

Faith's sense of time was being skewed by labor. "Are you sure, honey?" A twinge of doubt felt like the start of a headache. I *would* feel more confident if I could triple-check everything before they threw the switch.

"As long as you promise not to dawdle."

Patrice looked as if she were about to burst. "I insisted that Frank be at my side for all three of ours, and he had a company to run."

If something did go wrong with the experiment, I had the skills to affect a last-minute rescue. Soson wouldn't have a clue. "It means a lot that you offered, but I wouldn't miss Craig's birth for anything." I stood up and patted Faith's hand.

Faith groaned. Probably another contraction. When it passed, I dabbed her forehead with the cool cloth.

She took the cloth from me and gave it to Patrice. "No offense, but you're useless here. Who knows, if something goes wrong, you could be fired. Go to work. Just promise you'll be back for the big event."

"Really?" Faith knew me so well. I'd shown up late for too many dinners. "I promise." I sent a reply to Soson. "*Coming. Should be there in time.*" I slipped on my parka.

"Doctors have been wrong before." Patrice leaned over and wiped Faith's damp hair from her forehead. "Craig might pop out at any moment." She glared at me. "Can't you reschedule?"

16

"The availability of the linear accelerator doesn't work like a haircut appointment. They'll run experiments on time because there's always another one waiting." I checked Faith's expression as I zipped up, to make sure she still approved. She smiled. "Thank you for letting me do this. I'll be here before Craig is born."

"Maybe you'll earn another Nobel Prize." Faith grunted and gripped the sheets so hard her knuckles turned white.

"Another? I don't even have *one*." At work, Soson had passed along the unsubstantiated rumor that I'd been a nominee for a Nobel in Physics for my paper last year on process improvements in particle beam acceleration using plasma. It was a necessary prerequisite to my objective of creating heavy ions.

"But you will, some day. Now get the hell out of here."

Faith, ever the optimist. I waited until the current contraction passed. "I just want my experiment to work so doctors can step up the war on cancerous tumors."

Patrice's voice was sharp. "My neighbor, the over-achiever who's willing to miss the birth of his son."

I smirked at Patrice, leaned over and kissed Faith. "I'll be back as soon as the experiment is over. I won't even look at the results."

"I'm going to hold you to that." Faith blew me a second kiss.

I left the draped area.

Patrice followed. "Randy? What do you want me to do?"

Why was she asking *me*? She'd gone through this three times. My brain had shifted to the details of my experiment. All I could remember from our incomplete Lamaze lessons was rolling a sock filled with tennis balls on Faith's back. "Do for her what you wanted your husband to do for you. That's why Faith wanted you here."

"I thought she wanted her best friend by her side." Patrice's stare was intense. "I still think you should stay."

"You heard what the doctor said. I'll be back no later than noon." Even in this weather, I could easily be back within four hours. I pulled on my wooly hat. "Call me if anything happens. Now I really have to go." If I showed up late, I wouldn't be able to double check the settings and correct any last-minute glitches.

At the emergency room exit, I spied a husband and wife leaving with their baby, escorted by grandparents. It was already on my list to call my folks after Craig was born. As snowbirds in Florida, they might come back early to meet him.

I skated across the parking lot to Faith's SUV and wiped off the windshield with my sleeve. Behind the wheel, I pulled up directions to ChiLabs on my phone and evaluated the traffic conditions. Given the starting point and the snowstorm, my normal forty-five-minute commute to work was going to take longer. *Still doable.* I considered three alternative routes, each one a mess. I picked the one using highways instead of major streets. Plows should have cleared the way.

I struggled to concentrate on driving. Faith's condition filled my thoughts. How could she survive

18

hours of gut-wrenching pain? Would Patrice's presence help or hurt? I considered turning around but traffic in the other direction had slowed to a crawl. My visit to ChiLabs would have to be in-and-out so I could get back in time.

The route I picked turned out to be a bad choice. A multi-vehicle pile-up brought traffic to a stop. State police cleared a single lane to accommodate three converging ones, which made forward progress take forever. The estimated arrival time on my phone ticked up, flirting with nine o'clock. If I was lucky, the roads ahead would be clearer and there wouldn't be any accidents on the way back to the hospital.

Finally, I was through the bottleneck. My phone beeped, a text message. I couldn't safely take my eyes off the road. I accelerated Faith's Honda through the slush. Temperatures were stable so the snow kept accumulating. Traffic was heavy but moving. I signaled for the exit and sped along the frontage road until I got to ChiLabs entrance. Ruts in the snow confirmed that many employees had already arrived.

In the parking lot, maintenance workers had dutifully plowed overnight, pushing snow to the edges, creating mountains that filled parking spaces. Unlike me, other workers had left early to get to work on time. I drove through the entire lot looking for a space. That early in the day, no one was leaving. In fact, some were still arriving. Available spaces were quickly occupied. My watch read 8:56. I had to park and get inside before my experiment started.

Backup lights on a car parked down the way identified an about-to-be available space, but I didn't have time to wait for it.

There was only one empty area near me and it wasn't designated for parking: the top of a small dirt mound directly over the secondary target area for the accelerator. Not the one my experiment would be using.

I hesitated for a second before deciding I had no other choice. The formerly parked car sped towards me, as if we were competing for the same destination. *Back off! You had a parking space!* With my foot to the floor, I bounced Faith's car over the curb and onto snow-covered grass. The SUV shimmied up the slope, throwing up snow and sod. Front wheel drive got me to the top, facing two adjacent office buildings. I turned off the car, unbuckled, and pulled up my collar, ready to run directly to my office from which the experiment would be initiated. The other car parked directly behind, his brights blinding me in the rear-view mirror.

My watch vibrated, an alarm I'd set to go off when the experiment was scheduled to start. Nine o'clock on the nose. "Shit!" I sank into the driver's seat. So much for being there.

I checked the text message I'd gotten en route. From Soson, it read, *"Do not come! Have a pleasant day, snowed in with your beautiful bride."*

That's how he referred to Faith, even after eight years of marriage. At least I could go in and find out why Soson warned me away. After all, it's my project! Maybe one of the analysts would give me a glimpse of the preliminary results. That would take only a few minutes, and then back on the road. I had time. According to the doctor, Craig was taking his.

The headlights of the car behind me swerved away. I glimpsed the taillights of a sedan as it vanished in the direction of the parking lot exit.

As I gripped the door handle, my nose detected a smell that reminded me of the time Faith burnt vegetables in the oven, smoky but slightly sweet. Although the car had warmed up during my commute, a chill permeated the cabin. The SUV bounced as my fingers clung to the frozen steering wheel. My lungs rejected super-cold air. I shivered as dust rose from the footwell, obscuring my legs. Through the windshield, a speckled fog, like sand being whipped by the wind, swirled clockwise and obscured my view. Faith's SUV was getting sucked in. No choice but to ride it out. I reattached my seat belt and gripped the door handle with my left hand, the edge of my seat with the right. The vortex swallowed the hood. My eardrums ached at the sound of a million crickets. I tensed, closed my eyes, and held my breath, expecting I wouldn't survive.

Day 1

[2] Friday, April 12, 2019

When I opened my eyes, the sun's reflection glared in the rear-view mirror. The whirlwind had vanished. I was still in Faith's SUV on the mound facing the ChiLabs towers. *Faith!* I unbuckled and whipped out my phone to call the hospital. No service. "Shit!" When I opened the door, it creaked and fell off its hinges. A burnt rubber smell triggered my gag reflex but I stifled the urge to vomit.

I stepped out of the cabin into balmy air, green grass under my shoes. Where did all the snow go? I slid off my parka and tossed it onto the seat. Faith's SUV sat on bare rims, the tires shredded into piles of thick rubber bands. The hood, roof and quarter panels had been chafed with streaks down to bare metal. What the hell happened? I checked my watch. *9:03 AM.*

I ran down the hill to find a phone inside and call the hospital. Something seemed different about the ChiLabs building. Dirtier? As I ran up the concrete steps to the front entrance, a young woman gazing at a phone with a huge screen glanced up from beneath a White Sox baseball cap. Green eyes and turned-up nose. A shove and the revolving door jammed. Only because people don't usually sit on the front stairs, I took a second look over my shoulder. She'd brought the phone alongside her head. A second push and the revolving door rotated. I pulled my building pass on a lanyard from my pocket and hung it around my neck.

Instead of a blank beige interior, wall-sized displays above padded benches in the lobby showed videos of talking heads, presumably scientists, interspersed with diagrams of atoms and cartoonish simulations. Was this the wrong building? Amazing that anybody could have made all those changes overnight. It should have taken weeks.

A rent-a-cop security guard sat at a tall desk behind a computer monitor in place of Hannah the receptionist, who'd been the public face of ChiLabs ever since I'd been hired. If she'd planned to retire today, I hadn't heard. Shouldn't we have thrown a going-away party?

I pulled off my hat and approached the counter. "Good morning." Instead of Hannah's visual check, a flat glass scanner waited to verify me. I leaned forward and ran my security badge over the surface. The machine buzzed. I pulled the badge from my neck and swiped it a second time. Same result. "I think your scanner is broken." I held out the badge so the guard could see it.

The guard leaned closer. "It's one of ours all right but it's not active."

"Check again." I made direct eye contact. "I work here."

"I only go by what the security system tells me." He gestured at a cluster of young people, not much older than college age, cued up behind me. "Can you please step aside so others can get by?"

"Yeah. Sure." I stepped out of their way and listened to a series of rhythmic beeps as they passed.

24

Faith must be worried sick. I checked my phone for address book and calendar data. *Still intact. Just no cellular signal.* When the other employees cleared, I returned to the guard's desk. "I'll deal with the security department later. Can I use your phone?"

"They're for internal calls only."

"Really? My wife is in the hospital giving birth. Or maybe our son's already been born. Anyway, I need to talk to her, and my phone doesn't get a signal."

"Congratulations." He nodded me out of the way with a twitch of his head. Another group of employees had gathered, and I was in the way again.

My badge slipped from my hand. I picked it up and hung it around my neck. Why did we need an automated system when Hannah did a fine job?

Through the picture windows, it didn't look like winter. Where did all the snow go? No way it could have melted that fast. The young woman on the steps was gone.

Before I could step back to the guard's desk and continue our negotiation, I felt a tap my shoulder. "Something I can help with?"

I recognized his Russian accent before I turned around. "Soson! Thank god. I need to call the hospital."

Soson grabbed my upper arms, his ruddy complexion darkening. "You look the same."

"Of course, I do. I saw you yesterday." I rubbed the stubble on my face. "Faith and I were concerned about the pregnancy, so I took her to the hospital. When I got here, some weird storm hit her SUV. Did you see it?"

"You know, comrade, no one else had confidence you would return, but I did." Soson scanned the open-air lobby. "We need to get you out of sight." He ripped my hat from my hand and pulled it onto my head. "People here think you are dead."

"I'm not dead. Just a little late." Out of habit, I looked at my wrist. *Still 9:03.* Great time for a watch battery to die. "How did the experiment go?"

Soson led me silently to the glass window, away from a growing parade of inbound employees, his arm tight around my shoulders.

"Sign me in so I can take a quick look at the preliminary results. Then I've got to drive back to the hospital before Faith gives birth."

Soson shook his head. "We ran it. Eight years ago."

I rolled my eyes and waited for Soson to expose one of his practical jokes with a baritone belly laugh. "Not funny."

"You must tell me about the experience. What did it feel like?"

"You mean that whirlwind? Damn cold. Give me your phone already. I have to call Faith to see how's she's doing."

Soson glanced out the window, as if distracted. "Faith was at the hospital eight years ago, not today. No need to hurry." He scanned the first floor. "No place private down here, and believe me, you would not want others to see you."

Soson's nonsense pissed me off. I had a pregnant wife in the hospital, and he was playing Hide the Employee. He threaded his arm through mine, signed me in as a guest and hustled me to a table near a window in the far corner of the empty first-floor cafeteria. I'd spent many hours there pondering the details of my project while enjoying the view. My office upstairs was a converted storage closet. No windows.

"*V nogakh pravdy net.*" When Soson spoke Russian, he knew he was obligated to translate for me. "Come, sit down." He patted a plastic chair hidden from view by a huge potted plant. "Coffee?"

"What are we doing? Stop stalling. I have to get in touch with the hospital."

"No." He paused. "You don't." He pulled out his wallet. "My treat."

My stomach growled. When I tried to take off my woolly hat, he pushed it back down. Perspiration ran down the back of my neck. "Sit and do not move."

"Fine but make it quick. Iced coffee." My body needed something more. "And one of their pecan caramel rolls. I missed breakfast."

While he placed the order, I watched an army of faces walk by, some familiar but most not. If Soson refused to loan me his phone, maybe one of them would let me make a call. Sunlight forced its way through dirty windows, reflecting off the laminated table. I couldn't get over how drastically the weather had changed for a January. Something was messed up, and it wasn't global warming.

Soson came back carrying a tray with a chocolate-covered doughnut, my roll, our drinks, and his change.

"Thanks." I grabbed my roll and the piece of wax paper it sat on. With one bite, gooey caramel, crunchy pecans, and warm, soft dough satisfied my craving. "*Now* can I use your phone to call Faith?"

"I do not advise it." He warmed his hands on his cup of hot coffee. "There is no good way to tell you, *tovarish*, but to tell you. You are dead."

"Stop saying that." I lifted my cup of iced coffee to my face. "Dead men can't argue with colleagues."

Soson wore an emotionless expression. "I am serious. You have been gone without a word for eight years. Faith had you declared dead in absentia. Reason enough not to rush headlong into a complicated situation, yes?"

I glanced out the window. The lush grass and warm temperature didn't match the climate when we'd left the house. "What's today's date?"

"Maybe you should ask what year." He slurped his coffee and pulled back as if he'd burned his tongue. He dumped two packets of sugar into his cup. "Go ahead. Ask."

"I feel like an idiot. Okay, what year is it?"

"2019. The month is April."

"Bullshit. It's 2011. See?" I pulled out my phone. Still no service. "What did management install last night? A cellular dampening field?"

Soson picked up a quarter from the tray, examined it and handed it to me. "Check this."

The coin read MOUNT RUSHMORE with the date 2013. It looked like some kind of commemorative. "This doesn't prove anything." I slid it back. "If it's 2019, what were the results of my experiment?" I glanced up in the direction of my lab on the fourth floor. "What volume of heavy ions was generated?"

28

"Bad news, I am afraid. None of them appeared. I am sorry. I know you slaved over—"

"That can't be." Ten years of details gushed from memory. "I developed the equations. The fabrication folks built the plasma frame to generate additional acceleration. I ran simulations over and over until I got the particle streams correct. Damn it! If I've been gone eight years, then I need time off to be with Faith and Craig. When I return to work, I'll get back into the queue for a future test and debug the experiment while I'm waiting." I extended my open hand. "But right now, there's even more reason to call my wife."

Soson stared at me across the table with the same somber expression he'd worn when he told me his father had died. "No more experiments, I am afraid. Your grant was terminated. Eight years ago." He nibbled at the edge of his doughnut. "Are you feeling all right? Any effects?"

"From the storm? I'm fine but Faith's SUV is in really bad shape. Some kind of whirlwind, like a vortex, attacked me." I rubbed my hands on my pants. If this wasn't a prank, then what was it? There had to be a scientific explanation. "It might have been eight years for you, but it was only a fraction of a second for me." The words didn't make sense to me even though I'd said them. Even if I *was* in 2019, I wasn't going to claim I'd time traveled without being able to prove it. "How do you know about the storm?"

"There exists a gap in your experience of time." Soson's facial muscles strained, as if holding back one of his toothy smiles. "We had a nice memorial service, although without a body—"

29

"How could you do that?" I'd had enough of this bullshit. I pulled back my empty hand. "I didn't die. I'm *here*."

"Yes. Now." Soson clenched his teeth. He'd had them straightened and bleached. "Please, do not misunderstand. I am delighted to see you."

"Glad to hear it." They were crooked and stained yesterday. How did this get so screwed up? "You say I disappeared?" Grass instead of snow. Warm weather instead of freezing. Soson's repaired teeth. The building lobby. My brain battled with the anomalies, threatening a headache. *Damn, how did I lose eight years? Faith's been alone raising Craig?* I stood. I had to go somewhere, do something to fix this.

Soson's paw clamped around my wrist. "Sit. I will tell you the story."

I took a seat and folded my arms across my chest. Soson was one of the smoothest talkers I'd ever met. His whispers into the ears of the Board members cemented my original grant. "Okay but give me the executive summary. I've got to talk to Faith and let her know I'm all right."

Soson sat tall in his chair. "When you didn't return to the hospital that day, Faith called me. She said she couldn't reach you on your cellphone. I told her I'd received your text message, that you were coming despite my warnings, but I hadn't seen you. I did not want her to get worse upset in her condition so I told her I would care for it."

Soson's messages echoed in my memory. "Why *did* you tell me not to come?"

30

"Driving that morning was life-threatening. Besides, a husband's place is at the side of his wife when she is at a hospital. Allow me to continue."

Soson wasn't above pranks, but never this elaborate. Was he wearing false teeth? I felt a chill despite the climate-controlled environment. "Assuming I vanished, did anybody look for me?"

"Faith reported your disappearance to the Schaumburg police. Officers were asked to report anything relevant. I did likewise down here after Faith's call. The blizzard made things difficult. You and Faith's SUV simply vanished." Soson wove his fat fingers together, the same gesture he'd made when we discussed difficult problems in the past.

"What you're saying is impossible." I had no logical explanation for the whirlwind sandstorm or the radical change in climate.

Soson's body heaved with a deep breath. "I myself drove around until the wee hours of the next morning, following every route I could think of between here and the hospital."

If Soson was being honest, then where had I been for eight years? It felt instantaneous. "I wasn't—anywhere. I was in 2011, and now it's 2019? This is pure crazy." I folded my arms on the table to cushion my pounding head. I couldn't handle impossibilities, like dividing by zero.

"Everything will be all right. You will need to accommodate many changes, but I know you well." He poked a fat finger at me. "You will thrive. You have important work to do. And I will be at your side, as always."

I looked up at his smiling face, unwilling to share his optimism. "Listen, everything I've learned in particle physics revolves around one immutable fact: nothing travels faster than the speed of light. Isn't that what makes time travel possible? Yet you sit here and imply that's exactly what I did."

"Perhaps there are other ways to move through time that have nothing to do with the speed of light. Did you consider that?"

My brain was in no shape to travel down that line of inquiry. If eight years had passed, I had a lot of catching up to do. "Tell me about Faith. Did she give birth?"

Soson nodded with a faint smile. "The evening you vanished, I received a call from some woman, that Faith had given birth to an eight-pound baby boy."

Probably Patrice. Finally, some good news! "Terrific! I'm a father!" I had to talk to Faith, hear her voice. Craig's coos or cries. *No, wait.* Craig would be eight years old. We could talk, father to son. "Faith must be worried sick."

"She was, for a long time. Until last year."

"Is that when she had me declared dead?" I wrapped my arms around my body. "Faith gave up on me?" I longed for the parka in the SUV.

"It was seven years, *tovarish*. How long would you *expect* her to wait? Your disappearance, or abandonment as she eventually viewed it, was particularly difficult for her. She believed your promise to return and then you were gone without a word."

"What about Craig? How is he doing?"

"I have nothing to share. Faith refuses my calls and does not respond to my emails." Soson shrugged his shoulders. "The last time I spoke with her was just after the death certificate was issued. It was a courtesy call to inform me."

I used to make sure Soson joined us for occasional family dinners and weekend outings because living alone wasn't healthy. Hadn't Faith gotten to know and like him? After all, that was the point. Why didn't she maintain a relationship with him after I supposedly vanished?

Soson took a slurp of coffee. "I suspect, given Craig's DNA, that he is an above-average eight-year-old boy growing up in a single parent household. That has become more normal these days."

Soson's face had accumulated a few more wrinkles since the last time I'd seen him. Were there more strands of gray in his hair? Maybe time *had* passed. Eight years? "Even more need to call Faith and explain." I reached to remove my hat.

Soson put his hand on top of my head. "Explain to her like you explained to me? That you were— nowhere?"

I'd never lied to Faith, and I wasn't about to start now. "All right, then at least let's go upstairs and let whoever is my Director know I'm back. He can get my ID reinstated. After a reunion with Faith and Craig, I can get back to work."

"Impossible. You are, how they say, persona non grata. Management relied on my confident projections when they funded you over other promising projects from a blanket research grant. You knew quantum fields and particle physics better than anyone in this building." Bits of chocolate broke off his doughnut as Soson took another bite. "They were devastated that your experiment yielded bupkis. Then you vanished. For all they knew, you ran off embarrassed after wasting millions of dollars."

"And did what, live in a cave?" If I'd planned better, Soson wouldn't have been in charge in my absence. I would have made sure the experiment was successful. "You know me. My credibility is too important to make an unsubstantiated claim of time travel. I won't call it that until I can prove that's how I got here." If I couldn't make things right with management, I could do the more important thing. "My head is in no shape to deal with office politics. I've got to talk to my family."

"Let me tell you full, and then you can decide."

This is the executive summary? The plastic chair didn't yield when I stretched my back. I nodded and pulled at my roll, which had hardened and stuck to the wax paper.

"You would have been proud of Faith's determination. She printed flyers offering a reward for information that led to your whereabouts. When nothing of value came of the replies, she pestered the police to keep your missing person case open for years, well past when they normally would have categorized it an unsolved disappearance. The detectives who interviewed me, and there were many, asked if I thought you ran away for some reason."

34

I washed down a bite with ice coffee. "I hope you told them no. With my first child about to be born and my experiment to advance cancer tumor treatments—"

"Precisely. You had every reason to be here. When they failed to find you, Faith hired private detectives."

"She searched for me? That's amazing." I was proud of Faith for being persistent. It spoke volumes about our relationship and her commitment.

"In the process, she depleted your savings and retirement account. I offered her a loan at no interest but she refused. With no income, she still had mortgage payments, utilities, food, clothing." Soson spun a finger in the air. "After a few years, Faith was broke, financially and in spirit. The bank came for the house. She reluctantly sold your Audi."

"My TT?" She must have been desperate for cash.

Soson put his hand on mine. "Do not be selfish. She did not have food on the table. Hamza recommended—"

"That ignoramus!" He was a Middle Eastern leech, with a history of taking credit for others' work.

"Be calm. I only know as much as I do because he informed me." Soson put his palms together as if in prayer. "He advised her how to invest." His lips curled into the beginning of a smile. "Somehow, he saved the house."

Hamza meddling in Faith's finances made Soson's news even worse. He probably suggested selling the TT out of pure spite. "I'll bet you anything he was just waiting for me to be gone for him to make a move on Faith." When he'd visit my office, I'd catch him staring at the photo of the two of us on our honeymoon.

"You told me that Faith relied on you to handle family finances. There were plenty of con artists who crawled out from under the porch to swindle her. Hamza made sure—"

"Stop saying that name." Mister High and Mighty with barely a masters. "*He* became my wife's advisor? Why not you? I would have trusted *you*."

"I take that as a compliment. I offered and was refused. Politely." Soson pressed his lips tight before continuing. "Faith has always seen me as a cohort that took you away from her. Distracted you from your relationship. Long hours together here. Sharing your weekends."

"But you were alone. I wanted you to be part of a family. Was that so wrong?"

"In her eyes, I was guilty for keeping you two apart. It did not make things better that I reminded her of you when she was trying desperately to deal with the pain."

With no siblings of my own, I'd always pictured Soson filling a specific role. "So, you're not Craig's Uncle Soson?"

Soson flinched. "You must be joking. Me, an uncle?"

I couldn't put the puzzle together if I didn't have all of the pieces, or enough of a brain to manipulate the ones I had. "I have to go see Faith and make things right, especially if you're certain I won't be a welcome visitor in the executive wing."

"Do you think Faith will receive you with open arms? As I have tried to beat into that soft American brain of yours, she declared you dead after seven years. By law, she was not obligated to wait *that* long."

My heart ached and my brain pounded. I couldn't really be angry, given the circumstances. But no way was I going to give up on her or my son. Thinking about family triggered something I'd overlooked. "My parents! They must be worried sick." How old would they be now? It took only a moment to calculate. *Eighty-eight and eighty-seven.*

My chest went hollow when I saw Soson's serious expression reappear. "Your mother passed three years after you disappeared. Natural causes in her sleep. I attended the funeral. One of the few times I saw Craig. Faith would not let me speak to either of them. At a funeral, you do not make a fuss. Your father died a year later, from heartbreak I suspect. Faith did not come to that one."

I stared at my hands, which felt disassociated from my body. My parents were gone? Faith had written me off? An unfamiliar loneliness caught me by surprise. A part of me accepted Soson's premise, given empirical evidence. But now what? Where could I go? What could I do?

I stiffened my spine. "Screw the phone call. I'm going to see Faith in person." I had to make this right, so she'd know I wasn't dead after all. To bring her peace of mind. To see my son. "Hell, there's no law that says we can't have a conversation." I pictured the two of us renewing our vows with Craig as the ring bearer.

"And what will you tell her? The truth that you traveled in time? How credible is that? Or a fib? That you had a sudden urge to go off and find yourself on one of the most important days of your life?"

If my brain struggled to deal with how time travel could be real, how would Faith's? My shoulders slumped.

"Take my advice. *Shag za shagom*. Resolve your situation one step at a time. Get a lawyer, have the death certificate canceled or whatever lawyers do, and then at least you will be a person again." He raised his index finger. "I will make this easy for you." He pulled out his phone, tapped the screen, scrolled, tapped again and then spoke. "Tonya, *moya lyubov*, my best friend Dr. Randall Weinberg will call you to take care of something very important. Please treat him better than you would treat me. *Spasibo*." One more tap. "There, now you have a lawyer."

I'd lost track of the number of women that had passed through Soson's life. Why wouldn't he settle down? "One of your former paramours?"

"More than that. She was going to be *the one*. I could almost taste *khleb i sol'*. Bread and salt, a Russian wedding tradition." He stared into his coffee cup. "Leave it to me to make a silly joke that turned into an argument. Not to be." He looked up with sad eyes. "Unlike your old friend Soson, you have been lucky in love. Maybe you can win Faith's heart again. Then, Craig will have a father figure in his life. And I will maintain a suitable distance."

"Not just a figure. His real *father*." I chugged the rest of my coffee and stood. "Since you've made it

38

perfectly clear I can't stay here, I'm going home despite your advice. Can I borrow your car? Faith's is beyond repair." I held up my dead device. "And your phone, until I can get a replacement."

"I'd rather give you my molars, and they are permanent teeth." Soson rose from his chair. "I'll call you an Uber."

"What's that?"

Soson put his arm around my shoulder. "The world has changed, *tovarish*, in many ways. Too many to advise you about over coffee and a pastry." He struck one of his 'deep in thought' poses, his eyes focused on the atrium ceiling, stroking his chin. "Just your luck, an Uber will strand you, and you will call me to pick you up. I am too busy for such errands, even for my best friend." He pulled a small black plastic box on a keychain from his pocket as reluctantly as if he was giving up one of his kidneys. "It is against my best judgment but take my Tesla. It will be simpler and less expensive. If I see one scratch or dent when you return—"

"Then I'll pay for the repair." I hadn't heard of that brand.

"With what? You're dead. You have no money to your name."

I felt for my wallet in my back pocket. "I'll figure it out. Two doctorates must be worth something as collateral for a loan."

"After you are alive to sign for one. My *dragotsennyy*, my precious, is cherry red with personalized plates. It is parked at the recharge station."

"Recharge?" Truly electric vehicles had been prototypes, not commercial products.

"Plug it in when you return. Until you can get your phone repaired, use the built-in cellular service. Just ask the car to dial."

"You're kidding, right? Speech recognition in a car?" How much had technology advanced in eight years?

Soson nodded. "You have a major re-education ahead of you. Good thing I am an excellent teacher."

"Finally, this will make up for everything I taught you about physics."

Soson smirked and gave me a severely abbreviated course in operating his electric car including using a fob instead of a key. "It also has Internet. Everything else you will figure out, Dr. Science. Watch out for the accelerator. One of the things I love most is the instant gratification."

"I'll be careful." I tried not to make eye contact with familiar faces as we walked out of the cafeteria. I glanced up at the fourth-floor catwalk. "I'm just curious, what did they do with my office?"

Soson walked sideways next to me, a human barrier to oncoming traffic. "Sealed just the way you left it. Too small to bother with." He gave me a soft poke in the ribs. "The truth is, no one wants to go near. Maybe they think they too will disappear."

"When I come back, I'll need access, so I can check the settings, readings, and results myself." After eight years, I didn't have a job. Would ChiLabs consider taking me back after an unexplained absence? "And I'll want to go downstairs and inspect the primary

40

accelerator myself." Maybe one of the hardware modifications required for my experiment had malfunctioned.

"Did you not know? Management would not allow the plasma frame to be installed in the mainline and perhaps interfere with other experiments."

Nobody bothered to tell *me*. "Then where *did* they install it?"

"In the secondary tube that aims at a target beneath the front parking lot."

"Under the mound?" The sand vortex had showed up precisely at the time of my experiment after I'd parked Faith's SUV there. Did that cause me to leap eight years? The beam should have been aimed straight at the target, not at an angle. "Now I *really* have to get into my office."

"What you ask is difficult. Security is much tighter since you vanished. Employees were afraid of being abducted. That was one of the more popular theories about your fate."

That explained the rent-a-cop. "They were wrong. I'm here."

Soson planted his palm on my chin and turned my head away from oncoming people. "Not so loud." After the group had passed, he pressed the fob into my palm and wrapped his fingers around my hand. "When you get back, we will celebrate your return over dinner. My treat."

I nodded. "And we'll plan our next steps. By the way, can you have someone tow Faith's SUV off the mound before management figures out whose car that is? The tires are in shreds."

41

Soson maintained a nonchalant expression. "I will have it moved somewhere out of sight. Drive safe. Please. And send my best to Faith, assuming she is willing to see you." He signed me out at the security guard's station, and then took a glance out the front glass panels.

I kept my head down. After I exited the revolving door, I noticed Soson pacing inside near the lobby elevator, wringing his hands. If I had really jumped ahead eight years, he hadn't seemed at all surprised at my return.

[3] Friday, April 12, 2019 (continued)

Although I was well versed in Nikola Tesla's work, the only thing I remembered about the carmaker named after him was a prohibitively expensive roadster that seemed more like a science fair project than a commercial vehicle. I'd seen a Chevy Volt at the Chicago Auto show nine years ago, but that was a hybrid with a gas engine that recharged its battery. Had the car industry solved battery and range issues? I bet none of those electric cars had manual transmissions.

Soson's car occupied the middle charger spot between two other electric vehicles. The license plate—SOSON—made it obvious. Damn, the car was sleek and redder than red. I unplugged the charging cable as instructed. The charging door closed by itself. When I approached the car, silver door handles extended out from the body. How many other strange things was I going to run into? Bad choice of words when I'm about to be behind the wheel of Soson's new baby.

I stared at the humongous screen attached to the dashboard. What a distraction! How would I be able to drive and keep my eyes on the road? This was straight out of science fiction. Then again, so was time travel.

I used the electric controls to position the seat to accommodate the differences between my height and Soson's. He'd advised me that the car started by pressing the brake, not very intuitive. For everything else, he told me to refer to Support under the Menu button on the large screen. I knew how to drive a car, gas or electric.

No engine noise. The silence was freaky.

As I pulled out of the parking lot and pressed the accelerator, g-forces left all of my thoughts behind. The vehicle rocketed way past a legal speed. I cut pressure by half to keep me close to the posted limit. Soson's other advice was also spot on. The car braked when I pulled my foot off the accelerator. Soson had called it regenerative braking and advised that he almost never had to touch the brake pedal.

My memory provided the route from ChiLabs to home. I'd driven it just yesterday, at least, from my perspective of time. Lane changes in advance to avoid merging traffic took no thought. Instead, I considered how I'd approach Faith. If I'd really been gone eight years, I couldn't just walk through our front door and yell, 'Hi Honey, I'm home.' I might give her a heart attack.

When the car beeped and displayed a road icon, my arm muscles stiffened. Evidently I'd drifted out of my lane. I eased the wheel to the left. Not as much road feel as my Audi. The driver's screen showed cartoonish vehicles in front, on the sides and behind. *Damn thing is trying to act smart.*

Maybe I'd just ring the front doorbell and say nothing. A silent hug? Let her get over the shock of seeing me? Soson had made it sound like she'd been through a lot after I space-folded or whatever I did. I finally decided it would be best to call ahead.

When Soson told me the car had voice recognition, I almost laughed in his face. What the hell. "Call Faith."

The car responded, "Faith is not in your contact list."

Given what Soson had told me about their relationship, that wasn't surprising. The fact that the car understood what I'd said, however, was amazing. "Okay, call—" and I dictated my home phone number.

It rang four times before I heard an answering click. "Faith?" I held my breath.

"We're sorry; you have reached a number that has been disconnected or is no longer in service."

"Hang up." Damn it, she'd changed our number.

The hiccupping siren and flashing red lights in my rear-view mirror made my stomach clench. *Shit!* I pulled over to the shoulder and lowered the driver's window.

The officer's approach reflected in the driver's side mirror until he stood at my door.

"Can I please see your driver's license?"

I dug it out of my wallet and handed it over.

He looked at it, blinked and looked closer. "Did you know this expired six years ago?"

I couldn't tell him I'd jumped ahead eight years. He'd never believe me. *I wouldn't.* "Actually, no. I just got back. Uh, to town. Into the country." The lie burned in my throat. "I've been away."

"That's no excuse. How fast do you think you were going?"

I hadn't been focusing on the dashboard while attempting my call to Faith. I shook my head instead of guessing. "My friend loaned me his car for the day, and I'm not used to it."

"Next time you borrow a car, check it out first. Registration and insurance?"

I pulled those documents from the glove compartment and handed them over.

"I'll be right back." The policeman retreated to his vehicle.

I watched him in his squad car through the rear-view mirror. After a few minutes, he returned and handed me the documents. "We called your friend Mr. Grudovich. He confirmed he loaned you the vehicle." He scribbled furiously onto his ticket pad. "There's a $1,000 fine for an expired license, plus another one hundred and forty dollars for going twenty-three miles over the posted limit. Mail your check to the address on the back and get yourself a new license ASAP. Do you know where the closest Secretary of State vehicle office is located?"

"Yes sir. Elk Grove Village." I'd stopped there a couple of months back—years back—to renew a license plate sticker for Faith's car. Faith's car, which I hoped was no longer sitting on its rims on the target mound at work.

"There's a closer one, next door to Woodfield Commons East."

I was very familiar with Woodfield Mall but had never heard of the Commons, East or West. "Is that in Schaumburg?"

"You *have* been away, haven't you?" He handed me the tickets. "Under normal circumstances, I couldn't let you drive away, not without a license. But the owner of the vehicle explained that you were under a great deal of stress. Personal issues. You shouldn't be

46

driving under those circumstances." He handed me my license. "I'm exercising some judgment. Don't make me sorry. Get this replaced immediately. Drive safe and have a nice day."

I waited until he'd driven off. Still on the shoulder, I placed the tickets on the passenger seat and slumped against the steering wheel, my heart racing. Soson had pulled a miracle out of his Cossack hat. Maybe he'd also float me a loan because I couldn't cover an expense that large. Not right now. I felt lucky to have escaped a more severe penalty.

Soson's advice rang true. I needed to become a real person again. "Call my lawyer," I said.

"Your lawyer is not in your contact list."

What was her name? I tried again. "Call Tonya."

She answered on the second ring. "Smirnov Legal Services. How may I help?"

Her voice reminded me of melted chocolate, dark and smooth. I identified myself and explained that after seven years away, my wife had me declared dead in absentia and I wanted to get that reversed.

"The legal term is vacated. Why were you gone so long, without as much as a phone call?"

I swallowed hard and forced out an enhanced version of the story I'd told the policeman, that I'd been in isolation on a special assignment, with my passport confiscated, and just got back.

"You were a prisoner? That sounds terrible. Not my typical case, but I can do this. Gather up all of your documentation. Birth certificate, certified is best, passport, bank account records, et cetera. Oh, and take down this address of Precision Biometrics." Tonya dictated it.

I scribbled it onto the front of a Starbucks receipt I'd saved in my wallet. "What do *they* do?" A series of unfamiliar numbers filled the back.

"They will take your fingerprints and send them to the authorities. This is probably the most important evidence to get you through the process."

"What *is* the process?" All she'd given me were tasks.

"I get us on the calendar of the judge who granted the death in absentia decree. I present your fingerprints and other evidence that you are alive. He or she vacates the original order. Voila!" She paused. "You are Soson's best friend?"

"A very good friend. We've worked together for years."

"He never mentioned you. But that is *to proshlo*. You speak Russian?"

"No." Since Soson usually volunteered translations, I'd only picked up a random word here and there.

"In English, you would say water under the bridge. You call from Soson's number. Is he there?"

"I'm calling from his car." Was she still interested in him? Maybe I could put in a good word, but not without his permission. "He's letting me use it until I can get one."

"Then you must be a very good friend. He never let me drive his 911 even once."

I wasn't surprised that one of Soson's previous choices had been a Porsche. If I had one, I'd never trade it. "When I get a cellphone, I'll text you my number. Are you calling from your cell?"

"Yes. In the meantime, I will investigate which judge we have to see. My goal is to under-promise and over-deliver."

"Sounds good to me."

"I will speak with you later."

I relaxed a bit knowing that I was on my way to becoming a living human again. That was something positive I could tell Faith, but that wouldn't be enough to restore her trust. What else could I do on short notice? Maybe flowers?

The memories of holding her hand in the hospital, her lips against mine, were vivid, as if they happened just yesterday. I pictured Faith rushing into my arms, kissing me with bottled-up passion, returning my gentle caresses. Except she'd been alone for eight years. Soson had described how she'd held onto the possibility of my return. That proved how strong our love was. It must have been Hamza, pushing her to declare me dead. Still, her reaction to my return was not predictable.

After my exit from the expressway, I wasn't confident in visiting Faith without a plan. The last thing I wanted was to shock her, and I had no clue how to eliminate that possibility.

Familiar roads took me past unfamiliar strip malls and freestanding stores. Places I'd depended on in the past, Mom and Pop places with acceptable prices and great customer service, had been replaced by bigger retailers, many I didn't recognize. Depending on

Soson's car phone wasn't going to hack it, even for the short term. Tonya would need to get in touch as she worked my case. Maybe CellNation, my phone provider and carrier back in 2011, could make a quick fix and get my phone operable. In the meantime, I could reconsider my return home.

I parked in a large shopping mall lot and directed the dashboard to "Call CellNation."

Someone answered, "Best Cellular, Danny speaking."

"I'm trying to get in touch with CellNation."

"Oh man, they went out of business years ago. Why, do you have one of their phones?"

"Yes, and it doesn't get a cellular signal."

He chuckled. "No wonder. CellNation phones only worked on their proprietary network. Whatever you have won't work on any of the carriers we support. I'd be happy to sell you a new phone."

I listened to his sales pitch as I snuck my wallet out of my back pocket and checked my cash. "How much do they cost?"

"I've got phones that start at one hundred forty-nine dollars and up, plus your monthly service fee."

"Nothing cheaper?" I had to conserve my cash.

"Maybe you should buy a Pay As You Go model. They're cheap and available everywhere." He hung up.

Evidently I wasn't Danny's kind of customer.

I decided to get some clothes at Carson's, at least shirts, pants, underwear, and socks. I tried the Tesla's voice recognition once more, "Call Carson's." I'd ask for the address of the closest store after they answered.

"A number for Carson's is not available."

What's been going on the last eight years? I leaned back and watched people come out of a Target store carrying plastic bags. After I locked Soson's car, I went inside.

The store offered men's clothes at lower quality than Carson's, but I couldn't be fussy. Plus, the prices were good. I chose business casual slacks and polo shirts, plus underwear and socks. While waiting to check out, I saw a display of cellphones in plastic bubble packaging. The price for the least expensive model with a five-inch diagonal flat screen made by ZTE was twenty-nine ninety-nine. Perfect! I added that and a card with extra minutes to my cart.

Instead of scanning the items myself like many people were doing, I stood in line and waited for a clerk. How far have they taken this in 2019? Do-it-yourself haircuts at barber shops? Self-performed surgeries for routine procedures like appendicitis? I preferred human interaction.

I left the store and checked my wallet. After my shopping, I was down to about a hundred and thirty dollars in cash, plus three useless credit cards, a debit card for a joint bank account Faith had likely closed, and a $100 Starbucks Card that Faith had gifted to me for my birthday in September last year. 2010, I mean. Most of its balance was intact.

Soson's in-car cellular came in handy when I had to call a 1-800 number to activate my phone. A voice robot stepped me through the process and read my new cellphone number. It had four eights, my lucky number, a positive sign. And I hadn't talked to a human the whole time.

I texted my number to Tonya and then called Soson's cell.

"Hello?"

"Hi, it's me."

"Me who?"

"Your colleague, back from the dead." I winced as soon as I made the quip. "Save this as my new number."

Soson paused. "Done. I did not delete your contact in my phone when you disappeared. Speaking of calling, have you called Tonya yet?"

"Yes, from your car. She asked if you were there with me. I said no."

"Even if I had been, no was the right answer. She is very focused as a lawyer. Conversation about me will distract. Have you seen Faith?"

I hadn't come up with anything to soften my arrival. "I'm on my way there now."

"I still advise against, but *delay to, chto dolzhen delat'*. Do what you must. I expect you to pick me up after work. I have chosen a very nice place for dinner."

Streets had fallen into disrepair since I'd last been in my neighborhood. I maneuvered around potholes and pulled up across the street from my house. Just seeing it made me feel like everything was back to normal, even though it wasn't yet. It was too early for Craig to be home, assuming he was in school. Eight years old would put him in third grade. I tried to remember where the local school was. Walking distance

52

or did a bus pick him up? There was no activity at Patrice's house next door.

My garage door opened and a woman in her early thirties came out, followed by a toddler a few years old. What are they doing in my house? I got out and crossed the street. "Excuse me. Do you live here?"

She pulled her cardigan sweater tight. "Who wants to know?" She eyed the Tesla over my shoulder. "You'll have to speak with my husband. He's inside. I'll go get him." She grabbed the toddler's hand.

In the middle of the day, her husband was likely at work. She'd probably run inside and double lock the door. Maybe even call the police.

I stayed at the end of my driveway. "Wait, sorry. I used to own this house. Did my wife sell it while I was away?"

She'd moved closer to the garage in tiny steps. "Her lawyer said you were dead." She looked me up and down. "You don't look dead."

"I hear that a lot." I forced a smile. "Listen, I know this is hard to believe. I had to leave the country on short notice. The people I was with wouldn't let me call my wife, to let her know I was okay." My made-up story was becoming too comfortable.

"Were you kidnapped?"

That sounded like a reasonable enhancement. "Pretty close." My phony story grew the more details I added. "They just released me. When did you buy the place?"

"A little over a year ago."

Soson hadn't told me Faith had sold the house. Maybe he didn't know. "I was hoping for a reunion, but

53

I guess that's not happening. Do you have any idea where she moved?"

"She didn't say a word at the closing. Her lawyer just handed her papers, explained what they were, and she signed them. She seemed distracted, like in some kind of trance."

I could only imagine how hard my absence had been on Faith. I couldn't let this be a dead end. Hamza must know where she is, but I'm not ready to let him know I'd arrived in 2019. "Do you know her lawyer's name?"

"No, but I'll go inside and get *my* lawyer's card." She glanced down at the toddler, who'd plopped down and plucked grass from the lawn. She lifted him up. "Be right back."

"I'll wait." The garage door remained open. I hoped she wouldn't lock herself inside.

I wondered what Craig was like at her son's age. Did he sit outside and pull grass with his hands? I paced the width of the driveway, recalling footprints the morning I backed out into the snow.

The woman returned. Her son wiggled and thrashed in her arms. She put him down. Immediately, he pulled grass again.

"Thank you." I closed the distance between us slowly so I didn't frighten her.

She leaned forward and held out the card. Her hand shook as I came within reaching distance. "Keep it. I can get another one." She backed up and pointed at the foundation. "Did you know there's a leak in the basement near the fireplace?"

"That means the gutters in back are overflowing. Just clean them out and you'll be good."

"Thanks. Your wife didn't disclose that at the closing."

That was my cue to leave. I was in no mood to come clean about all of the repairs I hadn't done. I slid the business card into my wallet.

Her son stuffed grass into his mouth.

"Jeremy!"

The little boy wailed. Saliva carrying bits of grass dribbled out of his mouth. She knelt down next to him, wiping off his lips. He didn't stop crying.

"Jeremy is very sensitive about scolding. We're trying to teach him about good behavior choices." She picked him up and held him against her chest.

"Again, thank you very much, and thank you, Jeremy." He ignored me, his crying tapering off.

Before I could cross the street and get into the Tesla, Patrice pulled into her driveway. Even though I wanted Faith to be the first one after Soson to know I'd returned, a conversation with Patrice would fill in the gaps about what happened at the hospital. As her best friend, Patrice would certainly know Faith's whereabouts and more about her current condition.

Patrice got out, opened her trunk, and hefted two grocery bags in her arms. When she glanced over and saw me, she dropped one of them. "Randy?" Her eyes darted from me to our house next door, to the Tesla and back to me. "Unbelievable! You're alive!"

"Very much so." Except in the eyes of the law. "Can we talk?"

"Are you kidding?" She pointed at the bag on the ground. "Would you grab that?"

I followed her through the side door, put the dampening sack of groceries on the counter, and sat at her kitchen table. "I think something broke."

"Who gives a shit?" She pulled up a chair. "You know, I never thought you were dead. And neither did Faith for years until she went into seclusion. You don't look a day older. Where have you been?"

I gave her the only explanation I had, my kidnapping story.

One eyebrow went up. "Really? Why did they finally let you go after all this time?" She propped her head up with her arms, forming an isosceles triangle.

My gut told me Patrice wasn't buying it. She always had a good bullshit detector for her husband's tall tales. "Maybe they were convinced that I'd given them all of the information I had? To be honest, I didn't ask." The lie was getting complicated. I'd invented some bad guys who wanted my expertise, held me captive for eight years, and then decided to just let me go. It was my story, and even I couldn't make sense of it. Still, more credible than telling her I'd time traveled. "I thought I'd find Faith and Craig next door. Do you know where they live?"

"Beats the hell out of me. You'd think Faith would want to keep in touch with her best friend. She sold the house without putting up a 'For Sale' sign. The first I knew was when the moving truck showed up. She wasn't even here when they emptied out the place. Some mid-Eastern guy was bossing the movers around."

Hamza!

"Every month I search White Pages websites but with no luck. And she either changed her landline number or got rid of it."

"I know. I tried calling before I drove over."

She pointed at the door. "Speaking of driving, is that your Tesla?"

"No, a friend loaned it to me. I don't have a car at the moment."

"Faith had your Audi, but she couldn't drive a manual." Patrice's pleasant expression faded as liquid spread on the surfaces of the brown paper grocery bag, or maybe it was the memory of me leaving for work while Faith was in labor.

"You should take care of that before everything falls out."

Patrice stood and emptied the bags, pausing with a thoughtful expression before putting each perishable item away. "I was so glad Faith asked me to be there for Craig's birth. Not only because you weren't. Childbirth was really tough on her, thin hips and all. At one point they offered a C-section but she wanted it natural."

"She got through it okay, right?"

"Yes, but exhausted and alone. When you didn't show up, she went into a panic. She called that Soson guy. They had to sedate her, or I swear she would have gotten dressed and gone out looking for you. Fresh from childbirth. In a blizzard. Without a car."

Patrice's story had me on the verge of tears. I silently berated myself for leaving. How could I have been so selfish?

Patrice opened a cabinet above the counter and put away boxes of cereal. "You have no idea how deeply depressed she got when no one could find you. Not just because you broke your promise about being there for Craig's birth. She didn't deserve to be a single mom."

"If there was any way for me to be there for her, I would have. Believe me. The whole thing was out of my hands."

"Good luck explaining that to her. Assuming she'll talk to you. The new neighbors found out from her lawyer at the closing that she had you declared dead. Have you met Jillian?"

"Yes, a few minutes ago."

"I was part of the Welcome Wagon committee when they moved in. She's nice, but she's no Faith."

"I'm going to try to find Faith though her real estate attorney. I have Jillian's lawyer's card."

"Good luck. When you finally get in touch, please tell her I miss her very much. I can't think of anything I said or did to make her act that way. My number hasn't changed."

"And she knows where you live."

"Hang on." Patrice ran from the room.

It sounded like Hamza had taken control of Faith's life, just like he'd tried to worm his way into my project. *Asshole!*

Patrice returned with a photo and placed it on the table in front of me. "It's not recent, but it's the only one I have."

Craig as a toddler sat on a park swing, his face similar to mine when I was his age. Faith knelt behind him, her blonde hair wild in the wind, her face stoic as

58

if she'd been afraid to smile. The photo had been taken in the fall, trees with red and orange leaves in the background. I studied it and reluctantly slid it back. "Thanks."

Patrice shook her head. "Keep it. Hopefully the next time I see her, I'll take a current one."

She was being optimistic, that somehow I'd repair things between us first and then the two of them. I held the picture against my chest. "Thanks." I needed Faith to accept me back into her life.

Patrice's smile returned. "You should come by for dinner some evening. Clark would be happy to see you."

Clark, her dullard husband whose only topic of conversation was Chicago sports teams' standings and statistics.

"As soon as I get settled." Wherever that was going to be.

[4] Friday, April 12, 2019 (continued)

I sat in the Tesla on my former street, my head against the steering wheel. I'd lost my status as a living human being, along with my wife, my house, and my job. Who could I turn to? Soson, by default.

From my wallet, I pulled out the business card for Jillian's lawyer, Jason Harrison, and dialed his number.

A nasal female voice answered the call, "Harrison LLC."

"Hi. My name is Randall Weinberg. Mr. Harrison met my wife and her real estate lawyer at a closing he attended for the buyer. I'm looking for her lawyer's name."

"Pardon me, but why don't you ask her?"

Catch-22. "That's my problem. I don't know where she is." Every time I thought about seeing Faith, my stomach did a back flip. To get into the right frame of mind, I pictured Faith cradling Craig in her arms after he completed his entrance into the world. *Eight years ago.* "I expect her attorney for selling the house would know where she moved. Can't you just look it up in your files? It was about a year ago." I repeated my name, Faith's name, our street address, and both of our Social Security numbers.

"I'm sorry, I can't divulge any information about Mr. Harrison's clients."

"I'm not asking for details about the transaction. I just want to let my wife know I'm okay. Can you ask Mr. Harrison to consider my request?"

"One moment, please."

I waited for what felt like half an hour for her to come back on the line. In real-time, it had been only six minutes. "Mr. Harrison remembers the closing as rather unique. Your wife told him that you were dead."

Because she'd just gotten a judge to make that so. "She was mistaken." The more I considered how she'd effectively left me behind and cut ties to all of her friends, the more I worried about how Hamza was manipulating her, and how he was doing it. Blackmail? Drugs? The sooner I found her, the sooner I could rescue her from his control.

"Mr. Harrison told me he thinks she deserves to know that you're alive. Let me check our records." She hummed some song I didn't know while she worked. If I knew how to operate the radio in Soson's car, music might provide a pleasant distraction from all the unanswered questions banging around in my head.

"I found it." She read me my wife's lawyer's name, Andrew Tobias, and his phone number. "Now that you're back, Mr. Harrison told me to offer his services for any legal work you require."

"No thanks. I already have a lawyer. Thanks for your help." I ended the call.

My call to Mr. Tobias went straight to voice mail. I left a message for him to call me at his earliest convenience. I wanted to let Faith know I was alive before anyone else told her, but a growing list of people already knew—Soson, Patrice, Jillian the neighbor and three lawyers, including Tonya.

It took about half an hour to drive to Precision Biometrics. Luckily, their business model was walk-ins only. A pleasant and efficient clerk named Gloria gave me forms to fill out. She offered the option of sending my prints to both the State Police and the FBI. I chose both because Tonya hadn't specified. The scans were electronic, not requiring ink. I was required to provide an email address for the results.

Given how things had been going, I didn't expect that my old MyPlace email address was still valid. "I don't have a current one."

"That's okay. I'll wait while you set one up on Google."

My fingers felt huge on the small cellphone screen. I stopped counting how many times I had to delete and retype misspellings. Who designed this user interface anyway? Finally, I got an email account established and shared the address with Gloria. She advised me that I might have the results as soon as Monday.

I choked when she asked me to pay a ninety-dollar fee. Tonya hadn't said anything about that. With this transaction, I'd cut my available cash to about forty bucks.

I needed a source of money for food and shelter. ChiLabs would have stopped my payroll direct deposits when I disappeared. No reputable scientific establishment would hire me after a background check reported that I'm dead. I got goosebumps every time I thought about my status.

The clock on the Tesla's huge screen showed I had hours to kill before I needed to drive to ChiLabs and give Soson back his car. He'd promised to take me to dinner, after which I'd need someplace to stay for the night. I wouldn't depend on his generosity, but I'd have to ask. I winced at the thought of spending the night in a homeless shelter or a shared room at the YMCA. Faith in hiding. Mom and Dad passed. All I had was Soson, and that didn't feel like a relationship I could depend on.

Damn, the year 2019 sucked.

Driving around in the vicinity of my neighborhood, I found a Starbucks in a strip mall on Roselle Road. A jingling sound in my pocket as I walked to the door reminded me that I still had keys to our old house. Presenting them to the buyers would freak them out even worse than my sudden appearance.

Inside, I used my Starbucks Card for a small coffee and one of their overpriced roasted ham, Swiss and egg sandwiches left over from the breakfast rush.

While I ate and drank, I couldn't stop thinking about Faith. How could she afford to buy herself a new place, wherever that was? She would have had to pay off the mortgage when she sold our old house. Another loan, without income? Maybe the proceeds of my insurance policy? Hamza might have advised that, but what did he know about money? His master's degree was in electrical engineering. I wouldn't even recommend him to add a wall outlet.

Bastard repeatedly asked for details about my tumor-treating particle project, as if he would have understood them. I considered a restraining order, but we both worked in the same tower on the same floor. Fortunately, I wasn't in his reporting chain, or I would have resigned. Dad always said to watch out for submariners, folks aiming to scuttle your career.

I hoped to take Craig on outings like Dad and I had shared, distant or nearby. Those trips gave us quality time to talk about big issues like life and death, or small things like keeping the gas tank filled. I scanned the dash for a fuel gauge. Instead, the charge level on the big screen showed 89%. When I was in high school, Dad used to drive us regularly to a nearby gas station on Chicago's North Side, more like a shack with a couple of pumps in front. He'd fill up and then hang out and chat with the proprietor, a guy he called CJ. They knew each other from school or maybe the Navy. As a kid, I didn't ask a lot of questions about their relationship.

After watching him and CJ work on cars, Dad insisted I take an auto repair class at community college while I was in high school. I passed with an A. That's when I found out that Dad's ulterior motive was for the two of us to do oil changes and other maintenance on our cars to save money.

The big event in CJ's life was being offered a GoTane franchise for cheap. That's when he moved up to Schaumburg, which was expanding as a community. Dad had helped with the paperwork. Once it was up and running, he drove us there to give CJ his business and catch up. When GoTane went out of business due to competition from Shell, Mobil and the other big oil companies, CJ was back on his own. God, that was so long ago.

Was CJ's station still in business after all this time? I had to know, if only to see a familiar face. I drove down Wise Road, one of Schaumburg's main drags, and found the building on Mitchell Boulevard about a block south. The post on the corner of his lot was missing the large rectangular GoTane sign, leaving an empty metal frame.

The building itself, plain brick with large picture windows and two bays for service alongside, revived memories from my childhood. CJ was someone Dad confided in. They'd had lots of quiet conversations in the back room of the station while I played out front with GoTane-logoed toy tankers and tow trucks.

Two old-style gas pumps that CJ relocated from his station in the city stood guard in front. GoTane had fought CJ about those and lost.

I parked alongside the service building and walked in. A bald old man sat in a textured cloth recliner eating peanuts in the shell, watching a twelve-inch black and white TV set with a rabbit-ear antenna.

"CJ?" I asked.

He didn't respond. I came closer and repeated my question.

He swung around in the chair, spilling peanuts into his lap. "Fill 'er up yourself and put cash in the fishbowl."

On a table near the front door, a glass jar stuffed with miscellaneous bills and a puddle of change at the bottom made it clear that others had followed his directions.

"I'm Randy Weinberg." My dad Seymour always went by his nickname. "Sy's son?"

He blinked and pulled glasses down from the top of his head. "Little Randy, back again? How the hell are you? Why, I haven't seen you since you were as high as a doorknob."

I'd been close to five feet the last time Dad and I filled up and caught up, but this was no time to correct him. "I was in the neighborhood and decided to stop by and see you."

"Well, you done seen me. Now go pump your gas like a good kid and leave me to my reruns."

I recognized the game he was watching. In December 2003, my father and I saw the Green Bay Packers play the Oakland Raiders live in Wisconsin. Brett Favre's father had died the day before, but he played anyway, passed for four touchdowns in the first half, and 399 yards total in a 41-7 win. I'd admired Favre for his ability to concentrate under emotional pressure.

"Wouldn't you rather watch something current?" I had no clue what was going on in the world. Maybe I could catch a news broadcast before driving to ChiLabs.

"Don't want no new-fangled technology. Cable services and Wee-Fee and all that stuff costs money. And since I don't remember most of the old games, they're new to me."

On the shelf below his TV set, someone had installed a VCR and provided a box of videotapes. So much for watching a local channel.

"Where you been all these years?" CJ held out a handful of peanuts, which I refused.

It was impossible to explain the details of my educational journey in terms he'd understand. After high school, college for a bachelors, a masters and two simultaneous doctorates in particle physics and quantum mechanics. "School." I added "A career. And I grew up," to my detail-free summary. My eight-year gap would be beyond his comprehension. Even I didn't understand it.

He looked me up and down. "Yep, you sure have. You got any kids?"

Could I claim one I'd never met? I swallowed hard. "One son, Craig, eight years old." I couldn't wait to meet him and start building a father/son relationship.

"Bring him by some time. Never too young to learn about cars. Put your car up on the rack and show him the right way to do an oil change like your father taught you."

Without a car or access to my son, I filed his invitation for some future date.

I worried that the old guy, much older than the last time I'd seen him, wasn't taking care of himself. The smell of gas and oil fumes mixed with body odor told me the place hadn't been cleaned in years and that CJ didn't care a lot about personal hygiene. "Where are you living these days?"

"Upstairs. There's two bedrooms. My boy Mickey ran off to Hollywood for stardom and never came back, so the second one is empty. Even got a bathroom. How about you? You got a place? A nice house I bet."

The house Faith sold had been very nice, but I aspired to own someplace nicer, in a better school district. Where *was* Craig going to school now? "Not at the moment. My wife and I are separated, and I haven't found a place yet."

"Oh, that's too bad. My wife died before she could leave me. Raised my son all by myself.

Not an easy task. Glad your young'un has both parents."

My stomach clenched. He didn't yet, but I'd change that. Faith had kept Soson away from Craig. She'd have to let me see him after the judge made me alive again, wouldn't she?

He stroked his chin, which suffered from several days of growth. "Well, given how much your Dad helped me setting up the franchise and all, it's the least I can do."

"What is?" Had he forgotten that the franchise failed?

"Lettin' you stay here, of course. My son's room isn't much and I'm a terrible landlord, but it's yours, if you'd like. At least it'll give you a roof over your head. Besides, I could use the company."

"You want me to stay here with you?"

"Well, I ain't moving out if you're movin' in. *Of course*, with me. God, young'uns these days have no sense. Thought your father would've taught you better. Nowadays these schools—"

My attention drifted when CJ mentioned schools. All I needed was the name of either Craig's school or his teacher and I could see him for the first time. I wouldn't have to tell him I was his father right away. I could just be a visitor to his classroom. "CJ, you're a lifesaver. I accept." After Soson and I finished dinner, I'd ask him to drop me back here. "How will I get in after the station closes tonight?"

69

"Show up and ring the bell. A couple of times, since I don't hear so good. It'll take me a few minutes to come down and let you in."

"Do you have a spare key?"

"Sure do. In the cash register."

I punched the NO SALE button on the antique cash register and the drawer rumbled open. In the far-right compartment, I found a key on a ring with a GoTane emblem. "I'll let myself in."

"Oh. okay. Didn't know you had a key."

I added his memory issues to my list of concerns. "Thank you so much. I'll see you later."

"Hang on there. I need to be sure you're going to provide my customers good service."

"Excuse me? You want me to work here to pay for my room?"

"There you go, showing that brain of yours *is* working. There's a car up on one of the lifts. Go change the oil. The owner expects their car before closing."

The idea of doing something tangible that had value seemed pleasantly grounded in reality. Nothing else in my life was making sense.

Why not do as he asked? I'd never solve the issue of the eight-year gap without getting into my office and examining the experiment's results. I was in a holding pattern about Faith until her real estate lawyer called back. I couldn't take any steps to be declared alive until Tonya got me a court date.

I went into the service area, rolled up my sleeves and examined my patient, a pristine 1958 Buick Roadmaster 75 Riviera in sunflower yellow with a white top. It must have been from a collection because no one would use it as a daily driver.

I found a wrench to open the drain and a sloped container to hold the old oil. Despite my best effort to stay clean, splatters dotted my shirt and slacks. At least I had new clothes from Target in Soson's car.

I figured out how to lower the car and fill the engine from a huge oil tank using an extended flexible hose. After I checked the oil level, I scrubbed my hands with a bar of gritty soap I found at the sink. A wave of satisfaction gave me goosebumps. Why did performing such a simple task feel so rewarding?

When I went back to the office, CJ was still watching the replay.

"All done." I pointed in the direction of the service bays. "Do you want to check my work?"

"Nah, I trust you. You're Sy's kid. Set yourself a high bar like your old man."

"I know you two were close." So that's it? I passed? "Do you want me to drive the Buick around the block, just to make sure?"

"I'll drive it later when I make a grocery run. Need to restock the pantry for two of us."

"In a customer's car? Should you be doing that?"

"What do ya mean? That beauty is mine." CJ's mouth broke into a big smile. Over the years, he had lost and not replaced a few teeth.

I didn't feel snookered. The process of working on CJ's car had lifted my spirits. "Okay if I change clothes before I go?"

"Sure. Use the upstairs bathroom. While you're up there, check out Mickey's closet. Might have left some clothes behind. You can use them if they fit. You two are about the same size."

"I will." I got my new outfits out of the Tesla, went upstairs, and washed. CJ had left some clean towels in a laundry basket. I borrowed one and changed clothes. I stacked my dirty outfit in the corner of the bedroom I guessed was Mickey's by the carousel wallpaper.

Out of curiosity, I opened the door of Mickey's closet. I found a variety of clothing styles, as if he'd dabbled with fashion. Brown corduroys. A pair of leather pants, which I wasn't going to use even if they were my size. Bell bottoms, a throwback to before he was born. A navy three-piece suit, which I expect he used for weddings and funerals. They all looked way too big.

On the floor, my foot bumped a cardboard box. I knelt down and rummaged through the contents, remnants of CJ's relationship with GoTane as a franchisee: an Owner/Operator guide in a turquoise and brown vinyl binder, one GoTane baseball cap, and a pad of empty reorder forms so CJ could buy supplies like branded cans

72

of oil and lube and GoTane shirts for him and his employees.

I nudged the box back into the closet, jogged downstairs and called to CJ, "I'll see you later tonight."

"You stayin' here? Sounds good to me. I could use the company. By the way, I think I saved a pair of Mickey's overalls, in case he came back. Might keep you from getting your nice clothes all dirty."

I felt stupid, not asking before I did the work. "Thanks."

Late that afternoon, I drove back to ChiLabs, watching to make sure I didn't exceed the speed limit while reacting to a variety of beeps as the Tesla attempted to communicate with me. Stay in my lane. Maintain an appropriate distance from vehicles in front of me. Why wouldn't it just let me drive? Didn't Tesla trust human beings?

One space was open in the recharging area, so I parked Soson's car there. It took a minute to remember how to open the hatch to charge the car but I got it plugged in.

I called Soson from the driver's seat. "I'm back, and your car is charging."

"Good. Did you see Faith or Craig?"

A hollow feeling returned. That had been my self-assigned task for the day, not performing an oil change. "No, but maybe it's better this way

73

for now. I can't just spring my return on her. I'll have to figure out a gentle way."

"You finally agree? Good. Dinner is on me tonight. You bought clothes? I would prefer not to dine with someone who has worn the same items for eight years."

I examined my Target outfit. Nothing fancy, but at least it didn't have oil spatters. "As a matter of fact, I did. And I found a place to stay."

"*Khorosho*. Good, I was worried you would ask me. Having you as a houseguest would cramp my style."

Soson had a reputation as a ladies' man. Or he used to. Despite that, many ChiLabs female employees agreed to date him until they figured out he wasn't looking for a serious relationship. Then they'd dump him. If anyone had a negative reputation at ChiLabs, I figured Soson was in worse standing than me, at least with female employees.

"I spoke with Tonya," I said. "She told me we'll have to go to court to get my death reversed."

"Ah, *tovarish*, if it was only that simple for the rest of us to get a do-over."

Some day after Tonya got my status repaired, I'll pump Soson for details about the two of them. "Can I come in and use a bathroom?" Once I got past building security, there wouldn't be anything or anyone to stop me

74

from visiting my office. Except maybe Soson, and I could handle him.

"Wait until the mass migration finishes. Then you can use the public facilities on the main floor."

"If you insist." I wanted Soson to provide a guest pass so I'd have a chance to go upstairs. I'd done a precise set of calculations in preparation for the experiment and checked them over a dozen times for the scarce opportunity to use the linear accelerator. I'd even memorized the plasma temperature and laser beam settings so there were no pieces of paper or removable media to lose.

I tried to remain patient while I waited for the building to empty.

[5] Friday, April 12, 2019 (continued)

I sat in Soson's car, alternating between watching the battery charge and playing a video racing game on the large screen. When owners of other cars came out to retrieve them, I looked away. After employee exits slowed to one every five minutes, I walked into the lobby.

A different guard than the one on duty that morning nodded.

Soson approached and swiveled his head, probably looking to see if the coast was clear. He made eye contact and muttered, *"Neryashlivyy mal'chik."*

I remembered that phrase from the time he'd chastised himself for dripping ketchup onto a white dress shirt while devouring a one-pound burger.

He ran one finger along my jawline. "You have grease speckles on your face."

I hadn't recalled seeing any spots above my neck. "That's what happens when you do an oil change."

He pointed. "Use the bathroom."

"Do you have anything that removes grease? That liquid pink soap isn't going to work." Dad used Lava. I showed him a couple of oil patches on my hands I'd missed.

"You did not stain my leather interior, did you?"

"I did my best to keep the car clean." Actually, I hadn't noticed.

"I will check in the equipment closet upstairs." He narrowed his eyes. "You want to get into your office, no?"

"You know I do."

"Not tonight. If I let you in now, we will never leave, and I could use a nice dinner. We will come back this weekend. Sunday? There will be few people here."

"Okay, I'll wait. But I'm holding you to your promise."

I waited at the public bathroom door while Soson fetched some generic cleaner from the equipment room. I used it successfully to wash the grease from my face and hands.

When I came out, Soson asked, "Where is this place you are staying? I do not want to pick a restaurant that is out of the way."

"I'm rooming at CJ's in Schaumburg."

"Who or what is a CJ?"

"He's an old friend." I described how I'd met him through my father.

"You will be living at a gas station? Odd choices you make." The parking lot was almost empty by the time Soson led me to his car. "We are dining at Geneva Country House. We could both use a beer, and they have a healthy variety."

Just as I handed him the key fob, my phone rang. I stopped short while Soson walked around his car. "Hello?"

"Mr. Weinberg? This is Tonya Smirnov."

That was quick. "Thanks for calling back."

"I learned that Cook County handled your wife's death in absentia motion. Judge Iverson at the courthouse in Arlington Heights presided. I got us on his docket Monday morning, as a favor. Eight AM sharp."

"I'll meet you there." I'd planned on locating and going to Craig's school as soon as I learned where Faith lived. Being young, I hoped he'd take my return in stride. "Thank you so much." I hung up.

Soson stood alongside his Tesla.

"Looking for damage?" I asked. "There isn't any. I did get a speeding ticket. And one for an expired license."

"*Da,* I spoke to the officer. It could have been much worse. Grand theft."

How many favors was I going to accumulate for Soson's assistance?

He unplugged his car from the charger. "The speeding ticket was partially my fault. I should have taken the car out of ludicrous plus mode. Who just called?" He got in and held out the policeman's documents I'd left on the passenger seat.

I slid in and took my tickets from Soson's hand. "Tonya. God, what a voice. I'm going to court Monday to get my life back."

"Don't tell me. You'll need to borrow my car again?" He shook his head.

"That Uber thing you mentioned." I held up my phone. "How do I contact them?" I'd have to figure out a way to pay for it.

"Using an app. I will show you later." He started the car. The headlights came on automatically.

Soson authoritatively announced the restaurant's name to the dashboard. A map appeared with the route, including alternative choices and traffic jams. As he pulled out from the charging station area, headlights from a blue car behind us momentarily reflected off the passenger side mirror, blinding me.

Rather than stare at the dashboard display, I used our time together to catch up. "Where are you living these days?" Soson had always tried to keep his commute short, especially because of winter driving hazards.

"When I saw you last in 2011, I had an apartment in a nice complex in Batavia. After my lease expired, I moved upriver to Geneva. Cute town with lots of nice restaurants on the river. After that, I relocated to St. Charles. I am loving it there."

Further north every couple of years. "Why do you move so often?"

"When there are no interesting women in my apartment complex left to date, it is time to relocate."

Evidently Soson's supply at ChiLabs had run short and he'd turned to female renters who were handy and didn't know his game. "Won't you ever settle down?"

"No need. Children only bring expenses and trouble."

"What if your parents had the same opinion?"

Soson glared. "*Mu'dak.*"

He didn't translate. "I'm waiting to get Faith's address from the lawyer she used to sell the house. He must know where she moved."

"Faith sold your house? There was no need, after Hamza got her affairs in order." Soson shot me a glance. "She could be anywhere."

I hadn't considered the possibility that Faith had left the immediate area. Her parents had passed away before 2011 and never met their grandson. I kept telling myself that despite turning her back on Patrice, Faith still had some roots that would keep her close.

Occasionally, I checked the passenger side mirror. The same car from ChiLabs' lot was still behind us.

"What is the matter?" asked Soson. "You removed all of the grease speckles."

"I could swear we're being followed."

"We should add paranoia to your symptom list." He pulled a metal cigar tube out of his suit coat pocket. "I bought this in anticipation of Craig's birth. It has only aged by now."

"Save it for when I'm declared alive." Now was no time to celebrate. "Tell me, how many cars have you owned in the last eight years?" I'd seen Soson trade in cars before their first scheduled oil change.

He pocketed the cigar. "Four. My Tesla is the latest, and it is amazing. I may keep it for a few months."

I'd been familiar with Soson's self-indulgence, but never at Porsche prices. Teslas couldn't be that much cheaper.

At the Geneva Country House, Soson requested a booth at the rear of the restaurant. Shortly after we chose from the beverage menu, the waitress delivered two frosty steins.

Soson hefted one. "Here is a toast to life. Literally. *L'chaim!*" He took a gulp and wiped his mouth.

"Thanks." I drank at a more leisurely pace, in between recounting the day's events.

"What will you do, after your status as a living person is restored?" he asked.

"Given the Labs atmosphere you told me about, I'll have to find employment somewhere else. I'd prefer to continue in research, but I'll go into teaching if none of the local labs are willing to offer me a position."

"What a sense of humor you have! Do you think there will not be a bidding war to hire you? Your thinking has always been ahead of the pack."

"I appreciate that." 'What' had happened to me was evident. 'How' it happened remained a mystery. While the creative side of my brain generated possibilities, the logical side shot them all down as absurd. *When two things happen*

81

simultaneously, it's reasonable to search for a cause-and-effect connection. "You examined the results. Do you have any idea what went wrong with my experiment? Maybe some setting got changed at the last minute?"

"That morning, Hamza escorted an entourage of senior executives to your office, talking like he was the primary researcher, not you. When I objected, he told me to be quiet. I do not believe he got close enough to the controllers to make any changes. In any case, you will see for yourself on Sunday."

"The only way he'll ever come up with something innovative is by stealing it."

Soson nodded. "Which is why you should keep your distance from him."

"I'll drink to that." I took a bigger swig of rapidly warming beer. Bitterness increased as the temperature rose. I scanned other tables. Along the windows that looked out on the parking lot sat a young woman who resembled the one who'd been on the Lab stairs this morning. At a distance, I couldn't see her eyes but they shared identical profiles, including a turned-up nose. Without her ball cap and ponytail, her hair fell around her shoulders. "Don't stare, but I think the young woman alone by the window followed us here."

Soson disobeyed my caution and gazed in her direction. "I don't recognize her."

"She must work at the Labs. Why else would she have been sitting on the steps?"

"Someone's daughter perhaps? Or wife?" Soson had nearly finished his beer.

"Are you sure you don't recognize her? She may have been the driver of the car that followed us."

Soson shrugged and took another longer look. "On second thought, she may be on the Labs' payroll. Martin, I think, something Martin."

"This can't be a coincidence. I'm going to go over and speak with her."

Soson put his paw on my arm. "No! You are dead, remember? Besides, if she did follow us, she will only deny the accusation."

The waitress brought Soson another cold beer.

I heaved a sigh as I held my stein in both hands and stared down into the yellow brew. "This is all my fault. I messed up the experiment and somehow it threw me eight years into my future."

"Do you hear yourself? You cite your experiment as the cause of your leap." Soson's face radiated joy. "Finally, you are talking time travel. *Malchik*, this is certain to get you a Nobel, even more important than a cancer cure."

"I guess so." I wasn't comfortable or confident, not until I had more proof than just my physical presence. Still, that solution fit. "Did anything in the results support that conclusion?"

"I am not qualified to assess such things. That would require a Nobel Prize winner." He smiled and drank.

"Cut that out!"

"You will see the report from the analytics team. They reviewed the experiment results in detail."

I lowered my voice. "If it was time travel, a lot of good it's doing me. At Faith's request, the government says I'm dead, and I have a son who I've never met." I nodded in the direction of the far side of the room. "And someone from Labs is following me."

"Too bad you cannot have a do-over." He broke eye contact.

"What are you suggesting? Go back to 2011 and make everything right?" I pulled Soson's mug from his grasp. "That's it. No more beer for you. How can you be so casual about physics? Shit, don't you remember anything I've taught you?"

"Eight years ago, you would have called me crazy for suggesting forward time travel. Now you admit, to me at least, you did precisely that." He reclaimed his mug. "Why should I suffer criticism for the natural conclusion? If there is forward, there must be backward."

I shook my head, unable to assemble a mathematical challenge to his claim. I was too tired, suffering a headache from the beer. Evidently, Soson had no such difficulty.

The waitress cleared the table and left our bill. Soson's plate was empty. Mine was still half full. Somewhere along the line, I'd lost my appetite.

"*Ty yesh' kak ptitsa.*" Soson pulled out his wallet without hesitation.

"Which means?"

"You eat like a bird. Next time, order from the children's menu."

"I have a lot on my mind, or hadn't you noticed?"

The young woman was still there, nursing a glass of white wine and nibbling at a plate of pasta. It wasn't likely a coincidence that she showed up on ChiLabs' steps and at Soson's choice of restaurant on the same day. That bet had worse odds than winning the Lottery.

"Once you get a job, you can pay for your own meals." Soson handed his credit card to the waitress and winked at her. She seemed to ignore the gesture.

"Fine by me." Tips of what looked like tickets peeked out from his billfold. "Are you going to the theater? Since when have you become cultured?"

"These?" He pulled them out and put them on the table. "Lottery tickets. Winners, I hope. Hamza talks about Powerball like a little boy at Christmas every time I see him."

Soson spent money like he'd already hit the jackpot, the opposite of my situation. "The easiest thing would be to come back to ChiLabs—"

"Perhaps I could put in a good word." Soson tapped his temple with an index finger. "Hamza would have to be a complete nincompoop to disagree with your return, no matter what your peers might think."

"Hamza would have a say in that decision?"

"What can I tell you? There was an opening for Senior Director of Facilities. As such, he would participate in research hiring decisions. Management chose him because he kept his nose clean."

"Hamza's nose was always brown. You realize, when I get a good paying job, I'll stop going to dinner with you."

Soson laughed, hiccupped, and laughed even louder after every subsequent eruption. People around us reacted with smiles of their own. The young woman across the room avoided eye contact and seemed displeased. Maybe her pasta was over-cooked.

After the waitress returned Soson's credit card, we left the restaurant. I peeked over my shoulder. Ms. Martin was visible through a window, watching our departure. I stifled the urge to go back in and confront her. Soson was right, that wouldn't get me anywhere.

He unlocked the doors to his Tesla. I slid into the passenger seat.

"You should get yourself a car." Dashboard icons appeared when he started the silent engine. "I can pick you up on Sunday and drive you to the Labs, but I cannot be your daily chauffeur."

"You're right, but there's a problem. With less than fifty bucks to my name, I don't think I'll be able to afford many Uber rides, let alone my own vehicle."

After a forty-minute silent drive, Soson pulled up at CJ's. The flickering OPEN neon sign illuminated the front door. "You are staying here? What, you sleep on a tire rack?"

"CJ's got a spare bedroom upstairs. And he's letting me stay for free." Except for some work around the garage.

"Beware of free. It never is."

"Will you be okay?" I asked.

Soson said, "Take me home" and a map appeared showing the route. "See, it is thirty minutes, almost all highways. The Tesla will drive most of the way by itself, so have no worries about me."

"Good night, and thanks." I got out and stepped away from his car.

When Soson drove off, I used CJ's spare key and let myself in. I felt my way around in the dim light. When I got halfway up the staircase, CJ greeted me, a pistol in his hand. "Whatcha' doin' here?"

I froze. "CJ, it's me, Randy. I stopped by to see you earlier. You gave me a key." I dangled it in the glare of a bare bulb. "You said I could stay in your son's room."

"Little Randy?" He lowered the weapon. "Yeah. Sure. Folks in this neighborhood think the place is abandon'. I've had break-ins before."

"I won't cause you any trouble." I followed him to the second floor.

Before I could retire into Mickey's room, he asked, "How many hours you gonna' put in?"

"Excuse me?"

"You know, to work off your food and rent. Pump gas. Wash windshields. Do the occasional oil change. My station is all about service."

"I'll be glad to help out around here as much as I can, but I have some personal stuff to work on. My life's a bit of a mess right now."

CJ nodded like a bobblehead doll. "Tell me about it. My sister, she says I should use the money I get from selling this place to bankroll my retirement. Someplace warm. Enjoy my late years. Easy for her to say. She lives with her kids and grandkids in Atlanta. This place is all I've got. I don't want to walk away from it."

"I know exactly what you mean." I'd had the same feelings when I visited ChiLabs, like I'd left something incomplete.

"We'll talk about the details tomorrow. 'Nite."

If he remembered. "Have a good night's sleep."

"I'll make pancakes in the morning. Mickey used to like my pancakes." CJ closed the door to his bedroom.

Does Craig like pancakes? Maybe I could bring him to meet CJ, like Dad did for me. Faith would never let me bring him. She'd be worried I wouldn't bring him back.

As I slipped under dusty covers, scenes from the book *A Connecticut Yankee in King Arthur's Court* forced their way into my consciousness. No happy ending there. I cast the concept aside, instead wondering how successful a student Craig was, and what types of kids he'd chosen to hang with. Was he a geek like me, or did he excel at sports? No matter what brought me to 2019, I couldn't wait to meet him.

Day 2

I dragged myself out of bed and headed downstairs to the smell of bacon. CJ had converted the storage room behind his front office into a kitchen. A laminated four-by-four slab of pretend butcher block, held up by two sawhorses, sat along one wall. Three metal folding chairs were tucked into the accessible sides. Two narrow tables flanked a freestanding sink connected to wall spigots by short lengths of garden hose. One table held a small microwave and a propane-fueled Coleman. A slanted griddle and a toaster sat next to each other on the other table, with a mini fridge on the floor below. Bacon sizzled, grease running down to a tray at the bottom. A squatty tarnished kettle rattled on the back burner.

The old man stood at the camp cook stove, one hand hovering over an open egg carton. "How do you like 'em? Scrambled? Over easy?"

Had CJ changed his mind about pancakes or forgotten? "You don't have to go to all that trouble."

"How you gonna' put in a full shift on an empty stomach? You ain't plannin' on leaving me alone on the weekend, are ya?"

I wished CJ hadn't remembered that I'd agreed to work for my room and board. "A full shift?"

"You have a bit of hearing trouble, too?" He raised his voice. "I said, a good breakfast will keep you going until you make a lunch run. I found a pair of Mickey's overalls boxed up in the garage. Wear those when you're on duty. Your eggs?"

"Sunny side up." I was still waiting on Faith's real estate lawyer for her address. If he called, I'd find a way to get there. CJ would have to tolerate an absence. I took a seat on a metal folding chair at the table.

CJ cracked two eggs into a hot pan. "Be ready in a second." He plucked two pieces of well-done bread from the toaster and put them on a GoTane commemorative plate in the middle of the table. "You know how to pump gas? Silly question, 'course you do. I take cash money only, round to the closest quarter. Hate them small coins. Can't roll them worth a damn. Money goes in the glass pickle jar near the door. If a customer overpays, that's a tip. Keep it for spending money."

"No credit cards. Got it."

"You remember anything what you learned when you came here with your Dad?" When the kettle whistled, CJ tapped instant coffee from a jar into a GoTane mug and poured in boiling water.

"A little. And I took an auto maintenance course at the local college." Decades ago.

"Good. Some folks still appreciate our customer service." He put the coffee on the table in front of me. "Milk? Sugar?"

"Black is fine."

"Might need to do an oil change if the need arises." He massaged his fingers. "Harder for me to loosen them oil plugs these days."

"I think I can handle it." I'd had no problem changing the oil in his Buick.

He wagged one of his fingers in my face. "And we don't do work on any of them fancy new models with electrics under the hood."

"You mean electric vehicles, like Teslas?"

"Hell no! All them cars that got rid of carburetors and such. Ain't trained on them. And I won't buy the expensive diagnosis boxes." CJ put a knife and fork on the table near me.

CJ was limiting engine services to very old cars, given that most manufacturers had moved on from carburetors a long time ago.

"Understood. I need to make a call this morning if that's okay."

"On your own phone?"

"Uh—yeah."

"Then it don't matter. You can even make long distance on your own dime." CJ slid the eggs, with broken, runny yolks, onto a plate. "There you go. Ketchup and hot sauce in the fridge." Then he left me alone to eat.

After breakfast, I found two printed phone directories in a cabinet under a wall phone behind the service desk. On a slim chance

I might find Faith listed, I searched the White Pages for her address. Her name didn't appear but mine did, for our old house. Then I checked the date on the directory: 2009. Given the state of CJ's office, why wasn't I surprised?

To verify the second-hand information Soson had shared about Faith and my bank accounts, I got Territory National Bank's number from the Yellow Pages. Employees kept transferring me until I was connected to a clerk at the bank. When I inquired about our joint checking and savings accounts, he asked for my name, social security number and address.

After a moment, he came back on the line. "Our records indicate these accounts were closed." He paused. "The reason indicates death of spouse. This isn't a call from beyond the grave, is it?"

"Yes," I said. "Boo!" and hung up.

I changed into Mickey's overalls, which were large for my frame. I cuffed up the legs and tightened the shoulder straps to their limits.

Downstairs, CJ was standing in the kitchen doorway, the TV blasting away. If he wasn't hard of hearing from old age, then playing the TV at that volume would do the job.

"Saturday is our busy day, so keep an eye out." He returned to the kitchen.

"Sure thing." One blue bill and three green ones in the glass bottle weren't standard U. S. currency. Although I couldn't translate the words, the bills were clearly Russian, one 2,000-

ruble bill and three 200's. I brought them into the kitchen, where CJ was whipping up something in a frying pan.

"Did you see who left these?"

"Nope. Somebody pumped gas and paid with damn play money. Not the first time."

I waved them in front of CJ. "These are real, from another country."

"What am *I* gonna' do with it? You take 'em and see what they're worth."

"I'll let you know." I stuck them in my wallet. "I'll stop at a bank and have them converted."

During the first two hours of my shift, three cars came into the station. One stopped for directions I couldn't provide without doing a search on my phone. The second stopped to put air into one of his tires. I offered to help but he waved me off. The third, a black Chevy Blazer, pulled in and out without stopping.

I cleaned the store windows on the outside, wiped down the pumps, and swept the walk. I considered mounting a handmade wooden sign I'd found in the back of the service bay. It read "CJ'S GAS AND REPAIR." There was enough space in the empty metal frame at the corner of his property to accommodate it. The crumbling cement around the base wasn't a safe place for a ladder and I couldn't reach eight feet up the post without one, so I left it alone.

I considered what services the shop might be able to handle for newer vehicles and came up with oil changes, tire rotations and seasonal tire swaps, the same as CJ's list. I hated the swapping job, which is why I paid the dealership to do it for my Audi back in 2011. I hoped to be reconciled with Faith and Craig long before winter.

Finally, I went inside and approached CJ, whose eyes were fixed on a football game rerun from 1985. I recognized the names on the players' jerseys. Peanut shells littered the front of his shirt.

"Them Bears are something else." CJ cracked open another, letting the husk fall onto the floor. "They could take it all. I mean all the way to the Lombardi Trophy."

I didn't want to be a spoiler. "They're looking real good. Listen, there haven't been any customers all morning. I'll do an early lunch run if you'd like, but it'll have to be someplace within walking distance."

"Why? You don't drive?"

"Sure, I drive, but I don't have a car."

"That seems a shame." He waved his arm in the general direction of the space behind the building. "If you're interested, there's a junker out back. Somebody left it there. Don't know who it belongs to, and it ain't been driven except by Mickey once or twice. He didn't like driving stick."

I perked up. "I love manual transmissions."

"It's been sitting for a while. I ain't got no use for it so I just left it there, covered up. Go on, if it runs, it's yours. Mickey left the keys in the visor."

"Really? Thanks." Curiosity and excitement propelled me out the door and around the building. In the back corner of the property, a brown tarp with years of leaves, soot and other airborne debris covered something that had the shape of a small car. It couldn't be my Audi, could it? I peeked under the tarp. Someone had left CJ a New Beetle in bright yellow, the classic color. It reminded me of my beloved Audi TT, with similar rounded lines, just not the horsepower or amenities. I pulled off the tarp and coughed at the dust cloud. Its body showed crisscrossed abrasions, exactly like the scratches on Faith's SUV, but at ninety-degree angles. Quite the coincidence.

I found the key behind the visor, just like CJ said. I put the stick through the gears to make sure the transmission wasn't frozen. Then I put it into neutral and turned the key. Silence. I rolled a battery-jumping cart out from the service area. After a couple of minutes of charging, the engine coughed and popped until it got used to running again. I disconnected the jumper cables and drove the Beetle slowly around the building over a concrete lip and into the empty service bay. Just to be safe, I poured a can of gas stabilizer into the tank.

Before I got the Beetle up in the air, I replaced the battery and filled what looked like new tires to recommended PSI. Then I changed the oil, lowered it, filled it with regular gas from one of our pumps, and parked near the front corner of our lot. How easy it was for me to refer to the station as 'ours', not 'his.' Mickey's overalls were filthy, but I had a car to use.

I stuck my head into the office. "Thanks, CJ. That car is just what I needed."

"What car? Oh, that beater in the yard? It runs? Least I can do to repay your father. Sure, take it."

He'd forgotten his offer.

"Where you living now?" he asked. The game was in the fourth quarter, with the Bears on the verge of another historic victory.

"Upstairs. In Mickey's old room?" I was wearing his son's overalls. When he looked at me, did he see Mickey?

"Oh yeah. Good thing, you keeping me company. I forget stuff sometimes." A plate with crumbs sat on a folding table next to the lounger.

"It happens to everybody, eventually." The wall clock showed twelve-fifteen. "Sorry about that lunch run. Do you want me to get something now?"

"Don't bother. I made tuna salad. It's in the fridge if you want some." CJ's breath smelled like fish, and not fresh fish.

"No thanks. I'll find something when I take the Beetle out for a test drive. That's okay, isn't it?" I didn't want to upset my employer and get tossed out of my room.

"Nah. Go on. Young people need their freedom."

I wasn't necessarily thinking about myself as all that young. Maybe CJ was confusing me with his son because of the overalls.

I took a quick shower and changed into one of my new outfits, casual black slacks, and a grey short-sleeve polo shirt.

Putting the Beetle through the gears brought a smile to my face. I matched the speed of the cars around me, signaled my intentions, emulating a perfect driver's behaviors. I found a Starbucks a few blocks from CJ's for lunch. In between bites of my turkey and basil pesto sandwich, my phone rang. "Hello?"

"This is Andrew Tobias. I got your message."

My wife's real estate attorney, at last. I introduced myself and explained that all I wanted was his client's—my wife's—current address. As expected, he didn't believe it was me. We'd never met so how could he judge? I recited my date of birth, my Social Security Number, and the old phone number at the house.

"Faith said you were dead."

"I was away and couldn't get in touch. She had me declared dead after seven years, but now I'm back. Is this so hard to understand?"

"I was advised not to discuss the purchase with anyone." He spouted claims of lawyer/client privilege.

I interrupted. "Listen, Mr. Tobias, I don't want to know what she said about me, or details about the legal proceedings from the closing, how much she got for the house or anything else." I was curious if she'd created a new will. It would have made sense, with me gone. Was Craig the beneficiary? Who would be the conservator in the meantime? Not Hamza! "If I could have found her address online, I wouldn't be bothering you." Patrice told me she kept trying and failing.

Tobias paused. "What name did you search for?"

Then it hit me. Patrice might have only known Faith by her married name. What if she reverted back to her maiden name? "I'll try her name before we were married."

"I suggest you do, because you won't be getting any help from me." He hung up.

Living in my future was distracting. Those eight plus years had evaporated on my timeline. Even though I'd accepted that I was in 2019, I still couldn't reconcile time travel without understanding the cause.

I searched an Internet White Pages website and found her address in Schaumburg, listed under her maiden name. Thank goodness she still lived in the vicinity.

I examined my reflection in the window. I hadn't aged, as far as I could tell. I was still the

2011 version of me, with no discernable gray hair. A few strands, if you looked, but very few people got that close.

I finished my coffee and last bite of sandwich, waved to the barista in response to her smile and left the store. With a reasonable amount of money left on my card, I'd be back.

I sat in my car and reconsidered my plan to show up unannounced. The phone call to Faith had failed. *What about email?* I knew her address by heart and typed a brief message: *Dear Faith, You were right. I'm not dead. May I come and see you so we can talk? Love, Randy.* I pressed SEND. A moment later, I got a bounced message reply, that her email address was invalid. So much for advanced warning.

A florist shop caught my attention three doors down. Faith always swooned over a bouquet whenever I brought one home and it wasn't a special event.

I entered Patty's Pretty Petals and walked along their display case, looking for the right color. Faith loved pink, but most of the blooms were red, white, or yellow. Faith deserved a bouquet. Given the posted prices and cash in my wallet, I could only afford a single rose. I bought a pale red one, the best I could do.

I started the car, checked my mirrors, and pulled into traffic, the wrapped flower on the passenger seat. I hoped it would dull the shock.

Any time for hesitation ran out as a brick and glass four-story multi-unit building matching Faith's address confirmed my arrival. I parked my Beetle across the street behind a full-sized blue sports coupe, a Bentley Continental. Someone with money must live around here.

With sharp rectangular lines and a setback entrance in a nice neighborhood, I could see Faith choosing this place. New and contemporary, just her style. A reasonable size, not like some of those one-square-city-block buildings where all of your neighbors are strangers.

The landscaping was well maintained but there wasn't much lawn. Maybe we could sell the condo to break even and find a nice house with a yard. I enjoyed working around our former house, fixing small things that had gone wrong, feeling a great sense of accomplishment solving trivial problems.

As I crept up the concrete walkway with the rose in my hand, I imagined moving in. Did Faith choose one with three bedrooms, one for us, one for Craig and one to share as an office? The commute to ChiLabs wouldn't be much worse than from the old house.

I entered through glass doors into a ceramic-tiled vestibule with natural brick on two walls, an Ultrasuede couch, and an in-building intercom visitors could use to call residents. On the two-line screen, I searched the lists of tenants for Faith's maiden name, Watson. I often joked that I was her Sherlock, searching out suspect particles.

I forced my finger to press the CALL button. The phone rang. The problem of how to gently let Faith know I was alive came rushing back.

A familiar terse male voice said, "Yes?"

Hamza Bashir, the last person I wanted to speak with, was upstairs at Faith's condo in the middle of the day. Shouldn't he be at work pretending to be useful?

I was partially relieved that Faith hadn't answered. The anxiety of breaking the news to her had been deferred, not eliminated. "It's Randy. Randy Weinberg. Buzz me in so I can come up and see Faith. She needs to know I'm alive."

"I'll be right down."

"No, buzz me up." No reply. Then dial tone.

After I hung up, I noticed a box sitting against the wall addressed to Faith. Before I could read the name of the shipper, the elevator dinged. Hamza exited and strode towards the locked inner glass door of the foyer.

Wide white eyes on his olive face made it clear my presence surprised him. I expected we'd have a not so polite conversation and then go upstairs where I'd try to explain to Faith something that I didn't understand myself. What would I tell her? The same lies I'd been telling everyone, or the truth as I understood it?

Hamza opened the door just enough to slide his thin body through and let it shut behind him. Grey patches above his ears had doubled in size, in stark contrast to his short black hair. "I can always count on you to be in the wrong place at the wrong time."

"Is Faith coming down or are we going up?" I held up the wrapped flower.

"Neither." He ripped the flower from my hand, crushed it and threw it on the floor.

"Hey! That was for her." I looked over my shoulder at the lobby intercom. "I'll just call Faith and ask her to come down."

"Don't touch that!" He closed the distance until his face was inches from mine. "We must talk."

"Damn right we do. Me and Faith." I stepped over the ruined rose towards the inner door but he didn't budge. "I'm back, so consider yourself relieved or fired or whatever. I'll take things from here."

"For what reason? To put your family in jeopardy? That's not the Randall I knew." He crossed his arms. "You're not going to see Faith. Not today. Not ever."

I picked my words carefully. "You have no right to prevent me from seeing my ex-wife."

"She doesn't know you're here, and we're going to keep it that way, to protect both of you.

Soson wants something from you, something you must not give over."

"Soson is a friend and colleague." He *had* acted a bit strange since my appearance, but who could blame him? "He hasn't asked me for *anything*." Merely to accept that I'd time traveled.

"You have no idea what he is after. And what he will do to obtain it now that you've returned."

Hamza spoke gibberish. "Let's say you're right. But I don't *have* anything. No life, no job, no money. What could I give him?" Hamza's reaction to my appearance didn't match Soson's. "Did *you* know I'd come looking for my wife after eight years?"

He pulled a sheet of newsprint from his back pocket and held it up. "Look familiar?"

I scanned the front page of a *Daily Herald*, the local paper. The weather, cloudy in the mid-50's. "What am I looking for?" Headline articles about black church fires in Louisiana, a disabled boy being asked to leave a movie theater and a subpoena issued to President Hillary Clinton by a Republican-majority committee. *President Hillary Clinton?*

"The date!" He held it too close to my face. "Examine the date."

I pushed it back until the text was in focus. "Friday, April 19th, 2019."

"Today is Saturday, April 13. Do you not find this odd?" He leaned his face forward and tilted his head a bit, as if he expected me to buy into his nonsense.

"It's a phony newspaper front page. When we were dating, I had one printed up for Faith on her birthday with bogus headlines about her, to make her laugh." Was Hillary Clinton really President? "Speaking of Faith, can we go upstairs now?"

"Don't play coy. Who else but you could have brought a copy of the *Daily Herald* from 2019 back to 2011?" He put his finger an inch from my nose. "Don't you dare tell me you haven't time traveled. I just couldn't be sure of the precise date but here you are, eight years later and looking not a day older."

Soson also seemed to know I would appear. "You believe I've time traveled twice? Once to fetch the paper and once to bring it back to 2011?"

"Don't forget your third trip. You're standing here in 2019. Again."

The elevator dinged behind Hamza and the doors opened. Faith walked out wearing a short sleeve black blouse and black slacks, more beautiful than the first time I'd seen her. Is she still in mourning? She'd let her blonde hair grow out, well past her shoulders, with no apparent styling. She was thinner than I remembered, but my last memory was when she'd been pregnant. Still, her face was gaunt.

I shoved Hamza to the side and shouted, "Faith! It's me!" He tried to pull me back but he lacked upper body strength. The inner glass door rattled as I jerked the handle. She'd accept that

106

it was me the moment I took her in my arms. "Let me in!"

She stood like a scared department store mannequin, her eyes wide and mouth open.

Even though the glass was an impenetrable barrier, Hamza retained his grip on my arm.

She raised her hands to her ashen cheeks. She screamed and ran for the elevator.

"No! Don't go!"

The doors shut behind her.

I turned around to face Hamza. "Goddammit, why didn't you let me in?"

"She was looking for me, not you. She doesn't like to be alone. On workdays, I arrange for someone to come by for a few hours as company, to help clean, cook, do laundry."

"Why does she need help? She did all of that stuff when—when I was here. Why are *you* here at all?"

"She needed someone to watch out for her after you vanished. Your disappearance threw her into a depression like the doctors had never witnessed. She did everything she could to locate you, with no results, which drove her to even more extreme behavior."

His words chilled me. Faith had been independent, caring for the house while maintaining an active volunteering schedule. That was one of the things I liked about her from the start. As long as we had a place to live, food to eat, and transportation, Faith gave me plenty of slack to follow my interests while she pursued hers. I treated her with love and gentle care, and she did the same for me. "That's exactly the reason you should let me go up and help her."

"You are *not* the help she needs. The therapist is just starting to make progress. Faith let me take her out to dinner last week. Nothing fancy, a small Thai restaurant."

"She loves Thai food." A wave of sadness washed over me as I pictured them together.

"That was the motivation to get her out of the condo. And she did it without breaking down in the middle of the meal." He clicked his tongue, an obnoxious habit he hadn't overcome. "Now *you* show up. Who knows how many months you've set back her recovery?"

The elevator dinged. *Faith?* Another resident came through the open inner door and strode to the exit. I tried to get past Hamza but he blocked my path until the door clicked shut.

"Damn you. After Faith and I talk, she won't have to mourn me anymore."

"Too late for that. She'd clung to the hope that you'd be found but after seven years, she was emotionally and financially broke. The Nobel Prize money had been awarded but she couldn't touch it."

"Wait, what?"

"There are *many* things you do not know."

A Nobel for heavy ions that battle cancerous tumors would have been impossible. I hadn't conducted a successful experiment, so I couldn't have published a paper for consideration. Or had I and didn't remember?

Hamza inched his way to the locked door, as if worried I'd find a way to get through. "Your work on accelerating particle streams using a plasma frame won the award."

"It did? That was just a means to an end, no big deal. My director demanded that I write it up." Why hadn't Soson told me? Was it going to be some kind of big surprise over dinner?

"Believe me, I took no joy in my consult with Faith, but I had no choice." Hamza tucked the newspaper page into his back pocket. "She needed to put her past behind her and start a new life."

"With you?"

"No. Not with me. Men and women can have relationships that are not romantic in nature. But she is very fragile. She refused to sign the death certificate documents at the last minute. Until I explained the papers were necessary to open up your estate. Life insurance. The Nobel Prize money."

Not once did Hamza congratulate me for the prestigious award. *Jealous bastard.* "Okay, I understand why she did what she did. Maybe I even understand how you tried to help. Thanks for that. We can take it as slow as she needs now that I'm back."

"If it were that easy. After she accepted the fact that you were gone forever, she lost the will to go on without you. For a while, she was on suicide watch."

Shit!

"Fortunately, she has successfully closed the door to that part of her life." Hamza put his hand on my shoulder. "The closer your relationship to Faith now, the more both of you are in jeopardy. You are a logical thinker. Do you wish her or the boy harm?"

"Craig? No way." I needed to see him. "Is my son upstairs?"

"I was surprised when Craig asked to visit a friend today. Socializing with peers is a pleasant change from his isolation at home. Good thing he isn't here. He thinks his father died as some kind of hero. It's best for it to stay that way."

My skin chilled from an increase in adrenalin. "I understand that Faith might not be up to seeing me, but there's no way in hell you're going to keep me away from my son!"

"Then put our previous relationship aside and listen to me." He pulled out the newspaper and waved it in my face. "This is not phony. It is the front page of a newspaper I found in your home eight years ago."

"You're insane."

"Do you remember throwing away a newspaper the day Craig was born? The day you disappeared?"

"What?" I pictured myself that morning. "I went to take a piss." The ceiling light in the bathroom had been burned out. "Faith put a newspaper on the toilet seat for who knows what reason." Then it hit me. "You're not suggesting *this* was the newspaper on the toilet seat?"

"I am. It was. You brought this newspaper back to 2011 from this time period."

"No. That's not possible." This discussion resembled the one I'd had with Soson at the restaurant last night. "Something else must have happened."

"I would be pleased to hear an alternative possibility." He leaned against the glass door and folded his arms on his chest.

I hated Hamza's clipped tone of speaking and the air of superiority he wore like a Halloween costume over a body of scientific ignorance. "How did you get it, if it was in my bathroom trash?"

"Faith called my office from the hospital the afternoon Craig was born, to determine if I'd seen you. I had not, so out of concern I visited her. On top of your disappearance, she didn't have her updated medical insurance card. She sent me to retrieve it. I had to relieve myself at your home and I read the paper while I—you know. Many things didn't seem correct so I checked the date. That's when I figured out that you'd successfully traveled back in time."

"Whoa! You've got this all wrong. I haven't time traveled." It was less a lie, more like a statement unsubstantiated by mathematics. "And I don't have any intentions to do so."

"The space time continuum is a demanding mistress. I know you traveled forward in time to this year." Hamza leaned closer. "You can tell me, why did you bring this paper to 2011? And why did you return to 2019 afterwards? What is your end game?"

What had Soson said? Open your ears? "I didn't go back in time, and if presented with the opportunity, I won't."

"Except that you already have, at least once."

A trip backwards in time would explain why Hamza found the future newspaper in my bathroom. At the same time, wasn't that impossible? *Maybe not.* "Tell me again, why are Faith and Craig in danger?"

"Only collaterally. You are the target, for what you know."

"And what's this thing I'm supposed to know?"

"Why, how to travel backwards in time, of course."

I stood, speechless. Soson mentioned problems he had dealing with impossibilities. One stared me in the face. "Let me see that front page again. The bottom half."

Hamza held it up but didn't let go. Next to the winning lottery numbers, the address label in the corner made my stomach drop. "This paper was delivered to CJ's Gas and Repair."

"Where is that?"

I described the location. "He hoards old papers, but not ones from the future."

"Then we should wait until the nineteenth and see if this paper is delivered."

"How could it be delivered? You're holding it."

Hamza tucked the paper into his pocket and held me by my shoulders. "Promise me that you will not give them the secret to backward time travel. Who knows what kind of havoc they might wreak?"

Who are *they*? "That's easy. I can't share what I don't know."

"But you will learn, otherwise you cannot have taken this paper back to 2011."

Talking in circles made my brain hurt. He wasn't going to give up until I agreed. "Okay, if I accidentally learn how to travel backwards in time, I'll destroy all of my notes. That's going to have to be good enough." There were more important things to talk about. "Tell me about my son. How is he doing?"

"He is exceptionally bright, a young version of you perhaps. Responsible. Articulate. When we are both here, he spends most of his time in his bedroom reading or on the computer. It is his emotional well-being that concerns me."

"How? What have you seen?"

"He does not seem to be a happy child. What should we expect, with a despondent mother and no father? Faith's condition has had an effect on him. His teacher Ms. Sherman has

113

asked for a parent/teacher conference several times but Faith is in no condition to attend."

Ms. Sherman? "I'll go. I'm his father."

"No, you won't. He doesn't know you're alive. Imagine how Faith would react if Craig came home talking about his father. You have to stay away from him, for both his sake and Faith's. I pledged to her that I would do everything in my power to keep them safe, and that includes sane."

I needed to disclose my plans. "I'm going to court on Monday morning to have the death in absentia revoked."

"I understand completely. Being dead must be very inconvenient, but it was a necessary action at the time. Faith will not contest the procedure. But you are opening a can of worms. What will you tell the insurance company when they ask for their policy payment back? And the bank, who'll likely claim fraud? Who knows, the Nobel Committee might have questions as well." Another tongue click. "The whole framework will come crashing down. Think twice. Perhaps you are strong enough to handle the tumult, but Faith is not."

Soson had told me that Hamza had been promoted to management. "Can I get my job back at ChiLabs after I'm a real person?"

"And give you access to a facility that would allow you to develop exactly what you must stay ignorant about? Absolutely not. Keep your distance."

Hamza's demand came from some base of knowledge that required probing. "You seem to know a lot more about time travel than anybody, including me." He'd been in my office when the experiment went off the tracks. "Care to tell me what happened that morning?"

"Even now, you ask for an answer to the specific question which you must avoid. If your professional curiosity cannot be contained, I suggest you abandon your work in physics. Start a new life and a new career."

I didn't mention my upcoming visit to my office. "What do you suggest? That I sell TVs at Circuit City?'"

"They went bankrupt a year after you disappeared."

"You're smart enough to get my point." *Barely.* "Your plan to sweep me under the rug won't work."

"Fine. Assume a new identity. Pursue cancer treatments. All I know is, it will have to be without your family."

Our conversation about work reminded me of my financial situation. "I must not have planned well because I leapt forward in time without much money." I didn't find my words credible, yet they were consistent with the prevailing explanation.

Hamza pulled out his wallet. "I expected this." He pulled out ten crisp one-hundred-dollar bills. "There will be more for you later if you do as I say. Much more."

"Why don't you write me a check for half a million? My share of the Nobel Prize money?"

"Some of that is gone. Private detective bills. This condo. Extensive therapy for Faith and Craig. You left a devastated woman behind, and a son who has social issues. I invested the remainder. Money earning money."

I thought about my traffic tickets as I took the cash. "I could use a little more."

Hamza cocked his head. "For what reason?"

"Some unanticipated expenses since I've been back." I didn't share the reasons.

He pulled out eight twenties. "That's all I have."

The total covered the fines with twenty bucks left over.

Hamza extended his arm for a handshake. "We must cooperate. Faith and Craig deserve undisrupted lives."

I left his hand hanging in air. *Without me?* "I'll think about it." I'd never considered raising a toast to Hamza, but based on everything he'd done for Faith, I'd consider it.

Hamza took out his key ring and let it dangle from his hand.

I considered swiping it, unlocking the door, and going upstairs to plead my case directly with Faith. Except some of the things he argued struck home. I'd never taken even a moment to think about what would happen if I

116

died before her. Maybe because I wouldn't see the consequences like I was now. I had to think.

"One more thing. Do not interact with your associate Soson. With his promotion, he has a group of labs for which he is responsible. He might give you access based on your collegial relationship."

I'm supposed to stay away from the guy who's buying me dinner? "I'll try." I sauntered toward the exit and pointed at the box along the wall. "That was delivered for Faith."

"I'll bring it up later. Now, I must assess the impact of your appearance." I walked out of Faith's building and looked back through the front glass door into the foyer.

Hamza had waited until I was outside before he unlocked the inner door.

I pulled out the picture of Craig that Patrice had gifted me and studied it. Having confirmed where Faith lived, I could figure out the school at which Ms. Sherman worked and visit her. I hoped my son could cope with my return. Think of all of the experiences we'd share!

I put Craig's photo away and crossed the street. I understood Hamza's concerns but found them self-serving. Somehow, I needed to get past his blockade and speak to my wife.

117

By asking for more than a thousand, I had enough to get my driver's license renewed and pay my traffic tickets before the Secretary of State's office closed for the day. Except I miscalculated and had to make up the difference. My wallet was empty except for the Russian bills and a couple of singles, not enough to pay for a cup of coffee. Thank goodness for my Starbucks card.

I pulled into CJ's second service bay and got my phone out to call Soson. Hamza had cast doubts on Soson's motives. Only time would expose the truth.

I dialed Soson's cellphone number.

"Hey, *malchik*, how is it going? Are you alive yet?"

Soson loved to pull my chain, and my current circumstances provided him many opportunities. "My court date is Monday, remember?"

"Ah, yes. When should I pick you up for dinner?"

He'd presumed that our dinner dates were a regular thing, his version of being helpful. "No need. I've got a car to use. A real beauty." I petted the dashboard and got dust all over my hand. Maybe tomorrow, I'd give the Beetle a good interior cleaning.

"How about we pick someplace equidistant." Soson hummed. He was probably searching on his phone because the echo made it sound like I'd been placed on speaker. "One of my favorites. Tap and Grill. The Baker Hill Shopping Center, Glen Ellyn."

Hamza had warned me to stay away, but Soson had a huge role in this puzzle. "I'll find it." The name sounded familiar. "Six?"

"Six is good. I come straight after my shopping date."

My turn to poke back. "Anybody I know?"

"*Nyet*. You found a job yet?"

He never lets up. Was working at CJ's a job? "As a matter of fact, I have, not that it's any of your business."

"Then you will pay for your own meal?"

If I followed Hamza's advice, I could have avoided Soson's sharp banter. "Not tonight. I haven't gotten my first check yet." I didn't expect I ever would.

"See you later. Drive safe."

To be fair to CJ, I needed to spend more time working at the station. In street clothes, I could pump gas and not get dirty. I stood outside, waiting for a customer. Any customer.

A light-blue late-model Toyota Corolla pulled in alongside the building. As it got closer, I recognized the driver. Ms. Martin, from the ChiLabs steps and the restaurant.

I walked up to the driver's window. "Are you following me?"

"Soson told me where you are staying." She made a 'come closer' gesture with her finger. "Get in, we have to talk."

I wasn't going anywhere until I got some answers. "Why were you on the front steps yesterday?"

"It was my day to keep watch for you. I wasn't supposed to speak to you that morning or at dinner last night." Rosy color blossomed on her cheeks, exactly the shade of pink I'd looked for in Faith's rose. "By the way, my name is Louise. Call me Lou."

"But you can talk with me now? What changed? Are you a spy?" An SUV pulled in alongside the pumps. "Hang on a second." I approached and asked the driver if he needed any help.

"Nah, I know the drill." He got out and grabbed the nozzle from the closest pump.

"If you need anything, I'll be over there." I pointed at Lou's car." I walked over, opened the passenger door, and plopped down next to her. "Okay, what's going on? Are you working with Soson?"

"Yes, ever since you disappeared. Soson planned to introduce me after dinner tonight. I've been keeping everything I've done for the last eight years a secret. Now you're here, and I can't wait until tonight to share."

I sat sideways, facing her. "Okay, you have my complete attention." I couldn't hold back a question. "Were you a member of the analysis team that reviewed the results of my experiment?"

"That's where the story starts. I wasn't involved until the analysis team ran into a brick wall. I was Plan B, brand new to the company back then, fresh out of MIT."

"Soson told me none of my tumor-killing heavy ions showed up."

"That's true. As far as heavy ion protons? Bupkis."

She used one of Soson's words. "That's impossible. The experiment must have generated *some* cancer-killers!" I couldn't believe that after ten years of effort, the experiment was a total failure. How could I have screwed up so badly?

"I found something even better."

My head snapped up. "Like what?"

"The other analysts looked at the data starting when the stream made impact." She polished her fingernails on her shirt. "But *I* reviewed everything after the particle stream achieved speed. Tachyons showed up eight seconds *before* the initial impact."

"Impossible. Chrontins are only theoretical." The standard term was tachyons, but science fiction authors had polluted the word. I refer to them as chrontins. Particles essential to time travel.

"Not any more. We have evidence."

I must have misunderstood. "Before, not after?" Was this the proof I needed?

Lou nodded. "They sure did. Soson

121

insisted we keep the discovery a secret. Maybe that's why he's on edge. I don't know if anyone else in the world has generated any, and I haven't gone looking."

History has proven over and over that multiple scientists often come up with the same ideas simultaneously. Calculus by both Newton and Leibniz. The incandescent bulb by both Edison and Swan. Brownian motion by both Einstein and Smoluchowski. Would anyone else be paired with Hamza in future history books as inventors of time travel?

Lou sighed. "There, I feel so much better. You'll see the details tomorrow in your office."

"Soson told you he's getting me in? And you'll be there?"

"Uh-huh. Since you left, we've taken your results way further." She reached for the key, still in the ignition. "I'll tell you the rest tonight so you can be surprised in front of Soson."

My mind throbbed with anticipation. "No! Tell me now!" I had been struggling for facts on which to build a hypothesis that explained how I jumped forward eight years in time. *Now a young woman named Lou tells me my experiment generated time distortion particles.* "What did you do?"

She waved her hands in front of her. "Okay. Okay. First, we replicated your experiment to see if we'd get the same quantity of tachyons. And we did. We had no idea how many tachyons caused how much forward progress in time. After all, every test result had a built-in delay while we waited for the subject to reappear. Imagine waiting for an unknown duration to verify a set of parameters."

How about eight years? I was her first test case.

"After a series of tests using binary search, I came up with a formula to calibrate intensity of tachyons versus time displacement."

"Is that how you knew when I'd show up?"

Lou nodded. "Now we can fine-tune the combination of particle beam strength, plasma temperature and laser frequency to generate the precise density of tachyons to send something ahead in time." She beamed with pride at her accomplishment. "Our best success was a lab rat in a metal cage, who came through in perfect health one year after we sent him. The cage had scratch marks just like the ones on the hood of your SUV."

One more connection of my Beetle to time travel. Lou didn't describe her failures, which spoke volumes. Still, she'd recreated my experience on a shorter scale. I forced myself to accept time travel without corroborating formulas. *Too much empirical evidence to ignore.* "One thing. The beam in the linear accelerator travels horizontally. How could it hit my wife's SUV?"

"When I got to your office, the controller settings for the electromagnet bent the beam upwards. I've left it that way ever since. If it's not broke, don't fix it."

This whole scenario was broke. "What are your next steps?"

"Oh, I can't tell you that. In fact, I've already told you too much. I'm just a tech grunt with a good brain. Soson will get mad if I spill *all* the beans." She checked her mirrors and looked out the rear windows. "I need to get ready for tonight."

"Okay, see you later." I got out, reluctant to let her leave. I had many more questions.

Lou honked the horn, so I doubled-back to the driver's side.

She rolled down her window. "I need to come clean." She gripped the steering wheel so tight her knuckles turned white. "I've admired your work ever since my Physics teacher took his senior students on a field trip to ChiLabs."

"When was that?"

"Two thousand six. We never met, but the tour guide gave us a synopsis of the important projects in progress, and yours was at the top of the list. Because of your work and reputation, I studied physics in college. I'm working part-time on my master's degree, which is tough, but I'm planning on two doctorates, just like you."

"You've set some ambitious goals for yourself, but they should be yours, not mine."

"Like battling cancerous tumors? I was devastated when your project stopped." Her hands fell into her lap. "You see, my father was diagnosed with brain cancer a few years ago. He's getting treatments that keep him alive, but your work might have made the difference."

"I'm so sorry." If my experiment had been successful eight years ago, verification and randomized trials would have been completed in time to help her father.

"I hope you don't think I'm some kind of creep, following you around."

"More confused than worried. No one feels safe being followed. Good thing you've gone into physics because you'd make a terrible secret agent."

She laughed, so I laughed too.

"Okay, well, I'll see you later." She started her car. "And please act surprised. I don't want Soson to know I went behind his back."

"Like we've never met." I moved out of the way so she could make a three-point turn and leave.

I was grateful Lou told me about Soson's behavior after the discovery of chrontins. Why didn't he notify Chilabs' management? They would have been thrilled. I'd have to be careful dealing with him. Especially if Hamza was right and my actions put Faith and Craig in jeopardy.

That evening at the Tap and Grill, Soson's red Tesla stood out in a parking lot of white, gray, and black vehicles like a rare ruby. He was in the driver seat facing forward, his lips moving when I approached. He smiled at me, puckered as if making a kiss, pocketed his phone and opened his door.

"Chatting with your date?" I stepped back to give him room to get out.

"Oh no. Making another one for later tonight. But my best friend Randall comes first." He pointed at my Beetle. "Is *this* what you drive?"

"Something wrong with it?" I hadn't been using it very long but had become quite fond of it.

"Nothing, except you have to pay attention all of the time."

"Yeah, because I love driving, not just aiming." If by some miracle I got back to 2011 and prevented my leap forward, I wouldn't vanish. Faith and I would be financially stable and she wouldn't need to sell my precious TT.

"Come, let us celebrate your vehicle, the one that makes you work hard."

The hostess addressed Soson as Mr. Grudovich and took us to a booth near the back with a high padded leather surround for privacy. "This is where I always sit. Near the back, like

126

American gangster." He ordered two beers before I could tell him I wanted an iced tea.

Soson must have some insight into Hamza's circular statements about reverse time travel. Who else could I ask? "I'm confused about something Hamza claimed."

"You ignored my advice and met with him?"

"I couldn't help it. He was at Faith's condo. He showed me the front page of a *Daily Herald* published in 2019 that he said he found in my house in 2011. How could that happen?"

Soson's eyes opened wide and grinned. "Perhaps someone time traveled?"

No surprise. "Hamza accused me of bringing it there. But I don't know how to travel backward in time. Or forward, for that matter." Despite the presence of chrontins during my experiment.

Soson's expression told me he had answers and was hiding them. "Ignore logic for a moment." He leaned closer. "You *have* time traveled forward, of that we can be certain. And if Hamza is correct, a small possibility, you made a trip backward and brought the newspaper with you."

"Does that make this trip to 2019 my *second* visit?" The suggestion that I'd violated the laws of physics three times was ridiculous on its face.

"Consider the possibility." Soson pointed his fat index finger at me. "There's an old Russian expression—"

"From an old Russian?"

"*Chtoby dabit'sya uspekha v zhizni, nuzhno dve veshchi: nevezhestvo i uverennost' v sebe.*"

"Which means?"

"In English, you would say, 'To succeed in life, you need two things: ignorance and confidence.' Wallowing in uncertainty and achieving nothing will not sit well with you."

"Damn right it won't." He knew me too well.

The waitress interrupted as she placed two steins on the table and took our food orders.

Soson watched her swaying hips as she walked away. After she was out of sight, he said, "Fate has thrown you a fastball, *tovarish*. Swing for the fences."

"Since when do you use baseball metaphors?" I took a sip.

"Since the Cubs won the World Series in 2016."

I sputtered beer onto the table. "You're kidding, right?"

"And you missed the office betting pool." He took a slug.

I'd missed out on many things besides being with Faith and watching Craig grow up. *Damn!* When Craig got old enough to appreciate baseball, I'd take him to games like my dad used to do.

"Did you see Faith?" Soson pursed his lips.

"To answer your question, no. Hamza wouldn't allow me in. Faith came down looking for him, saw me and ran for the elevator in panic." My heart twisted.

"Now, will you keep your distance from him?"

"Your attitudes about each other are identical. Hamza advised me to keep my distance from *you*."

"What reason did my dear friend Hamza give?"

"He claims Faith and Craig are in danger because of me. Are they?"

Soson tilted his head. "It depends, *tovarish*, on your choices."

Soson and Lou both knew I'd time traveled and had kept it a secret from everyone. Including Faith. "You and I have been friends for years, working side by side. We've always had each other's backs, especially when Lab management had problems with our work."

"Do not forget. Many of those were initiated by Hamza, a very jealous man."

I didn't fall for Soson's diversion. "You suspected I was alive and didn't share that with my wife?" With that news, Faith might not have declared me dead or bottomed out emotionally.

"*Tovarish*, I am deeply sorry. I did not lie. Half-truths and withheld information, perhaps."

What was the difference?

129

"I was tempted to tell her at your mother's funeral, but she was having no part of me. Good thing because what would I have said? 'Do not despair. Your dear husband Randall is somewhere in the future. I do not know when?' No better than what you said to me. 'I was nowhere.'"

Hamza's clear message had been to avoid Soson and I'd ignored him. Soson's lies added to the reasons I should stay away.

"Do not focus on possibilities you can prevent. Instead, use your intellect to advance science." His hands covered mine, which disappeared in his grasp. "You must invent reverse time travel."

There it is, the reason Hamza told me to keep my distance. I stifled a laugh. "You might as well ask me to carry this building on my back. It can't be done. Laws of physics, remember?"

"I know you met with Louise, against my orders."

"Are you having me followed?"

"For your protection. She must have told you that tachyons generated by your experiment brought you here. Instead of dissipating harmlessly beyond the detectors, they were redirected and struck Faith's vehicle."

"But what *created* them?" The echo of my voice startled me. "My experiment wasn't designed to produce chrontins. They never showed up in my computations or simulations." *Who had access besides Soson?* "You said Hamza

130

was in my office that morning. Do you think he changed something?" I wouldn't have put sabotaging my experiment past him. Hamza had demonstrated his jealousy about my project and my wife. *Damn him!*

Soson guzzled his beer and wiped moisture from his upper lip. "I examined the settings after Hamza and his entourage left, but I had nothing to compare. You did not leave documentation."

I hadn't trusted paper or thumb drives. Instead, I'd memorized the settings, and hadn't been there to make corrections. "I need to verify all of this in my lab tomorrow."

"And you shall."

The waitress arrived with our food.

We ate in silence. With half of my patty melt and tots still in front of me, my stomach struggled to digest both my food and the danger Hamza had alleged. Would inventing reverse time travel have negative consequences for my family? I held the no-longer frosty mug in both hands. "I'm sorry, but I won't knowingly bring harm to my wife or son. Reverse time travel is a non-starter."

Soson wiped barbeque sauce from his mouth with a cloth napkin. "While you were away, without your guidance, I did a stupid thing, for which now we are both paying a price." He resumed eating.

"Oh yeah? What did you do?"

"I am embarrassed to disclose." He ran a hand through his wavy salt and pepper hair. "When I learned about your accomplishment, I felt obligated to reach out, to confirm the science. After all, I was your assistant, not the designer."

"Oh yes, a great assistant. Someone I thought I could trust."

"Then my subsequent actions will disappoint." He heaved a sigh. "A former colleague in Russia had been doing high-speed particle research before I left for America. I contacted him."

"And told him an experiment had generated chrontins? My god, do you know how stupid that was?"

"Not at the time." Soson hung his head. "I believed that we could discuss pure science without interference of politics. I did not know that an oligarch in the petroleum business funds him. And even though I never said the word 'tachyon', he understood our success."

"You told an enemy scientist we discovered a way to perform forward time travel? You've committed treason! And stop using that word. They're chrontins!"

"Do you not want to be understood by others in our field? Everyone else calls them tachyons."

"Well, they're wrong." I must have spoken too loudly because nearby patrons stared at our table. "If light particles are called photons from the Greek *phōs* meaning 'light,' it's logical to call time particles chrontins. Chron from the Greek word *khronos* meaning 'time.' What is a tachy anyway?"

Soson's stein, tipped up high, hid his reaction to my explanation. He wiped his mouth with the back of his hand. "My colleague has asked me to solicit your assistance..." He broke eye contact.

A familiar female voice said, "I heard you all the way at the reception station." Lou stood at our table, wearing sunglasses.

Arriving after our meal, as planned.

"Am I too late for dessert?" She glanced at Soson.

Soson thumped his stein on the table. "Right on time." He pointed to Lou with an open hand, as if directing a customer's attention to a product on a shelf. "*Malchik*, this is Louise Martin, ChiLabs analyst supreme. Louise, you know Dr. Randall Weinberg, if only by reputation."

Soson didn't let on he knew we'd already met. Maybe he was having *her* followed.

She nodded. "Nice to finally meet you."

"You see, Randall, I planned to come clean by introducing you to Louise at the end of our dinner."

I kept my previous conversation with Lou bottled up. "More than a little late, don't you think?"

"*Nyet.*"

Lou scooted in next to Soson.

133

"I apologize, my dear." Soson shuffled the silverware in front of them. "As you heard, I have shared your discovery of tachyons, what Randall calls chrontins. Please tell Randall what we have done while he has been away." He examined her face. "Are you all right?"

"On the way, I stopped by to see my father in the nursing home." She pulled off her sunglasses. Her eyes were bloodshot.

"How is your father doing?" I asked.

"Still suffering, thanks."

Lou's arrival interrupted our conversation about Russian involvement in Soson's scheme to invent time travel to the past. She repeated what she'd told me in her car at CJ's.

I did my best to act surprised while I focused on the consequences of time travel. I'd lost two relationships and both of my parents. It was my turn to fold my hands. "It's a tragedy I wasn't there when Craig was growing up. And to keep Faith from struggling for all those years."

"Then why don't you fix it?" asked Lou. "Go back, I mean. Together, we can figure out how."

Her too? She sympathizes with his suggestion? I expected she'd tried to invent reverse time travel ever since I'd been gone and hadn't succeeded. "It's not like all I have to do is make some coefficient of my particle specification negative or change the charge of the plasma buffer. This will take a complete reinvention of something I didn't intend to create in the first place."

Soson hiccupped and leaned forward. "Do this for your own satisfaction."

By having dinner with Soson the past two days, I confirmed it didn't take a lot of alcohol for him to become inebriated. "You can't be serious."

"Think of the benefits." He counted on his fingers. "You could show up for your experiment on time, prevent Hamza from messing with the settings, generate the cancer-attacking particles—"

"And improve the quality of my father's life." Lou stared. "For which I would be forever grateful."

Soson and Lou shared a knowing glance. They'd exposed their agendas.

When the waitress came by to clear our dinner plates, Lou ordered warm apple pie with ice cream.

Soson leaned closer. "When successful, you would be at Faith's side when Craig was born."

He'd articulately described the upside, something I'd already thought of. However, the consequences of giving Russians access to the secrets to traveling in time were unimaginable. They could go back and screw up the founding of the original thirteen colonies by helping the British win the War of Independence. Manipulate the results of World War II. My mind spun at the catalog of harmful possibilities. Unspoken were the risks to Faith and Craig that

Hamza mentioned. "Hamza warned me against researching reverse time travel. Maybe for the first time in his life, he's right."

"Your experiment proved that tachyons are real." Soson emptied the remaining beer in one swallow. "We theorized that you had been thrown forward in time, but we had no idea how far."

Hence Lou's calibration experiments. Being able to precisely set a target on the space/time continuum was a minor concern.

The waitress delivered Lou's dessert. She dug in with a spoon and hummed at the first taste. "All you need to do is harness chrontins in the backward direction."

"First of all, even though I admit I'm in 2019, and something changed my experiment to generate chrontins, I still need to assess the mathematical evidence." Maybe then I could revisit my equations.

"You will, *malchik*. Tomorrow."

I tried to get Lou's attention, which was focused on the plate in front of her. "You say you identified chrontins because they showed up before target impact. They could have been stray particles that escaped the beam. Nothing in my experience travels faster than the speed of light except for theoretical chrontins and neutrinos under special circumstances."

"You mean the MINOS collaboration?" Lou paused from eating and shook her head. "They corrected their initial results in 2012 after they upgraded their detectors. No neutrinos traveled faster than light. Aren't you going to mention quantum systems of an entangled pair?"

I was impressed with Lou's knowledge. "That doesn't count. Simultaneous synchronized changes over arbitrary distances don't transmit matter."

"Well, if you're going to be a Negative Nellie, I'm going to the little girl's room." She scooted out and walked a path among the tables.

I made sure Lou was out of hearing range before I leaned closer to Soson and asked, "You aren't seeing Lou socially, are you?"

"*Yesli by ya byl molozhe ili ona byla starshe.*" Soson shook his head. "Even I have limits on minimum age. She is but a child."

His statement relieved only a modicum of my anxiety. "You realize that *if* I figure it out, and I'm not saying I'll try, I'm not going to turn that capability over to any Russians, colleagues of yours or not."

"Sharing that secret is what I'm obliged to do, *tovarish*, or there will be consequences." Soson's somber expression and words chilled me. "And as compensation for payments already made."

Prepayments by some Russian oligarch gave Soson an added incentive to deliver. No wonder he was living high on the hog. Or maybe high on the bear. Soson was obligated, but I wasn't. "Tell your Russian contact that you were mistaken."

"With you as a living, breathing example? I am afraid I would have no credibility."

"Then just tell him I'm not interested." A bit of a lie, because the concept of going back and correcting this state of events intrigued me.

After a few minutes, Lou returned from the bathroom and sat on my side of the curved bench, leaving the remaining ice cream melt into a puddle. "Come on. You're the most brilliant particle physicist in the entire world. Maybe you didn't intend on creating chrontins, but with a couple of adjustments, your experiment did just that. Cool, right? You just have to figure out how to change the direction."

Under other circumstances, I might have appreciated Lou's unbridled enthusiasm for a physics dilemma. "It isn't as simple as that. You must be familiar with the Grandfather Paradox."

"Sure," said Lou. "Go back in time. Kill your grandfather. That means you weren't born. So how could you show up and kill him?"

"That's just the tip of the iceberg. We don't know the effects of even minor changes to the time stream." I sloshed the remnants of warm beer around in my stein but didn't drink. "Even though I want my 2011 experiment to execute without alteration, stopping Hamza from messing with the controls could have its own consequences." An image of Earth being sucked into a wormhole made me cringe.

"Or maybe an undisturbed experiment will do what you wanted in the first place and generate particles that will cure my Dad's cancer."

I understood her personal motivation. Her father could be one of many cancer patients whose lives would be saved.

She tapped her finger on the table. "My calibration formula makes it possible to target your destination within a day or so. At least forward. You have to try."

My major worry about traveling back before the leap forward was running into the 2011 version of me, who would still be there. How would that work? Not well, I expected.

Soson leaned close. "Randall, you are obligated."

He was. Not me. They were going to keep badgering me until I gave in. "Okay! I'll look at my test results tomorrow—the raw data, not your reports—and run some numbers of my own. But no promises." Had I agreed to look into the possibility of reverse time travel? *What am I thinking?*

Soson and Lou exchanged smiles. Their goals were complementary, and I could make both of them happy by inventing the impossible. Somehow, I'd have to exclude Soson's Russian buddies.

Soson grasped my hand. "It is so good to have you back!"

For his own selfish purposes. To bail him out. "With an ex-wife who disavows me, a son who's a stranger, and an impossible problem? I don't belong here!"

"So why don't you leave?" said an inebriated voice from the next booth.

Soson laughed so hard he gasped for air.

After Soson paid the bill, we all walked out to the parking lot, Soson and Lou side by side, me straggling behind.

Soson turned around. "See you tomorrow."

"Are you sober enough to drive?"

"It would take many more drinks to impair my capabilities." He winked. "Do not worry."

"You're going to get me into my office for sure?" I couldn't contain the anticipation of getting back to work, even if my experiment hadn't generated the expected results.

"I am a man of my word." He slapped his oversized hand on his chest.

Soson had told me my office was sealed off, but now he claimed to have access. Another half-truth?

He held up his palm. "But please, not first thing in the morning. I expect to have a late night, and likely a sleepover. It is not good form to rush out without providing your guest a handmade breakfast."

Based on his previous statements, he wasn't talking about Lou. "Fine. How about one-thirty?" I'd work at the station in the morning, stop at Starbucks for lunch, and work down the balance on my card.

"That is acceptable."

I didn't offer to shake Soson's hand and barely nodded at Lou. Soson's car was two spaces away. Lou walked further down the aisle.

Sets of perpendicular hood scratches on the Beetle reminded me of those on Faith's SUV. Had it been through multiple time travel experiences? When, and with who?

I sat in my car for a while before starting the engine. My curiosity had sucked me into investigating the possibility of backward time travel. The problem was too delicious to ignore. But if I was successful, how could I prevent Soson from sharing the technology with his Russian buddies? What a nightmare that would be!

My personal issues had to take priority. As I drove to CJ's, thoughts about becoming a living human again on Monday morning and stopping at Craig's school to meet him in the afternoon pushed all technical considerations from my brain. Maybe our son could break through to his mother, and we'd be together as a family.

Day 3

[10] Sunday, April 14, 2019

After I got out of bed the next morning, I checked Mickey's closet. Tonya had advised me to dress appropriately for court. The suit he'd left behind was too big for my frame. I should have known, given how his work clothes were at least two sizes too big. Since I didn't expect CJ would have anything appropriate in his closet, I needed to figure out some other solution.

The main floor smelled like CJ was making Chinese food for breakfast. I dressed for work in Mickey's overalls, jogged downstairs, and joined him in the kitchen.

"Howdy, sleepy head. We got French toast this mornin'." He pressed two egg batter-saturated hot dog buns against the griddle. "Ran out of vanilla, so I used soy sauce."

"Thanks, but I'll just have cereal." I found a dusty box of bran flakes in the cupboard and milk in the fridge.

CJ sat down, a just-cooked hot dog bun pretending to be a piece of French toast steaming on his plate. "You eatin' out again tonight?"

I considered CJ's situation, living alone for years. I didn't remember seeing Mickey when Dad and I visited. How much had my father's visits meant to him? "No, I'll be here for dinner."

"Great!" He sat up tall, as if someone had ordered him to attention. "I'll make my special spaghetti."

"I look forward to it."

With no customers in sight, I pulled the Beetle into the service bay to change the spark plugs. In the middle of the procedure, CJ hobbled in.

"Checking on your new employee?" I asked.

"Nope. Finally got around to doin an inventory last month. I'm short four tires. Why don't ya order replacements from RubberSideDown to make us even? Number's on the fridge. Put 'em on my account."

Given the low volume of customers, those must have been the ones Mickey installed on the Beetle. "Consider it done. And just a reminder. I'll be away from the station this afternoon."

CJ nodded, even though I wasn't sure he'd heard me.

Someone honked a car horn.

"Mickey, you got a customer." CJ shuffled back into his office.

For more peanuts and videos. *Did he read the name embroidered on the overalls?* I dismissed the reference.

An actual customer had pulled up to the pumps and lowered the driver's window. I ran over. "How can I help you?"

He gawked at the name on my overalls. "You're not Mickey. I've never seen anyone else working here. Is CJ all right?"

"He's fine. I'm staying with him for a while."

"That's CJ for you, always there with a helping hand. Fill it with regular." He popped the fuel door.

I got gas flowing, and then came around to wash his front windshield.

The guy turned out to be a chatterbox who'd lived in the neighborhood for years. He talked my ears off about how tough his life was and wondered how much fun it would be to "go back and relive my glory days when I was young and single."

My first thought was getting back to 2011. My second was Soson, living his glory days no matter his age.

I cleaned the rear window and put the pump nozzle away. The total read $34.88. I rounded up to the next quarter. "That'll be $35.00."

He handed me two twenties. "Thanks for listening. As long as you're around, keep an eye on CJ. He's not getting any younger."

I waved the two bills. "I'll get your change."

"No need. That's for CJ. Every dollar helps."

I stuck the two twenties in the glass jar and went back to my Beetle maintenance. When that was done, and since CJ hadn't specified what kind or size of tire he preferred, I ordered a set that matched the ones Mickey used on the Beetle.

After cleaning up for lunch, I wanted to stop at Five Alarm Dogs just minutes down Wise Road and wolf down one of their so-called famous Chicago Polish sausage sandwiches on French bread with all of the fixings. Given my cash situation, I settled for a turkey and basil pesto sandwich and something called strawberry açaí lemonade at the local Starbucks using my card.

When I arrived at ChiLabs, the parking lot was almost empty except for Soson's polished Tesla at a recharging station. He stood next to his car in jeans and an oversized knit sweater that looked like cashmere. He'd always worn a suit and tie at work, to appear professional. In his hands were a Dunkin Donuts bag and a paper cup.

I walked up to him. "Going casual?"

"I always do when I come into the office on the weekend. Which is never." He walked past a metal sculpture of Albert Einstein in one of his more thoughtful standing poses. Employees had often joked that they would have preferred one that had him sticking out his tongue, but I felt like those comments were sacrilegious to a great man.

In our last conversation, Soson had asked for an afternoon meeting because of a late date. "How did it go last night?"

"A gentleman never kisses and tells. But since we barely kissed, there is nothing not to tell. I do not think I will ask her out again."

We walked side by side up the front steps. "Have you figured out how we'll get in?"

146

He waved his security badge. "I can get in easily. It is getting you past security without being recognized that is the issue." He pulled a flat cap from his pocket. "Wear it low and it will hide some of your features."

I examined the label inside. "Is this authentic tweed?"

"Imported from England. I wore when I drove my Porsche Targa. All of the open top coupe drivers wear them. Jaunty, no? You should consider buying a convertible as your next car." He peered through the building window. "Although I am certain the company has changed weekend security services at least twice since you have been gone, they use the latest in facial recognition. Just remain silent and let me do the talking."

Soson walked through the revolving door first.

The ground floor was empty except for a weekend guard at the security desk. I missed Hannah and wondered where she was. Soson filled out the guest log and whispered, "To satisfy anyone who watches the security tapes."

We're being recorded too? I tilted the British cap up to look for cameras.

Soson pushed it down on my head. "Don't expose your face." He handed me a guest badge and signed me in as Rico Fermi. He hadn't lost his sense of humor. "Follow me."

The path to the elevator was as familiar as the stone walkway at my house, the one that Faith sold. Man, I loved that place.

I pressed the elevator button for the fourth floor before Soson could touch it. We rode up in silence.

When the doors parted, he stuck his head out. "The coast is clear. For now." He speed-walked to the bare door of my office, a repurposed storage closet.

"Someone took down my name plate."

"What did you expect after eight years? Besides, people in the building did not want to be reminded of your disappearance."

The long-gone small brass plate had hardly been a neon sign. My six by eight-foot office was not in a high-traffic area, situated at the end of a hallway. I pulled out my security badge, a reflexive response.

Soson put his hand on my arm. "Your card was deactivated forty-eight hours after your disappearance. Security protocols." He swiped his card and the lock clicked. "Be thankful they did not load a dumpster with the contents." Every other office door swung in. Mine swung out. It was a storage closet, after all. I pulled the door open.

Thousands of hours of work memories came at me like an accelerated particle stream. The wall to my left held my six-foot-long whiteboard, washed clean. Hadn't I left some last-minute notes for myself? In the back left corner stood the equipment rack. The size of my office didn't matter much because all of the major hardware for my experiment was housed in the basement: the linear accelerator, the particle source material, the target, and the receptors. However, I'd insisted that operation of the plasma frame, laser, and electromagnets be controlled by a rack in my office.

My parka hung on a nail on the back wall. "Did you bring that here?"

"I assumed you did not want to leave it in Faith's vehicle. Perhaps you will use it when the seasons change."

In the right rear stood my floor to ceiling bookcase, filled with 2011 state-of-the-art journals as well as my own published treatises. After eight years, technological advances must have made them obsolete. Science marches on or it doesn't survive.

My desk on the right just past the entrance held my desktop tower computer and two twenty-four-inch high-resolution monitors, side by side. The ever-present stack of open journals, notepads with scribbled ideas, and open manuscripts borrowed from my bookshelf were missing. The cleaning crew might have washed the whiteboard, but they never would have cleaned up or filed my papers and put manuscripts away. My rolling chair had been pushed all the way in.

Soson edged past me and pawed around my desk. "Where is it?" His eyes darted around the surface.

"Where's what?"

"I put it here, for when you returned. Perhaps Louise moved it."

Why had Soson let Lou into my office? "Would you please tell me what you expected and can't seem to find?"

"You won a Nobel in Physics." His lips curled into a smile. "It was supposed to be a surprise."

Hamza had spilled the beans yesterday, but that was none of Soson's business.

"I will ask her when she arrives." Soson's bushy eyebrows lifted and his eyes went wide. "*Pozdravlyayu!*"

The passage up the middle of my office was so narrow, he and I couldn't stand facing each other. Instead, he backed up so I could enter.

I shook my head. "A Nobel for improvements in accelerating particle beams using plasma was just a prerequisite."

"*Malchik*, you won a Nobel and are upset about the reason?" He pulled a doughnut from his paper bag and waved it. "I would accept a Nobel for finishing this." He took a huge bite and washed it down. "If it had not been for the one-point-one-million-dollar prize, Faith and Craig would have been out on the street."

I didn't care much about the award but the prize money had been a godsend for my family. "Okay, but why did Hamza feel obligated to take over Faith's finances?" I bet he stole from her. From us.

"Faith had been stubborn against his advice to have you declared dead sooner. The Nobel Committee reluctantly paid out the prize money during your absence but only because Faith appeared in person and

150

read your summary. By their rules, posthumous awards are prohibited."

I swung the door shut for privacy, pulled out my rolling chair, and sat down. Someone had raised the height and softened the seat back tension. *So much for a sealed room.* I flicked the power switch for the battery backup, into which all of my devices were plugged.

Hamza had mentioned that Soson had labs at his disposal. "Did you get a promotion and not tell me?"

"There was never a good opportunity. Besides, it would have come across as gloating, no matter how gently I said it. You did not need that on top of everything else." Soson jammed one hand into a pocket. "I am much more effective managing identified technology than inventing new ones. No hard feelings?"

Soson had been hired after me and was my junior for as long as we'd worked together. "I don't mind." The screen intensity lit up my desk. "If not for that, we couldn't have gotten in here. I'm just curious how it happened."

"When you disappeared, I was promoted to your position. Management was under the impression that since we worked together, I could pick up where you left off, to salvage their investment in the work. They quickly discovered that I had Peter Principled. You know the concept?" Soson leaned against my desk.

"Yeah. Promoted beyond your skill level."

151

He nodded. "I could not do anything you had done. They could not fire me because they had insisted on a contract when I immigrated, so they had no choice but to give me an available position."

"Which was a manager job. What about Hamza?"

"He was not good at supervising technical staff. Many of your peers complained often and loud enough for him to be kicked upstairs."

Irrational how the Lab seemed ready, willing, and able to promote as a solution for incompetence.

"You did not want to climb a managerial track, am I correct?" Soson nibbled at his half-eaten doughnut with an occasional swig.

"Damn right." I wouldn't have taken that kind of promotion if they multiplied my pay by—" The number of years I'd missed popped into my head. "By eight. The prompt on the screen waited for a user ID and password. "I can't sign in, can I?"

"Your ID was deactivated. Let me sign in."

I rolled back up against my whiteboard. Soson wedged himself between me and my desk, his large butt in my face.

It was taking longer than just signing in. "What are you doing?"

"You want to see the results, no? Then allow me to fetch them from my email."

After what seemed to be ages, he stepped to the side.

I pulled out a yellow legal-size pad and a mechanical pencil from my center drawer.

"You are so old school."

"What? These?" I held them up for examination. "How else would you suggest I take notes? On my whiteboard?"

"I take all of my notes on my phone. If there is a diagram, I take a picture."

"If my phone has a camera, I don't know how to use it, and typing on a tiny screen keyboard would be frustrating. I'd spend more time making corrections than entering information."

"You would get used to it." He held his device up to my face, a huge piece of glass with colorful icons. "Phones have changed dramatically since 2011. Why, this one has more raw computing power than that computer on your desk."

I was skeptical but turned to my monitors filled with Lou's open email messages to Soson, her analysis reports attached. "What's this? I told you I wanted to see the experiment data." In 2010, I'd purchased an expensive software license for a three-dimensional graphing program that could display the impact results from a particle collision. The graph could be rotated on all axes, so I'd be able to see the trajectories of the particles, zoom in to a particular one and click to get its measurements. Such a tool would save hours, even though other employees like Lou would be responsible for the analysis.

"Open the attachments."

Someone knocked on the closed door. I looked at Soson, who didn't show any panic.

The door opened about a foot and Lou stuck her face through. "Can I come in?"

"Of course, my dear." Soson took a step back, as if that would make room.

"Why not? The gang's all here." I double-clicked on Lou's reports and brought them up, one on each monitor.

"Sorry I'm late." A bag hung from her fingertips. "I stopped for coffee and a bearclaw." She slid behind my chair and joined Soson, between the bookcase and the whiteboard. "The room feels smaller with three people."

How much time had she spent in my supposedly locked office, and for what reason?

Soson backed up to make more room for Lou. "By any chance, did you move Randall's Nobel Prize medal?"

She pointed at an empty area between my two computer screens. "I left it there."

"It is missing. I do not know who could have taken it." Soson scratched his chin. "I will need to investigate."

"All I know is, it was here the last time I was in this office, about a week ago." Lou blushed. "I opened the box to sneak a peek. It was gorgeous."

"Can we please focus on the results of my experiment?" The first attachment showed one of those three-dimensional graphs, high-resolution and in color. Numerous particles with corkscrew

154

trails tunneled down the center. Their paths should have been straight lines."

I looked behind at Soson. "I thought you said the experiment didn't generate any heavy ions."

"Those are not heavy ions." Soson coughed.

"Then what are they?" I placed my mouse over the graph and tried to change the viewing angle. The whole document slid around on the monitor.

"It's a screen shot." Lou leaned over my shoulder. "I thought a three-quarters view was the best angle. Look at the second one."

The second monitor showed another graph, but this time the swirling particle trajectories had bent, angling upward. "Why are they doing that?"

"Those are the tachy—I mean, the chrontins. Lots of them, shooting up through the ceiling of the target area. The detectors only caught passing glimpses before they were gone."

"Are those the ones that appeared eight seconds before the particle impact?" I gazed at a phenomenon no physicist in the world would have predicted. And it was based on my experimental design.

Soson and Lou exchanged another one of their knowing glances.

I zoomed in on that graph. The time stamp in the corner showed 8:59:52 AM. "You told me but I didn't believe it." Questions pulled my mind in multiple directions. I desperately wanted to interact with the data, examine it from all sides, and in particular view an animation of the particles over time. I looked up at Soson. "These are important evidence, but they're static. No one can do further analysis from these snapshots. Where is the raw data?"

"Bring up AceLink." Soson pointed to the application list on the left side of the screen.

All of the expected apps were listed except for one. "What happened to ProjectMaster Pro?"

"We changed software vendors."

I opened the app, which produced a navigable project list for ChiLabs, sorted by date. "You've been busy while I was away." With repeated scrolling, I found my project near the end. "My listing is italicized. What does that mean?" I double-clicked on the name with no results.

"You see? All of the information for your project has been archived, safe and sound," said Soson. "What did you expect? That the company would waste online storage for eight-year-old results?"

"For them, it's eight-year-old garbage. For me, it's only forty-eight hours old and fresh." And vital if he wanted me to invent reverse time travel.

"Eight years, two months, and nineteen days, to be precise," Lou whispered. "Three thousand sidereal days, not solar."

Whatever those are. Lou and I would need to have a conversation about the details of her calibration, but for now, the experiment results took top priority. "Information in an archive can be restored. So how do we go about doing that?" I'd always been around after my experiments, so after the analysis and reports, I never thought about what happened to the raw data.

"We can put in a request, but Hamza would hear about it." Soson scratched his head. "*Govno*, given his level, he might even have to authorize it."

"Then we're stuck, because he doesn't want me anywhere near this place, or pursuing additional research on the topic of time travel. Excuse me." I squeezed past both of them and faced the rack-mounted controllers, next to a laminated poster for the 3rd International Conference on Nuclear and Particle Physics. Held in Dubrovnik, Croatia in 2010, I'd been invited to speak but refused. My cancer-curing project had priority.

I turned on the controllers and examined the settings. The numbers on the blue LCD displays didn't match the ones in my memory. "And Hamza changed these?" I examined the controllers one at a time. "The angles of the electromagnets were changed. The temperature for the plasma frame is too high. And the laser I had installed points straight down the particle pipe instead of along the inner surface, to eliminate contaminants. I'm surprised there were any results at all."

Lou stood shoulder to shoulder with me. "I left them alone, I swear. I thought if I changed

157

anything, I'd mess up the chrontin generation I needed for my calibration experiments."

I grabbed the legal pad from my desk. "I need to write down these settings." I was afraid if I memorized them, I'd eventually confuse them with the cancer experiment settings in my mind.

"Jot them in Notes on your phone. Or take a picture. That's what I did." Lou pulled up her phone's camera app and scrolled through a bunch of selfies until she got to a photo she'd taken of the equipment rack.

"Good idea." I examined the icons on my phone's screen, identified one that looked like a camera and took a picture of the current settings. *Not so hard.* They were identical to the one's in Lou's photo. "I never would have considered this controller configuration."

Lou leaned on my shoulder. "Together, do they make sense?"

I pointed at the plasma control settings. "Hamza increased the temperature by five percent. Still within operating limits, but unnecessarily high." I touched the faceplate of the laser control. "And this was supposed to be aimed at the edge of the tube to zap away ambient particles. Clear the path. Instead, it shot down the pipe, parallel to the streams, and then intersected with them at the crossing point. God, that could have boosted their acceleration at the last minute."

"Making chrontins!" Lou bounced on the balls of her feet. "Cool!"

"Two minutes ago, you exceeded my level of understanding." Soson looked up at the ceiling and sighed.

Lou pointed at the electromagnet control but didn't touch it. "Of course, the particle stream would escape at an angle with the magnets set this way."

"What do you think? Thirty degrees?" It was my best estimate based on a glance at the 3D graph on the monitor.

"Thirty-four degrees," said Lou. "The graphing program calculated it."

"Thanks for the correction. How did Hamza do this? And more important, why?"

"Let me describe a possible how." Soson leaned against the corner of my desk. "Hamza and his visitors were in your office that morning. Because of the limited space, I stood in the hallway. That is when he could have modified the settings."

"That still leaves the question why." Hamza's futzing might have caused a fire or an explosion. He got lucky. The only result was my disappearance.

"Perhaps to look good to management, showing his involvement?"

"Or to sabotage my last chance. To get me fired. Bastard!"

Soson slapped his hand on his chest. "He did not confide in me."

I looked at Lou.

"I wasn't even invited." She glanced at Soson, who nodded. "With these electromagnet settings, the chrontins shot up through the ceiling—"

Soson completed the thought. "And struck Faith's SUV, precisely where you were parked on the target mound."

The room spun. I'd been the victim of my own experiment. My unique collision configuration and Hamza's last minute setting modifications created chrontins. The evidence was indisputable, even without the underlying math.

"Now, with this proof, do you believe?" asked Soson. "You will easily earn another Nobel for this discovery."

"Not me. This is Hamza's work product." Knowing how I'd reached 2019 brought a moment of solace. My smile faded as I considered my time excursion's impact on my family.

Soson smiled back. "Yes he will, the self-absorbed bastard." He offered me his hand. "Are you ready to begin working on reverse time travel?"

I used his help to steady myself. "I'm not walking away. Not yet."

The Starbucks sandwich performed somersaults in my stomach. My head buzzed with ideas, and the two conspirators were a distraction. "I'd like to be alone for a while."

"Certainly. Louise and I will wait in my office upstairs. Do not dawdle. Someone could detect your presence. Call me if you need anything, or when you are ready to leave." Soson disappeared down the hall.

I felt Lou's eyes on me. "What is it?"

"The thing I told you before, about being a fan, Dr. Weinberg? That was the truth."

"Don't be so formal. Randy is fine."

"Okay." She leaned on the doorframe, half in, half out. "After I told Soson about the chrontins, he let me use your office to continue my analysis. I couldn't believe my luck. Spending time in the actual space where my hero worked. It was almost too much."

"I don't feel like much of a hero. I've let so many people down." Faith. Craig. Cancer patients. And either Soson or Hamza will be disappointed, depending on what I choose to do about reverse time travel.

"I'm sorry I rearranged things in your office. I forgot what was piled on your desk after I moved stuff to make space to work. And I used your whiteboard when I got stuck and needed to think."

"Great minds think alike. That's how *I* use it."

Lou folded her arms. "Every time I came in, I'd picture you at the board, spinning a marker between your fingers, and then streaming one of your original thoughts from your brain straight onto the board."

Boy, was she ever wrong. I'd come up with numerous incremental modifications before I got even close to a conclusive solution. "Too many times, I'd write something, decide it was useless and erase it, only to need it later."

She smiled. "The same thing happened to me. I can't calculate how many weeks I lost due to my own stupidity."

I nodded. "But I solved that problem." I pointed at a wide-angle camera sticking out from the top of the bookcase near the ceiling,. "One of the IT guys set up what he called a software daemon that wakes up once a minute when the computer is on and takes a picture. The name of the picture is the date and time. Later, if I needed something, I'd just scroll through the photos to rescue the erased stuff."

"I saw the camera but figured you were using it to broadcast lectures. It works like an automatic computer backup, except for your board?" She glanced at the camera, at the whiteboard, and back to the camera. "That's so cool. Do you think it still works?"

"Let's check." The computer had timed out from Soson's email account.

Lou reached into her shoulder bag. "Should I call Soson to sign you back in?"

"No, the photos are stored locally." I put one hand on a small dusty external disk drive at the rear of my desk. "I didn't want them on the network and have everyone view my failures." *Scattered among the insightful flashes.* I pulled up a file browser, selected the external drive and opened it. The computer took a minute to display a window. A scrolling list of files filled the screen, listed chronologically, many showing dates during the years I'd been missing. "It looks like your work was preserved for posterity, along with mine."

"It was?" She put her fingertips on her lips. "Oh no. Please erase them. I don't want you to see all the mistakes I made." That familiar pink tone returned to her face.

"Don't worry, I will." After I reviewed her work and figured out how she arrived at her calibration formula.

"If you want my help, I'd be happy to—no, that's just silly. Why would you need help from me? Never mind. I'll just wait upstairs in Soson's office."

"Before you go, there's something you could explain. The precise number of days I was gone. You calculated them?"

"Yes, after you reappeared on Friday. Soson and I weren't sure exactly when you would show up. Based on my successful tests, my calibration formula estimated your arrival within a range of four days, so we took turns keeping watch. As soon as you showed up, I called Soson and gave him the good news."

"And you said I jumped three thousand days?"

"Right. Lou took a deep breath, walked over to the whiteboard, and wrote '8.219178.' "Eight years, two months, and nineteen days, to be precise, with accommodation for leap years."

Lou's interpretation of the quotient was wrong. "So how did you derive your calibration formula?"

"By working backwards. I had to run a lot of tests to figure out how much the settings have to be reduced to yield specific shorter durations."

My brain ached as I contemplated her trial-and-error methodology.

"Now that you're here, I know that Hamza's settings yielded precisely three thousand days. I can use that to refine the accuracy of my formula. Important if you're going to use it for other time travels. You know, either forward." She paused, "Or backward."

Lou is definitely in Soson's corner. "Thanks for clearing that up." I wondered how Lou computed restaurant tips.

After Lou closed the door behind her, I scrolled through the photos of the whiteboard on the day Soson ran the experiment in my absence. Parts of his body appeared in many of the shots, in various candid poses. After a series of board photos with my last scribbles, Hamza and some people I didn't know appeared, trying to cram into the small space. It reminded me of a scene from a Three Stooges movie when the brothers tried to hide in a closet. I paused my review at a picture taken less than ten minutes before the experiment was initiated, mostly filled by backs of strangers. At the edge of the photo, Hamza's fingers touched one of the dials in the equipment rack. By the time the next photo was taken, he'd moved away, and in subsequent photos, he'd didn't appear at all.

I had proof that Hamza modified the settings before the experiment was initiated. I'd ask him why the next time I tried to see Faith.

I closed that photo, flagged it, and continued scrolling the file list to a photo taken about a week later. The camera caught Lou from behind, obscuring her work. The next one had a clear view of what she'd written on the board, a derivation of a formula I'd used in my experiment. Her changes didn't make any sense. Witnessing the mistakes she'd made threatened to bring on a headache. Did she know enough about string theory to understand what my formulas meant? Most of the other scientists in the building didn't.

I skipped ahead another week and checked out a picture. Then a month. All of the photos confirmed Lou's lack of particle physics expertise and a lack of intermediate math skills. According to her, she'd only succeeded in creating her calibration formula through a series of real-world tests. I saw no evidence of scientific method. How many hours of linear accelerator time did she consume with all of those particle collisions? And how did she get all of those test slots? I would've done it numerically, saving precious time and resources.

With chrontins evidently real and with a repeatable process to create them, could I engineer in what direction they would transport a subject? Without access to my raw data, I felt

166

stuck. I couldn't solve anything with the information I'd seen, so I called Soson's cell. "I'm done here, at least for now." As I waited, I dreaded the possibility that Lou would ask me to critique her work. What would I say?

Soson and Lou arrived at my door.

When I stepped into the hall, Soson locked my office. "Do not worry. I will get you access again, the same as today."

Soson called for the elevator. We rode down and got out at the first floor.

From the elevator bank, I noticed a different guard sitting at the tall security station where Hannah's desk used to be. I pulled the tweed cap low on my forehead.

Soson signed out first. Lou went second. I ducked as I handed back the guest building pass and wrote in my departure time.

"I never would have recognized you," said the guard. "It's not every day that a celebrity comes to visit."

I froze. "Excuse me?" I touched the brim of my hat, pretending to adjust it while obscuring my face. "I'm no celebrity."

Soson and Lou returned to my side.

The guard put his finger on the page where Soson had signed me in. "Oh, come now. You're world-renowned—Dr. Fermi. Except you've been dead for decades."

Lou interrupted. "Sixty-five years." She faced me. "You're not my only hero."

Soson's gag had backfired. Was a bad joke like this the cause of his split from Tonya? I lifted the brim of my cap and made eye contact.

The guard held out his hand. "Please show me some form of photo ID."

I pulled my fresh driver's license from my wallet and gave it to him.

The guard ran his finger down a list on a nearby clipboard. "You're famous, all right, Dr. Weinberg. Famous for being at the top of the 'people prohibited from entering the facility' list." He handed back my license. "What am I going to do with you, hmm?" He lifted the receiver of his desk phone.

Soson reached over the shelf and pushed the guard's arm until the receiver returned to the cradle. "You will call no one." He let go of the guard's arm. "It is a bit late to prevent him from entering since he is on his way out." Soson winked at me. "It is not like we can turn back the clock."

Yet that was exactly what he and his Russian colleagues were demanding.

The guard's stare at Soson suggested he was not in a playful mood. "What do you have in mind?"

Soson shoved me closer to the guard station. "Search him for contraband. I promise, he took nothing."

The guard came out and patted my chest, my legs on the sides and my back pockets. He acted as uncomfortable as I felt. When he stepped back, his face was red. "Nothing."

168

In the meantime, Soson had reached for the clipboard. "There is no date and time on this paper. For all we know this directive was published *after* Dr. Weinberg arrived, so he might not have violated any procedures. Why not pretend that you received this list after we departed?" Soson pulled out his wallet and slid a one-hundred-dollar bill under the visitor log. "For your trouble."

The guard looked both ways. "I guess I can't turn back time either. Get out of here, before I change my mind."

I tipped my cap and scurried to the exit behind Soson and Lou.

Outside, Soson wiped perspiration from his forehead.

"Are you okay?" I kept forgetting that everyone around me was eight years older. "Maybe you should sit down."

"I underestimated Hamza's precautions. There will be consequences if we violate his restrictions." Soson walked to one of the benches surrounding the Einstein statue. "This means I will never be able to get you in again. I hope you got everything you needed."

Lou sat beside him, her hands folded in her lap.

"Weren't you listening?" I shot Lou a glance. "No offense, but I got nothing."

She bit her lip and then raised her eyes. "I have copies of my full analysis report and a bunch of 3D screen captures at home, if you think they'll help."

Soson glared at her. "Removing those from the premises is expressly forbidden by policy."

Like conspiring with the enemy wasn't?

"The company shouldn't be angry. They got my after-hours work at home for free."

I would have preferred manipulating the raw data myself. With multiple screen captures, maybe I'd find something useful. "The stuff you have will be a good starting point." Better than an empty whiteboard. "Can you print them out?"

"How about I email them?" asked Lou. "It'll be quicker."

"*Nyet!* Taking them was bad. Exposing them to theft is worse."

I stared at my small phone screen. "Don't bother. I'd get eyestrain trying to read them."

"Don't you have a computer?" Lou asked.

I looked up. "Nope. Just this."

"I am not going to buy you a computer, *tovarish*. You would want a state-of-the-art model with maximum everything and dual monitors. Some things I can afford. Others I cannot." Soson straightened his posture. "If necessary, use one at your public library. They do not charge."

I had more modest requirements but there was no point in arguing. Besides, Soson had been very generous. "Maybe I'll do that." I'd avoid eyestrain by checking email and Lou's documents on a regular size screen. "Put them on a thumb drive." Her report and static screen shots of the

3D graphs weren't enough for me to reverse the process. "I guess I'll need to start from scratch." Using mathematics, not trial and error. I turned to Soson. "You'll have to get me time on CHUQ."

For the first time since we'd exited ChiLabs, he smiled. "He is so over-utilized these days, it is not funny."

Lou squinted, first at Soson, and then me. "Who's Chuck?"

"CHUQ, an acronym for COMPUTING HEURISTICS UNLIMITED QUANTA. A supercomputer in the IT building down the road, the one with no windows."

"I always use the full name. Other employees have mentioned Chuck, but I thought he was some math whiz I'd never met."

Ten years prior, I'd fought to get large chunks of access. Otherwise, it would have been impossible to compute the plasma frame's effect on the spins of strings, the basis for my enhanced protons. I turned to Soson. "Just a few hours."

"Hours? CHUQ slaved away at your formulas for five or six years. To be honest, I lost track."

It was as if I was being asked to work using only prime numbers. "What do you expect me to do? Perform the calculations in my head? Use some kind of desktop calculator?" I held up my phone. "Or this thing?"

The phone rang in my outstretched hand. I checked the screen. "It's your friend Tonya."

171

Soson grimaced. How bad was their breakup?

I answered the call. "Hello?"

"Mr. Weinberg? Your background checks have not come through. I don't believe they'll be available for court tomorrow morning. Do you have your birth certificate?"

I kept a miniature copy in my wallet. "Yes, and my Social Security card."

"Good. We will proceed with what we have. Our best evidence will be you, standing before the judge. He will not be able to dispute that you are alive and well. He may require a deposition to that effect, which we can create in his presence."

At least alive. "I'll see you bright and early."

"Yes. And please, make yourself presentable. First impressions?"

"Got it." I urged Soson to take my phone and speak with Tonya. He refused by raising a large open hand. When I checked the screen, she'd hung up.

"You do me no favors by trying to force Tonya back into my life, *tovarish*. She and I are finished."

I stashed the phone in my pocket. If Tonya was Soson's true love, didn't they deserve another chance to be together? "I just thought if the two of you chatted—"

He raised an index finger. "My new rule. In the future, I will manage my own relationships."

Lou stared at her hands, picking at her cuticles. "I think we're done here. I should go."

Soson scanned our faces. "Meet me later for dinner?"

"Sorry. I promised CJ I'd have dinner with him tonight. He could use the company." And I could use some downtime from Soson. "But the two of you can go ahead without me."

Lou looked away. "I'm going to reheat some leftovers before they spoil. Maybe some other night. Excuse me." She ran across the parking lot to her Corolla.

Something had spooked Lou. Maybe the conversation about Soson's love life.

My exchange with Soson about his promotion raised my curiosity about my own situation. I took Lou's place on the bench. "Tell me what happened, after I didn't show up here that morning." The statue of Einstein listened in.

Soson breathed a heavy sigh. "At first, management thought you had run away for some unknown reason. Then they decided you had been kidnapped by spies." He smiled. "Weeks went by and they received no ransom note. Meanwhile, I checked in with Faith every day. She wanted answers that I did not have. I could tell she was not doing well. I always thought of her as strong but silent."

"You only got one of those correct." In our personal life and her volunteerism, she was hardly shy about sharing her opinions. The only task she'd left for me was our finances.

173

"When I could not answer her questions, she accused me of being uncooperative or withholding information."

She'd been right. Soson knew that I'd time traveled. "But Hamza? She might have met him once at a holiday party. Why him?"

"You should be pleased. Hamza stepped up to help her through the trauma after she rejected my assistance. I would have continued to give help graciously." He patted my hand. "You know, you are like a brother to me? A younger brother."

A brother he'd coopted to do his Russian colleague's bidding. The incident at Faith's building haunted me. "Hamza wouldn't let me in to see her. And when she came down to find him, she took one look at me, screamed, and ran away in panic."

"What did you expect? How would you feel if *she* died and then appeared alive and well years later? Would that not freak you out?"

The thought of Faith dying chilled me, despite the warm spring breeze. "I expected that our love would persist through anything. Even an eight-year absence."

"You are such a romantic. Love. I do not go looking for it, and I keep my expectations reasonable. I am therefore never disappointed. And sometimes, my expectations are exceeded." He lifted one eyebrow, "Tonight perhaps."

Did Soson have dates every night? I didn't want to know any of the details. I considered his factory-line style of dating a failure by design.

Every relationship was expected to go nowhere, and therefore each woman eventually moved on. I felt sad that Soson had lost his true love over some stupid joke.

I stood and stretched. "Well, I'm going to have dinner with CJ and hit the sack early. I have court tomorrow."

"What are you planning on wearing? Not that?"

"I haven't taken care of it. Yet." So many more serious issues faced me.

Soson perked up. "Next to women, shopping is my greatest pleasure. Come with me." He led me to his Tesla and opened the door. "You have not *really* driven with me, no?"

I didn't understand what 'really' meant. "Where are we going?" I got in, buckled the seatbelt, and tightened it.

"To make you dapper. The judge will have no choice but to make you alive again, if only based on your sartorial excellence."

"This is nice of you, but I can stop at Mark Shale in Oakbrook on the way home. Their tailor knows me by name and makes off-the-rack look custom made."

"They closed about a year after you leapt forward in time." Soson took Kirk Road and flew down the ramp onto Interstate 88. "Check on your phone if you do not believe me. After eight years, that tailor might have passed away."

Every new revelation about the time gap slapped me in the face. Not just my parents gone. Who knows how many friends and family as well?

We passed a billboard advertising a forthcoming televised debate among sixteen possible Republican candidates for President. "Looks like we have another Clinton in the White House? How's she doing?"

"She is a vindictive witch!" After cutting across three lanes, he stomped the accelerator. My head jerked back. "She targets my former colleagues with financial penalties that cripple them. How your country could have chosen her over Donald Trump, I do not know. *Blyad!*"

"Don't blame me. I wasn't here to vote." Given the choice, I wouldn't have picked Donald Trump either. What a clown!

"Please not to mention your current Chief Executive again." Soson blasted past every car and truck on the road in silence.

"Do you charge extra for a thrill ride?"

"Not for close friends."

His jerky acceleration bounced my head against the seat. He took the exit onto Interstate 355 so fast, I thought he'd lifted two tires off the pavement.

When we got to the exit for Boughton Road, Soson's driving style returned to normal. He slowed, turned down Janes Avenue into a mall lot and parked in front of a Men's Warehouse store.

"*This* is where you're taking me?"

176

"Where would you prefer to shop? Target? We are not looking for small appliances or bedding."

Inside the store, the men's suit section contained a wide variety, all priced lower than Mark Shale.

Soson picked out a dark grey suit, a white shirt, a plain red tie, and black loafers. "There. Now you will look like a candidate for Congress. Most of *them* are alive. The judge should be very impressed."

I tried the outfit on in the dressing room. It wasn't a tailored fit, but there was no time for alterations.

I didn't complain when Soson swiped his credit card at the check-out station. Evidently, my new clothes fell within his budget.

When we got into his car, I said, "Thank you."

"Do not mention it. Just be brilliant and everything will work out for the best." He patted my hand like a concerned uncle and pressed the brake. "I will chauffeur you back to your cute little car."

"Will you be aiming for light speed again?"

"Nyet, as long as you do not mention your current Chief Executive." Soson stomped the accelerator to the floor.

I reached for a grab handle above my door. *Missing.*

"You should reconsider dinner. Pal Joey's is close by. We could catch up over drinks and have Louise meet us there. Great Italian."

"Sorry. I promised." I wrapped my arms around my torso.

"And you are a man of your word! But I insist dinner together tomorrow, to celebrate your reinstated personhood. In your honor, what cuisine would you prefer?"

"I haven't had pizza for eight years." In my reality, it felt like last week, when Faith and I carried out a large half veggie/half pepperoni during a fifty-degree hot spell in the middle of winter. I'd lowered the lights, lit candles, and opened a bottle of sparkling grape juice instead of Cabernet, her favorite. Who said that has to be the last date night we ever celebrate?

"Perfect! A Chicago spe-ci-al-ity. I will find the best place. You will call me tomorrow to finalize our arrangements."

If we get to ChiLabs alive.

I looked forward to a quiet dinner with CJ after my emotionally and intellectually draining visit to the Labs. Ignoring chrontins and time travel for one evening would feel like a vacation.

As I pulled into CJ's from Mitchell Avenue, I slammed on the brakes. The front window had been boarded up. *What the hell?* I parked off to the side and ran in. CJ was sweeping up glass and other debris from the wood floor and area rugs. Remnants of the glass pickle jar lay on the floor, paper money and coins scattered in the vicinity of the front door.

"What happened? There was dried blood on CJ's forehead and a rip in one pant leg at the knee. "Are you all right?"

"I'm fine. Somebody threw a brick through the window. It's around here somewhere. Woke me from my nap." Debris on the floor scattered as he dragged the broom in wide arcs.

"There's a cut on your forehead."

CJ reached above his eyebrow. "I tripped comin' down the steps. Musta' banged my head when I fell." He resumed his ineffective sweeping. "There's glass all over and I started dinner."

"First things first." I took the broom from his hand and escorted him into the kitchen. Pots occupied both burners. Using a first aid kit hanging on the wall, I cleaned his wound and assessed the damage. "You've got a bump and a cut, but it's not bleeding." I applied a band aid.

His knee was skinned so I cleaned it with a disinfectant wipe. "Why don't you sit for a moment while I clean up?"

He looked up with Bassett hound eyes. "I don't know why anyone would be angry with me. I sell gasoline."

"Who knows? There are a lot of crazy people out there. Who boarded up the broken window?"

"One of the policemen knew somebody. Did a nice job, but I miss the view."

At least the incident had been reported. "Do you have a vacuum cleaner?"

"Nope." He rubbed the back of his head. "Mickey made me buy a shop vac to clean up customer cars before we gave 'em back. Never figured out how to use the dang thing. It's in one of the service bays someplace."

I left CJ while I started to clean-up. I swept the scattered money from the floor into a brown paper bag. Then I stuck my head into the kitchen. CJ was shaping ground meat into patties next to the sink. "I can call for carry-out if you're not up to cooking tonight."

"Nope, I promised you my special spaghetti. Besides, you never know what they put in their stuff. Don't worry, we won't starve."

I entered the service bays and grabbed a pair of leather gloves. The shop vac in an unopened carton was buried under a stack of collapsed cardboard boxes in the far corner. I unpacked it and brought it into the office along with a trash barrel.

I wore the leather gloves to pick up the big pieces of broken glass and threw them in the barrel. The shop vac was effective in sucking up the small and medium shards from CJ's recliner and the floor.

CJ stuck his head around the doorframe. "How's it goin'?"

"Don't walk around barefoot. I'll have to clean glass dust off each bill and coin one at a time."

"Do that later. Dinner's almost ready."

While CJ worked in the kitchen, I used the shop vac along the baseboards and around the service desk. Outside, the boarding-up service had done a good job clearing debris.

CJ called out from the front door, "Time to put on the feedbag."

I left the shop vac and trash barrel in the main room. In CJ's kitchen, I pulled a metal folding chair up to his butcher-block sawhorse table on which he'd already set a GoTane-branded plate, a customer promotional item.

On his first trip from the stove, he brought over a colander. Steam clouded my vision as he dumped a pile of plain macaroni noodles on my plate. Hadn't he said spaghetti? On his second trip, he wielded a spatula and tossed a poorly formed hamburger onto the pile. This didn't make sense but I kept my mouth shut. On his last trip, he carried a different pot and ladled red sauce over the whole thing. "There you go, my Special Spaghetti."

The ingredients were indeed parts of spaghetti, configured in CJ's unique manner: macaroni instead of spaghetti pasta, and a burger instead of meat sauce. Maybe he'd forgotten what spaghetti looked like. I waited until he came to the table with an identical helping and sat down before digging in.

I used a knife and fork to cut up the burger as it wobbled atop the noodles. The patty slipped down the mound headed for the floor but I managed to rescue it. CJ picked up the whole burger with his fork, took a bite, sauce dripping from the bumpy patty, and put it back down, followed by taking a helping of elbow noodles with a spoon.

"Damn, I forgot the cheese." CJ pushed back from the table and stood. "Want some?"

"Sure." I expected that he'd pour some reconstituted Parmesan from a plastic cylinder.

Instead, he returned with a couple of slices of American processed cheese, peeled back the plastic on one slice and tossed it onto my plate, landing square on top of my meat and noodles. "There ya go. Doesn't taste the same without cheese." He unwrapped the second slice, laid it on his partially eaten burger and waited until I had a mouthful before asking. "You found a real job yet?"

I choked. "What makes you think I'm looking for a job?"

"Your Dad used to brag on you all the time. Straight A's and double promotions. Somebody with your smarts won't be satisfied working in a place like this. Your Dad musta' given you the talk about makin' your brains count."

"All of the time." My father had been one of my motivators and cheerleaders all through school and into my career. If I'd attended the Nobel Prize ceremony, I would have dedicated the award to him. Now he was gone. What I wouldn't give to be able to talk with him about my situation. Hell, with anyone on the outside of this craziness. Too bad CJ wasn't up to the challenge.

"Well, I'm in no position to give you advice. You're ten times smarter than me, and twenty on weekends. But you should make something out of yourself."

"I am. I mean, I will." *As soon as I'm legally alive again.*

I hadn't previously noticed the faded framed photo of CJ, his wife, and their infant son hanging on the far wall. I envied CJ. He'd had the opportunity to be there when his son was growing up. Faith must have had her hands full doing it solo. "So how was it, being both mother and father to Mickey?"

"Harder than the hardest job I ever had, including trying to run this place under GoTane's rules. From about the age of three, he was his own person. Wanted to decide things himself without thinkin' about what might happen. I stopped arguin'. After a couple of broken bones and a ton of scuffs and scrapes, he decided on his own to wear pads and protectors on that blasted skateboard of his."

I wondered how Faith was managing Craig's participation in athletics. Had she gone out into the yard and played catch? Given my own proclivities and lack of physical prowess, he might have turned into a bookworm. If I'd been there, he could have learned from my mistake of writing sports off as useless. I had witnessed many of my classmates building strong relationships with their teammates, something I never did with other intellectuals.

CJ finished a forkful of noodles. "Why aren't you with your family?" His face turned red. "I'm being too nosey, ain't I?" He nodded slowly. "None of my business. Families go through rough times. If you need to be apart from them for a while, you're more than welcome here. Truth be told, the place is pretty empty with Mickey gone. He says he'll come back to visit, but he never does."

"I'm sure he means to."

"Meaning and doing are two different things. You have kids?"

"One, a boy. He's very special to me." My heart tore.

"I can read your face, how much you love him."

My chest constricted. "Excuse me." I walked outside and forced myself to take deep breaths of cool, night air. How could I not tell Craig the truth about our relationship? I couldn't be sure how he'd take the news about a time-traveling father. Faith would hate me even more if I told him. I blew my nose and returned to the table.

"Hope it wasn't my cookin'."

I took a deep breath and forced a smile. "No."

"Where was I? Oh yeah, offspring. Mickey made it plain, he has no interest in taking over the family business. None of my relatives do either."

I thought CJ had retired in place. "Do you still enjoy running this place?"

"I like it just fine. But customers have lost interest. And the winters are unbearable." He shivered despite the warmth of the room. "The walls are concrete block, solid but drafty as hell. Costs an arm and a leg to keep the place heated during the winter. And the damn gas and electric companies keep jackin' up prices every month."

From the number of patrons I'd seen and the meager pile of paper money and coins in the pickle jar, I couldn't imagine CJ remaining solvent.

"If I had my druthers, I'd take my savings and pick up and move to someplace warmer. Florida, Georgia, someplace like that."

"What would happen to the station?" No matter the shape it was in now, CJ had poured his heart and soul into it. Terrible that GoTane hadn't appreciated that.

"I been thinkin' about that ever since you showed up. You and your pop, you were always

185

nice, stopping by and filling up, even when the price at the corner was cheaper." He pointed his fork at me. "And don't tell me you didn't, 'cause I know my competition. Can't beat their wholesale, the volumes they buy at. When you showed up, I figured it might be a sign from Helen."

"Heaven?"

"No, Helen, the housekeeper who used to look after me after my Betty passed on. It was like Helen saying, 'CJ, this nice young man has come to take care of the station after you're gone.'"

Gone? "Wait a second." How did I go from houseguest to beneficiary? The last thing I needed in my life was a run-down business that sucked cash like a black hole. "You'd put me in your will?"

"Heck no! You shouldn't have to wait 'til I croak. I'll sign the place over the minute I pick my retirement village. You just send me half of each month's profits."

If what I'd seen since arriving was any indication, there would be nothing to send.

He left the room and came back with a handful of colorful brochures. "Looky here." He fanned them out like cards in a losing poker hand. "Swimming pools. Tennis courts. Lounges with bars. All you can eat buff-etts." He licked his lips.

I couldn't picture CJ in tennis whites, running around a court, but I humored him. "These look really nice."

He sat and scooted closer, as if about to share a secret. "I've socked away a few bucks, from when GoTane bought me out of my contract.

See, I signed up for ten years. But after three, they wanted to dump me." He sat straight, hands on top of his head. "They couldn't, so I got me a lawyer who squeezed them good for a buy-out payment. Socked that money away into an investment that just keeps going up. 'Cept for when I need money to pay bills."

Retiring before his expenses depleted his savings made sense. But giving me the station and expecting some positive cash flow?

"What do you say?" He dropped his hands into his lap.

There was no need to get me involved. "Why don't you sell the station?" The land had to be worth something.

"Hell, no. I put my entire self into this business. I'll be damned if I'm going to abandon' it. You'd have to make one promise. That *you* won't sell it either."

"Never?"

"Well, that sounds unreasonable, even to my ears." He scratched at his stubbly chin. "How about five? You keep the place open for half a decade and then do what you will. By then, maybe I won't even remember the place, if that Al's Heimers disease takes over. Runs in the family."

There were other alternatives to giving the station to me, but this conversation wasn't the quiet time I'd hoped for. Dinner with Soson would have had different drama but significantly better cuisine. "That's a generous offer." After the judge rescinded my death decree, I'd figured that Faith and I would patch things up, get remarried to each other and raise Craig as a couple. Given her reaction at the condo, that was going to be harder than I'd thought. My employment could resume at some laboratory, an instrument manufacturer, or a local university. Operating a gas station wasn't in my plans.

I couldn't take CJ's offer seriously. He might not even be able to sign his business over to a guy the State of Illinois had declared as dead. "I'll think about it." Maybe I could find an alternative for CJ that didn't involve me.

"Good enough for now. More noodles?"

"No thanks. I'm full."

Before I left the kitchen for the front office, I put our plates and cutlery in the sink and rinsed them off.

CJ stood staring at his recliner. "Okay to sit? I don't wanna' get stuck in the ass."

"I cleaned it off. You'll be fine."

CJ slid a tape into the DVD player. Another old Bears game from 1985 appeared on the TV screen.

"You like football?"

No reply.

I hadn't paid attention to how the Bears did since Coach Mike Ditka left the team. If I brought their 2019 game scores back to 2011, I could bet on some sure things. Nah, that was something Hamza or Soson would do. Not me.

Along the wall near the recliner, three plastic laundry baskets overflowed with copies of the local paper. Hamza had flaunted the April 18th issue in my face. I knelt by the closest basket. The top issue of the *Daily Herald* was today's.

CJ leaned on the arm of his recliner. "Don't get 'em out of order. I want to read them chrono-illogically. Gotta' keep up with the news."

He was years behind. I was too tired to forage through the baskets looking for the one dated January 24, 2011, if CJ's collection went back that far.

"I've had a long day. I think I'm going to bed."

CJ eased himself out of the chair. "Hang on. Dang memory. You should see the brick they threw. I saved it for ya." He pulled it from the lower shelf of his service desk and handed it to me.

A heavily padded envelope was rubber-banded to the implement of destruction. I snapped the bands off. No postal stamps or markings, just my name printed on the front. "Thanks."

"Tell your friends to use the mailbox next time."

"Anyone who threw that brick is no friend of mine." I went upstairs to Mickey's room and opened the padded envelope. Inside were three objects: a grainy candid photo of Hamza Bashir with 4/19/2019 scribbled on the back, a sealed silver tube with red warning stickers in Russian, and a latex glove. I left the cap on the tube but squeezed it. The content was soft like ointment or skin cream. I dialed Soson.

"*Zdravstvuyte?*"

"Soson? It's Randy." I heard a woman giggling in the background.

"Not a good time, Randall. Whatever can wait until tomorrow, yes?" Soson's attention was focused on his female companion.

"I'm afraid not. Why would someone throw a brick through CJ's front window?"

"You disturb me about the actions of hooligans?"

I described the contents of the padded envelope addressed to me.

At a distance from the mouthpiece, Soson barked, "*Ukhodi!*" and then came back to the phone. "Unnecessary drama. Do not open the tube, under any circumstances! Promise!"

"Okay. Just tell me what this is about." My stomach digested itself, not CJ's Famous Spaghetti.

"Is there a date on the picture?"

"The nineteenth. Next Friday." Soson must have been familiar with this style of coded communication.

"Good, we have time. But I will not speak of this over the phone."

"CJ could have been killed. If you won't tell me now, I'll drive to St. Charles and we'll discuss this face-to-face."

"I do not know who is listening. If you choose to drive here, I will not answer the door.

Please, *tovarish*, put the package in a safe place and we will discuss tomorrow. Not your cute little car. Someplace it cannot be found."

My patience for Soson's games and riddles had evaporated. "If I'm in danger, I need to know *now*."

Soson raised his voice. "*Nyet*. We will speak of this tomorrow night, and you will decide. I may uninvite Louise from dinner, but we shall see. *Dobroy nochi*. Sleep well." He ended the call.

I'd been perceptive enough to distrust Soson the day my experiment was performed. Since then, my anger toward him had built with every conversation. How could I sit across from him tomorrow night and not explode?

Alone in Mickey's bedroom, I looked around. Where would a teenager hide something from his father? The closet. I pushed the box of GoTane paraphernalia to the side and crawled around, looking for a secret cubbyhole. At the back, a couple of boards weren't flush with the rest of the floor. They wiggled with a little pressure. Eventually I pried them up. A stack of adult magazines with nude photos had been hidden in a gap between the floor joists. I pulled them out and slipped in the padded bag. The magazines no longer fit so I tossed them into the box and shoved it back into place. I doubted Mickey would come back for them.

Soson's instructions made the contents sound dangerous and gave me the creeps. What kind of decision? On top of that, I still had an upset stomach. Could I even sleep now? I set an alarm on my phone so I wouldn't be late for my court date and crawled beneath the covers.

Thoughts bounced around in my mind like a Superball in zero gravity. Evidence of chrontins at the Lab. Soson's claim that "if there is forward, there must be backward." The attack on CJ and the ominous Russian package. My court date the next morning. And Craig.

I tried to remember my sensations as I'd passed through time. Cold and gritty, like I'd been scrubbed with steel wool. I curled up, forcing myself to ignore everything except how I'd feel when I reclaimed my life.

Day 4

[13] Monday, April 15, 2019

I showered, shaved, and dressed in the outfit Soson had purchased for me. The image reflected in the mirror was a bit startling, because I'd been wearing business casual to the Labs since the '90's.

CJ was in the makeshift kitchen holding a screwdriver, fussing with the camping stove. "Dang thing keeps on givin' me trouble. Can I make you somethin'?"

"No thanks." I pulled a box of corn flakes from the bookcase that acted as a pantry. "This'll do."

CJ turned around and stood frozen, staring. "You gonna' pump gas dressed like that?"

I'd become used to CJ's Swiss cheese memory. "I've got a court date this morning."

"You in trouble?" He put down the screwdriver. "Somethin' I can help with?"

"No, nothing like that. Do you have Internet service here?"

"Nope. Not like the phone company stops askin'. GoTane used to provide a Wee-Fee box as part of their deal. Mickey used it all the time with his lap computer. Screwed up his life, it did. That's why I run this place cash-only. Credit card companies can shove their fees. I keep the money tucked away 'til I can get to the bank."

Where does CJ keep the sales proceeds from the pickle jar? Under his mattress or in his freezer? I didn't ask.

"Anything else on your schedule today?" asked CJ. "Other than workin' at the station, I mean?"

I didn't intend to disappoint CJ so often. "After court, I'm going to school." I could hardly wait to meet Craig, and I had a plan to do just that.

"Ain't you already degreed?"

"Yes. Maybe too many for my own good. This visit is to see my son."

"You and the missus separated?"

"Yes." Until I could convince Faith to restart our marriage. I'd have to ask my lawyer Tonya about that.

"And she didn't give you any of them rights? I didn't have that situation. Betty died and I got Mickey. Did my best, I did. Made my share of mistakes too. Now he's gone and I'm alone."

Given his demeanor, I expected that CJ handled fatherhood the best he knew how. I would never consider raising Craig a burden, even if limited to shared custody. I put my arm around CJ. "I'll be back." The identical promise I made to return to Faith at the hospital echoed in my memory. A promise I didn't keep.

I drove to the Cook County Courthouse in Arlington Heights, made my way through the metal detectors and waited in the hallway outside the courtrooms on the second floor. A few minutes later, a dark-haired woman with severe curves wearing a navy-blue business suit, stiletto heels. and sporting Hollywood starlet make-up approached me. "Dr. Weinberg?"

"Yes. You're Tonya Smirnov?" I completely understood why Soson had fallen in love with her and was flummoxed about why he didn't try to get her back. I pictured them arm-in-arm, smiling at each other, like Faith and I used to do.

"The same. I searched for you on the Internet after our conversation. Quite a celebrity. Nobel Prize winner. One magazine called you—" She squinted at her phone's screen. "'—a combination of Edward Jenner and Max Planck, leading the charge for the future of medicine.' We can't have such an illustrious person declared dead in error, can we?"

Her smile made me optimistic that I'd regain my living status.

"You told me you had documentation, proof of your identity. Please show me." She shifted a Prada-labeled leather brief bag on her shoulder.

I pulled out my wallet and thumbed through the contents. "A miniature photocopy of my birth certificate. My photo ID from ChiLabs. An Illinois driver's license—just renewed—and some expired credit cards." I handed her everything.

"Very good. Even without your background check and fingerprints, I can get your status corrected." Her smiling expression shifted. She looked like she'd just eaten the last cookie in the bag. "I must tell you. I was obligated to notify your wife's attorney that we were bringing a petition today. I hope that is not a problem."

"I've been promised that Faith won't contest this." Why should she? "What harm would there be to her if I was being declared alive?"

"There are financial consequences. For example, any life insurance benefits will need to be repaid."

Hamza had said the same thing. "I don't care at all about the money. Hell, she can keep the Nobel Prize award, too. I just want them in my life."

"As for your relationship, I can refer you to specialists equipped to handle a reconciliation, assuming she's willing."

I mishandled seeing Faith for the first time at her condo. Soson had warned me to stay away, but I didn't listen. So had Hamza. "I'd like to try." Getting rid of the dead status was a great first step.

Tonya shook her head, her long black hair shimmering. "We should go in."

I followed her into the courtroom. In the gallery we sat side by side, Tonya with perfect posture. She scrolled through what looked like hundreds of email messages on her phone, her brief bag on her lap.

The judge at the front of the chamber paged through documents at his bench and then summoned two lawyers forward. The jury box was empty. No need for a collection of twelve random citizens to weigh in on my situation. I was declared dead but anyone could see I'm alive.

After a brief conference and a flick of the judge's hand, the two lawyers moved back.

The judge said, "Parties have agreed on a discovery schedule. See you back here in two weeks. Next case."

The bailiff called out, "In re the Estate of Weinberg."

Was this about money or the fact that I'd been declared dead?

Tonya put away her phone and tugged my arm. I stood and followed her to the judge's bench.

"Tonya Smirnov for the petitioner, your Honor."

"Proceed." The judge adjusted a pair of reading glasses, my paperwork in hand.

"One year ago, you granted a petition for letters of administration upon a presumption of death for Dr. Randall Weinberg, who had no contact with his friends or family for over seven years."

"I remember this case." The judge ruffled my papers. "Filed by the wife, if memory serves."

"Correct, your Honor. Faith Watson Weinberg. Her husband Randall had not been seen or heard from since January 24, 2011. Two police departments failed to locate him. His wife hired private investigators who combed the country, looking for him, with no results."

"She easily met the requirement for diligent inquiry. And seven years is the typical waiting period." His head bounced in a nod. "I ruled that the facts created a presumption in law that Weinberg died intestate on that date."

"Yes, and your court issued letters of office of the presumed-dead estate of Weinberg and appointed Hamza Bashir as independent administrator."

My stomach acid gurgled. Once all of this was over, I'd fire his ass from that responsibility.

"If it please your Honor, may I introduce Dr. Randall Weinberg." Tonya pointed at me with an exquisite fire engine red fingernail.

The judge peeked over his glasses. I smiled, nodded, and stifled a wave.

Tonya continued. "I brought him here as my prime witness, asking you to approve my motion to revoke those letters of administration."

"You're telling me this is Randall Weinberg?" He grunted. "Besides the physical presence of this gentleman—" He nodded in my direction. "—what evidence do you have to present?

Tonya opened her brief bag and took out all of the items I'd given her, plus another document. "As you can see, your Honor, Dr. Weinberg's previous employer required fingerprints and a background check for security."

The judge pawed through my items like a squirrel pushing aside leaves to find berries on the ground. "You're a modern-day Einstein, I take it"

I stood silent. Was I supposed to talk? A nudge in the ribs from Tonya's elbow was an affirmative. "No, your Honor. Just a capable particle physicist."

"I had Dr. Weinberg fingerprinted at Precision Biometrics, which will provide a certified copy of his prints. Their analysis will show that their set matches the one taken by his former employer." Tonya's voice became apologetic. "It might take a day or two."

The judge waved my birth certificate and driver's license. "Do you have an affidavit acknowledging that these items of evidence are, in fact, those of the person in question?"

"No, your Honor. I thought that, instead, you might place Dr. Weinberg under oath so he can testify in front of you as to his identity and as to the documents."

The judge cleared his throat. "Normally, I don't use court time for such things. And may I remind you that you promised me this would be a simple matter."

"It is, your Honor. I assure you that this is Dr. Randall Weinberg. A few questions under oath and this matter will be settled."

"I don't think so, Counselor. You will also want me to order Mr. Bashir to provide a full accounting of the estate and to turn over all remaining assets. Will he be joining us today?"

"No, your Honor. I've been advised by my client that Ms. Watson and Mr. Bashir will not be contesting our filing."

"Still, there will need to be separate hearings as to custody and visitation of the minor child."

"More hearings?" I whispered as I stared at Tonya's profile. "I thought the judge would see me and rule that I'm alive. Why is this so complicated?"

"Dr. Weinberg, the court has rules that everyone must follow." The judge sounded like my father giving me a lecture about studying hard for my SAT. "They're called laws. You have something similar in your line of work, correct? Laws of physics? I expect you don't go around violating those on a whim, do you?"

My current predicament of time travel seemed to be exactly that. "Not on a whim, your Honor."

"I'll discuss the next steps with you later, Dr. Weinberg," Tonya whispered. "First things first."

Soson had used the same phrase when recommending Tonya. I'd hoped the financial and custody issues would be relatively easy to negotiate. "Okay, you're the attorney."

"We've already spent more time on this matter than I'd expected." The judge called the bailiff over. "Might as well get this over with."

The bailiff demonstrated. "Raise your right hand." He recited the same words I'd seen on numerous TV shows.

"I do." I lowered my hand.

The judge stared at the documents in front of him. His lips skewed to the side. "2011, hmm? Just out of curiosity, Dr. Weinberg, where have you been the last eight years?" He pulled off his reading glasses and stared.

I was under oath, obligated to tell the truth. I couldn't repeat the lie about being kidnapped. That story would become part of an official record. Authorities would want to investigate. At the same time, I couldn't tell him that I was caught in a burst of chrontin particles and thrown forward eight years in time. He'd think I was insane. I'd lose all credibility. Besides, a good scientist doesn't publish a hypothesis without some proof. Tonya gave me a clear look of frustration.

I craned my head forward. "Must you know that, your Honor?"

He wiped off his glasses. "It's a reasonable question." His eyebrows dipped. "Where were you?"

"It's very complicated."

He squirmed in his chair. "Complicated? Seems rather straightforward to me. You had to be somewhere, didn't you?"

Clearly, I'd pissed him off. I considered exposing my leap through time, but as a layman it would sound like science fiction, or a made-up story to conceal some devious truth.

"Go on," whispered Tonya. "Tell him, he'll approve my motion, and you can move on with your life."

I returned my focus to the judge as I invented a viable excuse. "The government project I'm working on is covered by strict non-disclosure agreements. Do I *have* to tell you? Is it *required*?"

"No, it's not. But your sworn testimony under oath *is* required to turn these scraps of paper—" He picked up my ID's, birth certificate and license and let them flutter to his desk. "—into evidence."

The courtroom door opened.

"There he is."

Faith's voice. I whipped my head to see her walk in on Hamza's arm. *What are they doing here?* I knew she'd lost weight when I saw her at her condo, but this close, she looked even more fragile. Her longer hair partially covered her face from a carelessly arranged hairdo. With no makeup and dark circles under her eyes, she looked terrible. God, I still love her. I could make everything better if Hamza got out of the way.

When Hamza hesitated, Faith stepped forward, forcing him to escort her to the front of the courtroom.

"Excuse me, but do you have business related to this case?" asked the judge. "I'm in the middle of taking a sworn statement." He squinted and did a double take. "Wait, you're Faith Watson Weinberg, aren't you?"

Tonya threw me a puzzled look. "If it pleases your Honor, we didn't expect that Dr. Weinberg's ex-wife would be in attendance. May we have a moment?"

"Go ahead, but don't try my patience. Simple, hmm?"

"Thank you, your Honor." Tonya leaned close. At that distance, her perfume was overpowering. "Did you know Faith was going to show up?"

"No, that guy with her told me just the opposite."

Hamza helped Faith to a chair at the prosecution table and walked towards us.

Tonya and I met him halfway.

I stood close to Hamza, choking on the odor of curry and garlic. "You said you wouldn't interfere."

Tonya listened at my side.

"I told her lawyer to stay away. When Faith found out that you were coming to court, she became hysterical. The only way I could get her to calm down was to agree to bring her here. We're not contesting anything." Hamza glanced at Tonya. "Really."

A man in a pinstriped suit entered the courtroom, opened his briefcase on the prosecution table and approached the bench.

"Who's that?" I asked.

Hamza's shoulders slumped. "Her lawyer, from the original declaration. Damn!" He clicked his tongue. "He came anyway."

The judge tapped his gavel. "Ms. Smirnov? Dr. Weinberg? Can we proceed? Now?"

Hamza returned to Faith and helped her walk forward and stand next to her lawyer.

Tonya and I also stood in front of the bench, now part of a chorus line.

The man in pin stripes spoke. "My name is Andrew Tobias, your Honor. I represent Faith Watson, Randall Weinberg's former wife. She was the initiator of the original death order. I just found out about this hearing from Ms. Smirnov this weekend."

"You have standing in this matter," said the judge. "Are you here to refute the identity of this man?" The judge pointed at me. "He's obviously alive, and we were about to confirm his identity under oath."

"We're objecting on the basis of improper notice. Also, the petition lacks the required affidavit."

Tonya chimed in. "Because none was prepared. Dr. Weinberg was about to testify regarding his identity."

"In the matter of Dr. Weinberg's estate, Ms. Watson received the proceeds of his Nobel Prize award before your order was issued. She subsequently received insurance money as a result of your order and inherited all of Dr. Weinberg's possessions."

"You're a Nobel Prize winner?" asked the judge.

I nodded. No words were necessary.

"Please answer for the court reporter."

"Yes."

Tobias continued. "We request that you rule to continue the existing letters and hold a full evidentiary hearing to ascertain this individual's true identity. We request seven days to respond to the petition and prepare for the hearing. In the meantime, Mr. Bashir will prepare a full audited accounting of Ms. Watson's expenses against the estate for the last year."

"A week? I have to remain dead on the books for another *week*?" I leaned past Tonya and asked Faith, "Why are you doing this?" I hadn't intended on raising my voice, but that's how it came out.

The judge pounded his gavel. "Sir, please control yourself."

I stood at the bench, my fingers hooked on the ornamental wooden border. "I don't want any money. She can have it all!"

"There will be order in my court." The judge adjusted the glasses on the tip of his nose. "If you like, you may testify to that in the estate reconciliation hearing. I will not tolerate any further disruption in my courtroom."

A hollow feeling grew in the pit of my stomach.

"Well enough. Mr. Tobias, you've brought valid concerns to my attention."

I leaned over to see Faith. Her eyes were fixed on me. I'd seen that expression before, when I took the last of our frozen wedding cake to work and passed out pieces in the break room. At every wedding anniversary thereafter, I heard her complaint all over again. She snapped her attention to the judge and shouted, "My Randy is dead!" She threw her face into Hamza's shoulder, sobbing.

"Mr. Tobias, you might ask Ms. Watson to provide evidence for her accusation in the evidentiary hearing." The judge examined the faces of the people gathered before him and pulled off his glasses. "There's an issue of fact remaining as to the status of Dr. Weinberg and the identity of the individual in the courtroom claiming to be him. It doesn't help your case, Ms. Smirnoff, that you provided late notice and neglected to attach an affidavit to your petition. I'm continuing this case. Mr. Tobias, you have five days to file any written objections to the petition. We'll have an evidentiary hearing in seven days on my 9:30 call. That's all."

I remained in front of the judge's bench, Tonya at my side. "I'm still dead?"

The judge directed his comment to Tonya. "Please explain to your client that this hearing is over. I gave him ample opportunity to provide an evidentiary basis for his petition today, significantly delaying all the other attorneys in this room. He refused."

"He apologizes, your Honor."

On cue, I bowed my head.

"However, you must understand his frustration. How can he resume his life under these circumstances?"

"He brought this on himself. I asked a simple question, and evidently a highly relevant one, because he refused to answer."

Tonya extended her hands, palms up. "Perhaps, your Honor, it is personal or embarrassing."

The judge shook his head. "Perhaps. Still, despite multiple opportunities, you've failed to provide admissible evidence as to this man's identity. You've failed to provide proper timely notice to all parties. Mr. Tobias objects on those bases, as would any competent lawyer. You'll have another chance next week. This affords Mr. Tobias the opportunity to confer with his client before questioning your client under oath. You are dismissed. Next case."

"But your Honor—"

"I said, next case." He stuffed all of my papers into an envelope and handed-it to Tonya.

She grabbed my elbow and rushed me out of the courtroom. When she stopped in the hallway, she thrust the envelope containing my documents at me.

I stuffed the envelope into my suit jacket pocket. "Why didn't you tell me they'd ask my whereabouts?"

Tonya glared. "Because I thought you had an answer, the one you gave me on the phone, or was that a lie?" She pointed at the courtroom. "You torpedoed me in there."

If I'd told the truth, the judge would have sent me to an insane asylum and thrown away the key. "I wasn't going to invent something under oath and commit perjury."

"Why do you *need* to make something up?" She clamped her fingers around my arm. "Where in the hell *were* you?"

I was tempted to tell Tonya my time travel theory until, out of the corner of my eye, I saw Faith and Hamza at the far end of the corridor. "I need to talk to my wife."

"Ex-wife. And I strongly advise you not to interact with her."

Tobias finished a limp handshake with Faith and headed for the stairs. Hamza stood beside Faith, helping keep her on her feet.

I pulled away from Tonya's grasp. "Sorry, I have to go reason with her."

"Just like Soson to send me a self-destructing client."

I spoke over my shoulder. "As far as I'm concerned, you over-promised and under-delivered."

"Is that the way it is? Then we're done. I'll be filing a motion to withdraw as your attorney. You don't owe me anything, Dr. Weinberg. But tell Soson not to send me any more clients. My reputation can't afford it." Tonya strutted away, her hips and hair swaying from side to side, her stiletto heels clacking on the marble floor like tack hammers.

I ran over to Faith, who was still on Hamza's arm. "Faith?" I tried to make eye contact. "You think I deserted you when Craig was born, but I didn't."

She raised her head, her eyes shooting daggers. "You." Her pallid complexion came alive. "I should have known you wouldn't come back. Your work always came first."

"You gave me permission. Hell, you urged me to go."

"Not for seven years!" Tears streaked her cheeks. "You promised you'd be there for me. For us. And then you vanished."

"Faith." I reached for her hand.

She swung it away.

Hamza shifted Faith so I saw her in profile. "This is not the time or place—"

"Stay out of this!" I felt like breaking his hooked nose. My instinct about him working Faith to take control of her assets was spot on.

Faith stared off into the distance. "I waited for him to come back. Oh, how I waited, all of those months and years imagining the terrible things that could have happened. I saw his face every time I looked at Craig. And when I agreed to sign the papers—" She whipped her head and made eye contact. "—that *had* to be the end. Final." She poked my chest with her index finger. "You *can't* be my Randy. You *can't*." She pulled away, her head limp, her eyes closed.

"But—"

Hamza wrapped one arm around Faith's waist so all I could see was her back. "I told you. Stay away from her and the boy. You'll only make things worse." He leaned close and forced something into my hand. "Here's another thousand. There's more if you keep your distance."

Hamza stole money from Faith to pay me off! I cocked my arm, ready to throw the wad of bills in his face. Then I considered my situation. No job, no prospects, ongoing expenses, and a fragile living situation. I shoved the cash into my pocket, an advance on what a court would decide was rightfully mine.

Hamza escorted Faith to the elevator.

Faith wrote me off to survive. There was still Craig. I was determined to get to know him, and I had a plan to make that happen.

[14] Monday, April 15, 2019 (continued)

When I got back to the Beetle, I checked for new emails on my phone. One message confirmed that Precision Biometrics had sent my fingerprints to the authorities and Tonya. *One day too late, just like my Audi TT tire swap.* No other communication. It wasn't like 2011, when I'd get dozens of emails a day from members of the American Association of Physicists in Medicine or the Institute of Physics in the UK.

On my old personal email account, I used to cherish Faith's daily messages. The contents were never earthshaking, but those emails maintained our bond even when I was at work. At the time, I used MyPlace, an email and social presence platform. Whatever happened to that account? Had Faith continued to email me after I disappeared? It was worth checking to help me understand her mindset. I did a web search for MyPlace, expecting they'd gone out of business like Carson's, CellNation and Mark Shale. Except they hadn't. The "About us" tab said that a company named Evergreen Capital Ventures had acquired them, and the web listing showed a 1-800 number. I called.

"MyPlace is your place. This is Trip. How can I help?"

The representative's voice was young, upbeat, perky. Not like the stiff scripted service reps I'd spoken to in the past. Echoes of other voices in the background confirmed I'd reached a call center. "I haven't been on your service for a while. About eight years." Lou had computed the exact duration as three thousand days.

"I've heard longer. Customers enjoyed our services for a long time and then gave up on us for the competition. Not naming any names. I bet you want back in."

I liked the tone and attitude of this hip rep. "Exactly."

"We've got a simple procedure for that. Go to our web page, click on "I miss you" and fill out the form. We'll reinstate your account. Easy-peasy."

"With all of my old email messages?"

"Naturally. When a member goes idle, after a year we archive their information, just in case. Eight years? Man, where have you been?" His pause was too short for me to answer. "Never mind. Just give us about twenty-four hours to restore them. Data only moves so fast."

Not as fast as chrontins. "Okay. This is terrific."

"Listen, if you dig what we've got going on, tell your friends and relatives. There will be lots of cool features just down the road. We're trying to reclaim members just like you."

"Done. I'll fill out the form and log in tomorrow."

"Thanks for using MyPlace, your place on the Internet." He hung up.

If only restoring my experiment's raw data was so easy.

212

I searched for the name and location of the elementary school that served Faith's new address and arrived there after an early lunch at Starbucks.

A security guard buzzed me through the locked front door into a vestibule. "How can I help you today?"

"I'd like to speak with a teacher. Ms. Sherman?" I'd gotten her name from Hamza at Faith's condo. "My son is in her class."

"Sign in please, and I need a photo ID."

I handed my driver's license to him and then wrote my name in a logbook with the time and date.

He typed something into a computer. "She's on her lunch period, but I'll let her know you're here." With my license next to the keyboard, he typed some more, looked up and smiled, and then refocused on his screen. "She'll be right out."

I sat on a wooden bench, watching people walk through. Most of them had school passes hanging around their necks and only had to nod to the guard to get buzzed through.

A thin brunette in a plain white blouse and an ankle-length flower-patterned skirt came through the door. She stopped in her tracks when our eyes met.

I stood and approached her. "Ms. Sherman? My name is Randy Weinberg. My son Craig is in your class."

"Call me Elizabeth." She furrowed her forehead. "Wait. Is Craig Watson your son?"

"My wife Faith uses her maiden name. I guess she must have changed his as well."

"For security, I'll need to verify a few things—nothing daunting—so, when he finishes lunch, you can say a quick hello."

"You misunderstand. He and I have never met."

Her smile vanished. "Excuse me?"

"I've been away since he was born." No reason to tell her I was a dead man walking. "At the moment, Faith and I aren't together. There are some things I need to straighten out, after being gone so long."

"That's terrible." She toyed with the wedding band on her finger. "To be honest, Craig spends most of his time alone, not interacting with other students. I'm certain having his father in his life would help."

"I agree."

"You know, the statistics about what single-parent children succumb to is frightening. They're at risk for so many things."

I nodded. "I hoped you'd let me come to your classes and hang out, just for a little while each day. I won't distract him or the class but being able to spend time with him would be precious."

"I understand completely." She put a hand on mine and then pulled away as if to avoid getting burned. "But I'm afraid I can't do that. As you admitted, you and your wife are separated. Craig's safety must come first."

"I'm not taking him anywhere. I just want to be in the same room." Doesn't she believe I want the best for Craig?

"None of the other children would have their parents in attendance. There's bound to be a fuss and I can't afford one. You see, I don't have tenure."

I hadn't expected to negotiate. All I wanted to do was see my son and spend time with him. "If it makes any difference, ChiLabs reviewed my background extensively before they hired me. If you'd like something more recent, Precision Biometrics just sent my fingerprints to the State Police and FBI. A small misunderstanding." Why not get some value out of that ninety-dollar expense?

"What you ask is impossible. I'm very sorry." She took my license from the guard.

I sensed her compassion for my plight. I pulled out the photo Patrice had gifted me. "See this? It's the only picture I have of my son. Is it too much to ask to let me *look* at him?"

"I can't allow you on school property. We have rules."

There had to be a way to convince her. "Do you have kids?"

"Besides the ones in my classroom, no."

Maybe there was still a chance to get her support. "They go off to fourth grade at the end of the year, right?"

"I know what you're doing. Yes, I miss them, especially the ones I've gotten close to.

There are always a few. Craig will be one of those."

"Pretend that a few years after he leaves your class, you see him on the street or while shopping. How do you expect you'd feel at that moment?"

She stared at the floor while she formulated a reply. "A moment of joy." She raised her head, her eyes glossy. "I'd be filled with curiosity about how he was doing. And if he remembered me."

"I've never seen my son in person. Ever. But you can't figure out some way to make that happen and not violate your precious rules?"

"Hmmm." She cupped her chin. "There *is* a public sidewalk that surrounds the school, including the fenced playground."

That sounded like an opportunity. "When does your class take recess?"

She checked her watch. "In about fifteen minutes, immediately after lunch period, so the children can settle in for the rest of the day."

I imagined searching over a hundred anonymous faces. "How will I know which one is Craig?" He was only two years old in the photo Patrice had provided.

Her eyes flashed. "What if I were to pat one of the children on the head on his way out the door? Out of fondness?"

"Perfect. Thank you so much."

"One condition." The driver's license dangled from her fingers. "Under no circumstances will you engage him in conversation. Agreed?"

"Absolutely. Thank you so much." I took the license from her hand and walked outside.

I followed the sidewalk around the school, pretending to pay attention to the traffic, the houses across the street, the foliage of the trees, all while keeping an eye on the rear school doors. At the end of the block, a man with a flattop crew cut wearing a long-sleeved red Henley shirt and black pants leaned against the hood of his black SUV. He held a glossy-covered Hot Rod magazine in front of his face, exposing dirty knuckles.

Almost precisely fifteen minutes later, the bulky doors swung open. Dozens of children ran out, with no sign of Elizabeth. After the second throng of kids, she appeared in the door, overseeing her class's exit.

When a boy with scruffy brown hair appeared, she patted his head and glanced in my direction.

I mouthed, "Thank you."

His wrinkled T-shirt hung over his pants. Given Faith's condition, maybe she let him dress himself unsupervised. It took every ounce of self-restraint not to call out.

He walked around the playground alone, hands in his pockets, kicking random stones out of his path. I pulled out Patrice's photo and held it up. With puffy cheeks, the resemblance to his younger self was clear. I put the picture away and snapped candid shots with my phone's camera, a few full-body pictures and some zoomed to capture his face, with a pointy chin, like his mother. The man on the corner had his phone out, aimed at the playground.

While Craig meandered around, getting slowly closer to me, our eyes met. I put my phone away. After a couple of minutes, he approached the fence. Per my agreement with Elizabeth, I remained silent while staring at my flesh and blood, mere feet away. How awkward, standing there in silence.

"Do you always stare at kids? Are you some kind of pervert?" He bounced on the balls of his feet, perhaps prepared to run off if I made a threatening gesture.

I felt obligated to respond. After all, he'd spoken first. "Nope. Just enjoying a spring day."

Craig stared at the ground, dragging his shoe through the gravel. "Don't you have a job?"

I bit my lip and turned away. The truth stalled on the tip of my tongue. Craig deserved a complete conversation we couldn't have. "I'm a scientist."

Craig's eyes met mine. "My dad was a scientist before he ran away. Mom hid some papers, but I found them. His name was Randall."

I willed myself not to break down and tell him the truth. I didn't want to shock him, like I'd done by showing up at Faith's condo. I pulled my shoulders back and struggled to take my next breath.. "I'm a physicist who studies elemental particles."

"What are those?" His expression reminded me of Faith's when she'd try to handle a complicated bill. I decided not to give a lecture about the Standard Model of particle physics. "It's a specialty. Like there are some doctors in medicine who treat eyes, some do stomachs, other concentrate on feet." I lifted my leg and wiggled my shoe for effect. "I specialize in the tiniest pieces from which all matter is built. Even smaller than atoms." Could I have phrased that differently? Maybe an analogy?

"My mom has a bunch of doctors. I don't like them very much."

I tried to hide my concern about Faith's health that bubbled inside. Is that why she'd lost weight? "I'm sorry to hear that." It would have been tactless to ask Craig to provide details. Hamza would know, or perhaps Soson. "What's on your shirt?"

Craig pulled at the hem to stretch the front flat. "This is Sue. She's a dinosaur. Actually, a skeleton. I'd love to see real, live dinosaurs, but they died a long time ago."

With reverse time travel, I could grant his wish. "How long have you been interested in dinosaurs?"

"Since I was a baby. Mom bought a bunch of stuffed ones for my crib. Don't tell anybody, but I still have them in my closet."

Faith always had a thing for natural history. Those purchases must have been made after I vanished. "Did your mother take you to the Field Museum to see Sue?"

219

"No, Mom doesn't go out. Uncle Ham bought me the shirt as a present."

"Uncle Ham? Strange name."

"His real name is Hamza."

It was only a small gift, but the gesture still pissed me off. "You know there are lots of museums you should see." I pictured myself riding with Craig buckled into the passenger seat of the Beetle on an adventure to the Museum Campus. "If she can't get out, maybe someone else could take you."

"I'd have to get permission. Mom told me I shouldn't even talk to strangers."

Craig had broken Faith's warning. She would never agree. She'd be scared I would kidnap him and she might never see him again. "Maybe your teacher can take a field trip with the whole class." I'd ask to be one of the chaperones.

"She's never done that before."

My fantasy evaporated. From Elizabeth's expression on the stairs, I could tell she wasn't pleased. I shrugged, which I didn't think accurately communicated that Craig approached me and not the other way around.

Another woman, older, joined her. They had a brief conversation, after which they both went inside.

The bell rang, signaling the end of recess.

"I gotta' go." He bolted toward the open door.

I stood watching until the playground was empty and the doors shut. Was that it? One brief

220

conversation to last me, how long, forever? It wasn't right. I am his father.

The man on the corner was gone. I walked to my Beetle and pulled out my phone to look at the photos I'd taken of Craig. The ones at a distance made him look like just any other student. One of the close ones, in three-quarters profile, was good enough for a frame on my desk. If I had a desk.

Multiple issues nagging at my brain prevented me from enjoying the series. I needed to deal with everything on my plate, one at a time, or they would bother me forever.

I turned my attention to the padded envelope, retrieved Soson's number on my phone and called. "At dinner tonight, we've got some things to clear up. CJ could have been injured by a stunt like that."

"No hot date to interfere?"

I pictured Soson smirking. "You should talk." Did I offend him by having dinner with CJ the previous evening? I didn't try to describe CJ's Special Spaghetti. "What was so bad about spending one evening with my landlord?"

"Today, I am asking myself the same question. I hope your experience went better than mine. Now I will have to move sooner than expected."

Another failed relationship? "Faith and I had a great marriage, at least before I disappeared." She was the only woman I wanted in my life.

"Perhaps that will work out for the best. Tonight, I have the perfect place for pizza." Soson lowered his voice. "Is the package safe?"

"Yes." CJ wouldn't go looking for it. It seemed like Mickey's porn hadn't been discovered.

"Meet me at Pavers' Pizza in Elgin at five-thirty. It has a nice view of the Fox River. I told Louise to meet us there for dinner at six-thirty, so we can discuss the envelope over drinks before she arrives. You will need one, either during or after."

Does Soson expect it would take a full hour to discuss the Russian package? "Okay, see you then."

I checked my Google account. I had only one message, MyPlace telling me that all of my old emails had been restored on their service and were available for viewing. Now *that* was over-delivering.

I was excited to view the restored messages, like unearthing artifacts at an archeological site. At the same time, I was nervous about what I might find. I logged into MyPlace on my phone. Sure enough, my inbox was filled with numerous e-mails. As I scrolled through the list, I noticed that Faith's name appeared on many of them. I didn't want to strain my eyes, going through all of those messages on a small screen. They'd have to wait for a visit to the public library.

[15] Monday, April 15, 2019 (continued)

After changing out of my suit at CJ's, it only took about twenty-five minutes heading straight west on Golf Road to arrive in downtown Elgin. The restaurant was on the river, where Soson said it would be. Even though I had cash in my pocket, I still expected him to handle the tab. Who knew what expenses I might incur? I hadn't expected a traffic ticket in excess of a thousand dollars.

When I walked in, Soson occupied a stool at a small bar with his back to the door. Not his usual gangster position. I stood behind him and waited.

"You cannot be stealthy if I see your reflection."

Sure enough, a huge mirror backed the liquor bottle shelving. So much for not watching his back. Two other patrons sat nearby along the narrow surface.

Soson hesitated as he got off the stool. "We should get a table." He looked around the restaurant, gripping a rocks glass half-filled with amber liquid. "Not in here. Outside." He waved a hand to get the attention of the hostess. She escorted us out to a huge patio and pointed to a table at the back of the property.

"That will be fine." Soson led the way.

Our waitress took my drink order, a room-temperature root beer, no ice, and left us with menus.

"You will need something much stronger, my friend."

I waited until the waitress was out of earshot. "You said I'd have to make some kind of decision about what's in the package? Even without any details, my answer is no. Absolutely not." I didn't want anything to do with any Russians. Except Soson. "And I don't care what the question is."

He leaned back, his hands folded behind his head. "Fine with me. Are you alive now?"

Why did Soson drop the matter of the Russian package so easily? I answered him anyway. "Nope. The judge insisted I explain where I'd been for the last eight years. I didn't have the guts to tell him I came straight here from 2011."

"You are wise beyond your years. Instead of dinner, I would be visiting you in the loony bin."

"It sounds crazy, but given the presence of chrontins, there's no other explanation. I'm still dead as far as the State of Illinois is concerned. By the way, don't call Tonya. She got pretty pissed and dropped me as a client when I wouldn't answer the judge's question."

"I am not surprised. She gave up on *us* as a couple years ago."

The waitress returned with my drink.

Soson looked up from his menu. "We will have a wings appetizer." He asked me, "What sauce do you prefer?"

"Something sweet. Maybe teriyaki?"

The waitress wrote it down.

Soson asked for a sauce called Branding Iron, which I took to mean something much hotter.

"There's supposed to be some kind of hearing next week, but until then, I'm still dead." I took a sip of my drink. "I don't know who's going to represent me."

"I might know another lawyer."

Among the many women he's dated? Soson took great pride in adding to that statistic. I made it a point never to ask how many because I didn't want to know. He was dying to share. Let him suffer.

"As far as Faith is concerned, I'm still dead." I leaned my elbows on the table. "She might have even given the judge the impression that I'm an imposter."

"She came to the courthouse?" Soson's lips barely touched the glass, like a bird drinking from a rain puddle.

"Oh yes! With her lawyer and Hamza, like he was her caretaker or something. I guess when I vanished, she took it harder than I thought."

Soson nodded as if he suspected such. "It took much effort for Hamza to convince her of the fact that you were gone."

Could Hamza have brainwashed or drugged her? "You witnessed their conversations?" Back in 2011, Hamza and Soson acted like friends. Something must have happened to put them at opposite ends of the reverse time travel question.

225

"Every time he spoke to her, he would provide me a synopsis. He knew you and I were close. At least, during your first year of absence." He broke eye contact. "Nothing lately."

I yearned for insight into Faith's condition and her coping process. What she thought. What she felt. Maybe then I'd have a clue how to reconnect. "Besides the memorial service and my Dad's funeral, did you see her at all?"

"In the beginning, a couple of times a week, primarily to learn results of her search for you. She was so sure you would return with a logical explanation. I could tell that being alone with Craig, who was a really well-behaved baby, took its toll. During most of my few visits, she would plop Craig into my lap and take some time for herself. I did not blame her."

It sounded like he attempted to act like Uncle Soson despite his previous rejection of the concept. "I think what I miss most about the eight-year gap is not being there to be his father, a role model, to raise him the right way. I hope he's turned out okay."

"I have not seen him since your father's funeral. I took some photos of him on my phone. Alas, that was four phones ago."

Those pictures would have been precious. At least I had some current ones.

"If you have rejected the assignment, then I need the package from you."

The fact that Soson accepted my refusal so easily short-circuited my brain. "I expected you'd at least explain the contents."

Soson jerked upright in his chair. "What, *now* you are curious? You told me your answer. I accepted it. What is there to discuss?" He sipped his drink, whatever it was. "So where are you going to live? At CJ's gas station? Not a very nice place to bring a woman."

How many times am I going to have to ask about the package? "From my perspective, I've only been divorced for about three days."

"Remember, Faith has been a widow for a year but alone for seven more." He waved a fat finger. "But you do not need to be celibate. Men need female companionship. I predict you will run into someone who is a good match. Pretty, smart, and overwhelmed by your personality." He raised his glass, offering a toast.

I left my glass on the table. Soson seemed to be describing Elizabeth, Craig's married teacher. I banished the thought. My hope for reconciliation with Faith had sputtered, based on her behavior in the courthouse, but hadn't burnt out. The shock of seeing me upset her. If only I could explain it, everything would be all right. Once she calmed down, she'd realize we were meant to be together. How this was all just a horrible accident that left both of us wounded. A life together remained possible.

Soson revisited his drink just as the waitress delivered the wings appetizer to our table with two sauces.

"Ready to order?" She pulled out pen and paper.

Soson specified two large thin-crust pizzas, one with sausage and mushrooms he knew we both liked, and one with vegetables that must have been Lou's preference. "Please have them ready at six-thirty."

As I dipped one of the wings in the dark brown teriyaki sauce, I couldn't hold back my curiosity. "Tell me, what did I refuse to do?"

"*Again,* you ask?" Soson nodded. "*Da.* You deserve to understand the consequences of your decision." He leaned closer and lowered his voice, even though there were no other patrons nearby. "The package contains the means for you to kill Hamza Bashir."

I choked on a lump of chicken and skin. "What?"

"The tube of gel is a potent nerve agent. Apply it to Hamza's skin and then walk away. Oh, and discard the protective glove."

It took a lot of coughing and a long suck of my drink to clear my throat. "I don't like that guy, but kill him?" He'd been looking out for Faith, an activity I didn't expect and appreciated.

"The oligarch for whom you will be inventing backward time travel requires leverage. On you. Something that puts him in control of your behavior. Blackmail for murder works quite well, I am told." He leaned back in his chair, staring. "As long as you work diligently on reverse time travel, you will not be implicated for murder. Fail or subsequently refuse to cooperate and he will turn proof of your deed over to the police."

"I want to hear this from his own lips, if it's so damned important."

Soson shook his head. "You ask the impossible. Meeting him tips the balance of power, which he will not allow."

"Then *you* tell me, why kill Hamza? *His* alterations to the controller settings in my office caused time travel?" *This makes no sense.*

"The oligarch did not share his reasoning with me. Only his expectations. He will be surprised that you do not want to take advantage of this opportunity."

Soson didn't seem to be appropriately upset. "Too bad for him." Murder? No way! "Have you seen things like this before?"

"Yes, unfortunately. People in Russia with power and money want only one thing: more of both. Reverse time travel would make the sponsor in question both excessively powerful and wealthy."

"That guy is insane if he thinks I'll kill for him."

"There are consequences, *tovarish*. Always consequences. If you choose to kill Hamza by Friday, that ensures your cooperation. Given your knowledge and Hamza's results, he expects you will be successful within six months. Perhaps he will extend the deadline if you make demonstrable progress."

"Starting with my original research, a bunch of static screen shots, and Hamza's settings? That's impossible. Doesn't he know that I didn't invent forward time travel? That Hamza's futzing changed the results of my experiment?"

"He does not care. His best people have not been able to even replicate what Hamza achieved, let alone traveling backwards. He depends on *you*."

"I just told you I won't do it. There goes their leverage."

Soson took another sip. "Your choice merely changes their tactics. Let Hamza live, and you have sixty days to achieve the expected result or your son dies."

"What?" I jumped out of my chair, sending it flying. "He must be out of his fucking mind! They'd kill Craig?" I couldn't focus. How did I get caught up in this mess?

"Faith is next, after a sixty-day extension. And Louise, sweet girl, after another sixty. One death or three. Their continued existence depends on you. One way or another. It is your choice."

I stumbled backwards and tripped over my chair, landing on the hardwood deck. It wasn't difficult to think some Russian would kill for the ability to time travel in any direction, but to put pressure on me like that? "Blackmail or threats to kill family and friends won't make results happen quicker. That's not how science works!"

Soson's face was serene, as if enjoying a picnic on a summer's evening. I struggled to my feet, pulled my chair up to the table, my body shaking. "I'm afraid to ask what happens if six months isn't enough."

"Then he will expand the circle to people you have interacted with. Your landlord, CJ, perhaps. Your son's schoolteacher?"

This was beyond crazy. "Elizabeth Sherman? I only met her today."

"That does not matter to him. All he wants is results, as soon as possible. Trust me. He is not a patient person."

Or an ethical one. I'd become a walking death sentence for anyone I might meet. A fatal linear progression. "It would have to stop sometime, wouldn't it?"

"Disappoint him long enough and he will conclude that you will never give him what he needs. At that point, your life is worthless. He might arrange for you to go to prison, or he might deal with you directly. And *tovarish*, I can assure you, your death will not be painless. Nor will mine."

Soson was on the hook? "Shit!" I buried my face in my hands. "I don't want to be here."

A female voice said, "Soson told me you were looking *forward* to pizza."

Lou, who'd been escorted by the waitress carrying our order, stood at the table. Her eyes shifted as if waiting for one of us to acknowledge her.

"Sit down, my dear, we were just talking about a personal matter. Have a wing? The red sauce is like fire."

When the server asked if we wanted refills on our drinks, Soson nodded for both of us without asking me.

I wanted to dig deeper, to better understand my circumstance. Then I realized that Soson had told me more than I wanted to know, none of it useful in making a decision.

"How did court go? Want a sausage and whatever?"

I nodded.

Lou slid a slice of pizza onto a plate and placed it in front of me. "Eat it before it gets cold." She took a slice from the other pie for herself.

"I'm still dead, and I've lost my appetite." I had more to say to Soson. With Lou at the table, the best I could manage was an angry stare.

Soson served himself a slice of pizza from the raised metal stand. "My best friend here refused to tell the judge that he traveled forward in time eight years—"

"Eight years, two months, and nineteen days." Lou took a bite of a slice loaded with veggies.

I wobbled as I stood. "I have to get out of here."

"You cannot run from this." Soson downed the remainder of his whiskey.

"Why, is the pizza that bad?" asked Lou.

I scanned the room for suspicious people. I didn't know what spies looked like. Maybe the guy outside Craig's school. "Am I under surveillance?"

"By who?" asked Lou. "You don't look so good. Do you need a ride?" She stood. "I can ask them to box up some pizza to take with."

Additional exposure to me could move Lou higher on the target list. "No! I'll be fine."

"When will I see you again?" Soson waved his empty glass at the waitress, who evidently hadn't acted quick enough.

"I don't know. Maybe never." I stumbled across the patio and out of the restaurant. My car was still parked where I'd left it. When I got inside and put the key into the ignition, I hesitated. Had someone planted a bomb? No, they wanted me alive. I would become a statistic later, if I couldn't deliver reverse time travel on the Russian's arbitrary schedule. Everything was going to hell.

I didn't remember the drive from Elgin to CJ's gas station, distracted by my failure in court and the assignment to kill Hamza. Somehow, I made it in one piece. I trudged from the Beetle into the office.

CJ looked up from his recliner. "You don't look so good, Ricky."

Randy.

"Shoulda' been here for dinner. Made my Special Chicken."

My stomach lurched. "Maybe next time." I put one foot on the first stair and a hand on the railing, facing a mountain of a staircase.

CJ strained against the arms of his recliner and stood. "Before you go to bed—" He pulled Mickey's porn magazines from a pouch hanging off the arm of his chair. "—I found these in a box in Mickey's closet."

My ears burned. Better if he thought they were mine than his son's. "I'm sorry for bringing them into your home. I'll get rid of them."

"Hell, these ain't yours. They're Mickey's. I didn't have a problem, him using them for relief. Damn, all young men do it." He threw them onto his recliner. "I might just keep 'em, now that you pulled them out."

I breathed a sigh. "Sure. Whatever."

He leaned over and pulled something else from the pouch. "I found this in their place." CJ squeezed the padded envelope. "Wasn't this attached to the brick? Wondered why you were hiding it."

I gasped. A cold chill ran up my back. As if coaxing a child holding a grenade, I extended my hands, palms up. "Please, give that to me." I would never forgive myself if a toxin meant for Hamza killed CJ.

He reached into the envelope.

I froze, scared to take a step closer. "No!"

He tilted his head. "Just curious is all." He removed the silver tube. "Can't read the dang label. Is this some kind of fancy lubricant?"

234

The kid with a grenade was about to pull the pin. "Don't!"

He startled at the volume of my reply.

I forced myself to look calm and softened my voice. "I mean, you don't want to be messing with that stuff. Please, give it to me."

"All righty." He slid the tube into the padded envelope and tossed it towards me using an underhand throw.

I caught the envelope with pillow hands and exhaled. "Thank you. It's personal. Understand?"

"No sweat off my brow. If Mickey can have girlie magazines, you can have whatever that stuff is. G'night." He rolled up the porn, walked past me and headed upstairs.

I staggered into his recliner and closed my eyes, clutching the envelope to my chest. I smelled peanuts as I caught my breath and waited for my heart rate to return to normal. How could I dispose of this biochemical hazard without anyone getting sick or dying? People on bomb squads or FBI agents probably had methods, but no way was I going to get any authorities involved. If the oligarch found out, he might advance the timeline and kill all of my family and friends as a lesson. I would never be able to live with myself. The chill from my body radiated into the soft recliner padding. After all that carnage, he'd still demand I invent reverse time travel.

I must have fallen asleep in CJ's chair because I woke at one-thirty in the morning with the package still clutched to my chest. I went upstairs, put the envelope on Mickey's dresser and fell into bed without changing. I prayed emotional fatigue would help me fall back asleep.

Day 5

[16] Tuesday, April 16, 2019

The next morning, I awoke wearing yesterday's sweaty shirt and wrinkled slacks. A glance at the package on Mickey's dresser brought all of my anxiety rushing back. I was no murderer, even if the victim was supposed to be Hamza. I needed to get my priorities straight. While my status as dead or alive remained in limbo, I could still reconnect with Faith and become a father to Craig.

Satisfying some anonymous Russian by inventing reverse time travel was impossible without seeing the raw results of the forward time travel incident. Doing nothing wasn't an option.

In the shower, the possibility occurred to me that my thrust forward in time might be only temporary. At some random moment, I could be sucked back to 2011. Would that be a blessing or just make things worse? When would I arrive? At the moment I vanished, only to be thrown forward again in an endless cycle? At least in the movie *Groundhog Day*, Bill Murray discovered a way to end the repetition.

Instead of waiting for an involuntary return that might never happen, it would be better to find my own way back. I could invent reverse time travel and plan a deliberate jump to 2011. Maybe that would be the best outcome for everyone, despite the consequences of a paradox. I'd just have to keep any plans away from Soson and his Russian contacts. I chastised myself for pure speculation. The challenge and issues demanded more thought.

Before I went downstairs for breakfast, I needed to find a safe place for the envelope. Under the floor again? Too obvious. In my Beetle? What if someone broke in and stole it? I decided to leave it in the top drawer of Mickey's dresser. I prayed that CJ hadn't forgotten last night's warning.

In his makeshift kitchen, CJ stood over a square frying pan that substituted for a griddle. "Mornin'. All gussied up again? Guess you won't be manning the pumps."

"Not this morning." I had dressed in a fresh outfit, a polo shirt, and plain slacks, for the library.

CJ lifted a one-inch-tall pancake onto a plate and put it on the table in front of me. "Everybody should have a good breakfast. Most important meal of the day."

I sat down and cut through. Although dark brown on the outside, the middle oozed raw batter. I pushed back from the table. "I think I'll skip it. I'm watching my carbs. See you later."

I stood at the doorway, ready to leave, except I felt naked. When I worked at ChiLabs, I always carried a soft-sided briefcase to work, mostly to transport notes to examine after dinner while Faith watched television. Didn't I need to bring something to write on, in case inspiration struck? If Faith saw me, she'd laugh, her husband the incessant scribbler. Except we weren't married anymore.

I ran upstairs, the treads complaining underfoot, and pulled out the box of GoTane items from Mickey's closet. The Owner/Operators Manual pages were printed on one side only. I flipped them over, blank side up. Voila, someplace to take notes.

I jogged down the stairs and found CJ in the recliner, munching on peanuts in the shell, the debris all over him and the chair. I swiped a GoTane-branded pen from CJ's customer service counter. "Is it okay if I use this binder?" I held it up.

"That thing still around? Hell, I would have pitched it if I knew it was here. They made me give back their stuff when they pulled the franchise. Everything with a GoTane logo that wasn't nailed down. Even pulled their damn sign. Go ahead, it's all yours."

I topped off the Beetle's tank. CJ's comment drew my attention to the signpost on the corner of the lot, an empty rectangular metal frame through which an unskilled quarterback could practice his throwing.

I stopped at a Starbucks along my route to the Schaumburg Library and bought an apple, a Grande coffee, and a slice of banana nut bread. As I drove, I replayed in my mind my conversation with Craig. I wanted to remember every word. His expressions. The tone of his voice. At least I had a couple of pictures from the playground to reinforce the memory. I finished eating in the library parking lot.

On the first floor, I located the public computing area, two long tables next to the adult collection, three machines per table. After showing my library card, which was woefully expired, a clerk at the checkout desk updated their system to restore my access. When asked if I was at the same address, I lied, said yes, and handed her my driver's license for verification.

I sat at one of the available computers and navigated to the MyPlace website. A redesigned home page with graphics showing people at work and play requested my user ID and password, a sequence of terms from a simple but obscure physics formula. My personal page displayed the wedding photo I uploaded over a decade ago and a count of over fifty thousand unread messages.

I slumped back in the chair. I'd never have the time or energy to read them all. How would I ever find the important ones? I decided on a divide and conquer strategy. I created separate folders at MyPlace for emails from Faith and Soson. Hamza would have restricted his communications to my work email. For the moment, I could ignore the remainder in the in-box, mostly advertisements and special offers long expired.

My request to sort the emails by sender spun the multicolored beach ball cursor. While that processed, I opened a second browser window and did a web search for recent articles about tachyons, just in case some scientist somewhere

240

on the planet had gotten close to what I had accidentally experienced due to Hamza's meddling. Only one physicist from CalTech used plasma as a accelerator but his particles hadn't reached the speed of light. He didn't report any tachyons in his results.

The web browser icon blinked, alerting me that the sort had completed. I clicked back to the MyPlace page and moved Faith and Soson's emails into their respective folders, sorted by oldest first. Then I opened Faith's folder.

The visible part of the scrollable list showed that she'd sent me one email every day, starting the day I vanished. Her first message, sent from the hospital that afternoon from her phone, told me that Craig had been born and was healthy. She expressed confusion about where I was and why I hadn't come back, hoping that nothing had happened to me, and that she'd notified the police. As I scanned the ones later that week, the messages pleaded for me to reply, and asked what she had done wrong to drive me away. I felt the desperation grow in her subsequent messages.

As I scrolled down, her messages slowed to a few times a week. Like entries in a journal, her emails provided a running status report, including Craig's infant behaviors and her activities to find me. Pestering law enforcement to keep my missing person case open. Hiring domestic private detectives to track me down.

Reading about her emotional journey weighed heavily on me. If there was only something I could have done to prevent that pain. Her experiences were in the past, and I could do nothing to change that fact. Unless I followed through with what the Russians demanded and invented reverse time travel but used it for my own purposes. Who knew what kind of problems that would cause?

I skipped ahead a few months. Messages dwindled to once a week, most of the content repetitive. At about the six-month mark, Faith mentioned an argument with Hamza, who advised her not to hire detectives in England, Germany, and Japan. I found myself mentally cheering Hamza on, preventing Faith from wasting money she couldn't afford.

Hamza! The task of killing him was still on my schedule. I couldn't forget that errand since Craig's life depended on it.

Faith's messages slowed to once a month starting on Craig's third birthday, the anniversary of my disappearance. The January message included a photo of our son. God, he had grown up so fast. I checked my phone for the time. I'd been sitting there for over an hour, and I still hadn't looked at any of Soson's messages.

I skipped to Craig's fifth birthday. Faith mentioned that, a few weeks earlier, she'd invited a few close friends including Patrice over for a séance, a futile attempt to get in touch with me from the beyond. The medium claimed she felt my spirit but told Faith I would not speak or show myself. That I didn't feel welcome and was intentionally avoiding her. Pure bullshit. I hoped she hadn't believed it.

The next month, Faith explained that Hamza had effectively taken over her finances when the bank threatened to take possession of the house. Her first argument with him was when she refused to file for a death certificate even though the lawyer he chose told her it would be easily granted. Good thing too, or the Nobel Prize would not have been issued. At least she stuck up for her beliefs. She also apologized for selling the Audi.

The most difficult email to read was the last one in the list, written just after the death certificate had been rendered after seven years. *"Dearest Randy, I've come to terms with the fact that you're not coming back. Hope does not spring eternal. I have to go on with my life, such as it is, without you. Hamza's been saying that for years. My therapist agrees that I've been irrationally optimistic. I will do my best with Craig so he would make you proud. Please don't blame me. I have to let go of you, despite the pain. Goodbye, my love, wherever you are."*

Tears clouded my vision. I hung my head. Faith had the courage to let go, and my arrival rekindled her torment. How naive and selfish I was, to expect a warm welcome.

I shivered and took a cleansing breath. I was curious about the messages Soson had sent, so I switched to his folder. There were a bunch of them the first week, multiple short ones, asking me where I was and to get in touch, a final one a week after I leapt, saying he hoped to see me eventually, and then no more. Based on his language, I was certain he knew I would return. How could he be so sure?

I searched the in-box, already sorted by sender, for familiar names. Patrice's were nestled between RoadWeek reports and notifications for ZippyRebate coupons.

Her first email cursed me out for not getting back in time for Craig's birth, promising to dress me down in person the next time she saw me. The next one, about a week later, pleaded with me to get in touch because of Faith's deteriorating emotional condition. She promised not to holler at me. A month later, the tone was conciliatory with no demands, just her commentary on Faith's deepening depression. On Craig's first birthday, she sent one telling me that she helped Faith decorate and bake for the event, followed by a renewed accusation that I had abandoned Faith at the precise moment she needed me. Thank goodness time had diluted her hostility. When she saw me on Saturday, she didn't pull a knife on me.

I signed out of MyPlace, drained. I didn't have the emotional strength or courage to kill Hamza. Not today. It would have to wait until tomorrow, at the earliest. At that moment, I needed a friendly face and willing ears. Soson was my only choice. Except he wasn't.

I dialed Lou. "Hey, it's Randy. How are you doing?"

"Fine."

I noticed the hesitation in her voice. A cautious expectation. "Are you free for dinner?"

"Oh, sure. Do you want me to pick you up?"

"No, let me make it easy. Pick a place near where you live."

She thought for a moment. "There's Tupelo's Rock and Roll Deli in Carol Stream. If you like Elvis decor."

"Sounds like fun." Maybe it'll distract me. "I'll find it."

"Great. See you there about five-thirty."

One of the librarians threw me a grimace for making a call in her hushed environment. I moved away from the public computing area to a table in the adult collection.

Alone, I opened my binder to the first blank page and tried to jot down formulas from memory that I'd used in my experiment. After each, I looked around at patrons walking past, sitting, and reading. Even the library held distractions if I allowed them.

I went back to my scribbles. Upon closer examination, every equation seemed to be incorrect, either missing a term or an exponent swapped with a coefficient. My mind wasn't engaging. No surprise, given the circumstances.

I repositioned the binder on my lap and pretended to be surrounded by an opaque bubble in an attempt to concentrate. I corrected every formula as best I could under the circumstances and simplified them, the next step. At every turn, the resulting transformations led to dead ends. Dividing by zero, which by convention yields infinity. Equations that required impossible conditions like faster-than-light speeds or massive gravities that would produce black holes. My thoughts about time travel in general were confounded by physical logistics: the rotation of the Earth in a moving orbit around the sun, and the movement of our solar system within our galaxy, ad infinitum.

Variables and constants swirled in my head. Some accidental or intentional set of conditions leapt me forward in the same location but to the year 2019. Where in time and space is that 2011 location now? After all, the planet keeps moving. If I *could* leap back, where might I end up? The calculations would need to be precise or I could end up in the middle of the Atlantic Ocean or in an orbit around Earth. And if I wanted to prevent Hamza from ruining my experiment in 2011, I would have to get to work early enough to stop him. Precisely the moment when Faith needed me. Would space/time even allow me to modify the past?

I reexamined my notes. If I was going to recreate my work from scratch, I had to concentrate. Not as easily done in the quiet of a public library as I'd thought.

Would my process have been better if I'd worked with a knowledgeable partner, as opposed to Soson whose contributions were nods at random intervals? I'd chosen to be a loner with my tumor proton radiation project so that outsiders would assign all of the blame or all of the glory to me, however it turned out. My first project at ChiLabs, where I was the most substantial contributor but saw my name left off of the published paper, had determined my future behavior.

Recreating my work was the path to success, I knew it in my heart and soul. And the experiment would have worked if Hamza hadn't interfered. From Soson's comments and first-hand observations, Faith's life was also on Hamza's agenda.

Thoughts of Hamza and Faith contributed to the distractions. I turned to a fresh page and drew diagrams instead of formulas. My next alternatives were a Ouija board and a crystal ball.

Complaints from my stomach told me it was time to leave. Besides, I wasn't getting anywhere. I trudged out to my Beetle, drove to the same Starbucks, and skipped a full lunch. Instead, I dawdled over coffee and an almond croissant, reading through the formula attempts in my binder, but instinctively distracted by images of Craig and the sound of his voice. Would I ever see him again?

I headed south on Bloomingdale Road and made it to my destination way too early for my dinner date. The restaurant's lot was filled with cars, which forced me to circumnavigate. I passed the front neon fascia twice before finding a parking space.

I sat in the Beetle and closed my eyes. I must have dozed off because the next sound I heard was a fist pounding on the driver's window. "Hey Randy! Wake up!"

Lou stood outside my door. I rubbed my eyes and got out. Instead of leaving the binder on the passenger seat, I brought it along. My formulas and inventing reverse time travel would be topics for discussion.

Lou led the way to the entrance, a hemp tote tucked under one arm and her shoulder bag slung over the other.

A two-story jukebox headstock towered alongside the entrance. Inside, Tupelo's was one of those order, pay and pick-up places. I palmed the wallet in my pocket as I scanned the overhead menu.

Lou nudged me. "Order whatever you want. My treat."

"I can pay." Before she offered, I considered buying *her* meal. The food was reasonably priced.

"Oh no! Soson would be very angry. He made it clear that you're our special guest."

The special guest who's supposed to invent reverse time travel for his Russian friends. As an intellectual exercise only, poking around with the concept kept my mind active and distracted from my wife's pain and my son's isolation. I said to a clerk with his finger poised above a tablet, "I'll have a New York style corned beef on rye with yellow mustard, lettuce and tomato, and an order of homemade chips."

"And he'll have one of your cherry phosphates," Lou turned to me. "They're to die for."

At the mention of death, I imagined my gloved hand smearing toxic gel on Hamza. The distractions of two Blues Brothers on a sofa and an Elvis statue in mid-hip swivel clouded over. I gripped my stomach to ease the sudden ache.

Lou placed her order for a Tupe single burger, Parmesan fries and a chocolate phosphate, paid for both of our meals, and led us to a table in the corner. She must have learned that behavior from Soson. Without him present, Lou and I could have a serious and private conversation about the predicament he'd gotten me into. One that threatened the lives of not only my family, but her as well.

"I brought something to show you." She pulled a copy of *Physics Today* from her bag. "There's a scientist at CalTech who used plasma to accelerate protons."

I took the magazine, dated June 2010, checked the table of contents, and thumbed to the correct page. "I found a reference to this on the Internet. Did you read the last paragraph? He didn't get the protons to light speed."

"But he got close."

I tossed the magazine on the table. "Now, if we only had his equations and not just some puff piece."

"You mean like this?" She took a hardboard-covered document from her hemp bag. The cover read, *Potential for Acceleration of Electrons in A Plasma Wakefield*, by Dr. Norbert Holtgrass, PhD, CalTech. "I called his office and they overnighted a copy of a journal article he's submitted for publication."

My heart pounded. "If I can't recreate my own work with Hamza's changes, starting with Holtgrass' attempt gives me a healthy start."

A voice over the PA system blared, "Order number 88 is ready to rock and roll. Order number 88."

Lou waved her receipt. "That's us. You dig into Dr. Holtgrass' work and I'll fetch our food."

I skipped the abstract and went straight for the formulas. His approach for creating and manipulating heavy ions was different than mine. I was ready to reject his work as useless when I reached a simplification of his primary formula that didn't make sense. Is it possible to make that kind of substitution? Our two approaches were like parallel railroad tracks headed for the same destination.

Someone pulled a chair alongside. Lou must've decided to sit next to me, except the body in the chair was larger and didn't smell the same.

"Funny meeting you here." Soson gazed around the restaurant. "I do not see a bar."

So much for private. "What are you doing here?" I put a napkin in the document to mark my place.

"Louise called and told me where she would meet you. I presume she wanted a chaperone."

"She has nothing to fear from me. Unlike you, I'm not shopping for female companionship." *Constantly.*

"What else have you been doing besides filling people's gas tanks?"

Soson's comments had slid from teasing to abrasive. "Can you please stop? I went to see Craig." He didn't need to know the embarrassing details.

"Schools have security. Were you allowed to be there?"

"No. I watched him on the playground from the sidewalk."

"Kovarnyy d'yavol. Crafty devil. Soon, you will assist Craig with his schoolwork. That is what fathers do, no?"

Soson was a mind reader or he knew me too well. "Elizabeth got upset when Craig started up a conversation."

"Oh, so it's Elizabeth, not Ms. Somebody? Is that another reason to go to school?"

"Absolutely not. Eventually, I'll get to know Craig. He's my son. What's the harm? Faith won't find out."

"Unless Craig goes home and talks about you. What did you call yourself?"

"I didn't give him my name. Only that I was a particle physicist."

"Much too obvious. Does this Elizabeth know that you do not have Faith's permission?"

"I told her Faith and I were separated at the moment."

A tray filled with drinks and baskets of food plopped down on the table. "What are you doing here?" Lou seemed surprised.

Soson merely grunted.

"I stopped to pump some ketchup." Lou slid into her seat across from me. "I can't eat fries without it."

"Randall was just telling me how he spoke to his son through a fence at school."

That special pink tone returned to Lou's face. "You did? That's terrific."

"What are they studying, *tovarish*?" Soson swiped a fry from Lou's tray. "Einstein's theory?"

"The standard third-grade curriculum, I guess. It didn't come up."

"*Bozhe moy*. How will you stand it?" Soson turned to Lou. "By the way, how much do I owe you? Never mind." He pulled a fifty-dollar bill from his pocket and put it on the table in front of her. "This should cover and give you some spending money." He stood and walked toward the

252

order counter, his eyes on the overhead menu display.

Lou's scowl indicated Soson had embarrassed her. "I didn't tell him where we were eating so he could join us and pay. I swear!"

"I believe you."

While I attacked my sandwich, munched chips, and drank what turned out to be a cherry-flavored carbonated beverage, Soson returned, towering over the table. "Louise found research similar to yours." He tapped on Dr. Holtgrass' documentation. "What progress have you made?"

"With inventing reverse time travel or plotting Hamza's murder?" When we were at Pavers, Soson talked about the assignment openly.

"What?" Lou shot up in her chair and dropped her sandwich. "What's this about murder?"

"Shhhh." Soson scanned the room. Then he bent and leaned close to Lou's ear.

She sat stone silent, her eyes wide. Her pale face told me he hadn't held back the details of the Russian blackmail scheme and our collective jeopardy.

When he was done, Lou said, "That's crazy."

"I can't kill anyone. Even Hamza." I pushed my plate away.

"Damned right!" Lou's voice was loud enough for others to hear. "We're scientists."

"You would be doing the world a service." Soson eyed our meals. "I cannot decide. What is good here?"

Lou retained her wide-eyed expression while she pointed at my plate. Her voice quivered. "The corned beef sandwich. Or their burgers."

"Not like I used to get in Serpukhov. I will find something." Soson went back to the counter to place his order.

Lou leaned closer. "You're not considering it, are you? I mean, with Craig in jeopardy—"

"I don't want Craig to die, but I can't take someone's life in cold blood. This whole thing is Soson's fault, yet he acts so unaffected."

"And he's on the list too!"

That was new information. I doubted that Soson's Russian colleague would harm him.

Soson returned to our table. "For eight years, Hamza has been influencing your son's development. That upsets you, no? What kind of person will Craig grow into if he continues?"

"I spoke with Craig today. He's a fine boy, and I'll be proud of him as a young adult and beyond."

"You are not jealous that Hamza is his primary male role model? I would not want him to impact my offspring, should there be any."

Lou's head moved as if following a ping-pong match. "Why are you talking about this? Of course, Randy won't kill anyone."

I stared at Soson. "You know me well. Have you ever thought that I was capable of murder?"

"*Da.* I heard you say precisely that about Hamza. Something like, 'I could just kill that man.' That was you, no?"

"He's pissed me off more than once. I was just blowing off steam."

"Would you prefer that your first conversation with Craig today be the last one? He will be killed if Hamza does not die by Friday." He pushed my plate closer. "You still have two days. Do not decide now over food. It will give you indigestion."

"Too late." I felt the corned beef, chips, and drink churning, threatening to come up.

A voice rang out, "Number 92 is looking to boogie. Order number 92."

Soson glanced at his receipt. "Ah, my dinner partner awaits." He stood and walked to the counter, shaking his hips as if dancing to a tune in his head.

"Is he being serious?" asked Lou. "Does someone expect you to murder one of ChiLabs' directors?"

"Killing Hamza doesn't make sense. Why wouldn't the oligarch threaten Craig directly? Or kidnap Hamza for his knowledge about forward time travel?"

Soson returned with what looked like a submarine sandwich overflowing with peppers. "You will be pleased to know that Hamza has not moved in with Faith. Although he has mentioned that he is getting tired of driving there every day to check on her."

Hadn't Soson told me he and Hamza were no longer on speaking terms? "I thought he hired caregivers."

"Evidently he has taken a personal interest. And according to him, there are four bedrooms. One for your wife, one for Craig, a guest room, and an office. So, there would be space for him—"

"Bite your tongue."

Soson stuck out his tongue and pretended to clamp down his teeth. "Faith is available. She could consider getting married again."

My pulse throbbed in my temples, a warning sign that I would get a bad headache soon if I didn't change the subject. "When can I get back into my office?"

Soson looked up from his sandwich. "Your closet? Ha! Never. You were there. What else would you need to see?"

"Raw experiment results. Research notes. Experiment designs. Lots of things I didn't collect because *you* said I could come back later." *I could do the intellectual work for reverse time travel and just not implement it, couldn't I?*-I pushed away the remainder of my sandwich and chips. "I'm not very hungry."

"Louise, may I compliment you on your choice?" Soson held his sub close to his mouth, ready to take another bite. "The food here is marvelous."

"Glad you like it." Lou turned to me. "Listen, my apartment isn't far from here. If you want, you can read my analysis and look at more screen captures."

Soson raised his eyebrows. "Ms. Elizabeth has some competition."

Lou looked at me, one eyebrow raised. "Who's she?"

"Craig's teacher is hot to trot with our Nobel Prize winner." Soson winked. "And now *you* invite him over."

"I told you, she's married."

Lou slapped Soson's shoulder. "It's not like that. I told you before, Randy's formulas are complicated. We might make more progress if he explains them to me."

Soson threw up his hands. "Far be it from me to interfere with scientific progress."

I followed Lou's Corolla to Rocky Ridge, her apartment complex, parked and followed her inside. She let us into her third-floor apartment and dropped her things on the dining room table. "Can I get you something to drink?"

My dinner was still processing. "Maybe a glass of cold water?"

She brought a soft-sided briefcase and a sweating glass into the room. "I printed everything at OfficeMart because I was getting eye strain from looking at your work on my computer screen." She removed a pile of papers from the case and pushed them towards me.

I paged through the stack. Lou had printed out the fundamentals of my tumor-busting research. "Why didn't you tell me you had all of this?"

"I didn't know how useful it would be. After all, I did my calibration work without it."

I nearly got up to hug her, but I didn't want to give the wrong impression. Especially after what she'd told Soson. "This is exactly what I needed." I grouped the papers into stacks: the oldest stuff that was subsequently revised collected in a pile on the floor, the material I'd refined just before the experiment sat in front of me.

"Maybe you could explain how you figured all of this out?"

Her request showed interest but naiveté. "Do you have ten years? At times, I didn't think I would ever come up with anything worthwhile." I explained, starting with spinning strings, the underlying material from which elemental particles are composed. "No one else in the world figured out a way to measure the spin of the strings, but I did. All of my work focused on taking advantage of those spinning strings, to accelerate particles to unheard-of speeds." Given that someone else had figured out how to use plasma for particle acceleration, I was no longer certain of my pronouncement.

Her eyes were wide with wonder. How much did she really understand? "In what direction do they spin?"

I hesitated. "I—I don't remember." I was afraid to react, to let her know that her question might be the basis for an approach to creating reverse time travel. Reverse the spins of the strings, reverse the effect on the chrontins? "I'll have to check." With a hint in my hands, I needed to revisit my equations, to see if they were still valid if the strings spun in the opposite direction. I knew that the math was too complex for paper and pencil, or even a computer if Lou owned one. "I need CHUQ."

"The supercomputer?"

"Exactly. One run, to test out the feasibility of a theory."

She took an awkward step back. "You mean you know how to do it?"

I turned away, so that she couldn't see even a hint of optimism on my face. "No, I didn't say that—"

She came up from behind, threw her arms around me and kissed my cheek.

I leapt up. "What was that?"

"I just—I thought—It's always been a professional dream of mine to work with you. And now, after analyzing your experiment results eight years ago, my wish has come true." She brushed a stray hair off my forehead.

I took her by the shoulders and held her at arm's length. "I'm flattered, I really am, but I'm no physics icon. Lord knows, I'm as imperfect as any man, maybe even worse." I walked into her living room and guided her to the couch. "We're not in the middle of a fairy tale. Our friend Soson has put me between the proverbial rock and a hard place. Lives are on the line, no matter what I choose to do. People close to me will die if I don't give the Russians what they want. With reverse time travel in their hands, history could be changed. Many more could certainly die as a result."

Lou's eyebrows drooped. "How do we prevent it?"

"There is no winning strategy. But my mind needs to know if reverse time travel is possible, whether I use the resulting process or not. Do you understand?'

"I think I do." She sat, hands folded. "I share your intellectual curiosity. I'm convinced that I can help, as your partner, if you'll let me."

"I appreciate that. I don't want to make the same mistakes."

"What do you mean?"

"By concentrating so much on work, I failed my wife. I don't want to fail anyone else, and I don't know how to avoid it."

Lou stood and extended her arms. "I'll do whatever you need to test your theory."

I rejected her unspoken offer for a hug. We could be partners without actions that could be interpreted as emotional. "Got anything with caffeine? This is going to take a while."

Day 6

[18] Wednesday, April 17, 2019

I woke the next morning in Mickey's room. Variables and constants, integrals and derivatives danced in my mind. After hours of pencil pushing, I hadn't reconciled my formulas for tumor-killing protons with Holtgrass' efforts. The need to tutor Lou as we went slowed me down. In the end, we were left with a small set of equations that required validation using CHUQ. Lou promised me that, one way or another, she'd find a way to run them and get me the results. From her sly smile, she had something up her sleeve.

The issue of Russian expectations for Hamza's murder remained. Although the deadline approached, I convinced myself that it wouldn't be necessary. That my mind was agile enough to invent a resolution that didn't require me to take his life. So far, that epiphany evaded me.

I showered and got dressed for school. CJ would have to understand how many things on my calendar took precedence over waiting around to pump gas or wash windshields. Assuming any customers showed up.

With a bowl of corn flakes and milk in my stomach, I parked in Craig's school's visitor lot and walked over to the adjacent teacher vehicle area. About ten minutes later, I saw Elizabeth pull in driving a Mini Cooper. I waited until she was out of her vehicle before I called out. "Elizabeth." I waved and walked over.

"Mr. Weinberg. Randy. What are you doing here?"

"I need to know about my son. Since I can't see him for myself, indulge me for a moment."

"I went home and looked you up. You're brilliant, a Nobel Prize winner. And you've been declared dead. You look identical to the newspaper photo from 2011 that reported you missing. Are you sure you're not a fake? Someone *pretending* to be Dr. Weinberg to get access to Craig?"

"It's the real me." Elizabeth needed to understand my situation. "Faith had me declared dead, so I'm dealing with that complication."

"That should be easy enough. I mean, you'd stand in front of a judge, right, who could see you're alive?"

"It wasn't that easy."

"What was his problem?"

"I wouldn't tell him where I've been for the last eight years."

"Give me a break! Why not just tell him and have the death certificate revoked?" She struggled to face me. Her responsibilities pulled her towards the building. "Were you doing something illegal, that you withheld the details?"

This was an opportunity to come clean, to set my phony story aside. Could I share my time travel incident with a stranger? Despite my behavior, her eyes still reflected the awe in which

262

she held me. "Okay, but you should be sitting down for this."

She crossed her arms. "I'll stand."

I took a deep breath and then spoke. "A vortex of chrontin particles transported me here."

"Huh?" She squinted. "What are you talking about?"

I resorted to a term I hated. "Tachyons? Time travel?"

"Wait. What?" She covered her mouth with her fingertips "Oh my goodness!"

"Now you see why I couldn't tell the judge the truth. He would have sent me to a psychiatric institution."

She dropped her arms and faced me. "Chicago Behavioral, most likely."

"Do *you* believe me?" I held my breath.

"Why would I have any reason to doubt a Nobel Prize winner in Physics? That explains the lack of aging. Why haven't I heard about your discovery in my science newsfeed?"

I relaxed, one person I didn't have to lie to. "It's too dangerous to announce to the general public. I've shared the secret with just a couple of colleagues. I face many questions for which I don't have answers."

"All right." She stepped away and pulled her shoulders back. "Yesterday, you went back on your promise. Someone as brilliant as you must understand the phrase 'no conversation.' Were you *trying* to get me fired?"

"I didn't lure him over. He came over on his own and spoke to me."

"I might have expected. Someone standing outside the fence would catch his attention."

Better me than the guy in the red Henley shirt. "What was I supposed to do, pretend I didn't understand English? He asked me a question, and I answered him." I would have kept on chatting for the remainder of the school day or longer. "By the way, I didn't disclose that I'm his father."

"Thank goodness." She checked her watch. "I've got to get inside and prepare for my classes."

"As his father, I need to know. Is he getting good grades? Getting along with others?"

"He's an excellent student, well behaved, and intellectually inquisitive. He asks more questions in class than anyone else. Sometimes, I have to research the answers. He relates better with adults than his peers. Although, he recently volunteered to assist another student with his science fair project."

'That's a good sign."

"Yes, Oliver certainly needs the help. Craig told me, at home, he's responsible for getting dressed, making his own breakfast, completing his homework, and studying, as well as some chores. He carries significant responsibility, but I've never had a conversation with his mother."

"She's closed off communication with me and her friends." Or Hamza has. "It sounds like *she's* not doing very well."

The older woman I'd seen before stood on the front steps of the school.

"Oh, oh!" I froze in place.

She stared at Elizabeth.

"That's the principal. I told her about most of our conversation yesterday. She predicted you'd show up again."

"A smart woman." And another adversary.

"I have to go." Elizabeth turned and jogged through the lot, across the street and up the stairs.

I didn't wait around to witness their interaction, or a security guard dispatched to throw me off school property.

As I ran to my car, I wrestled with the missed opportunity to tell Craig I was his long-absent father. Would I get another chance, given Faith's attitude and how his school wouldn't cooperate? I had no idea how an eight-year-old would react to such news. Would he reject me as a liar, like his mother had? My heart wouldn't survive that outcome. What if he went home and asked Faith about a scientist he spoke with? What would she tell him?

So many complications. Worse than the number of variables in my computational dilemma because they involved feelings and emotions. Impossible to solve with mathematics.

Lou's promise to get us access to CHUQ echoed in my head. Maybe she planned on getting Soson to change his mind so we could verify our reverse time travel approach. After all, *he* desired that outcome.

Otherwise, Hamza would have to die.

[19] Wednesday, April 17, 2019 (continued)

In the parking lot of Craig's school, I sat in the Beetle and called Soson.

"*Malchik*, Louise was very excited this morning but a bit distracted. She told me that you burned the midnight oil reconciling your work with that thief from CalTech who copied you. I had to ask her questions twice. Even then, I did not hear convincing answers. Tell me, have you figured it out?"

I disliked Soson's intrusive attitude, whether directed at me or others. "Holtgrass did his own work. I tried to do mine. And no, I don't have anything to confidently share."

"Do you not think it odd that—"

"Simultaneous invention, that's all. If that *hadn't* happened, I would have been surprised." If it had happened in Russia, I wouldn't be in this mess.

"Did you sleep over?"

"What? Listen, I don't ask about your relationships with women. Don't ask about mine." I backtracked, not wanting Lou's reputation disparaged. "No, I did not sleep over." Her kiss on my cheek was none of his business.

"But you are making progress, no? *Something* happened between the two of you last night."

Soson was crazy if he thought I was going to talk to him about my evening with Lou. Even if something had happened, I would never tell him.

"I have an idea, or maybe just a concept, but it's far from a solution. Even if I had a fully developed approach, which I don't, it would require validation. Are you sure you can't get me even a few hours on CHUQ?" Had Lou already approached him? My request felt redundant.

"Hamza would certainly notice if either Louise or I made a formal request. He warned you to stay away from us, so your intention would be obvious, even to him."

The details of my conversation with Hamza in Faith's lobby were fresh in my memory. He hadn't closed the door to future communication. "Maybe if I see him and ask. I'll appeal to his scientific intellectual curiosity." Assuming he has any. I also had questions only he could answer.

"Yes, by all means." Soson's voice spiked like the high note of an operatic soprano. "Bring the toxin. Ask for a computation window on CHUQ. The worst he can do is refuse. Then put him out of our misery. Without Hamza to reject the request, you will gain access and achieve your validation. Perfect!"

I thought Soson knew me. I'd never consider harming an insect. Yet, Soson thinks nothing of asking me to kill a human being. In all the time I worked with him, I never suspected he had such a ruthless, maniacal nature. "Give me his phone number. You have it, don't you?" I could meet with Hamza without murdering him. As long as he didn't piss me off.

"*Da*, Hamza gave it to me when he began tending to Faith, as a precaution." He read me the number.

I put it in my phone's contact list along with Soson's and Lou's. "Thanks."

"Let me know when it is done. My friends will want to know, so they cancel their plans."

To kill Craig? "Oh yes. Absolutely." *Could I trade one life for another?* I hung up on Soson and called Hamza.

He answered on the fourth ring. "Yes?"

"It's Randy. It's important that I meet with you." I attempted some reverse psychology. "How about I come by Faith's condo?"

"After the way she reacted in the courtroom? No. Absolutely not." I heard his obnoxious tongue click. "My preference is to keep you away from the Labs, but we can meet at my office. Do not come through the front door. Do you know the service entrances along the main accelerator tube?"

"If they haven't moved them." Years ago, I walked alone through the underground corridors to see where the plasma frame would be installed. Except someone changed the location and didn't tell me.

"They are still in the same places. I'll make sure the door labeled L2 is unlocked. Follow the tunnel to the emergency stairwell and walk up. Ninth floor."

Damn, the executive suite. "I'll see you after lunch. One o'clock."

269

"My calendar is clear." He chuckled.

I saw nothing funny about him having time to see me. "Later."

I swung by CJ's before heading south. I needed to bring the toxin if I decided to murder Hamza. Could I really take a human life? I kept telling myself how wrong it was, and then remembered the threat against Craig. A fair trade, my son's life for that of a pain-in-the-ass. Would a jury see it that way if I ended up in court? A case of self-defense one-step removed perhaps? I wasn't sure I had the nerve to go through with it.

CJ was asleep in his chair, peanut shells scattered on his chest. I snuck upstairs, grabbed the padded envelope, and left without waking him. No matter what happened to me, when this was all over, I wanted to make sure he was taken care of. It wouldn't take a lot of effort to sell his station, maybe only for the land, and get him relocated down to a nice senior facility near his sister in Atlanta.

I stopped at a familiar Starbucks in the vicinity of the Labs. Because of the balmy 70-degree weather, I ordered a tall, iced-coffee and a sesame bagel. One of the baristas seemed to recognize me but wrote "Rudy" on my cup. While I drank, munched, and people-watched from an outside table, I mentally gathered my questions for Hamza and prepared as best I could to take his life.

270

Would the toxin kill him right away? I don't think I could watch him die in agony. Soson instructed me to walk away after the deed was done. Would some Russian agents arrive and clean up the crime scene? Another slurp of iced coffee went down bitter.

Weren't there cameras all over? Someone was sure to figure out I was the last one to see Hamza alive. For a task that Soson said would be simple, it had become as complicated as inventing reverse time travel, and that was only theoretically possible.

At ChiLabs, I parked the Beetle in a lot close to the underground accelerator tube, took the padded envelope and walked along the grass looking for service entrance L2. My body cast a shadow on the rusted metal cover. As promised, it was unlocked. I climbed down the access ladder into the dimly lit passage. Without a flashlight, I made my way slowly through the tunnel. I hid my face behind my hand whenever I passed any employees. Unnecessary since all of them were focused on their own work.

At the end of the walkway, the entrance to the staircase was marked with a glowing red EXIT sign. That door was also unlocked. I made my way up the stairs, pausing at every landing to regain my breath, hoping not to run into any employee seeking privacy in the stairwell.

All the way up, a question kept going through my mind: Why did the oligarch want

Hamza dead? How was he a threat? I had a long history of reasons to dislike the man, but I couldn't recall him ever mentioning foreign involvements with the exception of his native country of Pakistan. Maybe something would come up in our conversation to provide answers.

I peeked out at floor nine. My heart beat double-time. There didn't seem to be much activity, or it was confined to the rooms that lined the corridor. Through Hamza's open door, I watched him scurry around an office strewn with open cardboard boxes. His desk was a battlefield of mementos, magazines, and haphazardly stacked paper.

I knocked on the doorframe. Before he looked up, my feet didn't respond when I willed them to run away.

"Randall!" Hamza waved his arm. "Come in. Shut the door." He removed a box from one of his two visitor chairs, emptied his leather swivel and sat down. "First, I want to apologize for the drama in the courtroom. Faith's lawyer thought she needed to know you were going to have the judge revoke the death certificate."

Small consolation that Hamza hadn't told her. "Did you convince her it was me she saw in the condo lobby?"

"I thought so. After her lawyer's call, however, she threw a fit and insisted on going to court. I didn't understand her motivation, since she said she no longer wanted anything to do with you. I did my best to talk her out of it, but you know Faith."

Damn right I did, better than Hamza. "She didn't make things easier for me with the judge, that's for sure."

"Speaking of making things easier." He removed an envelope from his center drawer and tossed it over his cluttered desk. "Here's another thousand, with my thanks. And it won't be the last if you continue to do as I ask." He clicked his stupid tongue.

I took the envelope and put it in my pocket. "Yeah, about that. You said Faith and Craig were in jeopardy because of me, and you were right. Soson told me that Russian agents will kill my family one at a time if I don't invent reverse time travel."

"I told you to avoid that man. He is dangerous, nothing but trouble."

"They have a list. Craig first, and then Faith. After that, if I don't deliver promptly, Louise Martin, who works here, would be next."

"Louise in analytics? I know her. She's done work for me before." Hamza remained stoic despite the list of likely casualties. He stroked a red leather box on his desk.

"Followed by Soson. And then you." Truth was, Hamza was first, by my hand. He deserved to feel jeopardy. "They'll target anyone within my circle of family, friends and acquaintances."

Hamza didn't flinch. "Let them try. I now have the means to protect Faith, Craig and myself." He waved an arm and smiled. "Haven't you noticed I am packing? I resigned effective tomorrow because I won the PowerBall lottery, thanks to you."

"I didn't have anything to do with that." I muttered, "Congratulations."

"Don't you see? One hundred nineteen million dollars can purchase absolute anonymity. Faith, Craig and I will disappear." He paused, but his grin didn't fade. "I'm sorry to hear that Soson and Louise may come to harm, but that is not my problem."

Winning that much in the lottery meant Hamza didn't need to steal from Faith. Why would he take care of my family all those years if money wasn't the reason?" Was there some sincere emotion on his part? That no longer mattered. Could he really hide my family where the Russians wouldn't find them?

Someone knocked. "Excuse me." Hamza went to the door and opened it a crack. "I do not want to be disturbed."

A middle-aged man I'd never seen before stood outside the office. "There's something that requires your attention, Mr. Bashir."

He looked over his shoulder. "I am not off the payroll just yet. I will be right back."

As soon as he left, I pulled out the latex glove. My hands shook so bad, I could barely get my fingers in. I unscrewed the cap from the tube of gel and applied some to my protected fingertips. The package slid to the floor at my feet. A friendly handshake or touch of his arm would deliver the fatal toxin and get Craig a reprieve. I'd have to move quickly and take advantage of the element of surprise.

Hamza came in, slammed his door, went around to his side of the desk, and tossed the red leather box in front of me. "No more pleasant chatter." My name, embossed in gold with fleurs-de-lis in the corners, decorated the top. Something had put a significant gouge in the side that split the leather. "Do you know what this is?"

I had an educated guess but said, "No. I've never seen it before in my life." I let my hands dangle between my legs, out of sight below the desktop.

He remained standing on the opposite side. "Open it."

I fumbled with my left hand to lift the lid. Inside was my shiny gold Nobel Prize medal. I stared at the image of Alfred Nobel in left profile with the dates of his birth and death. "Where did you get this?"

"Faith asked me to place it on your desk in your office so you could see it when you returned. At that time, she still clung to the hope you would come back to her. But that's not where landscapers found it a week ago. It was on the mound just outside the main entrance."

"Well, I didn't put it there. I wasn't even in 2019 until last Friday." My mind raced. I knew that Soson and Lou had been using my office during my absence. "Maybe someone broke into my office and put it outside?"

"For what reason? So that groundskeepers would run over it with a lawnmower? No, there is more to this—" Hamza's expression soured. "The mound over the secondary target." His tongue clicked like a snare drum. "You son-of-a-bitch! *You* sent it backward in time!"

"Me? I couldn't have. I don't know how to do that." Soson had expected the box to be sitting on the desk in my office during my recent visit, but it was missing. My medal found outside and the 2019 issue of the *Daily Herald* in my bathroom in 2011 proved that someone had or would invent reverse time travel. Would that someone be *me*? I hoped I wouldn't be too late to prevent all of the threatened deaths.

"It must have been you. Who else do you know who has traveled in time?" Hamza paced, shaking his head. "How could you? You'll ruin everything!"

What would I ruin? I prepared for quick contact before Hamza threw me out of his office.

"I'm begging you, please don't continue doing Soson's bidding." Hamza plopped into his chair, his palms on the desk. "I don't expect anything from you as compensation for supporting Faith all these years. In my mind, perhaps I thought she would become fond of me."

The idea of Faith and Hamza as a couple made me sick. "Did she?" Was I ready for the answer? His bare hands were out of reach.

"I learned the hard way that no one will ever replace you in her heart." Another tongue click. "I tried my best, but it wasn't enough. And now she will die, after rejecting both of us."

"Die? Faith is going to die?" My gloved hand hung limp. "What are you talking about? How do you know that?" Had someone sent him another future newspaper with Faith's obituary?

"Being murdered might be a blessing." As he looked up, a tear escaped his eye. "Faith has pancreatic cancer. It was diagnosed during her annual check-up last year. Much of your prize money has been spent on doctors and hospitals. The best treatments she could afford. Chemotherapy temporarily slowed the progress of the disease but didn't eradicate it. Despite her doctors' best efforts, she has only a couple of years left to live, at best."

I forgot how to breathe. Faith had cancer? As I raised my hands, I realized I still wore the glove smeared with toxin. I let them drop. Hamza was an asshole, but he'd spent seven years as a companion and the last one as a caregiver. That came from a selfless place I didn't think he possessed.

I slumped in the chair, bent down to reach the padded envelope, and put my gloved hand inside. With a grip of the glove from the outside, I slid my bare hand out. "Soson didn't tell me she was ill."

"You continued to speak with him after I explicitly ..." He waved off the rest of his

277

comment. "Soson does not know of Faith's disease. I kept that from him. From everyone. However, Craig is smart enough to have figured out his mother is seriously ill." The pitch of his voice had dropped.

Craig's comments about doctors fell into place. Faith's weight loss and lack of strength made perfect sense. The cancer consumed her body from the inside.

"I will honor my offer to keep them safe. With my lottery winnings, I can afford to take Faith and Craig away where no one will ever find them."

Including me. If I don't know, I can't be forced to tell. A wave of relief passed through me. "If you can do that, it'll be a miracle." For some unknown reason, the Russians demanded Hamza be murdered by Friday. He didn't have much time to skip town with my family. "Okay. Please take them somewhere the Russians won't find them." Maybe someday, when the Russians had given up looking, I could find Craig. Or die trying. "When can you leave?"

"As soon as I can secure a location and formulate a travel plan that leaves no discernible trail. I sold my condo and was going to move into Faith's guest room, but this threat changes everything. And don't worry about Craig. After Faith passes away, I'll treat him like my own son."

"That won't be good enough." At that instant, I wished I hadn't taken off the latex glove so I could have slapped his face. With Hamza's plan, I would be separated from my son, and Craig would be burdened with Hamza for his entire life.

Before I could say anything else, Hamza stood and rummaged through several boxes. "Don't you have one more question?"

"Yes, as a matter of fact, I do." One that had bothered me since I arrived in 2019.

He stood tall, his chin out. "Ask it."

Images of Hamza in my office just before the experiment flashed into my mind. "Why did you mess around with the controller settings in my office before the experiment?"

"Mess?" Hamza laughed out loud. "You think I have no skills at all?" He pulled a familiar copy of *Physics Today* from the box in front of him, the same issue Lou had given me. "Have you seen the article about the CalTech professor who tried plasma boosting?"

"Dr. Holtgrass' work? Yes. Why does that matter?"

He waved the publication as if it was a red cape and I was a bull. "After reading it, I identified what was necessary to give your particle stream a last moment kick. Laser pulses timed to infiltrate just prior to impact. I also boosted the plasma temperature, just a little."

Maybe Hamza was more knowledgeable about physics than I thought, or he used Dr. Holtgrass' approach and got lucky.

He folded his arms. "I was on my way to leap forward from the mound above the secondary target when you got in my way. Fortunately, you gave me what I wanted, and I didn't have to leave 2011."

Was Hamza in the car I beat out for the parking space? "If you went to the future, how were you going to get back?"

"Ask your buddy Soson, but only after we've departed." Tongue click. "This was all his idea."

"Oh, I sure will." Soson had played me for a sucker, and I wasn't going to let him get away with it. I held up the red leather box. "I suppose you want your *own* Nobel Prize?"

"No need. They pay a paltry one million. With one hundred nineteen, I don't care if anyone learns I invented the process for forward time travel."

Hamza's comment confirmed that he wasn't a scientist, just an opportunist out for a big payday. Due to his discovery of the 2019 newspaper in my bathroom, he believed I assisted.

"You won't complete your work on reverse time travel because you know Soson will distribute it to the people who now threaten you." He clicked his tongue. "Even if you are successful, they will kill you anyway."

Taking control of my situation and avoiding fatal outcomes felt like an impossible task.

Hamza drummed his fingertips on his desk. "Before you ask, I will not share my research or CHUQ results with you."

Without complete documentation, I only had an anecdotal account and his controller settings. Those weren't a viable starting point.

Lou's attempt to get time on CHUQ was critical. "I guess this is goodbye." I stood, the padded envelope dangling from one hand, the weighty Nobel medal box in the other.

"You brought *me* something? A going-away gift perhaps?"

I clutched the envelope to my chest. "This? No, just something I have to take care of."

I dragged myself out of his office and down nine flights of stairs.

The Russians' desire to kill Hamza made even less sense now. Hamza was a valuable asset, someone who had transformed my heavy ion experiment into one that generated chrontins and successful forward time travel. They could use that knowledge to their advantage. Perhaps even to create the process they desired.

My local Russian, Soson, had already proven himself to be a liar. Could he also be the ringleader? What if the demand from some anonymous oligarch to murder Hamza was another lie? Had Soson's relationship with Hamza gone so sour that he felt the need to eliminate his former friend? I couldn't depend on Soson answering honestly, no matter what questions I asked.

In the hallway alongside the accelerator, I paused at the bin for hazardous material incineration. Is Soson behind the threat to kill Craig? *Maybe Soson deserves the toxin.* I took a deep breath and dumped the padded envelope into the bin. *So much for being a murderer.*

I needed to get Faith and Craig out of harm's way soon, but I wasn't convinced that depending on Hamza was the best choice. Unfortunately, without resources, I couldn't think of an alternative.

In my Beetle, I filled my bulging wallet with the fifty-dollar bills from Hamza's envelope and squeezed it into my back pocket. I sat at an angle, my wallet like a rock under one buttock. This wouldn't work while I drove, so I pulled out all of Hamza's cash, folded it and shoved it into a front pocket instead.

If somebody like Hamza could figure out how to turn my experiment into a forward time machine launcher, I could invent backward time travel. Maybe I didn't even need his modifications, although I wouldn't let my ego exclude valuable technology because of the source. When I invented a successful technique, I couldn't leave behind the results of my work. All of it would have to be destroyed. I needed to talk this out with a colleague, and I chose Lou.

The Mandarin Bistro in Bloomingdale, my choice for our ritual evening meal, sat in a strip mall between a beauty supply storefront and a dental office. Just inside the entrance, Soson popped complimentary mints, a couple at a time.

I anticipated a negative reaction to my failure, but I couldn't assess the real consequences. If Soson could lie about other things, why not the threat to Craig? He pulled a menu from a bin near the cash register and read it.

I took a deep breath before approaching him. "See, this is nice."

He looked up. "If you prefer paper lanterns hanging from the ceiling, reproductions of dragons on the wall, and plastic flowers in vases."

He had lobbied for a Chinese restaurant in the city because, according to him, the food was marvelous. I didn't want to fight rush hour traffic on the Kennedy Expressway. Congestion had been bad eight years ago and must certainly be worse now.

If Soson expected me to pay, I could easily afford this place. I still had about three thousand dollars from Hamza but was worried about future expenses. Who knows what could jump up and bite me in the wallet? I hoped he didn't notice the bulge of bills in my pocket.

As expected, Soson asked for the last booth along the wall, adjacent to the bathrooms and kitchen. He insisted on ordering egg rolls and steamed pot stickers while I searched the menu for main courses. Despite our location at the rear, spring breezes from the front door floated our napkins on the table every time a customer came in to get their phone order.

Why hadn't Soson advised his Russian oligarch to ignore my family and me? He knew about Hamza's meddling and could have easily given them the name of the individual who'd developed forward time travel. Instead, Soson or his associate directed me to murder Hamza. None of this made sense. A slap with toxic gel would have killed a source of valuable information. Russians should have kidnapped Hamza and forced the secrets of time travel from him without hurting Faith and Craig.

"Should I put the funeral for Hamza on my calendar?" Soson sported half a grin.

"I didn't use the toxin. Hamza's willingness to care for my family changed my mind about murdering him."

Soson drummed his thick fingers on the table. "You had a task to perform."

"Hamza admitted to making changes to the controllers to create chrontins and forward time travel." I paused to let Soson absorb the news. He sat stone-faced. "Do you know what this means? You can let your Russian contact know that he needs to target Hamza for his time travel expertise. Not me."

"Surely you jest." He made a production of opening a paper napkin, flapping it, and placing it on his lap. "All well and good, assuming Hamza is smart enough to parlay his knowledge into a technique for reverse time travel, which we know he is not."

Soson was speculating. Didn't he believe Hamza's claim? Then how else did I get to 2019? "If Hamza made random changes, there's not much likelihood I would have been thrown forward in time.."

Soson leaned closer, his arms on the table. "Even if he knew enough to accomplish the feat, which I doubt, he has no viable credentials. No published papers that have survived scrutiny by his peers. No Nobel Prize. Anatoly would laugh in my face."

Was Anatoly a Russian physicist, one of Soson's former colleagues, the oligarch, or someone Soson invented? In my professional dealings, I'd never heard of anyone with that name. "It's the truth." Doesn't that matter?

"Anatoly knows that you and I are close. As close as brothers. He would presume that I lie to save you and your family. Perhaps even myself." He ripped open the paper sleeve containing plain wooden chopsticks, broke them apart, and laid them off to the side. "Such a preposterous claim about Hamza would have no credibility. For better or worse, they have bet all of their rubles on your ingenuity and creativity, *malchik*. Bragging about you may not have been the smartest thing I have ever done."

All of the pressure came rolling back on top of me like Sisyphus's boulder. "The son-of-a-bitch won the multi-million-dollar Powerball lottery this week. He was packing up his office when I visited. He claims he can disappear with Faith and Craig so that no one, not even your friends, could find them."

"If he is successful, that leaves me and Louise as their next targets." Soson stroked his chin. "This has become very interesting. How close are you to breaking through with reverse time travel? Within the next sixty days, I hope."

Looking for me to save his ass if it really *was* in a sling. "At the moment, I have only a glimmer of an idea. I'm far from doing the math, let alone validation and a trial run." Hamza's comment about the appearance of my Nobel medal outside before I arrived in 2019 echoed in my memory. He was convinced someone had transported it there from the future. "Besides, *if* I complete the formulas, CHUQ is unavailable to me." I wasn't about to share my progress with Soson. "I'm not going to get as many chances with the accelerator as Lou got." Trial and error must have taken her years, not days or weeks.

Lou hadn't shown up and I wanted to have a private conversation with her. What if she said something in front of Soson about the formulas we'd landed on? "Excuse me for a minute."

I went to the bathroom and sent Lou a text: *Are you joining us for dinner?*

About a minute later, she replied: *Not feeling well. Come by the apartment after.*

Okay. Bring you anything? I figured she'd have me carry out for her.

An ice bag.

Huh? *Sure.*

I returned to the table.

Soson held a pot sticker in mid-air over the wicker basket. "Everything all right?" He dipped it into a dark sauce and put the whole thing into his mouth. His speech was mumbled as he spoke. "Try one. Not bad for such a pedestrian establishment."

"In a minute. My stomach hasn't been the same since I arrived." Maybe some part of my digestive system leaped to a different year.

Soson used his chopsticks to place an eggroll on my plate. "This will make it all better. Tell me, how is the life of a grease monkey?"

"Fine, thank you very much. CJ's place doesn't have much of a clientele. Being on a side street doesn't help and there's no gas station sign."

"I expect given how long he has been there, most of his clients have died or no longer drive."

"Or bought new-fangled electric cars."

Soson gave me one of those 'one eyebrow tilted down' looks. "Tell me you did not enjoy driving my Tesla."

287

When I borrowed it, my left leg felt useless and my hand kept reaching for the stick. "It was comfortable but it demands too much control. I'll admit, it's damn fast."

His smile returned. "How is your relationship with Craig coming along? Have you told him yet who you are?"

"No, and I don't think that's in his best interest right now. A disclosure would rip the scab off any healing in Faith's household. He's doing very well in school and has a better aptitude for empathy than his old man."

"I never would have guessed." He chuckled under his breath.

The young waitress approached our table, pad and pen in hand. I ordered the house special chow mein while Soson ordered kung pao chicken.

"That dish is very spicy." The waitress couldn't have been much older than high school age.

Soson offered a sly smile and winked at her. "I know. The hotter the better."

So much for his minimum age rule.

Her shocked expression made any reply redundant. She scurried away. How would the cooks react to such a customer comment? Perhaps as a challenge? I took a bite of egg roll.

"What are your long-term plans for employment? Service station attendant at minimum wage?"

I felt a jabbing pain in my side. Maybe parts of my digestive system *were* damaged in the leap. "Don't be silly."

"Perhaps as a volunteer at a school? Is Craig's teacher pretty?"

An expected Soson question. "That doesn't matter. I told you, she's married." Was I even looking for somebody? Maybe if I stuck around. After all, at least according to the calendar, I'd been divorced for over a year and reconciliation looked hopeless. Within a nanosecond, I rejected the possibility. No one could ever replace Faith.

"After you solve our current problem, you must not waste your education on some mundane job. Not when you have so much to offer to the scientific community." He leaned closer. "I would happily recommend you for a senior position at a very advanced facility near Moscow."

"No thanks." Did he seriously suggest working for the people who threatened my family? "I'll find a job in my field as soon as I take another pass at fixing this dead status. Your lawyer friend Tonya dumped me, so I'll have to find someone else to take my case. Unlikely they'll work pro bono." Under the table, my fingers traced the lump of money in my front pocket.

"For the first time since our separation, Tonya sent me a text. Not only did she repeat that she never wants me to contact her again, but she also told me never to send her clients." He swiped another steamed dumpling. "You should try one while they are still warm."

Or before he ate them all. "I'm saving my appetite for my main course."

Soson checked his watch. Was that a Rolex? "I wonder where Louise is."

"When I spoke with her earlier, she told me she felt a little under the weather. We shouldn't wait."

"All right." Soson swallowed the dumpling whole. "You know, my friend, you left a very bad impression with Tonya. Do not worry. I am all out of former girlfriends in the legal profession. Tell me, does working on cars please you?"

Soson's questions gave me whiplash. "It would if I was doing that instead of pumping gas. I feel bad taking advantage of CJ. He's accepting my minimal hours as payment for room and board, so I'm getting the better end of our deal. Although, I have to stay away from his cooking. It's terrible. Maybe I'll volunteer to make dinner a few nights a week."

"And miss these joyful gastronomic adventures with your best friend?"

Was Soson my best friend? Does a friend set you up for blackmail? None of our dinners together had been positive. "With Hamza gone from ChiLabs, can my best friend allocate me a few hours on CHUQ?"

Soson choked on his third dumpling. "First, the answer is no. Second, are you kidding? How much undisturbed CHUQ time did you need to complete the calculations for your failed experiment? Months, correct?"

"My experiment would have been successful if Hamza had just left it alone. It wasn't my fault that he changed the settings to generate chrontins instead." I realized I'd raised my voice when the young waitress nearby looked up from her phone.

It was impossible to justify my computing request without divulging the specific nature of the workload. I only needed to verify the equations that concerned particle spins.

"If I ask, even with Hamza gone, management will say *nyet*. CHUQ is overscheduled for the next eighteen months. Why would I waste my breath?"

"Isn't saving lives, yours and Lou's, reason enough?"

He ignored my question and pointed a chopstick at my face. "See, that is why you would have been a terrible choice for my position."

Soson wasn't suited to be Director of Facilities either. His lack of attention to detail would eventually get him demoted or fired.

"Maybe you can wait a decade or so until quantum computers become commercialized. Those would solve your equations in minutes." Soson bit the end off his eggroll. "Of course, you will be celebrating your success at my graveside."

How could Soson make such a morbid comment in such a nonchalant manner? "I don't want you to die, but I don't want your friends to be able to wreak havoc with reverse time travel either."

"They are my business associates, not friends. If they kill me, I will deserve it based on reasonable, mutually understood terms."

Much too calm. Is his life threatened, or was that another lie? "Since when is blackmail reasonable?"

The waitress juggled her tray when she arrived with our food during our conversation.

"Can you pack mine to go?" I got up from the table.

"You are *that* ill?" For the first time that evening, Soson's face showed a modicum of concern.

"I'm not in the mood for another one of these."

"One of these *what?*" After great deliberation, Soson plucked a piece of kung pao chicken from his plate with chopsticks and put it into his mouth. Perspiration formed on his forehead. His face flushed as his jaws slowed. I expected to see steam come out of his ears. His throat bulged as he swallowed. He was going to finish what he ordered out of obstinacy.

"How is it? Hot enough for you?"

He nodded and gulped down half a glass of ice water. Not once did he pant or wave a menu at his face. He did pull at his collar several times as the peppers did their damage.

The waitress scooped my chow mein into a white cardboard container and put it into a brown paper bag.

Before she left, I told her, "My father will pay the bill." I looked at Soson, struggling to eat his meal. "Tell your Russian counterparts that Hamza is the time travel genius. I don't give a shit about your credibility. It's the truth. They should want him alive, not dead. Given Craig's life is in the balance, it's worth a shot."

Soson choked out "*Da,*" his face as red as a bowl of borscht.

On the way to Lou's apartment, I stopped at a QuikMed store and bought an instant cold pack from the first aid aisle. Without enough smaller bills to cover, I had to break one of the fifties. What did she need an ice pack for?

I rang Lou's third-floor apartment from the lobby. After she buzzed me in, I hurried up the stairs, worried about her condition. She greeted me at her door, leaning against the wall, a small towel in her hand. She looked pale and didn't make eye contact, like her mind was somewhere else. As she navigated us into her apartment, her hand caressed the wall.

I held out the cold pack. "Is this what you wanted?"

"Perfect." She activated it, wrapped it in the towel, held it against her back, and sighed.

"What happened?"

"You don't want to know. I got time on CHUQ, like we needed. The results are in my bag. I didn't want to email them." She hesitated and raised her eyebrows. "To me, they look promising, but you'll have to interpret them."

"That's amazing." I put my carton of Chinese food on her dining room table next to her shoulder bag. "I brought house special chow mein from Mandarin Bistro." My plan was to share the food since Lou hadn't joined Soson and me at the restaurant.

"Thanks. I'll warm it later."

I took a seat at the table, removed the CHUQ output from Lou's bag, flipped open the fan-fold printouts, and ran my finger over each line. The computer had run numerous simulations against the algorithms that represented my formulas. "The concept of reversing the spin holds up, at least on a theoretical level. CHUQ didn't find any outliers. No anomalies. No infinite results. I think we've got a good chance."

"Are you kidding me? You did it?"

Threats against my family dulled my reaction. "I guess I did, but it doesn't make Faith or Craig any safer." With a viable approach, I'd become more valuable. *Damn it.*

"If you can get the strings to spin in the opposite direction and leave everything else alone, you'll go backwards in time?"

"That's my theory."

She swayed, shifting her weight from one leg to the other. "Are you ready to leap? Where will you go? I mean, how far back?"

"Hang on, not so fast. CHUQ just verified that we won't destroy the universe if we reverse the spin of the strings, but I haven't figured out how to *create* the reversion. I only know how to measure spins, not affect them."

"That shouldn't be so difficult, for someone as smart as you."

Did Lou think I was a miracle worker? "Assuming I can figure out *how* to do it, we're sure to need additional hardware. Only then will we be able to run a test before I use it on myself." I flipped back to the first page of the report, just to confirm my analysis.

"Is Hamza dead?"

I startled at Lou's question. "No. I guess I'm not cut out to be a murderer. It turns out, his changes were intentional so he could travel forward in time. Except I accidentally interfered." Lou's grunt distracted me. Her condition reflected in her grimace. "You've got to tell me. How did you strain your back? Some kind of accident?"

"More like intentional." She sat next to me at the table. "I convinced the second shift manager Eric to cancel someone else's time slot by telling them that CHUQ had switched itself into self-maintenance mode and couldn't be interrupted. A fat lie, but effective. Then he ran your equations."

"How did you get him to do that?"

Lou looked away. "He and I have what you might call a history. We dated about two years after we were hired at the Labs. He was a good boyfriend. Took me out to places he knew I liked. Bought me the occasional trinket. Anyway, because of our previous relationship, I thought he might do me a favor."

"I still don't—"

Lou glowered as she faced me. "Let me just get this out, okay? I tried what the Russians are doing to us. I know some embarrassing things Eric has done in the past, so I threatened to broadcast those to his friends and co-workers, anonymously of course." Lou paused and pulled the cold pack off her back. "I wouldn't have followed through. I thought the threat would be enough."

"How did he react?"

"The asshole laughed at me. He said he couldn't care less who knew. Then he made a counteroffer. Looking back, I should have opened with sex."

"What?"

"I changed my approach and ran my finger down the front of his shirt. Repeated my request as a whisper in his ear. He must have thought this was some kind of excuse for us getting back together."

"You were just asking for CHUQ time."

"Right. Eric can be a little dense sometimes."

For someone in computing?

"He led me into an empty conference room, we both got undressed—"

"No!" *God, why?*

"It's not like this was our first time. About three months into our relationship, I consented to be intimate."

The explanation was getting personal. I covered my ears with my hands. "This is none of my business."

"But you asked!" Her eyes dropped to half-mast. "Back when we were dating, I learned that, for him, sex was all about how *he* felt. My pleasure meant squat. I broke it off soon after."

"I'm so sorry."

"He was so anxious to get between my legs again, he would have done anything I asked." She winced. "It wasn't a terrible experience but I wish we would have done it on something softer than a table."

TMI! "I never asked you to compromise yourself." Why couldn't I have figured out another way?

"I don't blame *you*. After all, *I* was the one who promised to get us time on CHUQ. I just wish Eric had one caring bone in his body." Her attempted smile failed. "I think my spine is out of whack."

Damn promises! My head weighed so much I could barely lift it. "I don't know what to say." I felt guilty, putting pressure on Lou to get computer time. I rubbed my hands on my pants. My fingers collided with Hamza's payments. Could Eric have been bribed instead? I should have pressed Soson harder for use of

CHUQ. After all, he demanded that I invent reverse time travel and then withheld the very resources to help make it happen. One way or another, I should have figured out an alternative.

"Just put my name on the published paper that documents reverse time travel. It'll do wonders for my career." She winked.

Lou would know that a published paper would be worse than handing reverse time travel to the Russians. Imagine if everyone had access to the technology. Multiple people traveling forward and backward in time made my head hurt. I might be able to help Lou achieve the fame she deserved, just in a different way. I needed to give that some thought.

She stood and repositioned the cold pack on her back. "I need to stretch."

It was clear Lou wasn't interested in eating any of the chow mein, so I put the carton in her fridge. After hearing her story, I had no appetite either.

She followed me into the kitchen. "How do you know that your wife and Craig will be okay when you turn the process over to Soson's friends?"

She's an optimist to think that we can make this happen. "I don't. That's why I'm trusting Hamza at his word, that he'll use his lottery winnings to protect them from harm."

She ran her hand over the faux butcher-block countertop and lifted her eyebrows. "Do you know *how* he won the Powerball drawing?"

Pretty obvious. "He picked all of the right numbers." I wandered back to my documents on her dining room table and took a seat.

Lou followed me. "With a lot of help. About five years ago, Hamza asked me to analyze a special project he managed, one that involved Soson. I went into his office to discuss what he needed. In retrospect, the work sounded like your heavy ion experiment. Anyway, he got called out of the room. A *Daily Herald* laid on his desk, so I leaned over to read the headlines while I waited. One article reported an investigation into President Hillary Clinton about the attack on our embassy in Benghazi when she was Secretary of State. Obama was the current President, so the headline made no sense."

"Was the paper dated April nineteenth, 2019, this coming Friday?"

"How did *you* know?"

"Hamza showed me that front page when I went to see Faith. He accused me of bringing that 2019 paper back to 2011." He implied that was the newspaper I threw out the morning Faith went into labor. Given how distracted I was by our conversation in the condo lobby, I hadn't paid a lot of attention to the details.

"Huh? But that means you've already traveled backward in time. When did you do that? And why do we need to figure it out again?"

I squirmed in my chair. "That's a paradox. I haven't done either. The idea we've been pursuing is as close as I've come."

"The other thing I noticed, Hamza clipped one of those reminder notes next to the lottery numbers on the front page."

A newspaper from 2019 would show winning numbers years before they were picked. *Shit.* That's why Hamza wanted to leap forward in time, and why he

299

thanked me. He didn't want me to invent backward time travel because he was worried subsequent leaps might change something and screw up his big win. "Selfish bastard!" For a fleeting second, I regretted that I hadn't applied the toxic ointment. Taking care of Faith didn't seem connected.

"While I was in Hamza's office that day, I pulled out my phone to take a picture of the front page but he came back too quickly. He thinks you made him a multi-millionaire?"

"Let him believe what he wants. I don't care, if it gives him the resources to successfully hide Faith and Craig from the Russians."

Lou shook her head. "I don't think they'll stop looking, no matter what he does. Something will expose their location."

Over dinner, Soson had shared information about Faith that only Hamza would know. Despite Soson's warning to stay away from Hamza and Hamza saying the same about Soson, they clearly continued to talk. "Hell, Hamza might slip and accidentally give someone a clue to their whereabouts."

"We can't trust either of them. Maybe we can figure out a place where no one can find my family."

"And where would that be? Who has ever disappeared without a trace?" Jimmy Hoffa and Amelia Earhart popped into my head. Clearly, *they* were dead.

Lou paused. "You mean, besides you?"

Time travel was certainly one way to cause someone to vanish. Would that work? "With your help, I can send Faith and Craig forward in time, five—maybe ten—years. They'll vanish without a trace, like I did."

300

For the first time, I felt like forward time travel could be useful. Also, risky. "Of course, I would be older when I caught up with them. At least they would be alive. And safe."

"I can calculate when they'll arrive, so you can be there to greet them. Just like Soson and I were prepared for the reunion with you." Lou blushed.

Despite having a welcoming committee, Soson hadn't greeted me with cash or a place to stay. When it got close to their arrival, I'd do better. "Soson has been treating the death threat against himself so casually, I don't think he's in jeopardy at all." Did Lou know her name was on the list? "I think he's been in on this all along."

"Can we do this without Soson's help? He's bound to tell his Russian buddies everything."

"If Soson convinces them that Hamza invented forward time travel and has the knowledge they need, my family and I will be in the clear." I pulled out the lump of cash and held it up. "If not, maybe we can bribe one of my colleagues to relinquish their slot on the accelerator for our testing. And with Hamza out of the way, we shouldn't have any obstacles."

Lou plopped down into a nearby chair. "What do you need from me?"

"For starters, I'd appreciate your continued collaboration." As if reversing the spin of strings was a well-defined problem. "It could take a while." The Russians had promised to kill Craig if Hamza wasn't dead by Friday. Their deadline would be meaningless if I could shove Faith and Craig forward in time and out of harm's way.

"You've got it. In the meantime, gather your wife and son and bring them to the Labs tomorrow, as early as possible." Lou snatched some bills from my hand. "I'll bribe one of your colleagues for accelerator time and meet you there."

Was bribery viable? If I was approached to give up my time slot for a stack of cash, *I* wouldn't agree. Maybe one of my former colleagues will accept a delay to refine their experiment because they need the money. "Promise me you won't make another deal like you did with Eric."

She shook her head. "He's in computing tech support, not accelerator operations. Besides, I've learned my lesson. Just avoid Soson."

"You can be sure of that." My heart ached at Lou's sacrifice for our effort. I needed to act more like my son and pay her back. I pictured the accelerator tube entrance when I visited Hamza. Would he have remembered to lock it before he left? Maybe I could sneak Faith and Craig in that way. "You'll be safe?"

She nodded.

I left my carton of chow mein in her fridge and headed to the door. "Just curious, do you happen to remember the lottery numbers that won?"

"The paper won't be out until tomorrow, but the numbers should be on the Illinois Lottery site by now." She searched on her phone, walked over, and showed me the web page. "Here they are."

I wasn't certain that the winning numbers matched the one's from the 2019 newspaper. To keep track, I pulled out the Starbucks receipt on which I'd written Precision Biometrics' address and wrote the winning numbers on the back. If I traveled to 2011, maybe I could cut Hamza's winnings in half. Still, money wouldn't solve my problems. "See you tomorrow."

I drove to CJ's, more than a waystation but not quite a home. He wasn't on the first floor, and the door to his bedroom on the second was shut. He must have gone to bed early. I took a peek. He was curled up in fetal position, mumbling in his sleep. I couldn't make out the words so I eased the door shut.

As I got ready for bed, I imagined Faith and Craig in the Beetle, sitting on the grassy mound, waiting to be transported to the future. Once Faith and Craig were safe, I needed to disappear as well, either forward or backward in time. Lou and I faced the problem of how to modify the accelerator to reverse the string spin. We'd have to work expediently. If the hardware modifications took too long, Soson might get wind of our plans. Bringing Lou up to speed might slow us down initially, but the education would improve her skills and make her a more competent colleague.

In Mickey's bed, I tossed and turned, considering how I could fetch Craig from school and Faith from her self-imposed solitary confinement before Hamza whisked them away. Security at his school wouldn't make that easy. And I'd have to get upstairs into Faith's condo, much tougher with Hamza living there. Would my wife and son listen, even if I explained that coming with me was necessary for their safety? I lacked credibility but I had to convince them.

Day 7

Open fields and an occasional stand of trees along Interstate 90 were a nice change of pace from the overdeveloped areas I'd been driving through. I remembered when our town felt more rural with fewer malls and warehouse-sized stores. Now, retailers with the same names repeated every block, or so it seemed. If I needed a new mattress, some coffee, or a submarine sandwich, I was always within yards of a store to satisfy my needs.

I'd visited Craig's school, prepared to convince him to come with me. Except, after a long argument, Ms. Sherman disclosed that Craig had been excused for the day. Faith had taken him up to a family camp in Wisconsin to see if he would be comfortable going away for the summer. Ms. Sherman didn't know their destination, only that Craig couldn't stop talking about the chance to canoe on Lake Delton. A web search identified only one such facility, a place called the Osterman Retreat Center.

As I drove north, I considered how to convince Faith and Craig to come with me. At my first encounter with Faith at her condo, she'd been shocked at my return. At the courthouse, she wouldn't allow me back into her life. Or couldn't. Who could blame her, after an eight-year absence? This time, I had to make her believe I had her and

Craig's best interests at heart. Maybe remind her of my commitment by sharing some story? Odd things we said to each other during intimate moments on our honeymoon? Plans and promises that went unfulfilled? Better to avoid those.

I considered the risk of throwing them into a strange future environment. With me waiting, they wouldn't be alone. Still, I'd have to make sure they had sufficient resources. It was their only reasonable chance to avoid assassination.

As if it was confined to Wisconsin, rain hit the windshield only after I crossed the state line from Illinois. The wiper blades smeared water on dirty glass, something I neglected to care for when I filled the tank. Spraying windshield fluid helped cut through the grime.

A large wood sign confirmed my arrival at the property and indicated two entrances: one to the camp facilities and the second to the retreat center. Since camp wasn't in progress, I concluded that Craig's overnight was being hosted at the retreat center.

I didn't go to camp when I was a child. Summers were filled with either summer school or tutors, or the occasional family vacation by car. Funny thing, my family never traveled to Wisconsin. Maybe because it was so close, my folks didn't consider it much of a trip.

A gravel parking lot filled with pothole puddles appeared on my right, with a narrow asphalt path straight ahead to a sign that said

306

OFFICE. I drove along the path, carefully keeping my tires on the asphalt, rather than the grass on either side. It ended at a long building with a series of intermittent doors and lots of windows, likely some kind of dormitory. I ducked out of the car and ran for the office door. Inside, a woman at a desk greeted me with a smile. "Nice weather we're having. How can I help you?"

I shivered and sprayed water droplets all over the desk. "I'm looking for my son. Craig Weinberg. No, Craig Watson." Great way to raise her confidence, not knowing my son's name.

"Is there a problem?" She soaked up the water with a paper towel.

"Yes, something important I need to tell him."

"We don't like campers to be interrupted while they're here. It spoils the experience. Besides, can't you call your wife and give her the message?"

I played dumb. "Is she here?"

"Yes, campers under the age of ten must be accompanied by a parent or guardian at this program, to see if—Craig—is a good candidate for overnight camp this summer. You didn't know about this?"

"There's a lot going on in our lives right now." How had Faith gotten her act together enough to leave her condo for an event at this facility? Was this a temporary stop before they left for good with Hamza? A cramp twisted my stomach into a figure eight.

A young man in a hooded yellow slicker barged through the door and glared at me. "Whose car is outside?"

"Mine."

"We don't allow cars on the walking path. Please move it to the parking lot."

"Give us a second."

The woman leaned on her desk, her arms folded. "We don't have their schedule. They're at some event at the campgrounds across the river."

"That's it? Somewhere? That's no answer at all."

"I'm sorry you feel that way. Even if I knew exactly where they are, I couldn't provide you that information." She shook her head, as if chastising herself. "You understand, don't you?"

"Yeah, personal privacy." No one had cared much about that back in 2011. Folks would tell you anything. What caused all the focus on security and privacy during the years I missed?

The woman looked at the young man and then at me. "You should move your car now."

I scooted past the slickered young man, jumped into the car, and made a three-point turn. The tires sank into saturated grass. With a bit of struggling and sprayed mud, I got the car turned around. A quick downhill drive to the parking lot. Then a jog back up. Rainwater rippled down the path in waves.

Just before the office, a wooden sign pointed across the bridge to the camp. Attendees ran past me to escape the downpour. I ignored the rain, scanning for my family.

I was halfway across the bridge when I saw two people in silhouette at a distance, a woman with a cane accompanied by a young boy, both ignoring the precipitation. When they got a bit closer, I recognized Faith's distinctive gait. Not skipping the way she did on our strolls, or the joyous way she used to saunter around the house. I stood still, so as not to scare her into retreating. Craig recognized me first and pulled at his mother's hand. She stood frozen as he ran to me.

I crossed to the other side of the bridge, a soaked grassy field.

When he got close, he shouted against the rain, "What are you doing here?"

"I'm here to take you and your mother to safety."

He threw his arms in the air. "The rain doesn't hurt. We're just wet."

Given her attitude at the courthouse, Faith didn't want me to have contact with our child. She closed the gap, putting herself within the range of my speaking voice.

My eyelids battled the precipitation, blinking repeatedly as rain ran down my forehead. "I need to talk to you. It's important."

"You never give up, do you? Didn't I make myself clear? Leave me alone."

She'd preferred to accuse as opposed to converse. I reached out to her but she maintained a safe distance. "Please, Faith. It's life or death."

309

Faith shook her head, water sprinkling. "You're always exaggerating." She leaned closer to Craig but her voice wasn't a whisper. She wanted me to hear. "He did something very bad to our family, and we should never forgive him."

"No, Ma. He's a scientist like Dad, and he likes museums." Craig's uncertain expression didn't reflect his words. "Does that mean I can't talk to him at school?"

Her eyes flared. "You bastard! You knew I didn't want you to have contact and you did it anyway. Don't any of my wishes matter?"

I squatted, the back of my pants against soggy shoes, and spoke to Craig. "Remember when we talked about time travel? Well, I time-traveled on the day you were born. Now it's your turn. You and your mother."

Craig's eyes widened despite the pelting raindrops. "Wow!"

"You're going to see wondrous things." Wouldn't the world be a better place a decade from now?

Faith looked down. "Give me a break. Your excuse for disappearing is *time travel*? Ridiculous!"

I stood, my face a foot from hers. "Look at me. I'm the same as I was on the day Craig was born. How do you explain that?"

She blinked, the rain running down her face. "I can't." She stepped back, using the cane to steady herself. "This is about the money, isn't it?

Your precious Nobel Prize award. Ham warned me about you."

"Since I arrived, he's tried to keep us apart. I don't know how, but he knew I was going to be threatened and wanted to protect the two of you." Soson probably clued him in. "That's why he said those things about me." Given how he felt about Faith, there was some jealousy as well.

Faith created some distance between us, as if I were poison. "You're wrong. Ham wouldn't do anything like that. He's been nothing but a complete gentleman."

Yeah, right. "I hoped that we could reconcile. Put the past behind us." The words stuck in my throat. Was this the end of the line for us as a family? "I clearly see that's not going to happen. But I can't stand by and do nothing, knowing the two of you are in danger. Come with me. I have a way to protect you."

"No need. Ham told me we'd be leaving on an extended trip to celebrate his lottery winnings as soon as we got back from camp." Her hair tilted when she raised an eyebrow.

Is she wearing a wig?

"Ham told me the destinations are a surprise. This is a once in a lifetime opportunity for Craig."

Hamza was keeping his cards hidden, even from Faith. "I'll tell you why he's taking you away. People are threatening to hurt both of you to get me to do something for them."

"Mama?" Craig hugged his mother's leg.

Faith hugged Craig back. "Don't listen to him."

"Don't worry, son. I'll keep you and your mother safe." *If only she'll listen.*

"I don't believe you." She jabbed her cane into the wet sod. "Utter nonsense."

"Would you be pulling Craig out of school if it was just a trip?" I reached to touch Faith's cheek, like I always did when we had a crisis. She flinched and pulled her head away. My hand hung in the air.

"You know I've always wanted to travel. Ham is giving us the opportunity while I still have the time."

Has she given up the fight? How much time does she have? "I can use the same technology that got me here to send both of you into the future, where you'll be safe."

"What a load of bunk!" She lifted the cane and swung it in my direction.

When she tilted to the side, I caught her arm and helped her stay upright until the cane was back in place.

"You'll take us somewhere and lock us up, then have the courts declare us dead and find some way to inherit what's left."

My clothes were plastered to my skin. The slightest wind chilled me to shivering. "I don't give a shit about the money. I don't want you to die."

Craig's grip slipped. "*I* don't want to die." His sneakers slid on the muddy turf and he fell.

312

Faith reached out to help him stand with her free hand. I took him by his other arm.

She leaned over to hug him. "Neither of us is going to die, at least not from some fantasy boogiemen." She squinted through the downpour.

"Hamza told me about your condition. Who knows, they might have better treatments in the future." *Including mine.* "And I'll be here in the meantime, working on my tumor-killing therapy." *I could work on reverse time travel and heavy ions at the same time, couldn't I?* "We can fight this together." I pointed at the path. "I'm parked in the lot. I'll explain everything in my car."

Her weight on the cane drove it into the soggy ground. "You have your Audi?"

Faith's illness must have affected her memory of the sale. "No, it's gone." Could I distract her? "But *this* car is the same yellow. Would you like to see it?"

"Go away!" Faith waved her arm, unsteady on muddy turf. "Leave now, or I'll call for help."

Maybe if I explained better. "There are some bad people—Russians—and they want me to invent something dangerous. I don't want to, so they threatened to kill Craig, you, and some others if I don't agree to their demands. I don't want anything to happen to the two of you. Why won't you let me save you?"

"Russians? All this talk about dangerous Russians! More fake news!"

I knelt down again. This might be my last opportunity. "Craig?" I had to tell him before

Faith put some horrid spin on it. "I should have told you when we first met, but I was scared how you'd react."

Eyes wide, Craig waited for the disclosure.

"Randall!" Faith screamed. "Don't you dare!"

"Craig, I'm your father."

He blinked and looked up. "Ma?"

"He *was* your father." She wrapped her arms around him, plastering him to her side.

She's taking no chances, fearful that I'd steal him and run away. That wasn't what this was about.

I waited for a reaction from Craig. A smile. A kick in the shins. Something.

With each stroke of Faith's hand on his head, Craig's soaked hair drained onto his neck. "Patty did her best, lord knows. She knew what I was going through and coached me through the delivery without taking a break. But she couldn't be at our house every day after Craig and I came home."

I took small solace that she referred to the old house as "ours." "Soson didn't know you'd sold it."

"See, there's your Russian!" She breathed heavily and gave me one of her 'knowing' nods. "Ham, he knew how to take control. When the bank threatened to take the house, and when shysters tried to cheat me out of your prize money, he took care of things. Battling my disease has been difficult but choosing to leave you behind for good was the hardest thing I've ever done. A few papers to sign, and I could move on. So, I did."

She had to declare me dead to put those painful episodes into the past. My reappearance had revived them. "Faith, I wanted to be there when Craig was born more than anything in the world. But then your SUV got caught in some kind of time vortex and got sucked in—"

"Bullshit! You're a genius! You could have found your way back!"

I shook my head. If she wasn't going to believe the truth, any lie would be transparent.

"I hoped you were kidnapped." Her hair slipped to one side of her head. "Back then, I would have paid any ransom to get you back."

Maybe there was still a spark. "Faith, my dear Faith, I'm here now." I threw my arms open. "Let me try to make things right by saving you."

"The hell you can. I'll never forgive you for abandoning me just when I needed you most." She squeezed Craig. "When *we* needed you most. There's no place in our lives for you anymore. As soon as we get back, I'm going to have whoever gave you access to Craig fired."

If Hamza did his job, they'd never be back. "No one gave me access. Ms. Sherman pointed him out on the playground. Please, get your things and I'll take you to ChiLabs."

"She shares the blame and deserves to be punished."

Craig's voice was only slightly louder than a whisper. "But I like Ms. Sherman."

Faith had never been vindictive, just the opposite. She was the one who apologized if someone accidentally bumped into her at a restaurant. I had hurt her more than I knew. Maybe the pancreatic cancer had something to do with it.

Craig looked at Faith. "He's my Dad?"

I used the gentlest tone I could. "You must be confused right now. I get it. Me showing up after all these years—"

"I don't want to talk to you." He buried his face in his mother's side.

"Craig, I am so sorry."

He confronted me with damp, red eyes. "I don't care if you're my father. You hurt Ma." He threw his arms around her body. "I don't want to see you again. Ever."

Faith pulled the soaked wig from her head and hugged our son. "That goes for me as well."

A chill ran through my body, and not from soaked clothes. They ambled past me, Craig's arm linked in his mother's, Faith's drenched wig dangling from her hand. I felt helpless. They'd refused to be saved. Hamza might try, but I was certain that he would fail, either through greed or ineptitude.

There was now only one way to keep them safe. I needed to prevent this whole situation from happening in the first place.

I walked toward the path to the parking lot but couldn't help but glance over my shoulder. The pair had picked up their pace towards their housing, out of my life and into danger. By the time I got into my car, the water dripping down my face tasted salty. I pushed my hair back, wiped my eyes and placed a call to Lou. Time for me to go. They weren't coming.

As I pulled out of the Osterman Retreat Center lot, I recognized Hamza's Bentley pulling in, followed closely by a familiar black Chevy Blazer driven by the man with a flattop haircut. *Shit, now he's following Hamza.* With my fingertips, I wiped tears from my eyes as the wiper blades cleared the windshield.

My call connected. "Lou, it's Randy. How are you feeling?"

"Much better, thanks. I'm at ChiLabs. When will you be here?"

"Faith and Craig don't want anything to do with me."

She sounded out of breath. "What about the threats? You can't trust Hamza."

Or Soson. "The only thing I can do to make this right is prevent the whole mess from happening in the first place."

Her extended silence was deafening. "You're going back to 2011? Despite the consequences and likely paradoxes?"

"I don't know any other way to save them and prevent reverse time travel from getting into the wrong hands. The most unpredictable part will be dealing with a second Randy, who I presume is alive in 2011."

"But *you're* Randy from 2011."

"I'm Randy *after* the leap. I have to go back *before* Hamza modifies the settings on the controllers, generates chrontins and causes the time warp. That should mean, at least for a while, there'll be two of us. Of *me*." How effective could I be if I couldn't even refer to my own existence?

"How will you handle *that*?"

Unlike Lou, I didn't recall Soson ever asking questions like this to drive a technical conversation. "It would be best if I didn't directly interfere. Instead, I'll have to convince 2011 Randy to get to work early enough to stop Hamza, despite Faith's contractions." I played back that morning in my mind. "Hell, when Faith woke me with contractions, I chucked the 2019 newspaper into the trash. I'll have to make the 2011 version of me pay attention to the paper this time."

"What about an alternative? Why don't you switch places? Let 2011 Randy leap to 2019 while you show up at the hospital?"

"Interesting. I'll have to consider that." I was impressed by Lou's ability to think outside the box. "How are things going on your side?"

"Even before you told me that Faith and Craig didn't agree to travel to the future, we were screwed. I was unable to bribe anyone for access to the accelerator. As soon as they heard it was for you, they refused. In case you weren't aware, your colleagues don't like you very much."

I'd heard. "At least Hamza won't be hanging around, and Soson has some authority, which we'll take advantage of."

"Without telling him too much. Are you coming back to the Labs today?"

Rain let up the further south I drove. At this rate, clear skies would greet me by the time I reached Schaumburg. "No. I'm exhausted and soaked to the skin.

I'll be lucky if I don't come down with pneumonia. If we're going to invent a viable method of reverse time travel tomorrow, I'll need to get a good night's rest." Was that even possible? "So should you. No partying tonight."

Lou chuckled. "Like that ever happens."

"One more thing. Ask Soson to get in touch with his Russian contacts, tell them I'm working on the process and could use some more time. Maybe they'll cut us some slack."

"I will as soon as I'm off this call. But let's not depend on any leniency. See you tomorrow morning?"

"First thing. If you get there before me, ask Soson to let you into our office. And don't tell him anything about our approach."

"Our?"

"We're partners in this. See you tomorrow." I hung up.

Working closely with someone who engaged in the technical details, unlike Soson, was going to be an unusual experience. Collaborating with Lou so far had been very useful. I could bounce ideas off her, to get a different perspective.

Let 2011 Randy leap, so I could arrive in his place at the hospital in advance of Craig's birth? *Why didn't I think that would work out well?*

At CJ's garage, the OPEN sign pulsed neon red. I filled the Beetle's tank and put a one-hundred-dollar bill in the shoebox that replaced the smashed glass pickle jar. *Every dollar helps.*

CJ slept in his chair, crackling snow on the TV screen. I turned it off. The tape must have ended.

He rolled to his side to face me. "You back? I was worried."

"I'm fine, just wet. And a little hungry."

"Good. I planned on three squares a day for both of us, but you keep missing meals. Take whatever you want." He closed his eyes, mumbled, and dozed off.

I went upstairs and stripped out of my soaked clothes, dried off, and put on a pair of Mickey's oversized sweats. When the chill dissipated, I went downstairs to the kitchen. CJ had left his recliner, I expected for his bedroom.

None of CJ's leftovers looked appetizing. Some of them were glazed with green mold. I found a box of GoTane-labeled granola bars in the cupboard, well past their Best If Used By dates. Two of them softened by dunking into a glass of milk substituted for dinner. For dessert, a shot of whiskey from a bottle in one of the kitchen cabinets burned on the way down.

In bed, I couldn't fall asleep. What if I ran into myself in 2011? What would that do to the space-time continuum?

I shifted my thoughts to pleasant memories Faith and I had shared, to blot out our recent confrontation. Our honeymoon in Hawaii, running through the surf, playfully splashing each other as the waves rolled in. Volunteering to stock shelves at the township public pantry, side by side, something I never would have considered except for Faith's cajoling. Deciding we were both ready for a family, running into the bedroom and lying naked in each other's arms.

As I relaxed, I prayed I could change the past and make things right.

Day 8

[24] Friday, April 19, 2019

Wearing a bathrobe and slippers, CJ apologized the next morning for not making me a hot breakfast. "Musta' caught somethin' from a customer." He put his hand on his forehead. "There's some oatmeal packets in a drawer, I think, and I got a kettle here someplace." He walked out of the room but immediately came back in. "Forgot to tell ya, your tires showed up. They're by the service bay, waitin' to be put away. Don't recommend doin' that in your nice clothes." He patted me on the head. "Be a good boy." Then he shuffled back to bed.

I hoped CJ suffered from nothing more serious than digestive issues after consuming more than a sensible number of peanuts. His demeanor refuted that diagnosis. When I saw that the oatmeal packets were also branded GoTane, I planned instead on stopping for carryout from the nearby Starbucks.

A copy of the *Daily Herald* dated April 19th lay within ten feet of the front door. It was identical to the one Hamza had shown me, including CJ's address. Did he still have his copy, or did it vanish when this one was printed? There couldn't be two copies, right? I snatched it before CJ tossed it into his collection.

At ChiLabs, I parked near the access tunnels and took my Nobel Prize medal from the trunk. It belonged back in my office, no matter how Hamza had obtained it. I left the *Daily Herald* in the car.

I tried the same access door to the tunnels as last time. Locked! *Shit!* The 'do not allow' list at the security station, created by Hamza, would prevent Lou from signing me in. I called her cell, explained where I was, and asked her to rescue me.

"I've never been down there."

"You'll find it. The doors are labeled on the inside."

I paced while waiting for her to get downstairs and through the tunnel. About four yards away, a different access door popped open. Lou's head came into view. *Close enough.* I climbed down the ladder to join her in the passageway.

Lou hugged herself. "It's kind of creepy."

"Then let's get upstairs." We navigated the underground corridor and climbed up four flights. Between the staircase and my office, a few employees in the hallway greeted Lou. I turned my face away from them. Thankfully, none of them recognized me.

My office door was open. Lou had procured a second chair, which she placed in between my bookcase and the controller rack. Access to my shelves of documents was blocked, but I didn't expect that the answer to our dilemma would be there for the taking. I put the Nobel Prize medal between my two displays.

Her bright eyes were wide open when she handed back the bribe money I'd provided to get linear accelerator time. "This is yours. Now, where do we start?"

I stuffed the crisp bills into my wallet alongside the Russian ones. Damn, now *I'm* forgetting things. I promised CJ to get them converted to US currency.

"First, do you know if Soson was successful in getting us more time?"

She pressed her palms together between her knees. "He told me that he made two pitches to his Russian colleague. First, he identified Hamza as the inventor of forward time travel, as you asked. He said Anatoly couldn't stop laughing."

"Soson warned me they wouldn't believe it."

"Unfortunately, that also confirmed that Hamza was still alive. Second, that you were fully engaged on backward time travel, which made them happy. But only enough to delay action on their part until midnight."

"That's it? Midnight is no extension at all! I bet Soson didn't even try. Bastard! Then Craig is as good as—" I couldn't say the word. I needed to shake off my feelings of dread and focus on our work. "All right." I stood at the whiteboard and dragged an eraser across the clean surface. "Let's start with the mathematics that underlies quantum physics. And we have CHUQ's results as the starting point."

Lou's downturned mouth signaled dismay. "If you want my help, you'll need to start someplace I understand. I won't even be able to participate if you throw formulas up there. Sorry, but they would be mostly *gibberish* to me."

The eraser fell from my fingers. "What do you propose? Trial and error? With how many variables? That isn't an efficient strategy." I heaved a sigh and wilted into my chair. Had our partnership failed that quickly?

"Is that what you think I did?" She looked down her nose and smirked. "What you call trial and error were observations, hypotheses, tests, conclusions, and refinements. But that's *not* my point. Think about Einstein. He didn't start with equations." She tapped her temple. "His best work came from thought experiments. Then he worked up the mathematics."

"You're absolutely right." I'd practically memorized Walter Isaacson's biography of Einstein, except the parts about his marriages and philandering.

Lou gave me a thumb's up. "I'm only saying that if you put all of your focus on the numbers, you may be ignoring parts of reality that lead to a solution."

"You've made your point. You created a calibration formula, right?" *By trial and error.* I handed her my phone. "Put that in here in a note."

Lou typed her formula into my phone and then handed it back. "Done."

"Good. How do *you* think we should proceed?"

"With a thought experiment, of course, starting with your physical design to create tumor-fighting heavy ions. That's the base case that Hamza leveraged, right?"

I was flattered she acknowledged that my design was valuable. "We can build on what Hamza did to generate chrontins." I held the phone in my hand, prepared to document our progress.

"Like you said, time is our major constraint." Lou scooted her chair inches closer. "After your explanation, you can tell me your idea about reversing the spin of strings. Let's see where that takes us."

"Great." Lou's approach made perfect sense. I created a new note and tapped in what we just discussed.

"Okay, so start with your original experiment. What was your breakthrough? And can you explain it without math?"

"You don't know anything about my work, do you?"

"Only that it consumed your life for close to a decade, but nothing technical. My job was post-impact analysis, remember? I didn't have to know what happened before the results showed up."

Evidently, she created her calibration without those details. "Well, we don't have time for you to learn a decade's worth of my research. I'll focus on the most important concepts. For example, do you know what D-branes are?"

Lou scratched her head. "Dense ones? I'm guessing."

Did she think I said brains? "Not even close. It's a hypersurface in space-time. Endpoints of open strings are attached to D-branes."

"Boy, we got into string theory quick. What are strings anyway?"

I did a face palm. "I can't turn this into a class on superstring theory."

"I'm only trying to understand the basic principles. After that, I can help make progress on backward time travel. Give me a chance. I'm damned good at experimental physics, maybe as good as you are in theoretical."

"Okay." I stood up with a marker in my hand because I think better on my feet. "Instead of dimensionless points in space-time, superstring theory treats elementary particles as extended one-dimensional string-like objects. They're massless. The strings vibrate, and each mode of vibration corresponds to a different particle."

As I talked, Lou nodded. "While I waited for you to show up, I looked up the Standard Model of particle physics, because I thought we'd get to string theory sooner rather than later."

"Good. Ground we won't have to cover."

"Still, way over my head." Lou passed her hand above her body to emphasize her statement. "And you understand this stuff?"

"All too well. I ate, drank, and slept it since college. Let me shorten this to the executive summary, how I might describe it to Soson."

As if mentioning his name was a magic incantation, he appeared at my door. Good thing I hadn't transcribed any of the CHUQ formulas or results onto the whiteboard.

His ample body filled the doorframe. "Sorry I am interrupting this important conversation. I merely wanted to make sure the two of you have everything you need."

"Besides a decade? Yes, for the moment." I settled into my chair. "By the way, thanks for getting us a little more time, with the emphasis on little." I needed to hang onto every advantage. No way would I tip him off that I knew he was complicit.

"Be glad that they gave you anything. My former associates do not show weakness or negotiate. Might I stay and observe?"

I wanted Soson to make the decision to leave, so I gave him a reason. "Lou created our agenda for approaching the problem. The opening topic will be string theory. We can get another chair…"

Soson took a step back. "Never mind. I have other things to attend to."

He calls himself a physicist? "What projects did you work on in Russia?" *Perform Newton's apple-dropping?*

"Unfortunately, all of our work focused on atomic weapons. More effective bombs with broader devastation and lower radioactivity. An impossible combination. Yet, that was our mission. It paid the bills and came with substantial benefits. I will leave you to your task. *Spasibo.*"

When Soson was out of sight, I turned to face Lou. "I can't believe he put us all in jeopardy. How many years do you think he's been leaking my research to his Russian counterpart?" He betrayed our friendship. To think I wanted him to play uncle to Craig. Soson needed to stay ignorant. "Where was I?"

"Strings?" Lou leaned forward, elbows on her knees.

"Right! When I learned to measure the rotational spins of strings, I also learned how to force superstrings to span D-branes. With the proper configurations, the strings gain mass. Huge mass. Which makes their particles better tumor fighters."

"So far so good. What did Hamza change to create chrontins?"

"Oh, he was so proud of himself, he just blurted it out. He modified three settings, the temperature of the plasma frame I had installed to increase particle speed, the frequency and direction of the embedded laser, and the electromagnets to direct the resulting particles upward. I haven't done the math—"

"Not yet, but I bet you will."

I nodded. "It sounded like the higher temperature caused the stretched strings with significant mass to become coincident. When they approached the target material, the refocused laser added energy, which amplified their speed. The target plate generated chrontins in a uniform clockwise pattern, creating the aperture in space-time through which I was pulled." I continued documenting our discussion.

"Wow!"

"Are you still with me?"

"I think I understand most of what you said. That sounds like a wormhole." She tilted her head, staring at the phone in my hand. "Why are you writing everything down?"

"As a physicist, I depend on the certainty and precision of mathematics." I looked up from the screen. Lou's suggested approach helped me see things clearly. "When this is all done, I'll go back and create the formulas that underlie our accomplishment. Although I might have to do that in 2011, which is why..." I held the phone up facing her.

"So now we know how you got here. How do you reverse it?"

"With more time, I might compute a reverse energy field using the plasma frame temperature and laser like Hamza did."

"How about the CHUQ formulas?"

"Those results gave me hope that reverse time travel isn't out of the question, but I'd be more comfortable going back to experimental design."

"That's like starting up a new ten-year effort. We only have today. Think *tactically*. Vibrations make strings spin?"

How well was I hiding my frustration with Lou's fundamental questions? "The term spin is a little deceiving. It's not a rotating motion. It refers to the polarity of elementary particles."

"Like magnets?"

"Exactly." Lou's analogy sparked a revelation. I'd been trying to reinvent the wheel from ground zero. By forcing me to think about the specifics of the problem and avoiding all of the mathematics, we might get somewhere quicker. I added to my notes. "Like the polarity of magnets but at a microscopic level."

"Terrific. So how do you change the polarity of a normal magnet?"

I had no clue. "There must be a way. A more relevant question is, how do we change the polarity of the *superstrings*?" All I needed to do was find the right factors to take the disruption in the opposite time direction, backwards instead of forwards.

The anticipation of success twinkled in Lou's eyes, just like one of my mathematics tutors in high school who taught that the answers were inside me. His role was to help me find them. Did Lou already know the answers? Was she only going through the motions so *I* could discover them? "By any chance, have you done this analysis before?"

"Me? Heck no." She paused, as if daydreaming. "Although, I have to admit, parts of these conversations echo in my memories." She pointed at the computer screen. "Maybe we should do a search. Concurrent invention and all."

"It wouldn't hurt to check the literature on superstrings." I didn't recall reading anything about changing polarity of strings in any 2011 dissertation, research paper or journal. Of course, back then, I wasn't looking. Now, I had the advantage of eight more years of research at my disposal. "Perhaps there's something relevant."

Soson must have logged into my computer for Lou when he'd opened the office. When the screen saver disappeared with a move of the mouse, a web page with the Standard Model of particle physics filled a browser window.

I searched my favorite physics research sites for papers and journal articles related to strings and polarity. "Good. I found a commentary on the question." I read the ResearchGate reply out loud:

"Now as to polarity reversal, this could be possible if the magnetic poles of elementary particles were present one at a time, that is, if their energy oscillates between increasing presence and decreasing presence at the particle's energy frequency."

"Can we do that?" Lou's expression reminded me of a child waiting to taste their first ice cream cone.

"Not one particle at a time. There are thousands of them delivered in a stream, and the particles inside can't be manipulated individually. We need a way to change them en mass." I clicked on the second result in the list of responses to my original query.

I stared at the screen. All of the relevant considerations were there for a different situation. Could we apply his technique to our problem?

"Randy? Randy?"

I dragged my attention from the screen. "Can it be that easy?"

"What? What does it say?" Lou leaned against my shoulder, her eyes on the monitor.

I put my finger on the screen. "A researcher named Michaud at *Service de Recherche Pédagogique* in France posted an answer to a question about reversing the spin of electrons. That's not precisely what we want to do, but I think the answer is informative. According to him, all we need to do is reverse the polarity of the electromagnets."

"Isn't that just swapping the power cables? I might have done that once in my high school AP Physics class."

I read the footnotes:

"It is theorized that particles seem to be born with spin as an inherent property, like the mass or negative electric charge of an electron. Spin is sometimes called 'inherent' or 'intrinsic' angular momentum."

I slumped in my chair. "It *is* too simple." I spun around to assess her reaction. Was she keeping up?

"We'll have to birth a new set of particles and influence their angular momentum, or polarity, at conception. Then we can use those particles, built specifically for our purposes, to populate the stream."

Lou's green eyes sparkled. "How do we do *that?*"

Another leading question. She *does* know! "The first part, what you call birthing, is standard operating procedure. We use a duoplasmatron. That's the device that manufactures the source material for the particle streams."

"We just need to influence the polarity of the particles it produces, thus the spin of their strings. What do we need to do that?"

I was now certain. Lou was stepping me through a procedure she already knew but I needed to discover. Is she that smart, or had she been through this discovery process before? With me or someone else? I dragged my mind back to the task at hand by documenting these articles and our conversation, a roadmap that would allow me to prove why the solution worked. *Assuming it does.*

I clicked back to the first article. "If we use electromagnets to oscillate the energy around the newly created particles, we should theoretically be able to change their polarity. All other factors left as is, the chrontins eventually created would point backwards in time instead of forward." I shivered as the possibility of going back to 2011 now seemed plausible. "Once the electromagnets are installed, we'll need to monitor the energy of the created particles so the oscillation covers the correct range." I stood and faced my whiteboard, prepared to write. Nothing came to mind. "That should do it."

"Let me play devil's advocate? Can we switch the polarity of the chrontins after they're generated?"

"You *are* good." I hadn't thought about that alternative approach. "Here's a question back at you. How successful do you think we'd be in capturing the chrontins to flip their polarity?"

Lou closed her eyes, tilted her face toward the ceiling and hummed.

She must be doing a solo thought experiment. "So?"

She turned to face me and opened her eyes. "It would be too late. They'd already be scattering. Is there even room for a mechanism to trap and flip them?'

I pictured the cramped secondary target area. "There isn't. I'm glad you continue to offer creative alternatives. I think we should go with our original solution." I confirmed I'd jotted down the correct steps.

"Okay, so we think we can generate chrontins that will send you back, and I already have the formula we can use to determine how *far* back. How are we going to test it?"

"Whoa. Let's not get ahead of ourselves." I went back to the accumulated set of notes in my phone. "First, we need the hardware in place without Soson understanding the details. *Then* we run a test."

Lou scratched her chin. "Does ChiLabs have any spare electromagnets?"

"There used to be back-up units for all major components in inventory, in case of catastrophic failure." I expected Lou's leading questions. "If that's still true, I'll have the maintenance technicians borrow a set for making our reverse-spinning strings. Someone will have to monitor the energy of the particles at the back-up duoplasmatron."

"Let me do that. One more thing we can hide from Soson."

"Great!" I celebrated our collaboration with a smile.

I called Soson. When he answered, I said, "I'll need a block of time on the linear accelerator after a few hardware changes."

"You are already moving towards testing? You perform miracles!"

"It's a test, not the real thing." Best to establish low expectations. "Who needs to approve the requests?"

"You are speaking to him. I offered to fill in for Hamza until a replacement for his position was found, and at my current compensation. Senior management were pleased at the arrangement."

"Great. Please put through an approved general work order to the maintenance team."

"For what, *malchik?*"

Boy. "Must you keep calling me that? I'm a grown-up."

"Would you prefer *starik? Old* man?"

"Never mind." I kept the specifications intentionally vague. "Just a few tweaks. Nothing major. I can't make this happen with software and settings alone."

"But what do I specify in the work order?"

It was a legitimate question. One slip, and I might provide Soson with something his Russian colleagues would find useful. "Just have them contact me. I'll provide the details so nothing gets lost in translation. But good news, you won't have to interrupt the use of the accelerator while the hardware modifications are being made."

"How is that possible? You must explain."

Does he have the capability to understand if I shared the details? "Listen, this might not even work. Remember my first linear accelerator test? No impacts at all? I'll explain the whole thing *if* it succeeds."

I heard typing. "I am, how you say, all over it. I am issuing an emergency work order as we speak."

"Good. We're still doing last-minute calculations. By hand."

No reaction from Soson about CHUQ.

More Soson typing. "The request has been sent. You will require the accelerator *after* the modifications?"

"*Da.*" *One of the few Russian words I know.*

"I will stand-by. If things run late, I will cancel my evening appointment."

Another of Soson's women? "Perfect. I'll let you know when the changes are complete."

"Randall, as a celebration for your progress, I am ordering lunch in for the three of us, to discuss how we will package all of this up for your client."

"There's no deliverable yet. I told you, I don't even know if this will work."

"I have confidence, *comrade.* By the way, after this successful test, I will be your first human subject." He hung up.

Lou cocked her head when I put down my phone. "He's good with this?"

"Soson is so pleased, he's buying lunch so we can eat and talk about delivering our results to the Russians. And he plans on being the first human subject. Just great!"

Lou looked at me with raised eyebrows. "That wasn't part of the plan, was it?"

"No." How could we delay Soson's demand?

Before we could discuss the issue, Lou, who seemed to know all of the questions and most of the answers, asked, "Once everything is set up, what *are* we going to send back in time, as a test?"

I sat at my desk and played with my Nobel Prize box, sliding it back and forth between my hands. My recent confrontation with Hamza in his office provided the answer. "How precise is your algorithm to compute the interval of time jumps?"

"Spot on. Just give me a window of a couple of days. Why?"

I held up the box. "I'd like to send my Nobel Prize medal back in time to before I arrived in 2019. Maybe Wednesday the tenth. Can you do that?"

She grimaced. "A specific day? Boy, I don't know if I can be that precise, but I'll do my best."

I pictured where I'd parked Faith's SUV. "It needs to appear outside on the mound above the secondary target area."

"Of course. That's where I launched all of my forward time travel objects when I tested my calibration. And you're sure this will work?"

"Yes, because it already did." The medal must have shown up as a result of this test. There was no other explanation of why the grounds crew ran over it that day. Simultaneous consideration of present, past, and future jumbled my thoughts.

"In the worst case, I'll err on the side of earlier. The thing is, I'll have to compute the settings just before we send it. My formula uses relative time, not absolute."

Subtracting one date and time from another didn't make the process that much more complicated. "I'll leave all of that to you."

"If you know that our procedure works, why not skip the test?" Lou swallowed hard and quietly said, "I can just send you back."

That cold chill returned. "First, it's my life we're talking about. And second, we're going to tell Soson the test failed. Spectacularly. And we might need time to debug our approach. The second test will be my leap."

"Brilliant!"

My mind was off in the future. "What I need you to do, as soon as possible after I leap, is destroy all evidence of our work. Soson will know what we did with hardware after the work order is completed. Hopefully, our paper trail won't be sufficient to recreate the procedure." I mentally ran through the steps. "At least he'll be ignorant about how we flipped proton polarity because you're doing that work."

"What work?" Lou smiled.

"And you'll change all of the controller settings to zero after I leap."

"I sure will. I've never seen Soson pay attention to the controller settings when we were in the office together. Plus, I'll delete the pictures I took of them as well, just to be sure."

Nodding agreement, I silently reviewed our plans. They were workable, but there was one issue nagging me. "I'm afraid we're not going to publish this and make you famous."

She shook her head. "I didn't expect it. If the Russians shouldn't have it, no one else should either. Even in benevolent hands, many terrible things could happen."

I'd been considering how to compensate Lou for her contribution. Leaving her stuck in an analysis job seemed demeaning and wasteful. She was so much better than that.

While Lou and I waited for Soson to bring lunch, a man in his thirties, wearing clothing that made him look like he worked part-time at CJ's garage, knocked on the doorframe. He stared at me with a huge grin on his face. "As I live and breathe, Dr. Randall Weinberg."

"That's me." Was he going to join the club of employees who wanted to know where I'd been for the last eight years? Maybe I should have shut the door, but the air in the room would have gotten hot and stale.

"Boy, never in my wildest dreams did I think I would ever meet you." A red security badge hung from his belt, indicating he was an employee, not a vendor or contractor. "So, I'm Zach Stanton." He stood, all of his weight on his right leg, waiting for an acknowledgment.

"Do we know each other?" I glanced at Lou, but she didn't offer any assistance, tapping away on her phone.

He craned his neck forward. "We've never met, but your son Craig is in the same class as my son Ollie."

"Oliver?" The name clicked.

"Yep." He extended his arm for a handshake, which was more like pumping water.

Just when I thought my arm would fall off, he let go. "So, I just wanted to let you know how much me and the missus appreciate what Craig is doing, volunteering to work with Ollie on their science project. They might not win any awards, but your son is a winner in our book."

I choked up and forced out, "You're welcome," followed a second later with, "I'm very proud of my son."

341

"So, why I'm here." He pulled a folded paper from his back pocket. "Mr. Grudovich sent down a rush order for some installation work. Except there weren't any details." He shifted his weight to his left leg.

"Yes, I need electromagnets from inventory to be installed on our back-up duoplasmatron."

Zach scratched his head. "So, we've never done anything like that before. You know, we're strictly hardware guys. Is somebody from engineering going to help out?"

"Yes." I gestured at Lou. "This is Louise Martin. She'll be overall coordinator."

She looked up from her phone. "Sorry, I was just taking notes for the control system app. Call me Lou."

He did a combination salute and head nod. "So, is this a rush job?"

"Absolutely." The clock on the computer screen read just past noon, less than twelve hours left before some Russian assassin took my son's life.

"Well then, I'd be happy to call in a second crew so we can knock this out for you. The least I can do for the kindness your son has shown to my Ollie."

"I apologize for the short notice. It's very important." For Craig and me. "How long do you think it will take?"

"With two crews working non-stop?" He checked his watch. "Maybe five hours." Another weight shift.

Can't this guy stand still? The last thing I wanted to do was cut things close, with Craig's life in jeopardy. "Would a third crew get it done any faster?"

"Nah, they'd just trip all over each other. We'll get it done. I promise."

I checked my watch. Still 9:03. *Why do I bother?* "Okay, five hours, but it's got to be done right and on-time. Work with Lou so she can get the control software installed as soon as your work is complete for a test run this evening."

"Got it." He nodded too many times. "So, Lou, will you be working up here?"

"Until you give me the go-ahead to come downstairs and do the software installation."

More head nodding. "Okay, well, I'll call in that extra crew and get to work ASAP." He ran down the hall and took the stairs.

Lou looked at me. "I guess the elevator is on the fritz again."

Soson walked up with an armful of bags, struggling for breath. "I did not know your preferences, so I ordered a few choices." He paused to inhale and exhale a few times. "Burger. Chicken. Pork. A veggie sandwich for you, my dear." Soson handed Lou a bag marked "V." He dawdled in the doorway. "I would like to join you for lunch, but there is no room here, and I do not expect you are taking any breaks."

I opened the bag labeled "C" and sniffed. "Smells like barbeque chicken."

"I love the food at Backyard Pit. And I get frequent buyer points. I am pleased you made your breakthrough so quickly." Soson's breathing returned to normal. "What is your confidence level?"

I glanced at Lou, who had ripped open the brown bag and used it as a paper tray for her sandwich. I did the same and unwrapped mine. "You know how these

343

things go."

"That I do." He focused on Lou. "After five years of computations using CHUQ, Randall ran his first heavy ion test. No impacts. None."

Lou stared at me. "Why did you wait so long?"

"I didn't want to waste time on the accelerator." I was the butt of jokes until three years later. With a revised set of formulas, my next test showed I was on the right track. "No time to do the math, so it's a crap shoot." I'd already seen the successful results, the incident with my medal. I wasn't stupid enough to tell Soson about my recent CHUQ verification nor cavalier enough to jump into the chrontin beam untested with my son's life at stake.

"We work well as a team." Lou held out her fist for a bump. I complied. "Randy and I have complimentary skills."

"Yes, I need coffee and Lou gets it for me."

She scowled. Didn't she understand I was protecting her?

"How about your documentation?" Soson checked both of us for a response.

As expected, he wanted to ensure the Russians got our detailed work product. "I'll put everything together in a nice bundle for Anatoly." *Like hell I will.*

"Oh no, it is going directly to his sponsor, the oligarch who struggles to fund him. Stupid sanctions. Anatoly told me in the utmost privacy that you both will be receiving bonuses once the financial shackles are off. How do you like that? But please do not let on that you know."

"In dollars or rubles?" I smiled. "Just kidding. It's

very generous of the oligarch or whoever." Lou had finished her sandwich. "Listen, I'd love to chat, but I have things to do to prepare."

"I could not be happier. Two of my favorite people, collaborators on an Earth-shattering breakthrough."

That's exactly what I was scared of: Russians shattering Earth's future by modifying the past. "Zach Stanton was already here. I apologize, but I asked him to bring in a second team, so the work can be completed before our deadline." I had no issue spending Labs funds to save my son's life.

"*Sovershenno nikakikh problem*. No problem."

Lou stood and threw her trash in the garbage. "How much lead time do you need to schedule the accelerator for our test run?"

"Thirty minutes. I will not leave my office this evening. Felicia will just have to understand."

The next victim in Soson's sequential search for feminine companionship.

Soson turned and spoke over his shoulder. "By the way, you must use the stairs. The elevator is out of commission. Again." Soson took his dinner bag with him and walked down the hall towards the staircase.

Lou stood with fists at her waist. "I fetch coffee?"

"After I'm gone, I don't want you to be the oligarch's next target. Let Soson believe that this is all my work, for your own safety."

Lou's arms dropped to her sides. "Oh. Thanks, I guess."

I finished my sandwich and squirmed in my chair. "I can't sit here for five hours. I'll go nuts. Besides, there are things I need for my leap. Is it okay to leave you here? I promise I'll be back in time." *Why do I keep saying that? Haven't I learned my lesson?*

Lou wiped her mouth with a napkin. "I've got this. I'll measure the energy from a known batch of new particles and get the electromagnets to vary only within a close range."

"You may have to try a couple of different settings to get their polarities to switch."

"No sweat. I excel at trial and error."

I'd seen and heard. I jogged down the stairs to the main floor. The same man with a flattop and dirty knuckles sat in a padded chair in the lobby reading the same glossy-covered Hot Rod magazine.

Instead of using the main door, I exited through the tunnel and ran outside. As expected, his black Chevy Blazer was parked a few spaces down.

How could I disable his vehicle so he couldn't follow me? I didn't have anything sharp enough to stab his tires. My feet kicked gravel. Inspired, I picked up two tiny pebbles and crept to the close side of his vehicle. I placed the pebbles inside the tire valve stem caps, replaced them, and listened for faint hisses of air escaping. Then I stood up, giving him an opportunity to see me outside.

I saw him run toward the exit, only to be stopped by security. I got into the Beetle and gunned it, out of the parking lot and down the access road. Somewhere along the highway, his tires would go flat.

Without an escort, I had enough time to gather a few things and say some goodbyes.

During my drive up to Schaumburg, I was

tempted to concentrate on my list of things for 2011 Randy to do, until the Beetle drifted into the adjacent lane. I course corrected and kept my attention on the road. It would be a disaster to get into an accident now and screw up the plan.

When I got to CJ's, I backed up to the garage and flattened the rear seat. Four new tires had been stacked at the front of the service bay. I imagined putting them on the Beetle after my jump back to 2011, since the ones on the car would be shredded. *Damn, they're not mounted.* The time vortex left bare steel wheels. I scrounged around the garage but didn't find any that fit. Why was this so difficult? I'd have to buy new wheels and have the tires mounted. With judicious placement, the bare tires fit inside the Beetle. I covered them with a plaid wool stadium blanket I found wadded in the corner of the trunk.

On my way into the office, I dropped nine hundred dollars of Hamza's handouts into the shoebox, to pay CJ for what I took. If I was successful, Hamza would never get his hands on the Powerball winning numbers. But I had them!

Before I could contemplate how I might use the money to help others, CJ crept down from the second floor one step at a time, hanging onto the railing with both hands.

I waited until he completed the descent before speaking. "I wanted to let you know, I'm leaving. I appreciate you putting me up this week."

CJ's gaze was off somewhere in the distance. "You just got here. You patch things up with the wife?"

"Something like that."

He faced me with a hint of a smile. "Hate to think my cookin' drove you away."

Did his eyes twinkle? "You did fine." No need to hurt his feelings.

He pointed up the staircase. "You want any of your things from Mickey's room?"

"Yes, my clothes." To avoiding unnecessary ripple effects, I'd decided to wear the outfit I arrived in from 2011 to limit the number of modified variables.

Upstairs, I dressed in the 2011 grease-stained shirt and pants and left my Target outfits on the bed. I returned to the main floor and put the spare key back in the cash register. CJ sat in his recliner, staring at a black TV screen. "I'm going now."

He spoke without turning his head. "Need anything for the road? Maybe a sandwich?"

"No, thanks. Everything I need is waiting for me." My pregnant wife, my house, and my project to kill cancerous tumors.

"Have a nice life. Stop by and see me any time." He struggled to his feet and hobbled toward the door. "Sorry to see my lucky charm go." He shook the shoebox containing customer payments. "Did you see this? Hundred-dollar bills! Haven't had sales like that 'til you showed up!"

I patted his back as if touching a blown glass figurine. "People out there care about you. Don't forget that. And I'll stop by as often as I can." I opened the door. "Is it okay if I take the Beetle?"

"The car out back?" CJ followed me outside. "Sure. Thing's been sittin' in the corner of the property for nigh onto a decade. No use to me." He rubbed his bald head.

"Guess you're not takin' me up on my offer for the station."

It slipped my mind that he'd asked me to take over. "No, I'm afraid not. But I agree you should sell and move to Atlanta."

"I will if I can figure out how to do that. Way too complicated."

"I'll send someone by to help, if that's okay." I could ask Lou to visit him after my leap, but if I was successful, all of this would change anyway, for the better.

"Any friend of Sy or Randy Weinberg is a friend of mine."

I gave CJ an awkward hug in which he didn't participate, got into the Beetle, and drove off. He waved, his reflection in the rearview mirror shrinking. With Lou's help and some of the lottery money, the quality of CJ's life would improve after my leap.

I wanted to stop at Starbucks so I could bid the employees goodbye, even if I didn't say the words. They had become familiar faces that provided friendly service and a place where I could shut out some of the distractions. With wheel-less tires, however, there wasn't time.

Stops at Pep Boys, Just Tires and Tire Discount World all yielded the same result: thousands of tires in stock and not a wheel to be found. *Shit!* Could I mount my new tires on the old wheels in ChiLabs' parking lot? I learned how in my car maintenance class but hadn't done it for years. Certainly not without the right equipment, and CJ didn't have the machine, or I hadn't seen it. A web search came up with a manual tire changer available at Harbor Freight, and it was only $40.

I drove to their closest store, the radio as my companion. Someone left it tuned to news, weather, and sports, which was fine for my purposes of ambient noise. Evidently, President Hillary Clinton had authorized another round of sanctions on Russian energy companies and their executives, and the affected individuals had issued a press release condemning her behavior. Soson had mentioned that as one of the reasons he hated her so much.

As a favor after I bought the device, one of the Harbor Freight guys assembled the unit. I added an air foot-pump for another twelve dollars. I wedged both purchases alongside the tires in the back of the Beetle. Now I needed to tell Lou to adjust my target arrival time to allow for mounting the replacement tires on the existing wheels. The thought of doing that work in ChiLab's parking lot in the middle of a snowstorm exhausted me. What choice did I have?

At ChiLabs three hours later, the black Chevy Blazer was gone. A call to Lou got me into the building via the access tunnel. I brought the 2019 *Daily Herald* with me. *I'll need it when I leap.* The hike up four flights of stairs wasn't as bad as the ascent to Hamza's office. Boy, I was glad he was busy, planning for the disappearance of himself and my family. That plus his retirement would keep him out of our way.

Lou had traded her phone for a thin laptop. "Welcome back. I've coded the monitoring program and ran it in a test environment, as if connected to the sensors and electromagnets. Fixed a couple of bugs but now it's perfect."

I never trusted programmers who said their code was bulletproof. "As long as it works."

"Aren't you still worried about consequences?" Lou looked me up and down and frowned. "You know, disturbing the timeline?"

She must have noticed my oil-stained 2011 outfit. "The moment I decided to save Craig and Faith from harm by leaping back, I told myself, 'Screw the consequences'." I rubbed my hands as if washing them in a sink. "What I'm worried about is getting it right."

"You're going to let 2011 Randy leap and take his place with Faith, right, like I suggested?"

"I thought about that all night. I even dreamt about it. It was a creative idea, but there's a major downside. It leaves Hamza and Soson with time travel technology. They'll just threaten 2011 Randy, who'll reinvent reverse time travel to save his family. That's an infinite loop."

"You're right." She shook her head. "So silly."

"No, it's healthy to consider alternatives. This situation needs to end with one last leap back and no leaps forward, no matter how many times I've done this before." Had I accepted Hamza's interpretation of events? "This one will make at least twice, which makes me wonder why I failed the last time." I shook my head to clear it. "My concern now is being so compelling that 2011 Randy changes his behavior and prevents Hamza's meddling."

"Which means 2011 Randy won't leap. No Russians. No threats."

"Exactly! I plan to draft critical instructions for 2011 Randy while the electromagnets are fitted."

"I can't test my work until the maintenance guys are done. Let's talk through this. What will you tell your other self?'

I grabbed a legal pad and picked up a pen.

"Why don't you make a note on your phone, like you've been doing? Besides, you won't lose your phone like you might a piece of paper."

If I'd made multiple time leaps like Hamza claimed, maybe that's why I previously failed. "Okay." I pulled out my phone and created a new note. "At the top of the list, 2011 Randy needs to get to work before Hamza makes any changes. That'll mean he won't be able to take Faith to the hospital."

"Can someone else do that?"

That answer took no thought. "Yes. Patrice, our next-door neighbor. Faith wants her there anyway. In 2011, I called Patrice from the hospital and asked her to help Faith get through the delivery process." I pictured walking out on Faith again, this time before we left for the hospital. "In the short term, Faith will be pissed that I'm not taking her, but that'll ensure I show up for the delivery. A small price to pay. I'm adding 'Call Patrice and have her drive Faith to the hospital' to the list."

"You said you saw the 2019 newspaper in 2011 but threw it out?"

"I didn't look at the paper. It was just *a* paper. The bathroom bulb was burned out. 'Replace bathroom bulb.' And the paper was folded. Note to self, 'Open the paper up.' And 'Circle the publication date.'"

"Good. That will call attention to it. So that's it,

right? 2011 Randy will accept your advice and prevent Hamza from modifying controller settings, so he won't leap. Done and done."

"Maybe not. There's a lot more he has to do to make things right."

"What did I miss?"

There were things 2011 Randy would have to tell the 2011 version of Lou, but it couldn't hurt to tell the one at my side. "I'm going to have 2011 Randy give you the 2019 lottery numbers so you'll win one hundred nineteen million dollars."

"What?" Lou slid to the edge of her chair. "Are you kidding?"

"I'm serious. First, Hamza doesn't deserve it. Second and more important, by demanding that you destroy all of our notes about what we've done here, I'm denying your fame and fortune. The least I can do is give you some monetary compensation." I hoped that going back to 2011 didn't change the lottery results.

"Some?" Lou's eyes glazed over. "One—one hundred and nineteen million?" She looked like she was going to faint. I rubbed her wrists. "Stay with me here. It won't all be yours."

Her head snapped up. "What?"

"Five million off the top after taxes goes to my father's friend CJ. He's old, has dementia and deserves to spend the rest of his life in comfort. You—the 2011 version of you—needs to be instructed to find a senior community facility in Atlanta near his sister's house and move him down there. Oh, and sell his gas station. The property is worth something."

Lou wasn't focused on my words. It didn't matter

if this Lou understood, as long as 2011 Randy accurately conveyed the message to 2011 Lou.

Lou looked up, fresh from shock. "I was only twenty-two in 2011. I couldn't have handled a thousand dollars, let alone millions."

"The winning numbers will be picked two days ago, in 2019." I cringed at the mixed temporal reference. "You're so much more mature now."

Lou nodded. "I'll make sure CJ is cared for. Or at least, my 2011 self will." She scratched her head. "You know, this is complicated. You can't write it all in marker on the front page of the paper and expect 2011 Randy to blindly accept and follow your directions. Heck, he'll think it's a prank and toss the paper like you did the first time."

"He can't do that!"

"But he might. Is there some fact only you would know that you can add as a signature so he knows the messages are legit?"

It took only a nanosecond to come up with the perfect item. "Yep. Something we'll never forget." The only question I got wrong on my first college physics final had plagued me ever since. I knew how to compute the answer, but I blanked and never forgave myself.

Lou held up the newspaper. "Are you sure everything will fit?"

"I'll write small." I was quickly losing confidence that I'd be able to communicate everything necessary in writing. If I missed one critical item, the whole plan would fall apart. I had to be sure not to let that happen.

"And you're confident that 2011 Randy will have the patience to read a novel in the wee hours of the morning?"

I shook my head. "I'll have to come up with something else. Maybe I'll call him."

"You can't let him know you're there, right?"

What might 2011 Randy do if he knew another instance of him had arrived from the past or the future? "If he was *me*, I'd be curious as hell. I'd want to meet my other self and have a conversation." Two versions of the same person together could be as volatile as matter and anti-matter.

Our conversation was interrupted by a visit from Zach Stanton, who grabbed the doorframe before his momentum carried him into my lap. "So, we got it done."

"You didn't have to run up." Lou stood. "You could have called."

Zach blushed. "I didn't have the number."

"No matter." Lou snapped the laptop closed and put it on her chair. "Wait in the hall and we'll walk down together."

His face flushed as he backed away.

Lou stepped over to the controllers, pulled out her phone, and tapped away furiously. "Okay, I've used my calibration formula to compute the settings for sending the medal back to last Wednesday morning. Good?"

I nodded.

She checked her watch and adjusted the knobs. "There, now chrontins will be generated for the proper jump length forty-five minutes from now, at six. Hopefully, in the right time direction."

I put my hand on the desk phone receiver but didn't pick it up. "I'll call Soson and let him know we need an accelerator test slot at that time."

"He told us thirty minutes minimum, so there shouldn't be an issue. I've got to create a batch of fresh particles with the proper polarity anyway." Lou tucked her laptop under one arm.

I reached out my hand containing the Nobel Prize medal. "Don't forget this for the target mound."

"I know where to place it. During my calibration testing, I sunk a marker into the grass where the chrontins come up."

The same place I'd parked Faith's SUV.

Lou stroked the box as if it was her pet. "Someone is going to find this?"

"The grounds crew will, because they already did nine days ago," I enjoyed speaking about time in an odd way.

She lifted the lid. "This is pretty, and valuable. Are you sure you want to send this into the past? If something goes wrong, we won't be able to retrieve it."

"Trust me." I pulled my chair close to my desk to give Lou room to squeeze by. "It'll make it."

Lou closed the box. "Okay, let's do this." She left our office and accompanied Zach down the hall.

[27] Friday, April 19, 2019 (continued)

As soon as Lou left, I called Soson and told him I needed the accelerator for our first test at six. He agreed to notify operations they'd be cancelling the next scheduled experiment for priority work. Ours.

Rather than pace the length of my office, raising my anxiety about things that could go wrong, an infinite number, the available time allowed me to satisfy my natural curiosity and search online for things I had missed, in addition to the first eight years of Craig's life.

A wide range of events and changes in society surprised me: legalization of same sex marriage, explosion of social media platforms like Instagram, Facebook, and Snapchat.

Technology had made significant advances in the interim. Solid-state storage was commonplace, not only in thumb drives but in laptops and desktops as well. Although I hadn't noticed at the time, I was fairly certain Soson's Tesla didn't have a CD player. NASA had been successful in landing a robotic vehicle named Rover on Mars.

Four months after I jumped, Osama bin Laden had been brought to justice for an attack inside the US on 9/11 in 2001. The fabric of society seemed to have been torn by mass school shootings and violent disruption of events, including a bombing at the Boston Marathon. Maybe that's why the security was so strict at ChiLabs and Craig's school.

In 2016, by a slim margin, the American people had elected Hillary Clinton for President over Donald Trump, a reality television celebrity. I couldn't comprehend why the Republican Party had even nominated him to run. Evidently he lost because it was discovered that Russian hackers had penetrated social media for his benefit. I had trouble picturing Bill as First Gentleman.

Related to my own field, the CERN Large Hadron Collider had identified a Higgs boson a year after I'd leapt. That would have felt like a bigger deal except *my* experiment had generated chrontins. Speaking of accelerators, engineering breakthroughs promised smaller and cheaper ones for potentially one-tenth the cost.

Enough nostalgia. I turned my attention to the pre-jump task list for my trip. I had already gathered replacement tires from CJ's and the front page of today's issue of the *Daily Herald*. I still hadn't decided what message I would leave for 2011 Randy, so I grabbed a marker from the whiteboard tray and stuck it in my pocket.

Lou walked in just before 6:00. "The source particles have been generated. Looking good."

"Thanks." I brought up the linear accelerator user interface on my computer screen. My project was first in queue, to be run using the alternative target area. "It's time." I clicked the button labeled CONFIRM. Lou hung over my shoulder.

For me, this was a familiar process. Lou, as an analyst, might not have been present during a linear accelerator test before.

The customized proton stream came up to speed. A special interface element, added for my unique hardware configuration, showed the status of the plasma frame. The laser also showed operational. Because particles can accumulate on the inner surface and create friction with the accelerated stream, ChiLabs had installed lasers in all linear accelerator tubes to clean debris. Hamza had changed the settings so my laser aimed straight down the tube.

Lou's eyes were fixed on the real-time status changes. "They've reached impact velocity."

The evidence of the collision was a scrolling list of messages generated by the particle detectors, followed by a message "EXPERIMENT CONCLUDED."

"I'm going outside to check the mound." Lou ran from the office.

I knew what she'd find. The medal would be gone.

She reappeared eight minutes later, breathing hard. "It vanished."

"Just as expected. Except we'll tell Soson our test object didn't move."

She pointed at my desk. "Wait. What's that?"

The box with my Nobel Prize medal sat between my monitors, just where I placed it after Hamza gave it to me. I held it up in one hand. "The test worked."

Lou snatched the box and shook it. "But why is it here? Didn't we send it back?"

I'd hoped Lou would figure out the sequence of events. "When the medal was found Wednesday morning by the lawn crew, it was delivered to Hamza, who gave it to me yesterday. I brought it here and placed it on my desk between the monitors. Since those events have already happened in this timeline, it's right where it should be." I tried not to show my surprise at the first time travel I'd seen, apart from my own.

"Weird! What's going to happen to *you*?"

"My time travel and this one both delivered their subjects to their original physical location, the mound outside. My Beetle should show up there as well." I stood. "It's my turn. Adjust the settings."

She scooted past me and stood at the rack of controllers. "What date do you want to go back to?"

I added up the time needed to prepare and mount replacement tires, drive home, leave the newspaper, call Soson and get back to the Labs. Faith had woken me at just past four, by which time I had to be done and out of the house. "Midnight should give me enough time. To be precise, Sunday, January 23rd at midnight, so my first full day back is Monday, January 24, 2011." *Craig's birth day.*

"Got it." She made a note on her phone. "It'll take about half an hour to generate more source particles."

"That matches well with Soson's lead time."

"Okay, so I'll compute the settings based on a departure time of ..." She checked her watch. "... 7:00 p.m. on the nose. You and your Beetle should arrive on the target mound in 2011 at midnight." Lou tapped at her phone and then turned dials on the controllers.

"Great." I wiped damp palms on my pants. Despite my growing confidence in Lou, mistakes happen. This had to work.

Lou pulled up the folding chair and sat. "After you and the Beetle leap, what's going to happen to the car?"

"You mean after I drive home, leave the 2011 Randy my warning, and then return to the Labs?" She didn't need to know about my intended stop at CJ's if there was time. "I can't just leave it in the parking lot,

360

can I?" I looked up the phone number for emergency automotive services near my old house. Northwest Towing, a Schaumburg company, had been in business for three decades. "I'll have a company tow it to CJ's, where I found it." I put their number into my phone and made sure the wad of bills was still in my pocket. "Thanks for raising the issue."

I called Soson and told him we'd need another accelerator test run at 7:00 p.m. sharp. "For what purpose? You have everything figured out, yes? I have a packed bag and am prepared to depart."

"You're not going anywhere. The test failed." I toyed with the Nobel Prize medal box. "But I think I've found the problem. I made a bad calculation. Another test, and then maybe we'll know." I wanted Soson to feel responsible for the phony failure, one that delayed his plans for time travel. "If only we had used CHUQ to verify the supporting equations instead of doing them by hand."

"You and your mathematics. Always showing off."

How little Soson understood about physics. *It's all math.* "Tell your Russian colleague or the oligarch or whoever that I should have reverse time travel figured out by his deadline. No killing necessary."

"Oh." Soson paused. "Yes, of course."

If Soson could lie about his relationship to Hamza, then I could mislead him with a clear conscience. "After this confirming test, I'll provide the equations and equipment settings in a complete report. But please warn your buddies that my solution was specifically designed to work on the equipment here at ChiLabs. It

361

could fail miserably on any other linear accelerator, and I won't take responsibility."

"They will not accept that. You could give them a false solution that way."

"Who knows what kinds of equipment they use? A successful test here will have to be good enough. If they're smart, they'll be able to apply the concepts anywhere." They'd failed to recreate Hamza's work.

"*Da.* I am curious. What are you trying to send backwards?"

I grabbed a bound set of bimonthly journals from my bookcase. "*Advances in Physics* Volume 59."

Soson's voice boomed. "How appropriate. *Then* I will depart."

"Fine by me. After you leap, I'm going away for a long vacation, alone. I think I deserve it. Faith doesn't want to ever see me again. Craig hates me. Even you don't want me around. I'm an unfortunate version of someone you used to like."

"You are wrong, *malchik*. I *never* liked you."

He hadn't said it in his joking tone. In my time leap forward, I'd learned to hate *him*.

"And you will provide complete documentation before I depart?"

"Yep. I've got it all in my phone." I winked. "Lou was pleasant company, but I figured this out on my own."

"Randall, the solo scientist. My colleagues will appreciate receiving your documentation."

Damn right, because if I failed, eventually the Russians would target him. And I thought Hamza was self-serving. "Answer one question for me. I've never known you to be a risk-taker. Why would you volunteer? Even after one successful test, things could go catastrophically wrong."

"Like you had a mission to kill Hamza, for which you failed, I too have a mission. Fortunately for me, it is political, not technical. I will succeed." The call ended.

Given how Soson felt about Hillary Clinton and her sanctions on his Russian colleagues, I had a good guess as to his mission. He planned to change the election outcome.

Lou shook her head. "In seven years, I never saw this side of Soson."

My heart ached at a destroyed relationship. "Neither did I, for as long as we worked together." I held up my phone containing all of my notes before putting it in my pocket. "I'm taking this with me. Russians in 2011 won't be looking for me."

"I heard you lie about my involvement. Now I understand what you said about fetching coffee. Thank you for trying to keep me safe." Lou squirmed as she leaned on my bookcase. "Are you sure you've thought of everything?"

Her uncertainty was well-founded since I forgot about dealing with the Beetle. "*Now* I have. Only one chance to do this correctly." The warning echoed in my head, as if I'd been cautioned before. "I'll make sure it works." *This time?*

Just like at home, I patted my pants to make sure I hadn't left anything important on Mickey's dresser. "Wallet. Keys. Phone with my notes, which I'm taking. My old 2011 phone. Marker." I checked inside and waved the Starbucks receipt. "Lottery numbers." The wad of bills from Hamza was still in my pocket. I picked up the *Daily Herald* and put it under my arm. "For my message to get 2011 Randy to change his behavior."

"Sorry, but it still bugs me that Hamza had a copy of that 2019 newspaper. Have you figured out how that happened?"

"No. *I* don't remember doing it. Traveling back in time at least once, was that what Hamza said? I may already be in an event loop."

"You *have* done this before?" For the first time, Lou looked terrified.

"Hamza thinks so. But it doesn't matter how many times I've leapt forward or gone back." *Assuming my previous attempts failed.* I pulled out my phone and to see the pictures I took at school. "Craig will learn to love me as his father, just like Faith loved me as her husband. And they'll be safe."

Before I could leave the office, Lou asked, "If you're jumping back into January, won't you be cold in short sleeves?"

"Oh yeah." I reached behind her and took my parka off a bent nail that acted as a coat hook. "Thanks. I don't expect I will enjoy changing four shredded tires without this." I considered what else I might correct on this leap. "You said your father was diagnosed with cancer a few years ago?"

Lou stood at the controllers, entering the settings for my jump. "Yes. He was diagnosed in 2016."

"Before we met, you already knew of my cancer work, right?"

She nodded as she tapped on her phone.

364

"If I can, I'll try to have 2011 Randy give you a head's up about annual cancer screenings." I'll leave the same instruction with 2011 Randy regarding Faith.

She remained focused on her work. "Something else to cram into your message?"

"Sure, why not? Seriously, early detection cases have a better chance. Even if I can't add that to the list, at the first sign, bring your father to me. He'll be one of my first human trials."

Lou looked at me as if I'd asked a riddle. "You understand, the 2011 version of me won't know to do that."

"Yeah, right." I shook her hand. "Do you realize if I'm successful, this will never have happened?"

"And if it doesn't work, I'll be standing here, wondering what to tell Soson when he asks how soon he can leap."

"That's easy. No matter what happens to me, if Soson asks for the details of my work, profess ignorance. Tell him 'Randy wanted to do everything himself.' He won't question that answer because that's what he'd expect, and I reinforced it earlier."

"And your phone? The one with all of the details that won't be here?"

"Act surprised. 'Darn, Randy must have taken it with him.' Just like in 2011, he won't find me." I stepped out of my office and then turned around. "Just to be safe, immediately after I disappear, go directly to Zach Stanton and have his teams disassemble the electromagnets from the duoplasmatron and put them back in storage, like they'd never been used."

"Got it." Her eyebrows furrowed, and her lips spread into a broad frown. "How can you be *so sure* the 2011 version of you will understand and follow your directions?"

"Because he thinks and acts like me. Hell, he *is* me. He'll execute on *my* orders because he wants the same outcome as I do."

"If you say so." She took one step and opened her arms. "Nice working with you. It's been an honor."

"The honor was mine." I held a colleague who had contributed to our mutual success in a loose hug. "A piece of advice. Don't settle. You've got a great career ahead of you." Of course, if I was successful, that message would be more appropriate for the 2011 version of Lou.

She backed out of the embrace. "Just stay inside the car. Safe leaping."

I wouldn't want to be out in a time vortex without protection. "Is there any other kind?"

I ran down the stairs and stuck my head out on the first floor for one last look at the 2019 version of the lobby, and to make sure the flattop spy hadn't returned. No sign of him. Adrenaline made all of my senses sharper. The motors in the animated signs whirred like lawnmowers as the panels changed. Splashes of fish in the pond sounded like ocean waves. I escaped through the tunnel to avoid the security guard.

When I got to my Beetle, I shoved my parka into the passenger seat and drove it onto the mound, putting the car directly above Lou's marker.

The tires would be shredded, like last time. That was the reason for the four replacements jammed into the back. I hoped the time shift would be kind to the structure of the vehicle. The scratched paint indicated that it had been through time jumps already. Would it survive another one?

I pulled my 2019 phone containing all my notes and reminders from my pocket. My index finger instinctively reached out and tapped photos. I flipped through shots I took of Craig on the playground. Even a stranger would be able to tell he was a combination of Faith and me. My hair color and eyes. Her nose and chin. *I'm doing this for you, son. You and your mother.*

I decided to call Lou before the clock struck seven, just to let her know I was in position. From the access road, a car with its headlights set to bright entered the lot. Even with illumination from only a few light poles, the Bentley Continental was obvious by its design. It was the same make, model, and color as the one I saw parked in front of Faith's condo. *Hamza? Shit!*

He parked in his space, got out and glanced at my car on top of the mound. For a moment, I thought he might rush the car and drag me out. I made sure the doors were locked and held my breath. Instead, he ran toward the building.

I called Lou's cell. *Please answer.*

"That was quick. What did you forget?"

"Hamza just showed up. I don't know if he'll head for Soson's office, the accelerator, or my office."

"What should I do?"

"There's a lock on my office door. If he can't get in, he can't interfere with the settings. Soson is on the eighth floor. I've got to call him. Bye."

A call to Soson took one tap.

"Is there a problem, *tovarish?*"

The revolving door slowed to a stop. "Hamza is in the building. He may be headed either to your office or the accelerator."

"I will not be able to walk down eight floors in the time it takes for him to get to the basement. I will call security and have him intercepted."

"Lou is locked in my office. Please, don't let him interfere."

"I will not!" He hung up.

The clock in the Beetle read six fifty-five. All we had to do was thwart Hamza's attempts to interfere for five minutes and I'd be gone. My leg bounced in anticipation, urging the minute hand forward, but with no success. Would Hamza try to break into my office? *Lou must be terrified.* I prayed for Hamza's apprehension.

At six fifty-nine, I breathed a sigh of relief. Two men in uniform escorted Hamza out the front door. He took only a microsecond pause before he ran straight towards the Beetle. The clock read precisely seven. Nothing.

What's happening? Why the delay?

Hamza scurried down the steps. I put my fingers on the key, still in the ignition. I couldn't allow him to stop me. The welcome sweet smell of burnt vegetables appeared at the same time as the plastic steering wheel chilled. I pulled my parka over my body, anticipating the cold. Familiar dust rose from the footwell. The speckled fog erupted in front of me, blowing Hamza off course. He lost his balance and tripped over the curb.

Counterclockwise winds blew particles in a cone-shaped vortex, my path home. When cricket noises started, I hastily plugged my ears. My skin itched. Soon, the front hood was no longer visible. I closed my eyes, held my breath, and welcomed myself to 2011.

Day -1

[28] Sunday, January 23, 2011

The venue was familiar, the main auditorium at ChiLabs. I stood facing a room filled to capacity. Behind me, a whiteboard as large as the stage was set up to be my canvas. Marker in hand, I turned my back to the audience and transcribed the derivation of my formulas, based on universally accepted string theory and quantum mechanics principles. When successful, energized protons would pass through the human body without causing damage but would attack tumorous cancer cells using a kind of self-guiding radar. I must have been holding my breath as I wrote because I needed a series of quick inhales to remain alert and on my feet. When I turned to the audience, there was no reaction. People sat silent with frozen stares. I smelled shredded rubber.

I opened my eyes. My Beetle was parked on the target mound at ChiLabs, snowflakes dancing in the wind, scattered lights illuminating the empty parking lot. I felt a chill permeate the cabin. Shit, I was naked! My clothes, both of my phones, and my parka, all missing. So was my money, hundreds of dollars. *My clothes hadn't vanished when I leapt forward.* The keys dangled from the ignition and the 2019 *Daily Herald* lay on the passenger seat. I groped for the blanket in back. The tires and mounting tool were gone as well. *What the hell?*

I wrapped the blanket around my body as I got out. The Beetle's tires had been shredded into rubber ribbons, as expected. The paint job now sported a pattern of intersecting scratches. I danced from foot to foot as I examined the useless car. With a deadline to get to my house before 2011 Randy woke up, I was screwed.

My feet tingled on frosty grass as I ran down the hill. Then across the pavement and up the steps to the front door of ChiLabs. *Locked!* I couldn't see anyone in the lobby. *Shit!* Is this how things end? I die of frostbite, unable to prevent 2011 Randy from getting thrown into 2019? So much for reverse time travel. I leaned my back against the glass wall. My fingers fumbled with the blanket as they became numb.

Someone tapped from inside. I spun around. Murray, the night shift custodian.

His speech fogged the glass. "Hey, Doctor Weinberg. We're closed. Why are you naked?"

"Murray! Can you let me in?"

He mumbled something I couldn't hear and then fumbled through his keys, hanging from a retractable cord attached to his belt.

As soon as he unlocked the door, I bolted inside. "You're a lifesaver."

He scratched his head, his fingers tilting his ball cap. "What happened to you?"

"I was mugged. They took everything. You wouldn't happen to have some clothes in your locker, would you?"

"Lemme see." His eyes wandered. "We got some stuff in lost and found, and I got an old pair of overalls I can borrow you."

"Great. Anything."

Murray led me to a tall cylindrical bin in a first-floor utility closet. While he went to fetch the overalls, I plucked a man's shirt, a pair of gloves, and some leather moccasin house slippers from the bin. When Murray handed me the denim overalls, I took everything into the bathroom and got dressed. I hung the blanket around my neck. At least I wasn't naked.

Even with a broken plan, I knew how to get to Schaumburg and home. I'd planned on using Northwest Towing Service to take CJ's Beetle back to his garage, once my errands were complete. *Why not now?*

I pulled up Hannah's chair at her familiar reception desk, a simple metal one. After I got Northwest's number from directory assistance, I called. The clock on Hannah's desk said 11:52 PM. I'd have to commend Lou on the effectiveness and accuracy of her algorithm, except the Lou I would meet today hadn't invented that yet. *And maybe never will.* Past, present, and future blended together like a Starbucks Frappuccino.

A gruff male voice answered. "Northwest. Where's your vehicle?"

I gave him ChiLabs' address. "Can you get someone here immediately?"

"That's outside our service area. I can give you the name of somebody who's closer."

I didn't need an argument. "My car needs to be towed to Schaumburg, so your company is perfect."

"What's wrong with the vehicle?" I heard pages flipping. "Dazzo's Auto Repair and Towing is less than two miles from—"

"Four flat tires. I just need it to be dropped off at—" I gave him the address of CJ's garage. Where else should the Beetle be?

"Mister, all of my trucks are already on the streets. You know that snow we got is just a tease, don't you? The real thing is coming fast."

"I know the weather is about to get much worse. *That's* why I need to get my car to Schaumburg as fast as possible. Humor me. What'll you charge for what I just requested?"

"Assuming I can find somebody who's available." He hummed for a second. "Two twenty-five. Fifty bucks base fee, seventy-five hook-up fee, and four bucks a mile times twenty-five miles, one way."

I was penniless "I tell you what. I'll pay the driver *twice* that if I can ride along in the cab. And a bonus for a lift home afterwards. It's in the same town as the address I gave you."

"That won't make a truck appear out of thin air."

"Three times your rate. Rounded up to seven hundred and fifty dollars."

His voice lost the rough edge. "Are you serious? Sure, if you want to waste your money." He repeated ChiLabs' address.

"Right. It's a yellow VW Beetle."

"Make, model and color don't change the price. You want texts for driver status?"

"Don't bother." They'd be useless without a phone.

"I'll be there ASAP. Thanks for the business." He hung up.

Maybe I should have offered him more, just to be sure.

My stomach complained. I spun in Hannah's chair and looked around for something to eat. Whenever I passed by, she was always munching—cookies, popcorn, or nuts. On the bottom shelf of her side bookcase behind knitting needles holding a sweater-in-progress, I found an unopened box of Girl Scout Thin Mints. *She'll have to forgive me.* I broke open one of the two cellophane tubes inside and helped myself to a couple, and then a few more. Before I knew it, I'd eaten all of them.

As Murray walked by, I put the half-empty box away. Without my security badge, I needed his assistance. "Murray, can you let me into my office?"

"Sure thing, Dr. Weinberg."

We took the elevator up to the fourth floor. Murray let me in.

It was just like I had left it on Friday. A half-completed formula on the whiteboard. The controller settings perfect, just as I'd left them. A stack of open physics journals I reviewed at the last minute stacked on the corner of my desk.

While I waited for the tow truck, I dialed my parents' number down in Florida. I needed to hear their voices, even at the cost of waking them. No answer. Florida was one hour later, but my folks should have been home. I hoped nothing had happened to them.

About forty-five minutes after my call to Northwest, I returned to the lobby and sat in Hannah's

375

chair. A tow truck with a row of flashing yellow lights above the cab pulled into the lot ten minutes later. I ran out of the building and waved them over, although they should have recognized my car from the description I'd given the dispatcher. They parked with the back of the truck facing the base of the mound.

The driver of the truck came over. "Weinberg? I'm the guy you spoke with. Can you confirm the destination?" He held out a work order on a clipboard.

It was CJ's address. "That's right."

He looked me up and down for a few moments, taking in my overalls, slippers, and the blanket over my shoulders. "You know, Halloween was two months ago." He squinted, snowflakes in his face. "All the way to Schaumburg?"

"Yes, I'm dropping it off for a friend."

I hoped my strange outfit wasn't cause for him to renege on the lucrative job. Given how badly my plan was messed up, I didn't have time to waste. "Just take it to the address I specified."

"You said seven fifty, right?" He wiped his runny nose on his sleeve.

"Yes, with a bonus. If you take me home afterwards, there's an extra fifty bucks in it for you. It isn't far."

"I'll see, depending on my backlog when we get there. Payment due up front."

"Put through a charge for eight-hundred even." I recited my credit card number, expiration date, and PIN from memory. "It's good, I swear. I left my wallet in my other pants."

"I should've said cash when we talked earlier." With his lips in a sneer, he put my information into his phone and pulled a business card from his thermal bib overalls. "You need something, any time, any place, you call Northwest." He wrote me a receipt. For two hundred and twenty-five dollars.

He clomped up the hill and stared at the tires. "Good thing you told me about the flats, or I wouldn't have brought wheel dollies." It required two trips to his truck, but he brought four curved metal plates with wheels to the Beetle. I watched in awe as he placed one under each bare hub and jacked them up until the Beetle could be rolled. He pushed from behind while I walked alongside and steered until the car was on the pavement. He extended the ramp, attached a chain to the Beetle and pulled it onto the flatbed. Then he strapped it down.

I stared up as sparse snowflakes twinkled in the parking lot lights. My mind was back on the issue of how to communicate everything 2011 Randy needed to know.

"Hey, you're the one who was in a hurry." The driver stood at the door of the truck cab. "Get in or I'll leave you here."

I scurried into the passenger seat.

The driver put the truck in gear with a grinding shift. "Those tires weren't flat. They were cut to smithereens. How'd you do that?"

"It's a long and ugly story. I'd rather not repeat it, if you don't mind."

"For eight-hundred bucks, you won't hear another word from these lips."

The driver was true to his promise.

The first wave of snow had formed a skim of white on the highway. Salt trucks lined the route, prepared to go into action in a few hours after more snow had accumulated. Over at least the next six hours, the intensity of the storm would increase, leaving what I expected would be record amounts of snow on the roads.

Why did everything disappear when I arrived in 2011? I'd brought some of the items with me, but others like the tires had come from 2019. There had to be some rule of time travel that I didn't understand. Maybe more than one.

The flatbed truck pulled up at CJ's gas station with its GoTane sign in place. The OPEN sign was off and the lights were out.

"Where do you want me to dump it?" asked the driver.

"There should be an empty spot in back along the fence." I got out and confirmed that the area where the Beetle had been parked was vacant. "Right there."

The driver pulled forward and then backed up, aiming the ramp.

If I put the Beetle on CJ's lot, only to make use of it in 2019, where did it come from in the first place? Either I had acquired it in a previous jump that I didn't remember, or I'd created the world's first non-fiction causal loop.

The driver unstrapped the Beetle and rolled it into place using the tire dollies. Then he lowered them and put them away.

I reached into my pocket for the keys. *Still there.* Remembering CJ's original instructions, I tucked them behind the driver's visor and grabbed the 2019 newspaper.

I asked the driver, "What time is it?"

"1:55."

I didn't have time to dawdle. A light came on in one of the upstairs rooms. Damn, the noise must have woken somebody.

CJ, eight years younger than the last time I'd seen him and wearing a bathrobe, tottered out of the front door of the station with a flashlight. "What's going on out here?"

"Hi, CJ. It's Randy Weinberg, Sy's son. Sorry about the noise, but I was—"

Before I could finish the thought, he hastened over and threw his arms around me. "Well I'll be!" He ran his hand over my arm. "Come on in. You must be frozen."

The tow truck operator retracted the ramp, got into the cab, waved, and drove off. *Shit, there goes my ride home.*

CJ led me by the arm through the front door.

I stepped across the threshold into the office. No glass jar or shoebox for customer payments. The recliner was there, but in better shape. No peanut shells on the floor, as far as I could tell. And no laundry baskets full of newspapers dating back years. In fact, the place looked well-maintained and clean.

"Now I know who wakes the rooster." He waved his arm, beckoning me. "Come on in and sit a spell."

I had to make this a quick visit. "I was in the neighborhood and had the urge to stop in. It's not too early, is it?"

"To see the son of one of my best friends? No way. I'll put on a kettle."

I'd planned on stopping to see CJ, only *after* I'd taken care of things at home, and if time allowed. But this was CJ. I followed him into the storage room that was still his kitchen, with the same makeshift table. The appliances looked newer. He put on a kettle and gestured me to sit. "So how are your folks?"

The wall clock read 2:08. I could afford a few minutes. "Fine. They're in Florida." *Where they go every winter.* "Snowbirds."

"Your Dad and I talk about once every three months or so. Make you something to eat? When you and your Dad used to come by, you loved my cookin'."

I had no memories of that. "I don't have a lot of time."

"That's the way things are these days, everybody in a hurry. In the old days, people would take the time—"

I heard footsteps on the stairs. A young man stuck his head into the room. "What's going on, Pop?"

CJ's son Marty. I hadn't seen him for over a decade.

"Randy, do you remember Mickey? Mickey, this is Randy, the son of one of my best friends. His dad got me up and running in this location."

How could I have forgotten his son's name? I waved. "Hi."

"Nice to meet you." Mickey yawned. "I'm going back to bed. I'm opening tomorrow, remember?" Pounding of heavy feet told me he was going upstairs.

CJ got up, filled two GoTane-branded ceramic cups with instant coffee and hot water and put one in front of me.

I thought about CJ's situation with his son eight years in the future. "How are the two of you getting along?"

"I'm so damn proud, I could just burst. Ever since he graduated from high school, he's buried himself in his old man's business." CJ blew across his cup and took a tentative slurp.

In 2019, CJ had suffered with his son's acting career and the fate of his station. Had both of those been resolved because of my return to 2011? I stifled my joy at an improved outcome.

"Makes my heart feel good to know that this here station will be part of my legacy after I'm gone."

I drank a bit more. GoTane-branded food products hadn't improved from 2019. That made no sense. The wall clock read 2:35. "Listen, I'd love to stay and chat, but there's someplace I have to be."

CJ walked me to the door and opened it. He scanned the area around his modern gas pumps. "You got a car?"

With no tires, the Beetle was useless. "No, but my house isn't all that far from here. The walk will be good for me." If I didn't freeze to death.

"Without some kind of jacket? What would your father think if I let you do something dangerous like that? I'll take you. Heck, I'm already up." He rummaged around in his closet and pulled out his son's varsity jacket, with red fleece body and white leather arms. "Wear this for the ride." Still in his robe, CJ drove his Buick out from the service bay and pulled up in front of the station.

I got into the passenger side. "This is very kind of you." I gave him my address.

"Small potatoes compared to your father helping me get set up with GoTane. They make lots of demands on a sole proprietor like me, but they seem fair. Just wish they didn't keep raising sales targets. Someday, Mickey might not be able to keep up."

I knew how that story used to end in 2019. Maybe that too would change. All I could do was make sure that 2011 Randy told 2011 Lou to provide for CJ in his later years if he needed it. God, this communication was going to be way too complicated. "She runs nice."

"Just changed the oil. Can't be too careful with these antiques." CJ pulled up across the street from my house. "It was kind of you to stop by. Send my regards to your father."

"I will." I choked up. I didn't expect to be able to see my parents before my fate arrived, in whatever form that took. Maybe I could make time to call them again. I took off Mickey's jacket and put it on the passenger seat.

After CJ pulled away from the curb, I paused to look at my house before I crossed the rutted street. Snow had picked up since I'd left ChiLabs. The lights inside were off. Randy and Faith would be snuggled under their comforter for less than two hours until her contractions got bad enough to wake her.

Without Randy's keys, how was I going to get in? I rolled the 2019 issue of the *Daily Herald*, stuffed it into my back pocket and shivered as I walked up the snow-covered front walk. Had I hidden a key somewhere? My mind was foggy. I checked under the welcome mat and dug into the dirt-only flower box Faith had me hang near the front door. Nothing. I doubled back and across the front of the garage, making footprints in the snow. I knew the entrance code, but the noise of the motor would wake them. I walked toward the backyard. Perhaps they'd left the back door unlocked.

Just before the walkway reached the patio, I came to a door that we never used on the far side of the garage. I tried the knob. It wasn't locked, but the door seemed stuck. I put my weight against it and it slid open a crack. I pictured piles of stuff stored in the garage, to be dealt with some day. Moving that mass enough to slip inside required repeated pushes with all of my weight. After half a dozen shoves, the door was open just enough for me to slip through. I felt my way in the dark through neck-high stacks of boxes, furniture and who remembered what else.

My Audi TT sat next to Faith's SUV. What was it doing here? I flicked on the overhead light. The Audi sported winter tires, prepared for driving on snow. Had 2011 Randy made an earlier appointment, or did the dealership get it done quicker? A change, but not relevant. My mission remained the same: convince 2011 Randy to do things differently this time.

I tried the door that led into the house. Unlocked! I opened it ever so slowly, cursing myself for not oiling the hinges. Still, I was at the opposite end of the house from the master suite, Craig's future bedroom and my home office.

I took off my slippers to avoid tracking dirt and slush, which Faith despised, but also to be quiet. In the family room, Randy's wallet and keys were in their expected spot, in his wooden valet, a gift from Faith on their last anniversary so he wouldn't misplace his things. His cellphone was plugged into an outlet, charging. *So that's where everything went. Or stayed.* Is that why I couldn't have those items in *my* possession? Because I arrived at a time where they already existed? Did that mean there was no Randy Weinberg in bed with Faith? No, I showed up before Randy leaped. He must be here, asleep. The microwave's clock read 3:04.

I slid the step stool from its place alongside the fridge and took a replacement bulb from the pantry. Then I carried both items up the hallway to the guest bathroom and shut the door so I wouldn't wake anyone.

When I tested the switch for the ceiling light, it came on. *What's going on here? Who changed the burnt-out bulb?* My haphazard outfit was a joke. I placed the 2019 issue of the *Daily Herald* on the closed toilet seat and knelt. *Damn, no marker.* I killed the light and crept into Randy's office, where a ChiLabs coffee cup held pencils, pens and a permanent black felt tip.

Back in the bathroom with the door closed and the light on, I tried to remember all of the things I needed to tell 2011 Randy. Even incomplete in my mind, the list was daunting. Lou had been correct: writing all of these instructions on the front page would overwhelm him. Instead, I kept it short and sweet: "*CRITICAL! Meet Soson at work immediately. Patrice must take Faith to the hospital.*"

Below those words, I wrote, "*Two identical sleds start moving in different directions at the same time from the same point.*" That was the one question we'd gotten wrong on our Physics 101 final exam in college, something only *we* knew. In that moment, we froze, unable to do the calculation. We regretted that error ever since.

I circled the date in the masthead and wrote "Time travel is real." That would have to be good enough. I turned off the light, leaving the stool in place for Randy to stub his toe so he wouldn't miss the message written on the newspaper. My curiosity begged me to take a look at the couple in bed. I crept down the hallway and eased the door to the master bedroom open a couple of inches to confirm my prediction. Faith lay on her side, cradling her stomach with one arm, sound asleep. The other side of the bed was empty, the blanket and comforter cast aside. I didn't hear any noise from the master bathroom. Where was 2011 Randy? Both cars were in the garage, so he hadn't taken a joyride in the snow.

The absence of a body next to Faith brought momentary panic and then overwhelming but stifled relief. There *was* no 2011 Randy. No one to convince.

Just like 2011 Randy's possessions couldn't be in two places at once, space/time had prevented two of me. The burden, to communicate with an earlier version of myself, vanished. I didn't have to get 2011 Randy to change his behavior. I was in control. Just me, doing the right things. This time.

Day 0

[29] Monday, January 24, 2011

My task had gotten infinitely easier. I could achieve the results I wanted through my own actions. Without the list I created on my 2019 phone, I'd have to execute the necessary actions from memory. *No problem, I've got this.*

My first critical but simple decision. Should I get into bed and let Faith wake me, or leave for work? I knew where the former led—to an unplanned trip to 2019. Although it felt cruel to leave Faith alone, Patrice could keep her safe. I had to trust that she could. Otherwise, arriving late would allow Hamza to interfere with my experiment, repeating a vicious cycle. Preventing Hamza from messing with the settings before the experiment had to be my priority.

In Randy's home office, I pulled my 2011 outfit from his closet, underwear and socks from the dirty clothes hamper. His building pass hung from a hook on the wall. I slipped that into my pocket and made my way back through the kitchen. I bagged my makeshift outfit, which I'd return to ChiLabs' lost and found later. Randy's charger blinked at me, reminding me to take the phone. I put on his watch and filled my pockets with the rest of his stuff. Although my stomach growled, I had no time for breakfast. I found granola bars in a familiar upper cabinet and slid one in my pocket.

One question remained. What to do with the bathroom? I sure as hell wasn't going to leave the 2019 newspaper or the step stool. I fetched both. I slid the stool back into its place alongside the fridge. The newspaper came with me.

Faith's moan wafted down the hallway. Damn, are her contractions early? I needed to leave. As expected, Randy's parka hung in the front entry closet. No, *my* parka. There was no 'him.'

I put on my shoes and entered the dark garage from the family room and disconnected the overhead door from the motor, allowing me to lift the door without making much noise. I slid into the TT, its bucket seat comforting. The car's engine rumbled to life. In reverse, the Audi rolled back onto the snow-covered driveway. I put the TT in neutral with the parking brake set, flicked the pulley lever, and closed the garage door manually. The motorized belt would reconnect by itself.

I drove down my street, pulled over and took a deep breath to prepare for a difficult call with Patrice. Given how she pushed back at Faith's suggestion I go to work in the original timeline, I expected she'd subject me to severe verbal abuse.

"Hello?" She'd answered my call with a just-woken drawl.

"Patrice, it's Randy from next door." I kept talking, preventing her from responding. "I need a big favor. Faith is having contractions. We had no idea Craig was coming this early, and I'm not home." Not a lie and designed to convince her I had no choice. "Someone needs to get her to the hospital immediately."

"Don't say another word. I'll get dressed and take her. She wanted me there anyway, for my experience."

"No, it's because you're her best friend. If it's easier, take Faith's SUV."

"No problem. My car runs fine."

Her husband Clark grumbled in the background about being woken. Patrice told him to shut up.

"It's snowing heavily, so please drive carefully," I added.

"That's the only way I drive. How soon should Faith expect you?"

I added three hours to the time of the experiment. "Noon, I hope. Sooner, if the weather breaks and the roads are cleared."

"Where in the hell are you? Never mind, Faith wasn't due for a few weeks yet. Now don't you get *yourself* into an accident. I'll take care of our girl. Be safe." She hung up.

I exhaled. Not as bad as it could have gone. If I got to the hospital by eleven or eleven-thirty, at least Patrice would consider me a hero. Faith would still be pissed, but she'd get over it when I stood beside her at Craig's birth.

I passed the intersection where Faith and I had been delayed by an accident. No cars, no police. *Too early.* It took about fifteen minutes to get to the Interstate, which I anticipated would be clearer than when I'd originally driven it. Snow accumulated on my windshield. An increase in flakes told me that the snowstorm was beginning to intensify.

At that moment, Patrice was helping an upset Faith get ready for the hospital. If everything worked out the way I planned, I could stop Hamza, have a quick celebration when my experiment worked—and it *would* work—and head straight to the hospital. That way, I would be with Faith when Craig was born.

Using what I remembered about road conditions and traffic accidents, I avoided the inevitable congestion by exiting early and using state roads. Municipal plows had been out at least once, evidenced by uniform banks of gray snow. I made good time.

When I pulled into the ChiLabs' parking lot, the only activity was plows clearing the accumulated snow. I called Soson.

"Why do you call me at this hour?" His voice was raspy. "Do you know what time it is?"

I checked my cellphone. "Yes, just about four-twelve." Earlier than his text messages to stay away. "I need you to meet me at the Labs at six.'"

"Why in the hell would I do that, *malchik*? Your experiment is scheduled for nine."

"Listen, I don't ask you for favors very often." That much was true. His help often led to rework on my part. I guessed his credentials from his former employer in Russia had been exaggerated. "And don't call me *malchik*. You live, what, fifteen minutes away? I've given you plenty of time to get ready."

I heard a familiar deep female voice in the background complain. It sounded like Tonya. I must have woken her too.

"I have company." He lowered his voice. "And she has expectations for this morning. You understand?"

A quickie before he left for work? I didn't want to think about it. "This is important. Life and death important." A situation he would cause eight years in the future.

"All right, all right. I will break her bad mood with a joke. Tonya loves my sense of humor."

Was this the incident he mentioned, a quip that caused their break-up? "No! Don't make a joke. If it flops, she'll feel even worse about you. Promise her an expensive dinner at Les Nomades instead." I took Faith there for dinner when I proposed. "Insist you have to work early this morning. Don't disappoint me."

"Easy for you to spend my money. The things I do for your friendship. Of course, *tovarish. Vse chto tebe nuzhno*. Whatever you need from me."

Friendship? BS! "See you at the Labs. Drive safe, it's snowing like crazy and the roads are slippery. Six o'clock sharp." I expected he might be a few minutes late, but still early enough to stop Hamza.

I turned on the overhead light and took a good look at the front page of the *Daily Herald* from 2019. Why hadn't *it* disappeared? It wouldn't be printed for three thousand and six days. Hamza had insisted that he found it on the toilet lid in 2011. Maybe it belonged in this timeline because of a previous time travel excursion. Impossible to know for sure. The headlines remained the same but something seemed wrong with the lottery numbers. More changes? I pulled all of my Starbucks receipts out of my wallet. I hadn't written on any of them. I grabbed a pen from the glove box and jotted the winning numbers published in the *Herald* on the back of one and then put them away. The newspaper went into my back pocket.

Two hours weren't to be wasted. A rented security guard occupied Hannah's desk. When I flashed him my ID, he nodded me through. I headed upstairs to my office, turned on and signed into my computer. My experiment occupied the nine o'clock schedule slot. When

I logged into company email, there was one new message, sent late the previous evening. It was from Hamza, with a copy to Soson, that he would be bringing three people he called "dignitaries" to witness the experiment. He *had* advised me of his plans, just in an email I never read.

I tidied up my desk, wiped the whiteboard clean, locked up, and went downstairs. No one worked in the passage for the branch of the linear accelerator tube that led to the secondary target area. I ambled along its length, examining the curved metal pipe and attached electronics. The supports for the plasma frame were the only visible part of that enhancement. Electromagnets surrounded the tube at evenly spaced intervals. Everything looked clean and tidy.

I went back to the lobby and awaited Soson's arrival. While I waited, I checked my wallet. No Russian rubles. Two singles, plus my credit cards.

Headlights from an arriving vehicle grabbed my attention. A Porsche Targa. *Soson?* I expected that he'd still be driving his Lexus, which he couldn't stop raving about when he bought it. Had Tonya mentioned something about Soson's car?

That didn't matter. I needed to be civil to a man who stole intellectual property for a foreign adversary and put my family in harm's way.

I pocketed my wallet, stuffed my hands into my jacket, and went outside.

The Porsche pulled up alongside my Audi TT and Soson got out. "I would say good morning but that would be a lie."

"It's a glorious morning. I'm going into battle against cancerous tumors today, and Faith's in labor at the hospital."

"Then why are you here?" With his scowl and hunched shoulders, he looked like an angry bear. "The experiment will practically run itself. Do you not trust me to press the button in your absence? What about Faith?"

I used my previous experience as a script. "She urged me to be here. Our neighbor is with her. Besides, the doctor said Craig won't arrive for hours. I'll be here for the test and then hurry back to Faith's side. You know how precise the equipment settings must be. I have a feeling Hamza wants to interfere."

"Paranoia does not suit you, Randall. As a director at the company, he succeeds when *you* succeed. What motive would he have?"

Hamza had told me in his office: obtaining winning lottery numbers from the future. *None of Soson's business, assuming he didn't already know.* "I suspect he wants me to fail and then use my work as his own and claim success. That's why he's been in my face. Some of our colleagues have heard him disparage my work."

"Remember, this is the same Hamza who advocated that you receive the grant in the first place, instead of other worthy competitors."

Had Hamza's plotting gone back ten years? "Things change." I'd witnessed that over my week in 2019, much to my dismay.

"They always will, *tovarich*. By the way, I am glad I took your advice. My overnight companion was in one of her lawyer moods. Any joke, even an outstanding one, would have set her off. We have plans for an extravagant dinner tonight. Thank you, my friend."

"Glad to hear it." I hadn't planned that returning to 2011 would improve CJ's and Soson's relationships. I considered the changes happenstance good fortune. Why did Lou worry so much about consequences? Why did *I*?

Soson looked up at the flake-filled sky. "The snow comes down harder. News reports say this will be the heaviest of the season." He shivered, the fur on his coat quivering. "Do we have to be here this early? The experiment cannot be performed any earlier than the scheduled time. I expect the accelerator is in use as we stand here, freezing our *moshonki* off."

"I just want to make sure it goes well. Can you blame me?" I moved toward the revolving door. "If the cafeteria is open, breakfast is on me. Maybe they've got fresh pecan caramel rolls." I led, Soson followed.

"Since when are you so generous?" asked Soson.

I patted my back pocket to make sure my wallet hadn't vanished. "Because today is special." *In more ways than one.*

The rented security guard at Hannah's desk looked up from his magazine.

I waved my security badge in front of him.

Soson followed suit. "It will be just my luck the cafeteria will be closed."

We strolled in that direction across a spartan first floor. No wall-sized screens. No padded benches.

The guy behind the food counter waved. "Thirty minutes, gentlemen. Still setting up."

"No problem. Let's go up to my office." I strode toward the elevator. "I'll come down later and get your favorites." Those memories were still clear.

Soson unbuttoned his coat and stood beside me. "I know how you work. With precision to five decimal places. Everything is arranged for the experiment. Is it not too soon for the baby?"

I told him a modified version of my morning activities, leaving out all of the backward time travel bits. I'd woken up early in a cold sweat, worried about the experiment, slipped out of bed, got dressed and drove straight to ChiLabs.

"When this is successful—" Soson delivered a slap on the back that knocked me against the elevator buttons. "—and notice I said *when*, perhaps the Nobel Prize committee will consider this instead of your previous work."

I scratched my head. Soson couldn't know that I would win a Nobel for particle stream improvements using a plasma frame. "Don't count my award before the experiment is hatched. After all, this is our first full-scale test."

"You are a *bespokoynyy chelovek,* what you call a wart with worries."

395

The elevator delivered us to my floor. I unlocked the office with my security badge. "Have a seat."

Soson shrugged off his long coat, pulled the folding chair from against the wall and straddled it.

Before I settled, I checked the plasma frame controller, electromagnets, and laser settings again. All at their precise and designed values. "Perfect." I hung my parka on a bare nail in the far wall. Then I sat in my chair, still adjusted for my size and comfort.

With my body blocking Soson's view, I slid the 2019 *Daily Herald* into the top drawer of my desk and locked it. "What do you want this morning? The full boat? Eggs, bacon, hash browns, toast, coffee and a doughnut?"

"You must want something if you feed me so well." One of his eyebrows lifted. "A favor perhaps?"

"We'll see. Maybe later." I wanted Soson to feel indebted, even if only for breakfast. I was certain I'd need favors from him later. "You hang out here. I'll place the order and be right back." I took the elevator downstairs.

At the cafeteria, I placed an order for Soson's food plus a cup of coffee and a pecan caramel roll for myself. I remembered too late that the money from 2019 was gone. I had two dollars in my wallet, plus a folded up fifty-dollar bill behind my medical insurance cards, for emergencies only. "My buddy, the big guy that looks like Sasquatch, he's paying."

The cafeteria guy gave me a big grin. "I've seen you two lots of times. You're pranking him, aren't you? Sure, I'll go along for a laugh."

As I walked out of the cafeteria, I noticed Hannah at her desk near the front entrance. She stood, waving to me as if hailing a cab in a downpour.

I walked the length of the lobby. "Good morning. I have to apologize."

"For what?" Hannah hung her coat over the back of her chair.

"I got hungry earlier this morning and I'm afraid I went a little crazy." I pulled the empty cellophane sleeve from her wastebasket as evidence. "Once I ate the first cookie, I couldn't stop. I'll pay you back later."

"That's not necessary, Dr. Weinberg."

As I passed the cafeteria on the way to the elevator, the cook shouted, "Your order is ready. Total comes to twenty-one twenty. Is the big guy coming down to pay?"

Damn, that was too quick. Now that I was back in 2011, I had other resources like my checking account. I handed him the fifty. "Can you break this?"

"Sure." He snatched the bill from my hand. "Once the morning crowd shows up, I'll have plenty of small bills for change."

"Give me back twenty-five. Keep the rest for a tip."

He handed me the change. *I'll give the five-dollar bill to Hannah for the cookies I ate.*

I brought the tray upstairs. "Here you go." I put my coffee and roll on my desk and handed Soson the tray.

"This will taste even better because you paid for it." He smiled, his stained and crooked teeth showing.

I needed time alone, to remember everything I had to do. Details were already fading. I wouldn't be able to concentrate with Soson practically in my lap. I needed an excuse to get Soson out of my office. "When was the last time either of us verified the target area?"

"Last week." He took a forkful of eggs and potato and chewed while he spoke. "Why?"

"Check it. Go downstairs and make sure there isn't any debris or water leaks. With this snow, who knows what could go wrong if there's moisture."

"Me? Now?" He put down his fork. "Must I?"

"This is why I asked you to get here early. Check and recheck."

"But I have barely touched my breakfast." The tray teetered on Soson's lap. "My food will get cold."

He didn't deserve my patience. He was a traitor to the United States. A liar. A selfish man who put the life of my son at risk. "Now!" I tipped Soson's tray to the side. It slipped off, tossing his breakfast all over the floor. "Just do it!"

"What is wrong with you?" His eyes lit up. "The experiment, of course. You are anxious. Plus, Faith is in labor." Soson made his way past my chair, stepping in bits of egg and puddles of coffee. "I will ask housekeeping to clean this up."

"Not now. After the experiment."

With Soson out of the way, I typed into my phone as many tasks as I could remember. First thing, I'd have Soson fired or arrested. I'd want to get Louise involved early for analysis. I'd insist that Faith undergo periodic cancer screenings to catch her disease early. Same for Louise's Dad. I would find the time to help CJ dispose of his gas station after GoTane cancelled his contract. In 2019, I'd play the winning lottery numbers and win one hundred nineteen million dollars. I might even be able to prevent Louise's unsatisfactory relationship with Eric along the way. Small changes shouldn't ripple out into major catastrophes.

Out of the corner of my eye, I caught a glimpse of Soson lumbering up the hallway. He reminded me of a bear who'd failed to find fish in a nearby stream. Hungry. Angry. I shoved my phone into my pocket.

"You like to prank Soson? Sending me into the basement to look for leaks? It is dry, *malchik*, as dry as your sense of humor." He bumped into my chair as he returned to his seat.

"I needed to be sure. So much is riding on this experiment." *So much so, that a time traveling version of me came back to 2011 to make sure.*

I took a first bite of my roll, stood, squeezed past Soson, and stared at the controller settings.

"How many times are you going to do that this morning?" he asked.

"As many as I want to. Don't you want this to work?"

His dazed look made me worry. Had he messed with something else about my experiment, something I hadn't identified, or was he just hung-over? "How late did you party with Tonya last night?"

Soson squeezed his forehead, flattening his bushy eyebrows. "How do you know her? I did not tell you her name?"

Damn! I'd slipped up. "Yes you did, when you confessed that she'd be the one who could make you settle down. Remember?"

Soson's scowl faded. "Sorry. I am sensitive about her. Perhaps I, too, am distracted."

The likely cause was his collusion with Hamza. "Good thing I'm here. Who's available this morning from analytics?"

"I requested Cecelia Malmquist. She is senior in the department. The best." Soson nodded, as if congratulating himself. "In fact, I should get Cecelia to come and meet you." He checked his watch.

As good as Cecelia might have been, I wasn't going to depend on a stranger. "Listen, I don't doubt your assessment." Even if I hadn't had an alternative, Soson's use of her first name gave me pause. "I want Louise Martin instead."

Soson raised an eyebrow. "Who or what is a Louise Martin?"

"She's fairly new in the analytics group." That was an understatement. "But she comes highly recommended." By me.

"I must disagree. You deserve an experienced analyst for such an important experiment. Besides, I advised Cecelia that she would be involved. She was thrilled and spent some time getting up to speed on your project and the unique configuration."

"Before today? A bit presumptuous since it's *my* experiment. You'll have to be the one to let her down." Having Louise lead the analysis would mess up Cecelia's expectations and perhaps Soson's social life. "Get Louise up here. She's a quick study." She'd better be, even at eight years younger.

Soson grimaced and retreated to make his calls, leaving breakfast footprints on the hallway carpet.

Thirty-five minutes later, Soson returned to my office to confirm he'd notified both Cecelia and Louise. Our conversation was interrupted when Hamza appeared at my door at twenty minutes to nine. Three men in suits, the dignitaries who I barely recognized from photos in the ChiLabs annual report, accompanied him. Top executives or Board members, I didn't remember which.

The three men exchanged glances, possibly wondering how all of them could fit into my office.

Hamza's wide, glaring eyes spoke volumes. He expected Soson's text messages would keep me away but Soson didn't have a chance to send them today.

The man standing next to Hamza said, "We're pleased to be with you this morning. A momentous event, after all this time." He cleared his throat. "Tell us, what role did Dr. Bashir play in your project?"

Since when did Hamza have a doctorate? An advanced degree made him even more deadly.

Before I could say, "He didn't do a damn thing," Hamza answered. "Dr. Weinberg and I have worked closely, ever since the Labs awarded his grant." If Hamza noticed the mess on the floor, he didn't comment about it. He turned his attention to Soson, sitting in the metal guest chair. "Mr. Grudovich, could you please leave so we can enter and observe?"

"Of course." Soson stood and folded the metal chair.

"You're not going anywhere. Sit down!" I hadn't intended on shouting. I faced Hamza. "Mr. Grudovich is my colleague." *And a spy, but he takes up space.* "He's been involved in this project from the beginning."

Soson leaned closer and whispered. "Randall, please, these men have the power to terminate our employment. We are so close. Do not ruin this."

Precisely what Hamza intends to do. I made eye contact with Soson and pointed at the metal chair. "You understand English. I said sit."

Soson's shoulders slumped as he did what I asked.

I turned to Hamza at the threshold. "I'm sorry, but there's no room for anyone else. My office is off limits this morning."

He clicked his tongue. "Must I remind you, I am a director at this facility?"

"Yes, but you're not *my* director. I don't take orders from you."

Soson stood and put his hand on my shoulder. "No need to argue. I can return to my office and—"

I turned my head. "The hell you will." Soson's willingness to allow Hamza access to the controllers in my office confirmed my theory. They were in cahoots to turn my cancer-curing experiment into one that caused time travel. Why else would Soson be so willing to make room for his partner in crime?

The three men accompanying Hamza bickered with each other in the background. The nine o'clock event was to be one of science, not defiance.

I couldn't tell if they were more upset with Hamza

or me. *Who cares?* "Look at this place." I waved my arms to the side. My fingertips grazed the whiteboard. "The experiment we're about to perform requires some very precise settings on those controllers in the corner. How would you feel if someone, perhaps one of you, accidentally rubbed against the dials? Even a small change would subvert my experiment at the last minute." Hamza grimaced. "After all of the time and expense, you'd have no one to blame but yourself."

One of the entourage edged up to Hamza's side. "We can see fine from here."

"Perhaps just me?" Hamza didn't budge.

I placed both hands on his chest and whispered, "I know you want to modify the settings." Hamza's face darkened. "The last thing I need for you to do—is—"

"Futz around." I felt Soson at my back. Maybe I whispered too loud.

Hamza glared over my shoulder.

"I need to correct a misstatement, gentlemen," said Soson. "I swear that Dr. Bashir had no significant involvement with Randall's work." He put his arm around my shoulder, in solidarity. "The only thing Dr. Bashir did was complain about Randall's expenditures. The same thing he does with other projects. Now, can we please end this circus? There is real work to be done."

Why the sudden change in Soson's behavior? No time to speculate. The probability of success flowed through my body like electric current.

Hamza backed away, surrounded by a formerly friendly entourage that bombarded him with questions.

I didn't realize I'd been holding my breath until I gasped. I slammed the door. "That S.O.B.! Who knows

404

what would have happened if he changed any of the settings?" *Rhetorical question answered: time travel.*

Soson's face retained his dour expression. He was Hamza's cohort, and he knew that I knew. I imagined neurons firing in Soson's brain, attempting to invent a strategic alternative.

Our confrontation had filled the remaining time. I sat at my desk and brought up the linear accelerator user interface on my screen. "Scoot close, buddy. You're going to want to be an eyewitness." *That will keep you away from the controllers.*

My project was next in the queue, to be run using the secondary target area, as planned. I turned off my phone so I wouldn't be disturbed during the test.

Soson stood behind me. "This is your moment, *tovarish.*"

Tovarish my ass!

When the clock on my monitor showed "09:00:00," I clicked the button labeled CONFIRM. Soson and I waited in silence as various sensors reported on the state of the equipment. Protons released. Proton stream coming up to speed. A special user interface element, added for my unique hardware configuration, showed status and temperature of the plasma frame. The laser became operational, cleaning the inside surface of the accelerator tube.

Real-time changes held my attention. "They're approaching collision speed."

A familiar-looking young woman appeared in the doorway. A younger version of Louise, trying to catch her breath, diverted my attention for a split second. My eyes returned to the screen as she spoke.

"I got here as quick as I could."

Even without turning my head, I felt her eyes on me.

"Dr. Weinberg? I thought—I don't know what to think. Thanks for asking for me."

My screen displayed the real-time acceleration of the stream. "I want you as lead analyst on my project. It's underway, which means you'll have a ton of work in a few minutes."

"It'll be an honor."

The only evidence of the collision was a scrolling list of status reports generated by the particle detectors, followed by a message "EXPERIMENT CONCLUDED."

I spun in my chair. "And with that, I need to get to the hospital."

"What's wrong?" asked Louise.

"My wife is giving birth and I promised to be at her side when it happens." I wedged past Soson, ripped my parka from the nail in the wall, and tucked it under my arm.

Louise threw herself into my chair.

I slid behind her. "I'll check back with you in a day or two, after you've had a chance to—"

She scrolled through the detector messages, pausing as they advanced up the monitor. "There's some good stuff here."

I bent forward to examine the screen. "You can tell my results from those messages?" On previous occasions, analysts needed a complete set of raw results and days to extract any meaning.

"Not in detail. I'll need to plot the trajectories of the resulting particles, but several easily-identifiable heavy ions have shown up."

Soson stroked his chin. "Evidently, you chose your analyst well."

I glanced at Soson but asked Louise, "Were you briefed about my experiment?"

"Not formally." She blushed, a particular shade of pink I'd seen somewhere before. "I've read up about your work and chatted with other employees to understand your approach. To work with you, well, it's a dream come true."

"We'll do great things together."

She didn't take her eyes off the computer screen. "Give me time to examine the raw data before we get ahead of ourselves."

"Congratulations!" Soson pulled me into a soft hug.

"Premature, but thanks." Draining energy dulled my euphoria, as if I was less than my whole self. I went limp against the door frame.

Soson helped me to my desk. I slumped against it, in front of one of my dual screens, nudging Louise to the side.

"Are you all right?" Soson asked.

Louise waited silently while I blocked her view.

"Yeah, just a bit woozy. Must have been all of the excitement." I rotated my shoulders and then my head. "Better. I'll call you after I've held Craig in my arms. Don't expect me to be back at work for a while." I stood, pressed the power button on my phone and stuck the device back into my pocket. "Given how I just treated Hamza, I might not have a job when I come back."

"He would be a fool to fire you, *tovarish*. Management will be delighted with your results." He thrust one of his cigars into my hand. "Besides, family takes priority. We will continue working during your absence. Send my best to your lovely bride and the little one."

As I rushed down the hall, I pulled on my parka and checked my watch. *9:27. Did time travel recharge the battery?* Halfway to the elevator, my phone rang. Caller ID showed North Suburban Community Hospital. "Hello?"

"Mr. Weinberg, this is Laura, a nurse at North Suburban. I'm calling regarding your wife. I have an update about her injuries."

"What are you talking about? What injuries?" The word 'consequences' flashed bright in my mind.

"Your wife Faith and a female driver were in a vehicle accident. The doctors wanted to speak with you earlier but we had trouble locating your cellphone number, and then you didn't answer."

My phone had been off during the experiment. *Stupid!* I fumbled with it as I turned on the speaker and checked my texts. One from the hospital had queued up. A black hole in my stomach threatened to suck my body into oblivion. "How is my wife? What happened?" My mind filled in the details before she spoke.

"She's in intensive care. We've stabilized her and she's breathing on her own. As I said, they were in an accident. Your wife and the driver were lucky. An ambulance happened to be in the vicinity, and the EMTs were able to rescue them from the wreckage."

I didn't have to ask the location of the accident. I pictured the intersection. "And Craig? The baby?"

After a few moments, the nurse's voice dropped to a whisper. "I'm so sorry."

The phone fell from my hand. I slid to the floor and stared at the pattern of fake ceramic tiles. *Oh no! What have I done?*

Louise got to me first. "Dr. Weinberg, what's the matter?"

Soson arrived a second later. "*Tovarish?*"

I mumbled something about Faith and Patrice's accident. "Faith was badly injured and Craig didn't survive."

Louise knelt down next to me. "I'm so sorry."

Soson stood silent alongside, a hand on my shoulder.

I could barely breathe. "I need to be alone." I wiped tears from my cheeks.

"Come, my dear." Soson led Louise away.

My body shook. *This is my fault. Bad decisions!* Leaving Faith's side at a critical time. Delegating the task of driving Faith to the hospital to Patrice. Knowing her, she probably jabbered on about caring for Craig and didn't drive defensively. It should have been me behind the wheel.

In 2019, I left our perfectly healthy eight-year-old son behind to prevent Hamza from messing with my experiment. *I never thought Craig would die.* I never would have sacrificed him, not for anything. *I should have trusted my instincts, that reverse time travel had consequences. How could I have known the extent?*

I stuffed my phone into a pocket and steadied myself against the wall to get to my feet. Soson and Louise stood at the door to my office. "I'm heading for the hospital in case someone asks. And I'll be taking some time off, to care for Faith." And grieve over our loss.

Soson moved closer and half-raised his arms to offer another one of his bear hugs.

I wasn't in the mood. He figured it out and stepped back. Louise maintained her distance, biting on a knuckle.

"Of course, take all the time you need, *tovarish.*"

In 2019, he proved to me that he couldn't be trusted. Unlikely that changed, given his recent behavior.

I skipped the elevator, ran downstairs, and through the lobby. Hannah raised her hand to flag me down. No time to waste on conversation.

Faith needed me.

[32] Monday, January 24, 2011 (continued)

On the first floor of Northwest Suburban, I shouted at the clerk behind the reception desk. "Faith Weinberg!"

"Room 314. You can use one of those—"

I bolted from the desk, ran to an open elevator, and mashed the third-floor button. It trundled upward with a slowness that would have tested Job. When the doors opened, I careened down the hall, my eyes darting from sign to sign, looking for Faith's room. *Found it!* Before I could enter, a nurse came out and closed the door behind her.

I introduced myself as Faith's husband. "How is she doing?"

"She suffered head trauma from the accident. We're treating her infections with antibiotics. I've just given her pain medication, but you can go in." Sadness filled her eyes as she touched my arm. "You have my condolences."

"Thank you." I pulled the door open and slipped in. Faith lie in bed, her face pale, her eyes closed, swaddled in sheets and blankets. Tubes and wires connected her to a drip, and both heart and oxygen monitors. Her brunette hair cascaded across the pillow.

I crept to the edge of the bed at the pace of a machine's beep. When I reached her side, I took her hand in mine. In a whisper, I spoke her name.

Her eyelids fluttered. "Randy?" I leaned over and held her, my lips near her ear. I was speechless. There was nothing to be gained for either of us by confessing my guilt.

"Did they tell you Craig died?"

The word caught in my throat. "Yes." I didn't let go of her hand. "I got here as soon as I found out."

"The nurse told me they have people who can arrange for his funeral. That's what we should do, right? I mean, he has a name, and he was..."

Whimpering replaced her words.

I pulled back and saw her open eyes for the first time. Red, puffy. "It's a terrible loss, and we don't deserve it, but we'll get through this together." We'd never faced a tragedy of this magnitude. Perhaps I could give her some hope. "First things first, we need to let you heal." My voice broke. "Get your strength back and on your feet."

Her head flopped, side to side. "I don't think I'll ever be the same."

"Yes, you will. I'll have someone come in and help out around the house so you don't strain yourself."

Faith's pregnancy hadn't been easy. In hindsight, I should have done more. That damn experiment kept me away from her and my responsibilities at home way too much.

The hollowness returned. Faith and I had decided to have one child, part of our legacy to the world. A stupid, unpredictable side effect cost Craig's life. I'd seen him in 2019 as a vibrant and smart eight-year-old. He held such promise. This wasn't fair.

"The medications make my head foggy."

"Don't fight it. The rest will do you good. I'm not going anywhere."

Even if Faith agreed to get pregnant again, the baby wouldn't be Craig. He was the child we both

412

wanted. I didn't even have the pictures of him on the playground in 2019, only my fading memories. *Why can't we have* him?

I stood at Faith's bedside, her eyes shut, first holding her fingers, then placing my hand on hers, then slipping away as she fell asleep.

Coming back to 2011 eliminated eight years of Faith's worry and feelings of abandonment. In their place, the devastating loss of our child.

I left Faith asleep, cruised the hall, and found a chair in a corner near large windows facing a plowed parking lot.

Stopping Hamza from modifying the controllers' settings let my experiment be successful and proved that I could change the past. *I'm not satisfied with the personal consequences.*

Then it struck me. *Do I have to?* Why couldn't I time travel again, to prevent Patrice's accident? Faith and I would be cuddling with infant Craig instead of mourning him.

What would I need to do, to prevent Patrice's accident without letting Hamza get near the controllers in my office? Drive Faith to the hospital myself in my Audi as soon as she woke up? It might be just that simple. Or should we take her car instead? If I'd learned anything, just the act of traveling through time causes changes, like making a journey to a moving destination. Perhaps something subtler. Leave the Beetle on the mound instead of having it towed? Refuse CJ's offer to join him for coffee? Preschedule the towing company? Wear a different coat when I left the house? If Craig's death was a random byproduct of other changes, would any of these make a difference? Was there something firmly connected to his demise? The only way to find out is by trying. Craig's life was worth the risk.

How many of my notes about backward time travel, the ones I'd dutifully typed into my 2019 phone, did I remember?

I pulled out my 2011 phone. The small buttons slowed me down. I added everything Louise and I had talked about or done. Hamza's settings for the plasma frame and laser, as best I could remember them. Using electromagnets for—how *did* we use them? I couldn't recreate Louise's formula for calibrating time travel based on plasma temperatures and laser frequencies. She'd have to invent it, just eight years earlier.

I clutched the phone to my chest. According to Hamza, I traveled backward earlier and brought the 2019 copy of the *Daily Herald* with me. If that was one of my attempts, why didn't *it* work? And if I couldn't remember, how would I keep track of multiple tries and their results? Something else to figure out.

I had always been able to accomplish things others found impossible. Here was my chance to do it again and rescue my wife *and* son. The space/time continuum would fight me all the way. If on my next attempt Hamza succeeded or Craig didn't survive, I could try again.

I stared at the acoustical ceiling tiles above my head, a few with water stains, and considered the resources at my disposal. If funding became an issue, I had a lottery windfall at my disposal eight years in the future. I could pay facilities other than ChiLabs for my time travel excursions and still contribute towards CJ's comfortable retirement. Or make a down payment on one of those downsized accelerators of my own.

Louise had been instrumental in making reverse time travel successful. Did she help me invent the procedure in 2019, or had previous experiences taught her the answer? I'd demand to have Louise work with me.

My heavy ion project had to continue, to save lives. Today's experiment demonstrated that I was on the right path. Labs management wouldn't have trouble finding a replacement to continue my work. Any other physicist in the building would be delighted to be handed a successful project. Damn it, they can take all the credit.

Once I knew Faith was healed and stronger, I needed to correct the horrific mess I made. I dialed my office.

Louise answered. "Soson is here. I'm putting you on speaker. How's your wife?"

"Resting comfortably at the moment. When I get back in a couple of weeks, I'll need to tell you a story and get your input on making an important decision."

Soson's voice bellowed in my ear. "Of course, *tovarish*. I am at your service."

"I meant Louise."

"Me? Sure, but call me Lou."

I hung up and returned to Faith's room. For now, all my thoughts were for Faith—and Craig. The only thing that mattered was the present. The past could wait.

###

Made in United States
Cleveland, OH
16 August 2025

19192757R00232